BLOOD EAGLE

Blood Eagle

Craig Russell

HUTCHINSON
LONDON

Published by Hutchinson in 2005

1 3 5 7 9 10 8 6 4 2

Copyright © Craig Russell 2005

Craig Russell has asserted his right under the Copyright, Designs
and Patents Act, 1988 to be identified as the author of this work

First published in 2005 in the United Kingdom by Hutchinson

Hutchinson
The Random House Group Limited
20 Vauxhall Bridge Road, London SW1V 2SA

Random House Australia (Pty) Limited
20 Alfred Street, Milsons Point, Sydney
New South Wales 2061, Australia

Random House New Zealand Limited
18 Poland Road, Glenfield
Auckland 10, New Zealand

Random House (Pty) Limited
Endulini, 5a Jubilee Road
Parktown 2193, South Africa

The Random House Group Limited Reg. No. 954009

www.randomhouse.co.uk

A CIP catalogue record for this book is available
from the British Library

ISBN 0 09 180014 5 (Hardback)
ISBN 0 09 179709 8 (Airport/Export Edition)

Papers used by Random House are natural, recyclable products made from
wood grown in sustainable forests. The manufacturing processes conform to
the environmental regulations of the country of origin

Typeset by Palimpsest Book Production Limited, Polmont, Stirlingshire

Printed and bound in Great Britain by
Mackays of Chatham PLC, Chatham, Kent

To Wendy, Jonathan, Sophie and Helen

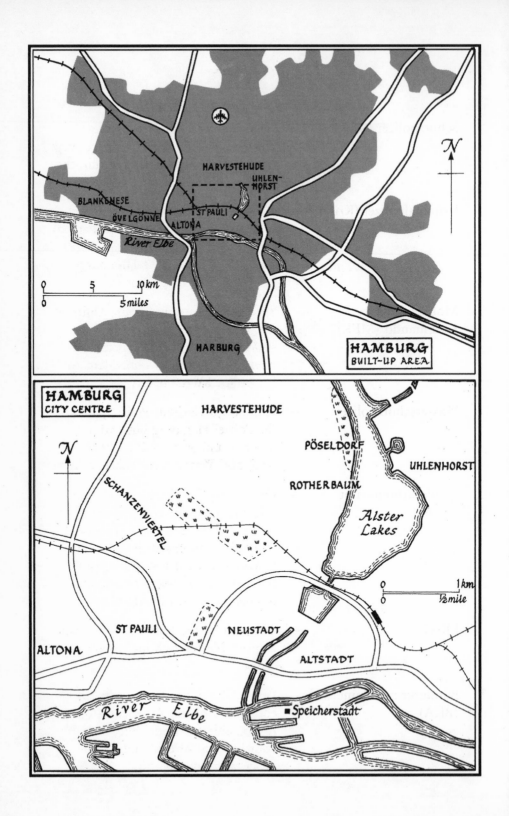

GLOSSARY

Schutzpolizei (SchuPo) – The uniformed branch of the German Police. In 2003, there were 6306 uniformed officers within the Polizei Hamburg

Kriminalpolizei (KriPo) – The plain-clothes detective branch of the German Police. Equivalent of the UK CID. In 2003, there were 1621 members of the Hamburg Polizei's KriPo department

Mobiles Einsatz Kommando (MEK) – Special Operations Group. Units of the Polizei Hamburg used for surveillance and armed response operations. Broadly equivalent to US police SWAT teams

Wasserschutzpolizei – Hamburg's Harbour Police, part of the Polizei Hamburg but with a different uniform. In 2003, there were 566 Wasserschutzpolizei officers

Landeskriminalamt (LKA) – Office responsible for the administration of all KriPo within each of Gemany's federal states. The LKA is divided into eight departments (LKA1 – LKA8) each responsible for a different aspect of criminal intelligence and investigation

LKA7 – The unit of the Landeskriminalamt responsible for fighting organized crime

Bundeskriminalamt (BKA) – Federal Criminal Bureau. Broadly equivalent to the American FBI, responsible for nationwide coordination of criminal intelligence and investigation

Bundesnachrichtendienst – (BND)	Federal Intelligence Service. The secret service of the Federal Republic of Germany, responsible for all national security matters and, since 1996, involved in the fight against organized crime
Polizeipräsidium	– Police Headquarters

KriPo Police Ranks: (in descending order):

Kriminaldirektor	– Chief of Police (Detective Branch)
Erster Kriminalhauptkommissar	– Principal Chief Commissar (Fabel's rank)
Kriminalhauptkommissar	– Chief Commissar
Kriminaloberkommissar	– Leading Commissar (Werner Meyer's and Maria Klee's rank)
Kriminalkommissar	– Commissar (Anna Wolff's and Paul Lindemann's rank)

State Officials and Departments:

Staatsanwalt	– State Prosecutor
Staatsanwaltschaft	– State Prosecution Department (equivalent of DPP in UK)
Erster Bürgermeister	– Principle Mayor (and in the case of Hamburg, Berlin and Bremen, the Head of the State government)
Innensenator	– The Interior Minister of the Hamburg Senat or State government

Nowhere were the Dark Ages darker than in the lands of the Viking. Powerful cults flourished: cults whose superstitions and bloody rituals revolved around the most arcane beliefs. One of the most horrific of these rituals was the rite of the Blood Eagle.

A rite of human sacrifice.

Part One
Wednesday 4 June and
Thursday 5 June

B L O O D E A G L E

Polizei Hamburg Mordkommission

From   SON OF SVEN
To   ERSTER KRIMINALHAUPTKOMMISSAR JAN FABEL
Sent   3 June 2003, 23.00
Subject TIME

TIME IS STRANGE, IS IT NOT? I WRITE AND YOU READ AND WE SHARE THE SAME MOMENT. YET AS I WRITE THIS, HERR HAUPT-KOMMISSAR, YOU SLEEP AND MY NEXT VICTIM STILL LIVES: AS YOU READ IT, SHE IS ALREADY DEAD. OUR DANCE CONTINUES.

I HAVE SPENT ALL OF MY LIFE ON THE EDGE OF OTHER PEOPLE'S PHOTOGRAPHS. UNNOTICED. BUT DEEP WITHIN, UNKNOWN TO ME AND HIDDEN FROM THE WORLD, LAY THE SEED OF SOMETHING GREAT AND NOBLE.

NOW THAT GREATNESS SHINES THROUGH ME. NOT THAT I CLAIM GREATNESS FOR MYSELF: I AM MERELY THE INSTRUMENT, THE VEHICLE.

YOU HAVE SEEN WHAT I AM CAPABLE OF: MY SACRED ACT. IT IS NOW MY SACRED DUTY, MY MISSION, TO CONTINUE, JUST AS IT IS YOUR DUTY TO STOP ME. IT WILL TAKE YOU A LONG TIME TO FIND ME, HERR FABEL. BUT BEFORE YOU DO I SHALL HAVE SPREAD THE WINGS OF THE EAGLE FAR AND WIDE. I SHALL MAKE MY MARK, IN BLOOD, ON OUR SACRED SOIL.

YOU CAN STOP ME, BUT YOU WILL NEVER CATCH ME.

I SHALL NO LONGER BE AT THE EDGE OF OTHER PEOPLE'S PHOTOGRAPHS. IT IS MY TURN AT THE CENTRE.

SON OF SVEN

Wednesday 4 June, 4.30 a.m. Pöseldorf, Hamburg.
Fabel dreamed.

Hamburg's element is water: there are more canals in Hamburg than in Amsterdam or Venice; the Aussenalster is the largest city-centre lake in Europe. It also rains throughout the year. Tonight, after a day when the air had lain over the city like a damp, stifling cloak, the heavens opened with vehemence.

As the thunderstorm outside flashed and growled its way across the city's sky, images sparked across Fabel's mind. Time imploded and folded in on itself. People and events separated by decades met in a place outside time. Fabel always dreamed of the same things: the untidiness of real life, the ends left loose, the stones left unturned. The unravelled ends of a dozen investigations would insinuate themselves into every corner of his sleeping brain. In this dream Fabel walked, as he had done in so many dreams before, among the murdered of fifteen years. He knew them all, each death-bleached face, in the same way most people would remember the faces of their extended family. Most of the dead, those whose killers he had caught, did not acknowledge him and passed by; but the dead eyes of those whose cases he had not solved gazed at him in bleak accusation and held out their wounds.

The crowd parted and Ursula Kastner stepped out to face Fabel. She wore the same smart, grey Chanel jacket as the last time, the only time, Fabel had seen her. Fabel stared at a tiny spot of blood that stained the jacket. The spot grew larger. A deeper red. Her bloodless, grey lips moved and formed the words 'Why have you not caught him?' For a moment Fabel was puzzled, in that vague, detached way one is in dreams, as to why he could not hear her voice. Was it because he had never heard it in life? Then he realised: of course, it was because her lungs had been torn out and therefore there was no breath to carry her words.

A noise woke him up. There was a rumble of thunder

beyond the picture windows and the soft crackle of rain on the panes, then the urgent trilling of the phone. Rubbing the sleep from his eyes, he picked up the receiver.

'Hello?'

'Hello Jan. It's Werner. You'd better get down here, *Chef* . . . there's been another one.'

The storm continued to rage. Electrical flashes danced across the Hamburg skyline, throwing out the black silhouettes of the Fernsehturm television tower and the spire of St Michaelis like flat stage scenery. The wipers on Fabel's BMW, switched to their fastest setting, fought to clear the windscreen of the barrage of thick viscous globs that exploded against the glass and turned street lamps and the headlights of oncoming cars into fractured stars. Fabel had picked up Werner Meyer at the Polizeipräsidium, and now Werner's considerable bulk was squeezed into the front passenger seat, filling the car with the smell of the rain-soaked fabric of his coat.

'This definitely look like our guy?' asked Fabel.

'From what the guy from Davidwache KriPo said, yep . . . looks like our guy.'

'*Shit.*' Fabel used the English word. 'So he's definitely a serial. Did you call forensics?'

'Yep.' Werner shrugged his vast shoulders, 'I'm afraid it's that asshole Möller. He'll already be there. Maria's at the scene as well and Paul and Anna are waiting for us at Davidwache.'

'What about an e-mail? Anything through yet?'

'Not yet.'

Fabel took the Ost-West-Strasse into St Pauli and turned into the Reeperbahn, Hamburg's Sündige Meile – sinful mile – which still glittered joylessly in the five a.m. rain. The downpour dulled to a heavy drizzle as Fabel swung the car into the Grosse Freiheit. Traditional indecency and imported middlebrow banality were waging war, and this was the front line. Porn shops and stripclubs were fighting a rearguard action against the invasion of trendy wine bars and musicals imported from Broadway or London's West End. Bright promises of 'Live Sex', 'Peep Show' and 'Hardcore Movies' competed with even brighter signs for *Cats*, *The Lion King* and *Mamma Mia*. Somehow Fabel found the sleaze less offensive.

'Did you get the message that a Professor Dorn has been trying to get in touch?' asked Werner. 'He said he needed to talk to you about the Kastner case . . .'

'Mathias Dorn?' Fabel kept his gaze on the road, as if the act of concentration would keep at bay the ghosts that stirred, somewhere deep and dark in his memory.

'Don't know. He just said he was Professor Dorn and you knew him at the Universität Hamburg. He's very keen to talk to you.'

'What the hell has Mathias Dorn got to do with the Kastner case?' Fabel's question was to himself. He turned into Davidstrasse. They passed the narrow opening of Herbertstrasse, concealed by a baffle of screens. Fabel had worked this district years ago and knew that beyond the screens prostitutes sat bleakly illuminated in their windows while the shadowy forms of browsing customers floated insubstantially in the lamplit drizzle. Love in the twenty-first century. Fabel drove on, passing through the pulse of dance music that bled into the night from the Weisse Maus in Taubenstrasse, and he pulled up outside the red brick ship's-prow front of the Davidwache police station. A couple sheltered in the doorway: the man was tall and lanky with sandy hair; the girl was petite and pretty, with spiky black hair and fire-truck-red lips. She wore an oversized black leather jacket. Seeing them in this context, Fabel couldn't help thinking just how young they both looked.

'Hi *Chef*,' Kriminalkommissarin Anna Wolff dropped into the rear seat and slid over, allowing her partner, Paul

Lindemann, to climb in and slam the door after him. 'I got directions from the Davidwache KriPo. I'll tell you where to go . . .'

They drove out of Davidstrasse. St Pauli's sham glamour now degraded into sheer seediness. The garish neon promises of libidinousness had the night to themselves and reflected bleakly on the rain-soaked pavements. The occasional pedestrian shambled along, shoulders hunched against the rain, resisting or accepting beckoned invitations from the spiritlessly enthusiastic stripclub doormen. Another turn: the descent continued. Doorways were now occupied either by gaunt and cheerless-looking prostitutes, some frighteningly young, others unfeasibly old, or by drunken down-and-outs. From one doorway an animated bundle of rags slurped from a bottle and yelled obscenities at the passing cars, at the prostitutes, at everybody and at nobody. And behind the doors, behind these blank, blind windows, the trade of flesh was conducted. This was Hamburg's eternal twilight: a place where human beings could be bought for any purpose and at any price; a place of dark sexual anarchy where people came to explore the murkiest corners of their souls.

As part of an investigation, Fabel had once had to watch a snuff movie. By the very nature of his job, Fabel usually walked onto the stage after the act had been concluded. He saw the corpse, the evidence, the witnesses, and from them had to build a picture of the killing: a slow envisioning of the moment of death. In this case, for the first time, Fabel was to become a witness to the crime he was investigating. He had gazed at the television screen, a vortex of fear and disgust swirling deep in his gut, as an unsuspecting porno actress performed her accustomed part with the usual insipid imitation of ecstasy. Throughout the loveless, crude penetration by three PVC-masked men, she moaned with transparently fake rapture, unaware of the denouement of this particular drama. Suddenly, with a swift and skilled single movement, one of the men tied a leather thong around her neck. Fabel saw the surprise and vague unease on her face: this was not part of the script, if these things were ever scripted, but she played along, miming heightened sexual excitement. Then, as the thong was tightened, her feigned ecstasy became a genuine terror. Her face blackened and she thrashed about wildly as her life was squeezed from her.

They had never caught her killers, and she had joined the accusatory legion of murdered who marched through Fabel's dreams. The video had been filmed somewhere near here, behind one of these blank windows.

Maybe another was being made now, as they passed by.

Another turn took Fabel into a residential street lined by four-storey apartment blocks. The sudden normality made Fabel feel disoriented. Another turn: more apartments, but this was where the normality ended. A small crowd had gathered around a police cordon, which in turn encircled a knot of police vehicles parked outside a squat 1950s apartment block.

Fabel gave a blast of his horn and a uniformed Obermeister parted the crowd. It was the usual mix of nobodies, faces blank or cheerlessly curious, some in night clothes and slippers, having dashed out from neighbouring apartments, some lifting themselves on tiptoe or twitching heads to see past their fellow ghouls. It was perhaps because he was so used to these crowds that Fabel noticed the old man. As Fabel inched his car through the huddle he saw him: he was in his late sixties, short – no taller than one metre sixty-five – but robustly built. His face seemed like a flat plane edged with sharp angles, particularly in the high cheekbones beneath the small, penetrating green eyes – eyes that, even in the insubstantial light from street lamps and headlights, seemed to gleam bright and cold. It was a face from the East, from around the Baltic or Poland or beyond. Unlike the others, the old man's expression held something more than a casual, morbid half-interest. And unlike the others, he wasn't turned towards the bustle of police activity outside the apartment building: he stared directly and intently at Fabel through the side window of the BMW. The uniformed officer moved between the old man and Fabel's car, bent over and peered in as Fabel held up his Kriminalpolizei shield. The uniform saluted and waved to another to lift the tape and allow Fabel through. When the policeman moved out of the way again, Fabel tried to find the old man with the luminous eyes, but he was gone.

'Did you see that old guy, Werner?'

'What old guy?'

'What about you?' Fabel asked Anna and Paul over his shoulder.

'Sorry, *Chef*,' answered Anna.

'What about him?' asked Paul.

'Nothing . . .' Fabel shrugged and drove through to where the other police cars huddled around the entrance to the building.

There were three flights of stairs up to the apartment. The stairwell was bathed in the bleak glow of wall-mounted half globes, one on each landing. As they climbed, Fabel and his team had to stop and flatten themselves against the stairwell walls to allow uniformed officers and forensic technicians to pass. On each occasion they noticed the grim seriousness on the silent faces, some of which were blanched by something more than the dismal electric light. Fabel could tell that something pretty bad waited for them at the top of the stairs.

The young uniformed policeman stood half bent over in a posture like that of an athlete who had just completed a marathon run: the tail of his spine resting against the door frame, his legs slightly bent, his hands spread out over his knees and his head forward and down. He breathed slowly and deliberately, staring intently at the floor at his feet as if absorbing every scratch and scuff on the concrete. He was unaware of Fabel's presence until the last moment. Fabel held out his oval Kriminalpolizei shield and the young policeman pulled himself stiffly upright. When he pushed back his mop of unruly red-blond hair it revealed a face that was pale behind its constellation of freckles.

'Sorry, Herr Kriminalhauptkommissar, I didn't see you.'

'That's okay. Are you all right?' Fabel looked into the younger man's face and rested his hand on his shoulder. The young policeman relaxed a bit and nodded. Fabel smiled. 'This your first murder?'

The young Polizeimeister looked directly into Fabel's eyes. 'No, Herr Hauptkommissar. Not the first. The worst . . . I've never seen anything like it.'

'I'm afraid I probably have,' said Fabel.

By now, Paul Lindemann and Anna Wolff had arrived at the top of the stairs and joined Fabel and Werner. A scene-of-crime officer, wearing his Tatort tabard, handed each of them a pair of pale blue forensic overshoes and a pair of white surgical gloves. After they had slipped on the gloves and overshoes, Fabel indicated the door of the flat with a movement of his head.

'Shall we?'

The first thing Fabel noticed was the freshness of the decoration. It was as if the short hall had only recently been painted. The colour was like pale butter: pleasant but bland, neutral, anonymous. There were three doors off the hall. Immediately to Fabel's left was a bathroom. A brief glimpse inside revealed it to be compact and, like the hall, clean and fresh. It seemed almost unused. Fabel noticed that the scant surfaces and shelves were uncluttered by the knick-knacks that tend to personalise a bathroom. The second door was opened wide and revealed what was obviously the main room in the apartment: a bedroom and living area combined. It too was small, and made even more cramped by the cluster of police and forensics in it; each doing his job in a bizarre dance with the others, arms raised, squeezing past each other in a clumsy ballet. As Fabel entered, he noticed that each face wore a solemnity that one would expect in such a situation but which is, in reality, rare. Normally there would be an element of gallows humour: that inappropriate black levity that somehow allows those who deal with death to remain untouched by it. But not these people. Not here. Here death had reached out and seized them, gripping their hearts with fingers of bone.

When Fabel looked over to the bed, he saw why. Somewhere behind him Werner muttered, '*Scheisse!*'

There was an explosion of red. A sunburst of blood had encrimsoned the bed and splashed across the carpet and up the wall. The bed itself was sodden with dark, sticky blood and even the air seemed heavy with its rich, copper odour. At the heart of the bloody eruption, Fabel saw the body of a woman. It was difficult to make out how old, but probably somewhere between twenty-five and thirty. She was spread-eagled on the bed, her outstretched wrists and ankles bound to the posts, her abdomen grotesquely deformed. She had been sliced open through the chest and the ribs pulled apart and outwards until they looked like the superstructure of a boat. The bony whiteness of the sheared ribs shone through the prised-open mess of raw flesh and glistening dark viscera. Two dark, bloody masses of tissue – her lungs – speckled with frothy, bright blood, lay thrown out over her shoulders.

It was as if she had been blown apart from the inside.

Fabel's heart pounded so fiercely that he felt as if his chest, too, were going to burst. He knew his face had blanched white. When Werner made his way over to him, squeezing past the police photographer, Fabel saw the same pallor on his face.

'It's him again. This is bad, *Chef*. This is really bad. We've got the mother of all psychos on the loose here.'

For a moment Fabel found he couldn't direct his gaze away from the corpse. Then, taking a breath, he turned to Paul.

'Witnesses?'

'None. Don't ask me how this much mayhem could be created without someone hearing, but this is the way she was found. All we've got is the guy who found her. No one saw or heard anything.'

'Any signs of forced entry?'

Paul shook his head. 'The guy who found her said the door was ajar, but no, no signs of forced entry.'

Fabel moved towards the body. It seemed so cruel that such a violent and terrifying leaving of her life should go unnoticed. Her terror had been a lonely terror. Her death – a death he could not imagine, no matter how graphically it was laid out before him – had been desolate, solitary, in a universe filled with only the cold violence of her killer. He looked beyond the devastation of her body to the face. It was spattered with blood; the mouth gaped slightly and the eyes were open. There was no look of terror: no fear nor hate nor even peace. It was an expressionless mask that gave no concept of the personality that had once lived behind it. Möller, the pathologist, masked and bunny-suited in his white forensic kit, was examining the sliced-open abdomen. He gestured impatiently for Fabel to move back.

Fabel pulled his attention away from the body. The corpse wasn't just a physical object, it was a temporal entity: a point in time, an event. It represented the moment that the murder had been committed and, in the sealed scene of crime, everything around it belonged either to the time before or to the time after that moment. He scanned the room, trying to imagine it without the swirl of police and forensic technicians. It was small but uncluttered. There was a lack of personality about it, as if it were a functional space rather than a home. A small, faded photograph sat on the dressing table by the door, propped against the lamp; the photograph was conspicuous as the only truly 'personal' personal effect in the room. There was a print on the wall, a female nude reclining, eyes half closed in an attitude of erotic ecstasy: not something a woman would usually pick for her own enjoyment. A wide, full-length mirror, fixed to the wall which divided the room from the room beyond, which Fabel surmised would have to be the kitchen, reflected the bed. He noticed a small wicker bowl on the bedside table: it was filled with condoms of various colours. He turned to Anna Wolff.

'Hooker?'

'Looks like it, although she isn't . . . wasn't anyone Davidwache vice knew about.' Anna's face was pale beneath the shock of dark hair. Fabel noticed she was making an effort not to look in the direction of the devastated corpse. 'But we do know the guy who called in.'

'Oh yes?'

'A guy called Klugmann. He's ex-Polizei Hamburg.'

'An ex-cop?'

'In fact he's an ex-Mobiles Einsatz Kommando officer. He claims that he was a friend . . . he has the lease on the flat.'

'"Claims"?'

'The local boys reckon he must have been her pimp.' It was Paul who answered

'Whoa, hold on . . .' Fabel's impatient expression implied he held Paul responsible for his confusion. 'You said this guy is a former Mobiles Einsatz Kommando member and now he's a pimp?'

'We think he may well be. He worked with the MEK special-operations unit attached to the Organised Crime Division, but he was kicked out.'

'Why?'

'Apparently he developed a taste for the goods.' It was Anna Wolff who answered. 'He was caught with a small amount of cocaine and sacked. He was charged and got off with a suspended sentence. The Staatsanwalt prosecutor was cagey about sending an MEK member to prison and anyway it was only a few grams of coke . . . personal use, he claimed.'

'You seem to know the story pretty well.'

Anna laughed. 'While Paul and I were waiting for you at Davidwache, we got the whole story from one of the guys there. Klugmann was involved in a couple of raids in St Pauli. Typical surprise attacks on Turkish Mafia drugs factories by MEK special units. Both times the premises were as clean as a whistle – they'd obviously been tipped off. Because they were joint operations with Davidwache KriPo, the MEK tried to pin the blame on Davidwache for being loose with security. After Klugmann was busted it all fitted together.'

'He bought his drugs with something other than cash?'

'That's what they reckon. The MEK tried to prove he'd been passing information on to the Ulugbay organisation but couldn't come up with any hard evidence.'

'So Klugmann got off with a slap on the wrist.'

'Yes. And now he works in an Ulugbay-owned stripclub.'

Fabel smiled. 'And as a pimp.'

'Like I say, that's what the local police suspect . . . and more.'

'I can imagine,' said Fabel. A former special-forces policeman would be incredibly valuable to Ulugbay: muscle *and* inside information. 'Should we look at him as a suspect for this?'

'He needs checking out but no, I doubt it. Apparently, he was in genuine shock when the local uniforms got here. We talked to him briefly at Davidwache. He's a tough-looking son of a bitch but he clearly hadn't worked out a credible story. Just kept saying he was a friend and had called around to see her.'

'Do we have a name for her?'

'That's the thing,' Paul answered. 'I'm afraid we have a mystery woman on our hands. Klugmann says he's only ever known her as "Monique".'

'Is she French?'

Paul half smiled, looking at Fabel to see if there was any sign of irony in his expression; he had heard of *der englische Kommissar*'s reputation for a British sense of humour. No irony. Just impatience. 'Not according to Klugmann. Sounds like a professional name to me.'

'What about her personal effects. Her identity card?'

'Nothing.'

Fabel noticed the bedside cabinet had already been dusted for prints. He pulled open one of the drawers. There was an oversized dildo and four pornographic magazines, one of which specialised in bondage. He looked back at the body: the wrists and ankles were tied tightly to the posts of the bed by what looked like black stockings. The choice had been practical and improvised rather than erotic and premeditated; nor was there any other evidence of the usual paraphernalia of bondage. The next drawer held more condoms, a large box of paper tissues and a bottle of massage oil. The third drawer was empty except for a pad of writing paper and two ballpoint pens. He turned to the head of the forensic team.

'Where's Holger Brauner?' he asked, referring to the forensic department's chief.

'He's on leave till the weekend.'

Fabel wished that Brauner had been on duty. Brauner could read a crime scene like an archaeologist could read a landscape: seeing the traces, invisible to everyone else, of those who had passed by before. 'Can one of your guys bag all of this stuff for me?'

'Of course, Herr Hauptkommissar.'

'There was nothing else in this bottom drawer?'

The duty forensics chief frowned. 'No. Anything we removed for examination and dusting has been replaced. There was nothing else.'

'Have you found her appointment book?'

Again the technician looked puzzled.

'She's been a hooker but not a street girl,' explained Fabel. 'Her customers will have been by appointment, probably made by phone. She must have had an appointment book.'

'Not that we've found.'

'My guess is that, if she had one, it was in here,' said Fabel, nodding to the open third drawer. 'If we can't find it elsewhere then it's my guess our guy took it with him.'

'To protect himself? You think she's been done by a client?' asked Paul.

'I doubt it. Our guy – and this *is* our guy – wouldn't be so dumb as to pick someone who has prior knowledge of him.'

'So this is definitely the same guy who did the Kastner girl?'

'Who the hell else could it be?' answered Werner, nodding towards the corpse. 'This is obviously his signature.'

A silence fell between them as they each sank into their own thoughts about the implications of this being the work of a serial killer. They all knew that they would not close the gap between themselves and this monster until he had killed again. And more than once. Each scene of crime would yield a little more: small investigative steps paid for with the blood of innocent victims. It was Fabel who broke the silence.

'Anyway, if our guy didn't take the appointment book with him then maybe Klugmann swiped it to protect the identities of his clients.'

Möller, the pathologist, had remained bent over the body, peering into the empty chasm of the girl's abdomen. He straightened up, peeled off his bloodied surgical gloves and turned to the Hauptkommissar.

'This is the same man's work all right, Fabel . . .' With a surprising gentleness, Möller swept the blonde hair back from the girl's face. 'Exactly the same form of killing as the other victim.'

'I can see that for myself, Möller. When did she die?'

'This kind of catastrophic dismemberment makes temperature readings –'

Fabel cut him off. 'Your best guess?'

Möller angled his head backwards. He was a good bit taller
than Fabel and looked down at him as if he were surveying
something unworthy of his attention. 'I would estimate
between one and three a.m.'

A tall, blonde woman, dressed in an elegant grey trouser
suit, emerged from the hall. She looked as if she would be
more at home in the boardroom of a corporate bank than
at a murder scene. She was Kriminaloberkommissarin Maria
Klee, Fabel's most recent addition to his team. '*Chef*, you'd
better have a look at this.'

Fabel followed her out to the hall and into a small and
extremely narrow gallery kitchen. Like the rest of the flat,
the kitchen seemed almost unused. There was a kettle and a
packet of teabags on the counter. A single rinsed cup lay
upturned on the drainer. Otherwise there was no trace of the
mechanics of living: no plates in the sink, no letters sitting
on the counter or on top of the fridge, nothing to suggest
that this space contained the cycle of a human life. Maria
Klee indicated an open wall-cupboard door. When Fabel
looked inside he saw that the plaster of the wall had been
cut away and a sheet of glass allowed a clear view of the
room beyond. He found himself looking directly at the gore-
sodden bed.

'One way?' Fabel asked Maria.

'Yep. The other side is the full-length mirror. Look at this.'
She squeezed past Fabel, reached her latex-gloved hand into
the cupboard and stretched out an electrical cable. 'I reckon
there's been a camera in here.'

'So our guy could have been caught on video?'

'Except there's nothing in here now,' said Maria. 'Maybe
he found it and took it.'

'Okay. Get the forensic guys to give it a good going over.'

Fabel made to leave but Maria stopped him. 'I remember, when I was a kid, my school went on a day trip to the NDR television studios. We were shown around a set for some TV show . . . you know, a *Lindenstrasse* or *Gute Zeiten Schlechte Zeiten* type soap opera. I remember how real the room looked – until you got up close. Then you saw that the sky beyond the windows was painted and the cupboard doors didn't open . . .'

'What's your point, Maria?'

'There's everything here you would expect from a call girl's apartment . . . but it's like a set designer's *idea* of what a call girl's apartment should look like. And it's like no one has really *lived* here.'

'For all we know this place *wasn't* lived in. It could simply be "business" premises used by a team of girls . . .'

'I know . . . but there's still something about it that doesn't ring true. Know what I mean?'

Fabel took a deep breath and held it for a moment before replying. 'As a matter of fact I know exactly what you mean, Maria.'

Fabel moved back into the main room. The scene-of-crime photographer was taking detailed shots of the body. He had set up a lamp on a stand; the stark light was focused on the corpse, making the blood spattered across the room even more vivid and adding to the sense of explosive violence. The young uniformed officer was still standing at the door, his gaze fixed on the corpse. Fabel placed himself between the young cop and the body.

'What's your name, son?'

'Beller, sir. Uwe Beller.'

'Okay, Beller. Did you speak to any of the neighbours?'

Beller's gaze had started to drift across Fabel's shoulder and back to the horror in the room beyond. He snapped himself back. 'What? Oh . . . yes. Sorry sir, yes, I did. There's a couple on the ground floor and an old lady immediately underneath. They didn't hear a thing. But there again, the *Oma* underneath is practically deaf.'

'Can they give us a name for the girl?'

'No. Both the old lady and the couple say they hardly ever saw her. The flat used to be owned by another old woman who died about a year ago. It was empty for about three months and then it was rented out again.'

'Did they see anyone come or go this evening?'

'No. Other than the guy who arrived at two-thirty, the guy who phoned us. The couple on the ground floor were woken up by the front door slamming – it's on a spring hinge and it closes with a bang that echoes a bit in the hall . . . but nobody heard anything before that. There again the couple on the ground floor were asleep and, like I say, the old lady underneath is a bit deaf.' Beller tilted his head to look over Fabel's shoulder towards the body. 'Whoever it was is a complete psycho. Mind you, she was asking for trouble getting mixed up in this game – bringing back all kinds of pervert off the street.'

Fabel picked up the dog-eared photograph that leaned against the lamp on the dresser. A worn fragment of someone's life, a real life. It was as much at home in this spiritless apartment as grit in an eye. The photograph had been taken in what Fabel guessed to be Hamburg's Planten un Blomen park on a sunny day. It was an old photograph, the quality was not good and it had been taken from a distance, but he could just make out the features of a mousy-haired adolescent girl, around fourteen. It was a face that was not ugly, not pretty, but one you would pass in the street without noticing. With her was an older boy, about nineteen, and a couple in their mid-forties. There was that feel of familiarity and ease between them that led instantly to the conclusion that this was a family.

'She's still a person,' Fabel answered without looking at the young Polizeimeister, 'still someone's daughter. The question is whose.' He took an evidence bag out of his jacket pocket and placed the photograph in it. Then he turned to Möller.

'Give me your report as soon as you can.'

Wednesday 4 June, 6.00 a.m. St Pauli, Hamburg.

On the way out, Fabel got Beller to go with him to the apartment downstairs. There was already a uniformed officer there, drinking tea with a bird-like old woman with paper skin. This apartment was an exact copy, in layout at least, of the one above. But decades of habitation had etched itself into the walls of this flat, until it had become an extension of the old woman who lived in it. In contrast, it was someone's death, not their life, that had made the only mark on the apartment above.

The officer rose from the armchair when Fabel walked in but Fabel motioned for him to relax. Beller introduced the woman as Frau Steiner. She stared up at Fabel with large, round, watery eyes. The combination of her gaze and her bird-like frailty made Fabel think of an owl. There was a table and chairs against one wall. Fabel pulled up one of the chairs and sat facing the old woman.

'Are you all right, Frau Steiner? I know this must be a shock for you. Such a terrible business. And I'm sure that you must find it disturbing to have all of us tramping around the place. So much noise . . .'

As Fabel spoke, the old woman leaned forward and creased her brow over her owl eyes, as if concentrating hard on his words. 'It's all right, the noise doesn't bother me . . . I'm a bit deaf, you know.'

'I see,' said Fabel, raising his voice slightly. 'So you won't have heard anything last night?'

Frau Steiner suddenly looked deeply sad. 'That's the thing, I probably did . . . I probably heard something but didn't realise it.'

'I don't understand,' said Fabel.

'Tinnitus. I'm afraid it goes along with my deafness. I take my hearing aid out when I sleep . . . every night I hear sounds . . . bumps, high-pitched whines . . . even sounds like screams. But it's just my tinnitus. Or rather, I never know whether it's my tinnitus or not.'

'I see, I'm sorry. That must be unpleasant.'

'You have to shut it out. Otherwise you'd go mad.' She shook her small, bird-like head slowly, as if too sudden a movement might damage it. 'I've had it a long, long time, young man. Since July 1943, to be exact.'

'The British bombing?'

'I'm glad you know your history. I'm afraid I have to live with mine. Or at least the echoes of it. I was caught outside when the first wave came over. Both eardrums shattered, you see. And this . . .' She pulled up a black woollen sleeve to reveal an impossibly thin arm. The skin was puckered and mottled pink and white. 'Burns on thirty per cent of my body. But it's the tinnitus that has marked me most.' She paused for a moment; a sadness seemed to well in the owl eyes. 'I cannot stand the thought of that poor girl crying out for help and me not hearing it.'

Fabel looked past the woman's head and took in the collection of old black-and-white photographs on the dresser behind her: her as a child and as a young woman, even then with owl eyes; her with a man with a shock of black hair; another photograph of the same man wearing what Fabel thought at first was a Wehrmacht uniform, then he recognised it as that of a wartime Police Reserve Battalion. No children. No photographs less than fifty years old.

'Did you see her much?'

'No. In fact I only spoke to her once. I was brushing the landing when she passed on her way up.'

'Did you talk to her?'

'Not really. She said hello and something about the

weather and went on up. I would have asked her in for a cup of coffee, but she seemed in a hurry. She looked like a businesswoman or something . . . very smartly dressed. Expensive shoes, as I remember. Beautiful shoes. Foreign. Other than that day, I only heard her on the stairs occasionally. I thought she probably went away on business a lot or something.'

'Did she have lots of visitors. Men, specifically?'

Her face creased in concentration again. 'No . . . no, I can't say that I saw much of anybody.'

'I know this is a very unpleasant matter, but I have to ask you, Frau Steiner – was there anything that made you think she may have been a prostitute?'

Impossibly, the owl eyes widened. 'No. Certainly not. Is that what she was?'

'We don't know. If she were, I would have expected you to see more men coming and going.'

'No, I can honestly say I was only aware of two or three visitors to the flat. But now you mention it they were all men, I never saw another woman.'

'Can you describe them?'

'No, not really,' she shook her head again, slowly. 'I can't even be sure if there were more than, say, two men visiting. I maybe saw the same person more than once.' She pointed past Fabel, down the hall, to the semiopaque bronze-glass panel in her apartment door. 'I just saw shapes through the door – figures more than anything.'

'So you wouldn't be able to recognise any of them?'

'Only the young man who sub-let the apartment to her . . .'

'That would be Klugmann, sir,' interjected Beller. 'He was the one who discovered the body and called us.'

'Did he come around often?' Fabel asked.

The old woman gave a shrug of her insubstantial shoulders. 'I only saw him a couple of times. Like I say, he could have been one of the figures I saw go up and down, or he was maybe only here the couple of times I saw him.' She looked towards the glass panel in the door at the end of the short hall. 'That's what it means to become old, young man. Your world shrinks and shrinks until it's reduced to just shadows passing your door.'

'When was Herr Klugmann's most recent visit, that you know about?'

'Last week . . . or maybe the week before. I'm sorry, I didn't really pay much heed.'

'That's all right, Frau Steiner. Thank you for your time.' Fabel rose from the armchair.

'Herr Hauptkommissar?' The watery owl eyes blinked.

'Yes, Frau Steiner?'

'Did she suffer terribly?'

There was no point in lying. It would soon be all over the papers. 'I'm afraid she did. But she's at peace now. Goodbye, Frau Steiner. If there is anything you need, please ask one of the officers.'

The words didn't seem to have sunk in, the old woman simply sat shaking her head. 'Tragic. So tragic.'

As they left the flat Fabel turned to Beller. 'You said you were first on the scene?'

'Yes, sir.'

'And there was no one hanging around?'

'No, sir. Just the guy who phoned us . . . and by that time the young couple from the downstairs flat.'

'You didn't see an older man hanging around?'

Beller shook his head thoughtfully.

'Even later, when the ghouls began to gather? A short, thickset man in his late sixties? He looks foreign . . . Slavic . . . maybe Russian.'

'No sir . . . sorry. Is it important?'

'I don't know,' said Fabel. 'Probably not.'

Wednesday 4 June, 7.30 a.m. St Pauli, Hamburg.
The interview room in the Davidwache police station was a study in efficient minimalism. The starkness of the white-washed walls was broken only by the door and a single window which would have looked out onto Davidstrasse, had its glass not been thick and cloudy, like a sheet of frozen milk, against which the daylight that was dawning outside was reduced to a vague bloom. One end of the interview table was pushed up against the wall, and four tubular metal chairs were arranged, two on either side, at the table. A black inter-view-recording cassette unit sat at the end of the table. Above it, on the wall, was a notice advising of exits and procedures in case of fire. Above that a sign forbidding smoking.

Fabel and Werner sat on one side of the table. Opposite Fabel was a man of about thirty-five with thick, greasy black hair combed back in glistening strands that continually slipped over his forehead. He was tall and powerfully built, his shoulders straining against the cheap black leather of his too-tight jacket. He had the look of a former athlete gone to seed: an incipient corpulence gelling around the waistline, the eyes shadowed, the skin pale against the black hair and two-day stubble; a face still square and strong, but beginning to show signs of sagging.

'You are Hans Klugmann?' Fabel asked without looking up from the report.

'Yes . . .' Klugmann leaned forward, hunching his shoulders, placing his wrists on the edge of the table and picking at the skin on one thumb with the nail of the other. A poise almost like prayer, but for its nervous intensity.

'You found the girl . . .' Fabel flipped over a few pages. '"Monique".'

'Yes . . .' The thumbnail dug deeper. One leg, resting on the ball of the foot, started to bounce in an unconscious twitch under the table. The action made the hands shake rhythmically.

'It must have been a shock . . . very unpleasant for you . . .'

There was genuine pain in Klugmann's eyes. 'You could say that . . .'

'Monique was a friend?'

'Yes.'

'Yet you claim you don't know her surname?'

'I don't.'

'Look, Herr Klugmann, I have to admit I really need your help here. I'm a very confused man and I'm relying on you to help me clear up my confusion. So far I have the body of an anonymous girl lying dismembered in an apartment where there's no trace of personal belongings other than a single set of clothes found in a wardrobe . . . no purse, no papers . . . for that matter there isn't even any food other than a litre of milk in the fridge. We also find *some* of the trappings you would expect in an apartment used for prostitution. And the apartment is located conveniently near, but not in, the red-light district. Yet there is no evidence of a lot of male visitors. See why I am confused?'

Klugmann shrugged.

'And on top of all that we discover that the apartment is officially rented out to a former police special-forces officer who claims not to know his sub-tenant's full name.' Fabel waited for the words to sink in. Klugmann sat impassive, staring at his hands. 'So why don't you stop jerking us around, Herr Klugmann? You and I both know that the apartment was used for the purposes of prostitution, but in some kind of highly selective way, and that this girl Monique didn't live there. Listen, I'm not interested in your arrangement with this girl other than in the information you can give me about her. Do I make myself clear?'

Klugmann nodded but did not lift his gaze from his hands.

'So what was her name?'

'I told you, I don't know . . . I swear that's the truth. All

I ever called her – all she ever called herself – was Monique.'

'But she was a prostitute?'

'Okay, maybe . . . I don't know . . . she might have been
. . . maybe part time. Nothing to do with me. She never
seemed short of money, so yeah, maybe.'

'How long have you known her?'

'Only about three or four months.'

'If you don't know her name,' Werner said, 'then there
must be others who do. Who did she hang out with?'

'I don't know.'

'You never met any of her friends?' Fabel asked without
disguising his incredulity.

'No.'

Fabel pushed a photograph of the first victim, Ursula
Kastner, across the desk. 'Recognise her?'

'No. Well . . . yeah . . . but only from the papers. Isn't she
the lawyer that got murdered? Was she done the same way?'

Fabel ignored the question and left the photograph sitting
there. Klugmann didn't look at it again. Fabel had a feeling
that he was deliberately avoiding looking at Kastner's face.
An instinct, somewhere deep inside Fabel's gut, began to
stir.

'What about Monique's address before she moved into the
flat?'

Klugmann shrugged.

'This is getting ridiculous.' Werner leaned forward. His
bulk and the brutality of his features gave his movements a
menace that often wasn't intended. In response Klugmann
straightened himself in his chair and angled his head back
defiantly. 'You are trying to tell us that this girl moved into
your life and into your apartment without you knowing her
full name, or anything else about her?'

'You have to admit, Herr Klugmann,' said Fabel, 'I mean,
as a former policeman, that it does all seem a bit strange.'

Klugmann relaxed his pose. 'Yeah. I suppose it does. But

I'm telling you the truth. Listen, it's a different world out there. Monique just, well, sort of appeared one night at the place I work and we got talking . . .'

'She was on her own?'

'Yes. That's why I got talking to her. Arno, my boss, thought she was an expensive hooker trawling our club and told me to send her on her way. We got talking and she seemed a good kid. She asked me if I knew somewhere she could rent a room or an apartment and I told her about my flat.'

'Why did you offer her your flat? Why don't you live there yourself?'

'I'm . . . well, sort of *involved* with one of the girls from the Tanzbar . . . Sonja. I was staying over most nights at her place because it was so close to the Tanzbar. After I leased the new place I moved in with Sonja while it was being decorated. Then I meet Monique, and she says she's willing to pay well, and in advance, for a decent place to stay. She also said it would only be for maybe six to nine months. So I thought it was a good way to make a few extra euros . . .'

'And you were to keep out of the way?' asked Werner.

'That was the deal . . .'

'So what were you doing up there at that time of the night?'

'I called up to see her. I did that now and again to check everything was okay. We got on . . .'

'You were making a social call at two-thirty in the morning?' Fabel asked.

'Neither of us worked normal hours.'

'What, exactly, is your job, Herr Klugmann?'

'Like I told you, I work in a nightclub . . . a Tanzbar. I'm an assistant manager.'

Fabel consulted the file again. 'Ah yes, the Paradies-Tanzbar off the Grosse Freiheit . . . that the one?'

'Yeah.'

'So you work for . . . ?'

'You know who I work for . . .' Klugmann looked down

at the thumbnail he was now excavating with the other.

Fabel pulled a second file out from under the first. He flipped it open and scanned the first page. Klugmann saw his own photograph at the top right-hand corner. His hunched shoulders sagged. 'Yes . . .' Fabel leaned back in his chair and eyed Klugmann contemplatively. 'Your current employer is Ersin Ulugbay . . . not exactly Hamburg citizen of the month, is he?'

'S'pose not.'

'It's an odd career move,' said Werner, 'from an elite police unit to the Turkish Mafia.'

'I didn't have much choice about my retirement from the police.' Klugmann smiled cynically. 'As you probably already know. Anyway, I don't work for any "Mafia". I know what Ulugbay's into, but I'm not into it. Ulugbay may own the bar, but my boss is Arno Hoffknecht, the manager. It's not much, I'm supposed to be an assistant manager but I'm really nothing more than a glorified bouncer. But I keep my nose clean.'

'Really?' said Werner. 'Interesting choice of expression. I don't know if your nose is really that clean.'

'What d'you mean?'

'When was your last line?'

The sinews on Klugmann's thick neck tautened. 'Fuck you, *Arschloch*.'

Werner's eyes blazed and his huge frame seemed primed to explode into violence. Fabel took the initiative. 'I hope you're not going to prove uncooperative, Herr Klugmann. That could make things look worse for you.'

'What do you mean "worse for me"? This has fuck-all to do with me. And you've got no proof otherwise . . .'

'You're holding something back.'

'For instance?'

'For instance, where is Monique's appointment book?'

'I don't know what you're talking about.'

'Or the video camera that you had hidden behind the mirror? What was that about? Blackmail or just making porn?'

For an instant Klugmann seemed taken aback. 'Look, I have absolutely no idea what you're talking about. No fuckin' idea at all.'

Fabel leaned back. Werner recognised the tag and leaned his bristle-haired bullet head forward, smiling. 'I don't like you, Klugmann . . .'

'Oh really?' Klugmann feigned hurt surprise. 'And I was thinking maybe we had some kind of future together . . .'

'I don't like you because you're a traitor and a crook. You crapped on this police service when you started selling your mouth to Ulugbay.' Werner leaned back and twisted his face in contempt. 'You stink. You smell of the fucking gutter, you live with a whore . . .'

Klugmann tensed and made a sudden movement forward. Fabel held up his hand. 'Easy . . .'

Werner continued, unfazed. 'You live with a whore, you rented your home out to another whore so that she could be ripped apart by some fucking maniac, and you work in a cesspit for a Turkish godfather. What's it like, Klugmann . . . what's it like when you look in the mirror in the morning? For Christ's sake you were a policeman – and, from what we can see of your record, a good one. You must have had ambition once. And now you're . . .' Werner gestured towards Klugmann, extending his arms as if he were holding something noxious at bay – 'you're this.' He pushed his face even closer to Klugmann's. 'You are vermin, Klugmann. I don't for one second think you're beyond doing what was done to that girl. And I don't for one second believe any of this line of crap you're feeding us about not knowing anything about her except her first name.'

Werner came to an abrupt halt. There was silence in the room. A balanced, calculated silence. Klugmann slumped back in his chair, one leg sprawled, the other still doing its little nervous dance. Fabel scanned Klugmann's face. There was the expected mask of disinterest: a studied boredom worn by countless others who had sat across the interview desk from Fabel over the years: an expression intended to convey a lack of concern, but Fabel could invariably see through it. As he regarded Klugmann, he realised that, in this case, he couldn't penetrate the mask.

Werner continued. 'You weren't a friend, and you weren't a customer . . . you weren't up there for a sly four-hundred-euro fuck, were you? From what we can tell about "Monique", she was way out of your class – and your price bracket.'

Klugmann didn't answer and stared at the edge of the table.

'And I don't believe that you are simply the unfortunate landlord of an anonymous girl who just happens to be butchered in the property you rent. So where does that leave us?' Werner persisted: 'Not a friend. Not a customer. That leaves . . . well, that leaves either you slicing her up, or that you're an enforcer for Ulugbay . . . that you were her pimp. I think you were up there to collect – and I mean more than the rent – and if she got out of line you'd give her a little slap. Isn't that about the size of it?'

Silence.

'Maybe you like your work. Maybe you get a hard-on when you knock these girls about a bit. Maybe last night was you having some special fun . . .'

Klugmann exploded. 'Don't be fuckin' stupid . . . You saw the state of that room . . . if it hadda been me I'd be covered in blood . . .'

'Maybe you took your clothes off before you had your jollies . . . Maybe we should have forensics give you a going over . . .'

'Do what the fuck you want . . . Okay, so I work for Ulugbay. That's got nothing to do with what happened up there tonight. It's got nothing to do with him and I'm not bringing him into it. You don't scare me like the fucking Turks scare me. You know the score . . . if they think I'm talking to you about them I'll end up in the woods with my face shaved off.'

Fabel knew the custom Klugmann was referring to, a favourite with the Turkish Mafia: someone who crossed them in a drugs deal, or who gave information to the police, would be dumped in the woods to the north of Hamburg. The hands would be missing, the teeth smashed and the face sliced off. It made identification of the victim difficult, sometimes impossible, and delayed investigations to such an extent that often the trail would be too cold to secure a conviction.

'Okay, okay . . . just calm down,' Fabel said. 'But you've got to see that you're the only person that we can place in her apartment . . .'

'Sure – for thirty fuckin' seconds. As soon as I saw her . . . like *that* . . . I came straight out and phoned you.'

'You didn't use her phone?'

'No. I used my cell phone. I couldn't stay in there. I had to get out.'

'You arrived about two-thirty?' Fabel asked.

'Yeah.'

'And you didn't touch anything?'

'No. I was straight in and out.'

'How did you get in? You have a key?'

'No. Well, yes, I do, but I didn't use it. The door was unlocked and open a bit.'

'Your call was logged by the Einsatzzentrale at two-thirty-five. Where were you before you called at the apartment?'

'At the Paradies-Tanzbar, working.'

'Until when, exactly?'

'About a quarter to two.'

'It doesn't take three quarters of an hour to get from the Grosse Freiheit to her apartment.'

'Had business to do . . .'

'What business?'

Klugmann held his hands out palms upwards and tilted his head to one side. Fabel picked up his pen and rattled it between his teeth.

'If you can't or won't tell us, that gives you the opportunity to kill the girl, get cleaned up and claim that you've just arrived and found the body.'

'Okay, okay . . . I went down to see a guy I know in the Hafen . . . bought some stuff . . .'

'From whom?'

'You've gotta be fuckin' kidding . . .'

Fabel spun a scene-of-crime photograph across the table. The scene had been captured in full colour, so vivid that it looked unreal.

'This is no joke.'

Klugmann froze, his face white. Memories were obviously flooding back. 'She was a friend. That's all.'

Werner sighed. Klugmann ignored him and looked directly at Fabel.

'And you know I didn't kill her, Herr Fabel . . .' The intensity faded from his eyes and his posture. 'Anyway, I got a taxi from the club down to the Hafen. The taxi guy waited for me while I had my meet and then took me up to the apartment. He dropped me off there about two-thirty. He can tell you all my movements from leaving the club to arriving at the flat. Check with the taxi firm.'

'We're already checking.'

Fabel closed the file and stood up. It seemed clear that Klugmann wasn't the killer; they had no solid grounds for detaining him, even as a material witness. But the interview had unsettled Fabel. Klugmann seemed everything he was supposed to be, but Fabel had had the feeling throughout that he had been looking at a map upside down: all the recognised landmarks were there, but they disoriented rather than guided. With both files under his arm, Fabel walked towards

the door and spoke without looking back at Klugmann. 'We'll
get forensics to examine you and your clothing anyway.'

Everything about Maria Klee was brisk and sharp, from her
clipped Hanover accent to her short, styled blonde hair. When
Fabel emerged from the interview room she was standing in
the corridor waiting for him. She had a sheet of paper in her
hand.

'How did it go?' she asked briskly.

Fabel was about to answer when a uniformed SchuPo
arrived to escort Klugmann to forensics. Klugmann's and
Maria's eyes met for a moment; Klugmann's eyes seemed
blank, as if Maria weren't there, while Maria frowned, as if
trying to work something out.

'You know him?' asked Fabel when Klugmann and his
escort were out of earshot.

'I don't know . . . I thought I recognised him, but I couldn't
say where I've seen him before . . .'

'Well, it is possible. He is ex-Polizei Hamburg.'

Maria shrugged again, this time as if she were shaking off
an irritating inconsequence. 'How did you get on with him
anyway?'

'He's obviously not our guy, but he's dirty. Everything is
just wrong about him. There's something he's not telling us.
In fact, there's a lot he's not telling us. How did you get on?'

'I talked to the manager of the Tanzbar, Arno Hoffknecht.
He confirms that Klugmann was there working until after
one-thirty.'

'Could Hoffknecht be covering for him?'

'Well, you have to see this guy to believe him. He is as
sleazy as they come. Made my flesh crawl.' Maria mimed a
shudder. 'But no, he's not covering for him. Too many other
people saw Klugmann throughout his shift. Davidwache
KriPo have also checked out Klugmann's claim that he went
everywhere in the same taxi . . .'

'He just told us the same story.'

'Anyway, the driver confirms that he picked up Klugmann at the club at one-forty-five, took him to a Kneipe in the Hafen – Klugmann told him to wait – then he dropped him at the apartment about half past two.'

'Okay. Anything else?'

'Yes, I'm afraid there is,' said Maria, and handed Fabel the print-out of the e-mail she had been holding in her hand.

Wednesday 4 June, 10.00 a.m. Polizeipräsidium, Hamburg. Fabel read it out loud again, then put the page back down on the table and walked over to the window. The briefing room was on the third floor of the Polizeipräsidium. The traffic below pulsed with the changing of the traffic lights: the reassuring rhythm of Hamburg life.

'And the e-mail was addressed to you, personally?' asked Van Heiden.

'Yes, the same as the last one,' Fabel sipped at his tea. He kept his back to the others and looked out through the rain, across Winterhuder Stadtpark to where the city centre jutted into a steel grey sky.

'Is there no way we can trace it?' asked Van Heiden.

'Unfortunately not, Herr Kriminaldirektor.' It was Maria Klee who answered. 'Our friend seems to have a pretty sophisticated understanding of information technology. Unless we actually catch him online, there's no way we can locate him. Even then it would be unlikely.'

'Have we had Technical Section look at this?'

'Yes sir,' said Maria Klee. Fabel still didn't turn but kept focused on the pulsing traffic below. 'We've also had an independent expert look at the e-mail. There's just no way we can track it back.'

'It's perfect,' said Fabel. 'An anonymous letter or note gives us physical evidence; we can look for DNA, carry out hand-writing analysis, identify the source of the paper and the ink . . . but an e-mail only has an electronic presence. Forensically, it is non-existent.'

'But I thought an anonymous e-mail was impossible,' said Van Heiden. 'Surely we have an IP address?'

Fabel was momentarily taken aback by Van Heiden's knowledge of information technology. 'That's right. We've had two separate e-mails, each with a separate Internet provider and identity. We followed both up and found out that our guy has hacked into what should be an impenetrably secure network and set up fake accounts. He then sends the e-mails through these accounts.'

Fabel turned away from the window. There were six people around the cherrywood table. The four principal members of Fabel's Mordkommission team – Werner Meyer, Maria Klee, Anna Wolff and Paul Lindemann – sat together on one side. On the other sat an attractive dark-haired woman of about thirty-five, Dr Susanne Eckhardt, the criminal psychologist. At the head of the table was Horst Van Heiden, Leitender Kriminaldirektor of the Polizei Hamburg: Fabel's boss. Van Heiden rose from his chair, a policeman as if it were his genetic destiny; even now, in his pale grey Hugo Boss suit, he managed to convey the impression of wearing a uniform. He took the few steps across to the briefing-room wall, upon which large, colour photographs, taken from different angles, showed the devastated bodies of two young women. Blood everywhere. White bone gleaming through gore and flesh. Two different women, two different settings, but the horror at the centre of the images remained constant: their lungs lay excavated and thrown out from their bodies. Van Heiden's eyes ranged over the horror, his face emotionless.

'I take it you know who I have waiting for me – for us – upstairs, Fabel?'

'Yes, Herr Kriminaldirektor. I do.'

'And you know he's been giving me hell to put an end to . . . to this.'

'I am well aware of the political pressures upon you, sir. But my main concern is to prevent some other poor woman falling victim to this animal.'

Van Heiden's small blue eyes glittered coldly. 'My priorities, Herr Kriminalhauptkommissar, are exactly where they should be.' He looked towards the images again. 'I have a daughter roughly the same age as the second victim.' He turned back to Fabel. 'But I can do without the Erste Bürgermeister of Hamburg breathing down my neck.'

'As I said, sir, we're all trying to nail this bastard as quickly as we can.'

'Another thing. All of this "spreading the wings of the eagle" and "our sacred soil" . . . I don't like it. It sounds political. The eagle – the German eagle?'

'Could be,' Fabel said, looking over to Susanne Eckhardt.

'Could be . . .' she confirmed. When she spoke her voice was tinged with a southern accent: Munich, Fabel reckoned. 'But the eagle is a potent psychological image in any culture, an icon for power and predation. The eagle could be his metaphor: observing, circling above, unseen by his prey, then swooping silently for the kill. It's more likely that he is motivated by some deeply sublimated and abstracted sexual drive rather than extremist political ideology. This man isn't a fanatic: he's a psychotic. There's a difference . . . although I must admit the religiosity of the e-mail – the sense of crusade – and the ritualised method of death bother me.'

'Are we looking for some crazed neo-Nazi or not?' There was an aggressive edge to Van Heiden's voice.

'I doubt it. I doubt it very much. The victims are not from non-German ethnic backgrounds, they are not the typical targets for neo-Nazi attack. But I cannot exclude it as a possibility. I think this is more likely to be a personal crusade . . .' Susanne

Eckhardt wore the expression of someone trying to remember where they'd left their car keys.

'What is it, Frau Doktor?' asked Fabel.

Dr Eckhardt gave a small, almost apologetic laugh. 'It's nothing . . . or at least it's nothing that would stand up to professional or even objective scrutiny . . .'

'Please share it with us anyway,' said Van Heiden.

'Well, it's just that this e-mail is a textbook example of a socially dysfunctional psychotic. I mean, it's all there: sentiments of social dislocation and isolation, a perverted, crusading morality, identification with an elevated symbol of predation . . .'

Fabel felt an electric ruffle through the hairs on his neck. Something else that was too right.

'I don't understand . . .' Van Heiden had clearly missed the subtext. 'You're saying the e-mail is clearly genuine. That it was written by our killer.'

'No . . . well yes . . .' Eckhardt laughed again, exposing perfect teeth that glistened like porcelain. 'I really don't know what I'm saying. Just that if I had sat down to write a missive from a serial killer, I would have included all of these elements.'

'You're saying it's fake? Or are you saying it's genuine?' The edge was back in Van Heiden's voice. 'I'm getting confused . . .'

'It's probably genuine. Two killings, two e-mails received. If it were a hoaxer or compulsive confessor, then his timing is too good to be true. I'm just making a point. No . . . an observation.' Her eyes scanned the room for support. She found it: Fabel was nodding thoughtfully.

Van Heiden blanked her. 'This last . . . escapade – do we have anything more to go on, Fabel?'

'This one bothers me particularly,' said Fabel. 'There are a number of anomalies. In fact, there are a number of things we simply don't know about the victim.'

'Like her identity . . .' said Van Heiden. Fabel couldn't tell whether or not he was being sarcastic.

'We're working on that.'

Van Heiden flicked through the pages of the report. 'What about this former Mobiles Einsatz Kommando guy that was involved with her? I don't like the idea of an ex-Polizei Hamburg officer running a prostitute. The media would love that.'

'Unfortunately we've had to let him go,' said Fabel. 'But we've put a tail on him. He'll be watched twenty-four hours a day. I am certain he's withholding evidence, but there's nothing we can prove.'

'Have you seen his service record?'

'I've just had it called up,' said Fabel, sitting down and leaning against the table. He slightly exaggerated the casualness of his pose: he knew his informality rattled Van Heiden and he enjoyed irritating him. 'I haven't had much time to look at it yet, but it would appear that Klugmann was a star recruit who showed a great deal of promise until the drugs charge. Before he joined the Polizei Hamburg he served as a Fallschirmjäger . . .'

'A paratrooper?'

'Yes. Perfect grounding for the Mobiles Einsatz Kommando,' Fabel gave a small laugh. 'Practice for doing all of your thinking with a gun.'

Van Heiden bristled. 'The MEKs perform a valuable function. And they are police officers just like us. What was Klugmann's military record like?'

'As far as I can see, it bordered on the exemplary . . .'

'A good man turned bad . . .'

'Or a highly professional thug changing sides . . . it all depends on how you look at it, sir.'

This time Van Heiden ignored Fabel's bait. 'You think he's holding back on us?'

'I can't for one minute believe that he doesn't know the victim's full name. But his alibi is tight. We need to confirm the exact time of death, but it's almost definite that Klugmann is out of the frame.'

'So why keep him under surveillance? Perhaps our resources could be better employed elsewhere?'

Fabel could sense the exchange of incredulous looks between his team members. 'Because, sir, we have a body without a name found in the most bizarre circumstances and Klugmann, I feel, is our best lead towards establishing her identity. Like I said, I believe he is hiding something. For all we know that something could be the identity of the killer . . . it could be that "Son of Sven" was one of the girl's clients.'

Fabel caught Dr Eckhardt's glance but ignored it: she knew that he was throwing up a smokescreen. It was obviously a ploy to get Van Heiden off his back. It worked.

'Okay,' Van Heiden said. 'But I'm more interested in the identity of our killer than of the victim. What else have we got underway?'

'We're still looking into the background of the other victim.' Maria Klee pulled some notes from a file. 'As far as we can see, there's no connection between them. A prostitute and a high-flying civic lawyer. It looks like he's picking them at random.'

'It may seem random to us,' said Dr Eckhardt, 'but to the killer there is a connection between them that we cannot yet see. Remember that we are dealing with a profoundly disturbed individual here: his logic is not the same as ours. It could be a similarity in height, the way they walk, the shape of their nose . . . however abstract, there is commonality that the killer sees . . . in fact perhaps *only* the killer will ever see.'

There was a pause before Werner chipped in. 'So that means?'

'That means every woman in Hamburg, whatever her age or background, is a potential target.'

Van Heiden scratched the grey bristle on his scalp. 'And so far we only have one potential link with the killer – this man Klugmann, who may or may not know him as a client of this latest victim?'

'There is another potential link.' Dr Eckhardt didn't look up from the table. Her arms lay framing her files. Everyone turned their attention to her. 'And that link is Kriminalhauptkommissar Fabel. Just as the killer has some abstract criterion in selecting his victims, he has chosen Herr Fabel as his . . . well, as his alter ego, his opponent in the game, as it were. In his eyes, Herr Fabel is a worthy opponent. He has chosen him as his nemesis. In fact Hauptkommissar Fabel has become an essential element in his fantasy, in his plan. He has made it clear that he intends to engineer the conclusion to this hunt –' she turned to Fabel – 'perhaps even by having you kill him. This declaration – *you can stop me but you will never catch me* – is a promise of something.'

'That I will have to kill him to stop him?'

'Perhaps. He clearly feels that the psychotic part of his personality is safe from you. He perhaps has a fantasy of immortality that you cannot reach, even by killing him. It's as if there is some kind of buffer between you.'

'I am a policeman, not an executioner.' Fabel paused, frowning. 'But why has he chosen me?'

'That I don't know. Again perhaps only "Son of Sven" will ever know the reason he has picked you . . . but . . .'

'But what?' asked Van Heiden.

Dr Eckhardt continued to address Fabel directly. 'Well, he feels *connected* to you. There is a chance that your paths have crossed in the past. Or maybe he is someone you know right now.'

'But that is by no means definite . . .' Fabel made the statement more like a question.

'No, not definite. It's just a possibility. This sense of connection may be based simply on what he has read about you, for example . . . about you or one of your cases and made his choice based on that.'

'But it could be someone whose path *has* crossed mine in the past, perhaps significantly?'

'I think it's a possibility . . . but only that.'

Fabel turned to Van Heiden: a look laden with meaning. Van Heiden shook his head. 'Not that old chestnut, Fabel . . .'

Fabel shrugged. 'I know. It's just I can't help thinking that it would fit: Svensson taunting me with this "Son of Sven" crap . . . telling me he's alive and that this is his work . . .'

Van Heiden shook his head 'Give it up, Fabel. Svensson is dead. He's been dead for nearly twenty years.'

'Who's Svensson?' asked Dr Eckhardt.

'History,' answered Van Heiden. 'Ancient history, and nothing whatsoever to do with this case. Someone long dead.'

'*Presumed* long dead,' corrected Fabel. 'Supposedly burned to death. But there wasn't enough evidence to prove the body was his. His name was Karl-Heinz Svensson and he was an evil manipulative bastard who maintained a cell of young female terrorists. He was a former member of the Baader-Meinhof Rote-Armee-Fraktion who set up in business for himself. At that time there were a lot of splinter groups who didn't share the Baader-Meinhof philosophy of going completely underground. There was the Movement 2nd June and the SPK, which predated the Rote-Armee-Fraktion, and there were the Revolutionäre Zellen, who combined active, deep-cover terrorists with "legals" working in plain sight. Then there was Rote Zora – which was exclusively female. Svensson borrowed from them all. He called his unit RAG – the Radikale Aktionsgruppe. Most of the girls he operated were in their late teens. He sent them out to plant bombs in the arcades by the Alster and to hold up banks.'

'Fabel and I have been over this before.' Van Heiden turned back to Dr Eckhardt. 'Because of the inconclusiveness of the identification of Svensson's body, Fabel suspects that he may have somehow come back from the grave to carry out these murders.'

'Is that what you believe?' she asked Fabel.

'No, not necessarily. Not really. I just think it's an option we should keep open . . .'

'I'm sorry,' said Dr Eckhardt, 'I just don't understand: why are you even considering this person as a potential suspect? I don't see the connection between a dead terrorist and these serial killings . . .'

'I admit it's highly unlikely. And I do accept what Herr Kriminaldirektor Van Heiden says – it probably *was* Svensson who died in the explosion. But it was the reference to "Son of Sven" that first started me wondering . . . and the continuous reference to eagles. Svensson's codename was "Eagle". Added to that is the weird relationship he had with women.'

'In what way weird?'

'He seemed to need to totally dominate them. He was supposedly physically intimate with all of his group. The press dubbed them "Svensson's Harem".'

'And what's the connection with you?'

'In 1983 they tried to hold up the main Commerzbank in Paul-Nevermann-Platz. There were three women, members of Svensson's splinter group. They were on the way out when they stumbled into two uniformed Schutzpolizei on foot patrol. There was an exchange of fire . . . two of the terrorists and one SchuPo were killed and the other badly wounded. I arrived on the scene as the surviving terrorist made a run for it. I chased her to the waterfront, called for her to drop her gun, but she turned and fired. She hit me in the side and I fired back: two shots in the face and head. She died instantly. Her name was Gisela Frohm. She was seventeen years old. A child.'

'I see.' Dr Eckhardt removed her glasses and seemed to appraise Fabel for a moment. 'I understand you making the link, but I have to say I think that even if this Svensson had survived, he would not be a natural suspect for these killings.'

'Why not?'

'He just doesn't fit the profile – in age, psychology, anything . . .' Dr Eckhardt pushed back a lock of thick raven hair that had fallen over her broad brow. She donned the spectacles again before reading from her file. 'We've got two indicators from which to build a profile of our killer: the physical evidence from the murder scenes and the content of the e-mails. The broad profile we have at the moment is: male, anywhere between twenty and forty, but likely to be under thirty. He is clearly intelligent, but perhaps not as intelligent as he thinks he is. Educated to at least Abitur level, he may be a graduate working in a reasonably responsible job which he nevertheless feels is beneath him. Or he may, for some reason, have been diverted from fulfilling what he sees as his full academic potential and is in a lower-grade technical position. If he is a graduate, this would, of course, nudge the lower end of our age range up to about twenty-six.

'As Frau Klee has already pointed out, he seems to be highly computer literate. He is likely – although not certain – to live alone. The description in the e-mail of social isolation and marginalisation is consistent with the typical profile. He is a loner: someone with a low sense of self-esteem. He feels that his intelligence is undervalued and his potential underdeveloped by the world around him . . . a world that he has now declared war upon. There may also have been an event – or a sequence of events – in his childhood or youth where a woman has humiliated or dominated him. Alternatively, there may have been an event where he blames his mother for failing to protect him from a domineering or abusive father. Whatever the event, it may have coincided with puberty when masturbatory fantasies may have revolved around violent revenge against women. In which case his loathing and fear of women has become indissolubly linked to sexual arousal. He may be sexually dysfunctional and impotent except when arousal and orgasm is precipitated by extreme violence against women.'

'But there has been no semen or even signs of penetration found at the scenes,' Fabel commented. The beautiful Frau Doktor returned his look by angling her face and peering over the top of her glasses.

'No. But that does not mean that he has not carried out a sexual act. He may have used a condom to prevent leaving DNA traces. What is more likely is that what this person does to achieve sexual gratification is so wildly removed from normal sexual function as to be unrecognisable. And, as I said, he may be impotent. The crime is sexual in nature, but the perpetrator may not himself recognise or acknowledge its sexual motivation. And a major element that emerges from the e-mail – and from the ritualised nature of the killings – is the religiosity of this act. It's some kind of ceremony he is committing for reasons more abstract than simple or immediate sexual satisfaction.'

Maria Klee interjected. 'Could this be more than one person? The way you're talking it's like it's almost a ritual. If it's not political, could we be dealing with some kind of cult?'

Werner Meyer gave a hollow laugh. Both women ignored him. Fabel gave him a warning glance.

'That is possible, but unlikely,' answered Susanne Eckhardt. 'If this were to be the actions of more than one person, then the profile of our principal – the person who is doing the killing – remains the same. Any other involvement would mean a manipulator . . . someone whose role fills the chasm left by the uncaring or abusive parent. In such cases – like the Leonard Lake and Charles Ng case in America in the eighties – one half of the pair has no self-esteem whatsoever, while the other is pathologically egotistical. But in this case, I think this is much more likely to be a solo crusade. He has spelled that out in his second e-mail. He is a lone wolf. And that, of course, is far more common than teamwork serial killers.' Dr Eckhardt paused, slipping the glasses from her face. 'This person is compensating for his low self-esteem through these acts. That is why I think it highly unlikely that Herr Fabel's terrorist would fit: wrong age, wrong motivations, wrong psychology, wrong politics . . .'

Van Heiden responded as if he'd received a mild electric shock. 'What do you mean, "wrong politics"?'

'Well, the basic psycho-profile I've outlined – the blaming of society for personal failings, the belief in a personal potential underdeveloped in an unjust world . . . almost everything, in fact, excluding the psycho-sexual trauma – also fits with neo-Nazi types.'

'I thought you said that this was not politically motivated?'

'Yes. I don't think it is. This man is probably psychosexually motivated to kill, but, like everyone else, he has political opinions. In his case these political opinions may or may not have become grotesquely distorted from his psychotic perspective and may even form a justification – an excuse – for these acts. At least in part. My point is that a left-wing terrorist such as Svensson wouldn't share the same profile.'

Fabel nodded his head slowly. 'I accept all of that, but what if *I* am the focus of all of this? What if he is engaging me in . . . well, some kind of challenge. I killed one of his women so he is killing women whom I, as a policeman, am supposed to protect?'

Susanne Eckhardt laughed. 'Now we're swapping roles, and I have to say that's pretty lousy psychology. It's a tenuous link to say the least.' She laid her glasses on the table before her, straightened her shoulders and tilted her head back, her dark eyes focused on Fabel. He felt awkward under her relentless gaze, fearful that his attraction to her might show. 'But if you're going to play psychologist,' she continued, smiling, 'then let me play policeman. You admit yourself that we're talking about someone who is more than likely dead . . .'

'Yes.'

'And in this latest e-mail he has described himself as having "lived his life on the edge of other people's photographs". It doesn't exactly fit with a headline-making terrorist with a harem of young female acolytes . . .'

Van Heiden laughed. 'Dr Eckhardt, maybe I should give you Herr Fabel's job . . .' He turned to Fabel, the smile disappearing as he did so. 'Now, Fabel, let's focus on living suspects.'

Fabel was still watching Dr Eckhardt. Her smile remained and she held Fabel's gaze, a hint of dark fire in her eyes.

'Well, as I said, I saw it only as a remote possibility.'

Dr Eckhardt donned her glasses again and scanned through her report. 'Another thing we should be looking at is previous unsolved rapes or attempted rapes. Our killer may have committed sexual assaults in the past as a prelude to the main event.'

'Have we looked at recent attacks such as the ones Frau Doktor Eckhardt has described?' asked Van Heiden. Werner looked across to Fabel, mimicking a 'now why didn't we think of that?' expression. Another warning look.

'Yes, Herr Kriminaldirektor,' Fabel answered. 'We have interviewed all known sex offenders that fit the broad profile. Nothing on them. Although there was a number of attacks on women in the Harburg and Altona areas last year that we haven't accounted for. We're re-interviewing the victims, just in case.'

'All right, Kriminalhauptkommissar Fabel,' said Van Heiden, 'keep me notified. In the meantime we have an appointment to keep.' He checked his watch. 'See you upstairs in ten minutes?'

'Fine.'

Fabel stepped over to the wall covered with the scene-of-crime photographs of the victims. The flash photography made the images unnaturally vivid: nauseous colours exploding across the glossy prints. They looked unreal, Goyaesque. But they were real: four long months ago Werner

and Fabel had stood on a cold and wind-blasted Lüneburg
Heath, collars turned up against the sharp edge of a wind
born in Siberia that had swept unimpeded across the low,
flat Baltic plain. It had been like a moonscape, the night illu-
mined by the stark glare of portable arc lamps, the chill air
crackling with the sibilant chatter of police radios. They had
gazed down at the mutilated body of the first victim, Ursula
Kastner, a twenty-nine-year-old civic lawyer who had stepped
out of her office and straight into hell. She had lain before
them on the heath with a gaping blackness in the middle of
her chest. The next day the first e-mail had arrived for Fabel.

He became aware of Maria Klee standing beside him.

'Why do they do it?' Fabel spoke as much to himself as
to her. His eyes ranged over the images.

'Why do they do what?'

'Why do they *comply*? The first victim seems to have met
with the killer by arrangement. Her car was found parked
and locked up in an autobahn rest station and there was no
evidence of a struggle or violent abduction. This second
victim . . . it's like she invited her killer in. Or that he had
a key. There's no evidence of forced entry, or of a struggle
at or near the threshold. I suppose, to a certain extent, you
can understand a prostitute being, well, welcoming. But
Ursula Kastner was an intelligent and safety-conscious young
woman. Why did they both comply with a complete
stranger?'

'If he was a stranger,' said Maria.

'If he follows the typical serial-killer profile then, as you
know, he will not pick victims that have prior knowledge of
him . . .' Susanne Eckhardt now joined Fabel and Maria.

'So why did Kastner go with him and "Monique" let him
in?' Fabel repeated his question. Maria shrugged.

'Maybe there was something about him that invited trust
. . .' Susanne paused, as if weighing up her own words. 'Do
you remember the case of Albert DeSalvo?'

Maria and Fabel looked at each other blankly.

'Albert DeSalvo. The Boston Strangler. He murdered a dozen women in Boston in the early sixties . . .'

'What about him?' Fabel's confusion was genuine.

'The Boston police asked exactly the same question you're asking: "Why did the victims let him into their apartments?"'

'So why did they?'

'DeSalvo was a plumber by trade. He would call at the door and say the apartment-block supervisor had asked him to call. If the victim was suspicious or protested, DeSalvo would simply say, "Okay," and walk away as if it was no big deal to him. Because the victims didn't want to cause trouble with their landlords, because DeSalvo obviously had the authentic tools of his trade with him and because he didn't push the issue, they would call him back and open the door.'

'So what are you saying?' asked Maria. 'That we should be looking for a plumber?'

Susanne sighed impatiently. 'No, not necessarily. But it is possible that he is masquerading as something similar. Something that invites trust, even though he is a stranger to the victim.'

Maria tapped her pen against her teeth. 'We know that this guy is, by his own admission, anonymous in appearance. Maybe he gets off on dressing as someone in authority before killing . . .'

'Now, that, Herr Fabel,' Susanne Eckhardt revealed her perfect teeth in a broad smile, 'is much better amateur psychology than yours.'

Fabel's eyes ranged over the images on the wall. 'Let's say he does embellish his ritual by dressing as an authority figure. What would epitomise authority to the victims, as well as gaining their implicit trust?'

Maria Klee stared at Fabel for a moment. When she spoke, it was almost a whisper. 'Oh, shit.'

'Shall I break the news to the Kriminaldirektor or will you?'

Before making his way up to Van Heiden's office Fabel made a call to LKA7, the special division of the Landeskriminalamt dedicated to the fight against organised crime. He arranged an appointment to see Hauptkommissar Buchholz, who commanded the team that targeted the Ulugbay organisation. There was something about Buchholz's tone that made Fabel feel that his call had been expected but was not particularly welcome. Buchholz agreed to see Fabel at half past two. After he had made the call, Fabel pulled out Klugmann's blue file – the one containing his Hamburg police-service record. There it was, as he had expected: Klugmann had spent six months – in fact the six months immediately before his departure from the force – working under Buchholz's direct command as a member of one of the Mobile Einsatz Kommandos.

Fabel had just gathered his papers together before heading up to Van Heiden's office when Werner stuck his bristle bullet head round the office door.

'Jan, we've had another message in from Professor Dorn. He's asking again if he can see you.'

'Did you get his number?' Fabel did not look up and continued to gather his files.

'Yep. He says he can help us with this case. He's very insistent, Jan.'

Fabel still did not look up. 'Okay. Arrange it.'

Werner nodded and disappeared. Fabel tucked the files under his arm and made his way out of the office and towards the elevator. As he did so he felt an unpleasant stirring deep in his gut, as he recalled the face of his old tutor. He could see it quite clearly. Then he tried to recall another face, a face that he also associated with the name Dorn, but found he could not.

Van Heiden's office was on the fourth floor of the Polizeipräsidium. Leaving the lift, Fabel was immediately faced with an attractive and smiling young receptionist in civilian clothing. Her butter-blonde hair was brushed back from her face in a ponytail and she wore a sober white blouse and black suit of skirt and jacket. Fabel could have been walking into a bank, except he knew that the pretty young receptionist was a Polizistin and would have a nine-millimetre SIG-Sauer PG automatic clipped to the waistband of her skirt. After confirming his appointment, the receptionist led Fabel along the hall to a large meeting room: a long rectangle with large windows along one side which looked out, as did the briefing room below, over the Hindenburgstrasse. A long cherrywood table was flanked on each side by black leather chairs. Three of the chairs, towards the top of the table, were occupied: Van Heiden sat between a squat, powerfully built man with short black hair receding at the temples whom Fabel did not recognize and an overweight man with sand-coloured hair and a mildly florid complexion that looked as if his skin had been recently scrubbed. Fabel recognised him as Innensenator Hugo Ganz, Hamburg's Interior Minister. Over by the window a fourth man stood with his back to Fabel, looking down at the flow of traffic below. He was very tall and wore an elegant suit that was not German, probably Italian. The three men at the table were in detailed, mumbled discussion, continually referring to notes that lay before them.

Fabel looked directly over the table at the unknown man. Van Heiden caught the look and made the introduction.

'This is Oberst Gerd Volker of the BND. Oberst Volker, Kriminalhauptkommissar Fabel. Please sit down, Fabel.'

Here we go, thought Fabel. The BND – Bundesnachrichtendienst – was the intelligence service, charged with protecting the Grundgesetz: the Basic Law, or constitution, of the German Federal Republic. It was the job of the BND to monitor terrorist and extremist groups, both right and left, active or dormant, in Germany's political landscape. And, since 1996, the BND had been involved in the fight against organised crime. Fabel's distrust of the BND was profound. Secret police are secret police, whatever initials you give them.

Volker smiled and reached across the table. 'I'm pleased to meet you Herr Fabel. I read a great deal about your work on the Markus Stümbke case last year . . .'

The two men shook hands.

'And this is Innensenator Ganz,' continued Van Heiden.

Ganz extended his hand; the scrubbed face did not break into a smile. 'This is a terrible business, Herr Kriminal-kommissar,' said Ganz, demoting Fabel by several ranks. 'I hope that you are employing all means at your disposal to put a stop to this.'

'Erster Kriminalhauptkommissar,' corrected Fabel, 'and it goes totally without saying, Senator, that we are doing all we can to catch this killer.'

'I'm sure you're aware that the press is whipping up public concern almost to a state of frenzy . . .' It was the figure by the window who spoke, turning at last to face the others. A tall, elegant, lean, broad-shouldered man in his early fifties, with intense blue eyes and a long, thin, intelligent face carved with vertical lines. His hair was as much grey as blond and expensively cut. Fabel, himself an admirer of fine English tailoring, reckoned that the expensive royal-blue shirt was from Jermyn Street, London. The suit was definitely Italian. The overall effect was more of taste and style than ostenta-tion. Fabel had never met the man before, but recognised him instantly. After all, he had voted for him.

'Yes, Herr Erste Bürgermeister, it has not escaped my notice.' Fabel spun the leather chair he was sitting on around to face Hamburg's first mayor and leader of the Hamburg state government, Dr Hans Schreiber.

Schreiber smiled. 'You're the one they call *der englische Kommissar*, aren't you?'

'Incorrectly, yes.'

'You're not English?'

'No. I can honestly say I haven't a drop of English blood in me. My mother is a Scot, my father was a Frisian. We lived in England for a while when I was a kid. Part of my education was there. Why do you ask?'

'Just curious. I'm an Anglophile myself. After all, they say Hamburg is "the most British city outside the United Kingdom" . . . Anyway, I find it interesting – that they call you the English Kommissar, I mean. It marks you out as . . . well, different. Do you see yourself as different, Herr Fabel?'

Fabel shrugged. He didn't see the point in this conversation and its personal tone was beginning to annoy him. The truth was he did feel different. All his life he had been aware of another, non-German aspect to his make-up. He resented it and treasured it at the same time.

Schreiber obviously sensed Fabel's growing unease. 'I'm sorry, Herr Fabel, I didn't mean to pry. It's just that I have read your service file and it's clear that you are an exceptional officer. I believe you *are* different, that you have an edge, an added perspective that others don't. It's why I believe you are the man who will stop this monster.'

'I have no choice,' said Fabel, and went on to explain his 'selection' by the so-called Son of Sven. As Fabel spoke, Schreiber nodded and frowned as if absorbing and weighing up every morsel of information, but Fabel noticed that the Bürgermeister's gaze ranged around the room. The motion gave the hooded, intense eyes an almost predatory look. It was as if his mind were in several places at the same time.

'What I want to know, Herr Hauptkommissar, is whether you actually have a strategy?' asked Innensenator Ganz. 'I hope we are not allowing this maniac to set the agenda. Proactive policing is what is called for here . . .'

Fabel was about to retort when Schreiber cut across him.
'I have every confidence in Herr Fabel, Hugo. And I don't
think it's helpful for us as politicians to dictate how the police
do their job.'

Ganz's pink cheeks reddened further. It was clear who was
in charge here. The odd thing was that, although Schreiber
had said all the right things, Fabel didn't feel totally convinced
that he did indeed have the Erste Bürgermeister's trust. Or
that he in turn trusted Schreiber.

Van Heiden broke what was becoming an awkward silence.
'Perhaps now would be a good time for Kriminalhauptkommissar Fabel to give us his report.'

Schreiber took his place at the table and Fabel ran through
a summary of the case progress to date. He punctuated his
report with images from the case file. At several points Ganz
looked quite ill; Schreiber's face wore a mask of practised
solemnity. Towards the end of his presentation, Fabel leaned
back in his chair and looked towards Van Heiden.

'What is it, Fabel? Is there something else you have to
report?'

'I'm afraid so, Herr Kriminaldirektor. At the moment it's
only a theory but . . .'

'But?'

'As I've already pointed out, there have been no signs of
forced entry into the second victim's apartment, nor has their
been any evidence of violent struggle at first point of contact
between the perpetrator and either victim. This has led us
to the conclusion that either he was armed and forced compli-
ance by threat, or the victims have, well, trusted their killer
in some way. The latter means one of two things: that the
killer is someone they already know – we think this highly
unlikely, given the profile we've compiled on our killer and
the disparity in the victims' backgrounds and areas of
residence . . .'

'And the second option?' It was Schreiber who spoke.

'The second option is that our killer disguises himself as some kind of figure that carries authority or implicit trust . . .'

'Such as . . . ?' asked Van Heiden.

'Such as a police officer . . . or a city official . . .'

There was a moment of silence. Schreiber and Ganz exchanged a look that was difficult to read. Van Heiden looked miserable. Volker remained expressionless.

'But that is by no means definite?' Van Heiden's question was more like a plea.

'No. It's not. But we have to account for the victims admitting their killer without a struggle. It could be that he turns up as a bogus workman with a plausible story, but our psycho-profile would suggest that he may enjoy the feeling of power over his victims that a police uniform or identity badge would give him.'

A deeper redness infused Ganz's cheeks. 'I'm sure I don't have to point out to you gentlemen that the Polizei Hamburg is enjoying anything other than a good press at the moment. Just yesterday I had a very – shall I say "vigorous" – discussion with the board of the Polizeikommission about what they see as institutional racism in the Polizei Hamburg. The last thing we need is some maniac wandering the streets of Hamburg pretending to be a policeman and ripping women apart . . .'

Fabel's patience snapped. 'For God's sake man, we can't help it if some psychopath has chosen to masquerade as a police officer – and it's a big "if". It's not something we are responsible for or have control over . . .'

'That's not really Innensenator Ganz's point,' said Schreiber. 'The point is that the public is going to become even more distrustful of police officers if they think there's a psychotic killer disguising himself as one.'

'Only if we're right, and then only if it gets out. Like I said, it's only a theory as yet.'

'I sincerely hope it's the wrong theory, Herr Fabel,' said

Ganz; he was about to continue but a look from Schreiber seemed to silence him.

'I'm sure that it won't become an issue,' said Schreiber. 'I have every confidence that Herr Fabel will track down this monster before long.'

Do you? thought Fabel. I'm not sure that I do.

'Of course,' Schreiber addressed Van Heiden directly, 'I do expect us to be able to report some progress as soon as possible. I know it's difficult for you gentlemen to take public concern too much into account – and nor should you – but I have to think about the press-generated perception of violent crime in Hamburg. Another serial killer is just one more reason for our female citizens to feel disempowered.'

Disempowered. Shit, thought Fabel, these people don't even speak plain German. Schreiber made towards the door. Ganz took the hint and rose from the table. Volker, the BND man, Van Heiden and Fabel all rose too.

'Please keep us fully informed of your progress,' said Ganz.

'Of course, Herr Innensenator,' answered Van Heiden.

After the two politicians had left, Fabel turned to Volker. 'May I ask, Herr Oberst, what the BND's interest in this case is?'

'Hopefully none.' Volker's over-broad smile did not somehow seem to reach his eyes. Fabel felt his distrust of the BND man deepen. 'I am working with the Besondere Aufbau Organisation set up here in the Präsidium. Herr Van Heiden has alerted me to the fact that there may be some kind of Rechtsradikale extremist political element to these crimes.'

Fabel nodded slowly as he processed the information. Why would a BND secret-service man working with the Besondere Aufbau Organisation have an interest in this case? The BAO was set up by the Bundeskriminalamt after the embarrassing discovery that a tiny apartment at 54 Marienstrasse in Hamburg had been the base for the terrorists who launched the September 11 attacks in the United States. At least eight of the terrorists, including the cell's leader, Mohammed Atta, had passed through the Hamburg apartment. The German government's response was the BAO. There were seventy Bundeskriminalamt specialists, twenty-five Polizei Hamburg detectives and six American FBI agents operating from the BAO; their exclusive focus was gathering intelligence on al-Qaeda and other Islamic terror groups. Fabel found that he resented having to discuss his case with someone whose brief was totally unrelated.

'I've already made it clear to the Kriminaldirektor that it is highly unlikely that these are the actions of some kind of neo-Nazi.' Fabel struggled, unsuccessfully, to keep his irritation out of his tone. Volker's smile remained in place.

'Oh yes, I understand that, Herr Fabel. Nonetheless, if there is any likelihood whatsoever that there is a political element to this, I think it best that the BND is kept up to date on the progress of the case. I promise to get in your way as little as possible . . . if you could just keep me informed, particularly of any developments that might signal a political element . . .'

'Of course, Herr Oberst Volker.'

Van Heiden stood up. 'Well thank you, Herr Fabel, I think everyone found your report informative.' He moved towards the door to see Fabel out. Fabel gathered his files and shook the hand Volker extended before making his way to the door.

Van Heiden held the door open for Fabel and as Fabel passed through, Van Heiden followed him out into the corridor. He lowered his voice conspiratorially as he spoke. 'And for God's sake, Fabel, let me know if you find anything that proves your theory about this lunatic impersonating a police officer. I don't like it. I don't like it one bit. Particularly when this latest victim seems to have been a prostitute run by an ex-Polizei Hamburg officer.'

'I will, Herr Kriminaldirektor.'

Fabel started to move away when Van Heiden placed a

gently restraining hand on Fabel's arm. 'And Fabel . . . make sure you tell me first . . . and inform me before you pass anything on to Oberst Volker.'

Fabel frowned slightly. 'Of course, Herr Kriminaldirektor . . .'

As Van Heiden slipped back into his office, Fabel stood for a moment in the corridor gathering his thoughts. There was something about the whole set-up – the involvement of Volker the BND man, the intensity of Innensenator Ganz's concern about any possibility of the killer masquerading as a policeman, and the way he felt the entire meeting had been 'managed' by Schreiber – that made Fabel feel that there was something more going on than his hunt for a serial killer. It was as if there were some other agenda to which he was not party.

Wednesday 4 June, 12.00 p.m. Mortuary of the Institut für Rechtsmedizin, Eppendorf, Hamburg.

The Institut für Rechtsmedizin – the Legal Medicine Institute – was responsible for all forensic medicine in Hamburg. All of the city's sudden deaths found their way to the Institut mortuary.

Fabel's gut lurched at the morgue smell with which he had grown familiar but to which he had never become accustomed: it was not the smell of decay, as one might expect, but a faintly disinfectant-rinsed stale odour. There were no bodies on the stainless-steel post-mortem tables and the bleaching striplights bathed the mortuary with a cheerless, unrelenting glare. When Fabel entered, Möller, still dressed in his green scrubs, was sitting at his desk, referring to handwritten notes and then peering at the screen of his computer. In between, he absent-mindedly scooped forkfuls of a ready-made pasta salad into his mouth from a plastic tub. He did not acknowledge Fabel's arrival.

'I wouldn't have thought eating was allowed in here.' Fabel pulled up a chair without waiting for an invitation.

'It's not. So arrest me.' Möller didn't look up from his notes.

'What do you have on the girl?'

'You'll get the report this afternoon.' Möller tapped the page he was writing with his pen. 'I'm doing it now.'

'Just give me the main points.'

Möller threw his pen down onto the desk and leaned back in his chair, sweeping his hands through his hair and then placing them behind his head. He eyed Fabel with his practised, superior look. 'Have you heard from your penfriend yet?'

'Möller, I don't have time for this. What have you got for me?'

'This is an interesting one all right, Hauptkommissar.' Möller picked up his notes. 'The victim is female, between twenty-five and thirty-five years old, one metre sixty-five tall, blue eyes, with brown hair dyed blonde. Cause of death was heart failure caused by shock and massive blood loss, in turn a result of the massive trauma to the abdomen. She was dead before the lungs were excavated.' Möller looked up from his notes. 'You reckon this young woman was a prostitute?'

'Yes. Why?'

'She had not had sexual intercourse in the forty-eight hours prior to her death. The other thing is that she obviously took very good care of herself.'

'Oh?'

'Her muscle tone was extremely good and there is a very low body-fat-to-muscle ratio. I would say she was either some kind of athlete or that she visited a gym frequently. She didn't smoke and there was no trace of alcohol in her blood. Looks like her diet was good, too: her last meal was some kind of fish with pulses and her blood lipids were very low.' Möller flicked through his notes. 'We've screened her for narcotics

– nothing. Notwithstanding genetic influences, if this young lady had not crossed paths with your "correspondent", she would have more than likely lived to a ripe old age.'

'Anything on the killer?'

'No forensic evidence of the killer's presence. As I said, no evidence of sexual intercourse nor of any other sexual activity. It's definitely the same killer as the other one – or at least, the method of killing is identical. The killer made a single incision which was caused by a powerful but incredibly accurate blow to the sternum, probably with some heavy, large-bladed knife, or perhaps a sword, after which the ribs were prised open and the lungs excavated. There were stress indicators and splintering on the sheared bone edges, suggesting a sweeping, forceful blow downwards. The separation of the ribs would have taken considerable physical strength, as would the single-blow incision. This is a man all right . . . and the arc of penetration suggests probably not less than one metre seventy tall, with at least a medium build.'

'That narrows it down to about ninety per cent of the male population of Hamburg,' said Fabel, without sarcasm and more to himself than to Möller.

'All I deal with is the physical evidence, Fabel. Although I am intrigued by the victim's obvious regard for her own health and fitness.' Möller laughed. 'I don't have the benefit of your experience of the underside of our city's life, but I wouldn't have imagined that the average Hamburg prostitute places much importance on her health – or that of her clients.'

'That depends. She appears to have been high-end – taking care of her body would be an investment in . . . well, her *product*. But you've got a point. There's not much about this victim that fits. Did my guys take her prints?'

'Yes, they were over earlier.'

'Okay. Thanks, Herr Doktor Möller,' Fabel made for the door. 'I'll get your full report this afternoon.'

'Fabel.'

'Yes?'

'There's one more thing . . .'

'What?'

'There's an old wound on the right upper thigh, outer aspect. A scar.'

'Bad enough to be a distinguishing mark that could help us identify her?'

'Well, yes, I think it increases your chances considerably. But it has more significance than that . . .'

'What do you mean?'

Möller turned back to his computer and punched a few keys. 'I've got the photograph from the digital camera loaded into my report. Here it is.'

Fabel looked at the screen. A picture of the woman's thigh, the skin bleached white. There was a round mark with a lateral scar and some puckering around it. It had the look of a faint and ancient lunar crater. Möller punched a key and another image appeared. This time it was the back of the thigh. Instead of being pale, it was a lurid purple-red. Post-mortem lividity: the body having lain on its back, gravity had drawn the blood to the lowest points.

'Do you see here,' Möller tapped the screen with his pen, 'the corresponding scar on the other side? They were very faint scars . . . perhaps five or six years old. Do you know what they are?'

'Yes, I do,' said Fabel. After all, he had two similar scars himself.

Möller leaned back again in his chair. 'I would think that that should narrow things down a little in identifying her . . . I mean, how many young women in Hamburg have been treated for gunshot wounds over the last ten years?'

It rained heavily. Despite the downpour Fabel felt the urge to get out into the open, to allow the rain and the moist air to purge his clothes and his lungs of the musty odour of the morgue. His car was parked a couple of streets away and by the time he reached its shelter his blond hair was plastered to his scalp. He drove down towards the docks of the Hafen district. Within a few minutes the vast cranes that lined the banks and quaysides of the Elbe started to dominate the skyline. Fabel called his office on his cellular phone and asked to speak to Werner, but got Maria Klee instead, who explained that Werner was checking in with the surveillance team who were tracking Klugmann. Fabel told Maria about the gunshot wound on the body and asked her to carry out a thorough search of records covering all Hamburg hospitals and clinics from about fifteen to five years ago. By law any hospital or medical professional treating a gunshot injury was obliged to report it to the police. Maria pointed out that there was a chance that, if this girl was a prostitute and had been injured in some kind of underworld shoot-out, then the wound may have been treated unofficially by some bent medic. Fabel told Maria that he thought that was possible, but not likely.

'Any other messages?' he asked Maria.

'Werner left a message to tell you that an appointment with Professor Dorn has been set up for tomorrow. Three p.m.' Maria paused. 'Is Professor Dorn some kind of forensics expert?'

'No,' said Fabel, 'he's a historian.' He paused for a heart-beat before adding, 'I thought he was history. Anything else?'

Maria told him that a journalist had called a couple of times: an Angelika Blüm. The name meant nothing to Fabel.

'Did you refer her to the press department?'

'Yes. I did. But she was quite insistent that it was you she needed to talk to. I told her that all press enquiries had to be handled by the Polizeipressestelle, but she said she wasn't looking for a story, that she needed to discuss a matter of great importance with you.'

'Did you ask what this matter was?'

'Of course I did. She basically told me to mind my own business.'

'You get a number?'

'Yep.'

'Okay, I'll see you when I get back. I've got an appointment with the Organised Crime Division at two-thirty.'

The Schnell-Imbiss snack stand was by the docks on the Elbe, dwarfed by the huddle of cranes that loomed above it. It comprised a caravan with a wide, open serving window and bright canopy. It was surrounded, at regular intervals, by parasol-topped, waist-high tables at which a handful of scattered customers stood consuming Bockwurst or drinking beer or coffee. There was a small newspaper stand next to the serving window. Despite the drabness of its surroundings and the weather, the Schnell-Imbiss managed to look both cheerful and scrupulously clean.

Fabel pulled up and ran through the rain from his car to the shelter of the canopy. A rotund man of fifty, with florid cheeks and dressed in a white overcoat and cook's hat, stood behind the counter. He leaned forward onto his elbows as Fabel approached.

'Good morning, Herr Kriminalhauptkommissar,' he said, with an accent that was as broad and flat as the Frisian landscape to which it belonged. 'And might I say you look like shit today.'

'Been a rough night, Dirk,' answered Fabel, his own speech slipping from strict Hochdeutsch into his natural Frysk. 'I'll have a Jever and a coffee.'

Dirk served the Frisian beer and the coffee.

'Have you seen Mahmoot lately?'

'No, not for a while, now that you mention it. Something up?'

Fabel sipped his beer. 'I need to talk to him, that's all. I'll give him a buzz later – if I can get a hold of him. You know what he's like.' Fabel sipped the thick, black coffee. It scalded his lips so he put it down and took another sip of the Jever.

'I take it this is your lunch?' Dirk nodded at the beer and the coffee.

'Okay, give me a Käsebrot to go with it. If you see Mahmoot could you let him know I've been looking for him? I know I don't need to tell you to be discreet.' Fabel looked past Dirk; on the wall of the caravan behind him was a photograph of Dirk, about fifteen years younger and slimmer, in his green SchuPo uniform. Fabel nodded towards the photograph. 'Don't you get hassle because of that?'

He handed Fabel a split bread roll filled with cheese and gherkin and shrugged. His smile broadened. 'Occasionally. Sometimes I get a rough crowd down here, but I find that my diplomacy usually works on them . . .' He reached under the counter and pulled out a large Glock automatic. Fabel coughed on his beer and looked around to make sure the other customers hadn't seen.

'For Christ's sake, Dirk, put it away. I'm going to pretend I didn't see that.'

Dirk laughed and reached out and down and slapped Fabel affectionately on the cheek. 'Now, now, don't get agitated, Jannik . . .' Little Jan. It had been Dirk's nickname for Fabel when they had served together. Despite Dirk's inferior rank as an Obermeister in the uniform branch, the Schutzpolizei, the young Kommissar Fabel had quickly recognised the wealth of experience the older policeman had to offer. Dirk had willingly shown Fabel the ropes. He had done the same for Franz Webern, the young policeman who had died the same day Fabel had been shot. Dirk had taken Franz's death very badly. When he had visited Fabel in hospital after the shooting, it was the only time Fabel could recall Dirk stripped of his infectious good humour.

The rain had stopped and the sun probed a shaft of light through the furls of cloud, etching the latticed shadow of the cranes' superstructure across the car park. Fabel paid for the Käsebrot, beer and coffee. He tossed an extra few coins down. 'I'll take a *SCHAU MAL!* as well,' he said, pulling a copy out of the news-stand.

'I didn't think *SCHAU MAL!* would be your thing,' said Dirk.

'It's not . . .' Fabel flipped the folded tabloid open. The headline slapped Fabel in the face.

MANIACAL RIPPER STRIKES AGAIN! POLIZEI HAMBURG POWERLESS TO STOP MADMAN! Underneath the headline was a photograph of Horst Van Heiden with the caption: KRIMINALDIREKTOR VAN HEIDEN: THE MAN FAILING TO KEEP HAMBURG'S WOMEN SAFE.

'*Scheisse* . . .' muttered Fabel. Van Heiden would be going through the roof. The editorial blasted the Polizei Hamburg and offered a reward for information. The centre spread was also devoted to the story. Another shrill headline proclaimed: WHO CARES ABOUT CATCHING THIS MONSTER? *SCHAU MAL!* DOES. WE WILL PAY €10,000 FOR INFORMATION THAT LEADS TO THE ARREST AND CONVICTION OF THIS MANIAC!

'What's up?' asked Dirk. Fabel tossed the paper across the counter to Dirk. 'Oh, I see . . . let me guess, this is your case?'

'Got it in one.' Fabel drained his beer and then his coffee and left the uneaten bread roll on the counter. 'Better go. Before Van Heiden puts up a reward for my hide.'

'*Tschüss*, Jan.'

Wednesday 4 June, 2.45 p.m. Polizeipräsidium, Hamburg.
LKA7 – the Organised Crime Division – is separated from the rest of the Hamburg Polizeipräsidium by heavy security doors, which in turn are controlled from a security desk. Closed-circuit security cameras sweep the corridors leading to LKA7, and everyone approaching the department is watched by the armed officers manning the security desk. A

secure environment within a secure environment; a police station within a police station.

The fight against organised crime in Hamburg had become a secretive and violent game. Immigrant Mafias – specifically Turkish, Russian, Ukrainian and Lithuanian – were involved in a constant struggle with indigenous German gangs for control of the two most lucrative criminal markets: sex and drugs. There was even a special department LKA7.1 devoted to the fight against Hamburg's Hell's Angels, who had carved out a piece of the organised-crime market for themselves.

LKA7 had, as a consequence, developed a reputation for secrecy itself. It was a war, and the mentality of the division's officers had almost become more that of soldiers than policemen.

Fabel approached the screen door and pressed the buzzer. At the command of a speaker above the door he identified himself and held his police ID up to the camera. A harsh electrical buzz and loud click confirmed his permission to enter. An older uniformed officer of massive build and with a shaven head awaited Fabel at the security desk.

'Someone will be along shortly, sir.' The desk man smiled. He was clearly out of practice. 'They will take you along to see Hauptkommissar Buchholz.'

Fabel had just sat down at the small reception area when another huge man approached. His blond hair was cropped almost to the scalp and muscles bulged under the stretched fabric of his black polo-necked shirt. The broad shoulders were braced with a tan leather shoulder holster which held a massive and non-regulation Magnum automatic. As he approached, the muscleman smiled, exposing a row of perfect white teeth. The question 'Does it bite?' flashed through Fabel's mind.

'Good day, Herr Kriminalhauptkommissar. I'm Kriminal-kommissar Lothar Kolski, I work with Hauptkommissar Buchholz.'

Fabel stood up and found himself still looking up at Kolski as they shook hands.

'Please follow me, Herr Fabel, I'll take you along.'

Kolski made small talk as they walked along the corridor. Fabel found the experience surreal: walking along beside a heavily armed hulk who chatted about the weather and how he was looking forward to taking some late leave. Gran Canaria, probably.

Buchholz's office was one of a uniform row that lined the corridor. Whereas the other offices in the row had two work-station desks facing each other, obviously shared by teams of two officers, Buchholz had an office to himself. Kolski held the door open for Fabel to enter, and Fabel felt like an insignificant satellite orbiting a vast planet as he slipped past Kolski's bulk into the room. Behind a large desk with a computer terminal was a man in his mid-fifties. He was balding, and what was left of his dark hair was trimmed to bristle that, in turn, extended into stubble which darkened the lower half of a tough face. His nose looked as if it had been broken more than once. Fabel had heard that Buchholz had been a boxer in his younger days and he noticed framed photographs on the wall behind him: the same face but more youthful; a slimmer but still-powerful build. Each photograph showed the youthful Buchholz at a different stage of his amateur boxing career and his nose at a different stage of destruction. One photograph showed a teenage Buchholz, in boxing kit, holding aloft a trophy. It was captioned 'Hamburg-Harburg Junior Light-Heavyweight Champion, 1964'.

'Come in and sit down, Herr Fabel.' Buchholz half rose from his seat and indicated one of the two chairs opposite him. Fabel sat down and was surprised to see Kolski pull up the other chair. 'Kriminalkommissar Kolski leads the Ulugbay team,' Buchholz explained, 'he can probably tell you more than I can.'

'There may be nothing to this,' Fabel began, 'but as part

of this murder inquiry I would ideally like to set up a liaison with the LKA7 – that would obviously be yourself, Herr Kolski. The victim was, we believe, a prostitute, and possibly working for Ulugbay – through a man called Klugmann . . . an ex-Polizei Hamburg officer.'

Buchholz and Kolski exchanged knowing looks.

'Ah yes,' said Kolski, 'we know Herr Klugmann rather well. Is he a suspect in your inquiry?'

'No. Not at the moment. Should he be?'

'This is a serial killer, you reckon. A psycho?' Buchholz asked.

'Yes . . .' Fabel flipped open the file and handed a scene-of-crime photograph to Buchholz. Buchholz studied the picture in silence before passing it to Kolski, who gave a long, low whistle as he took in the image. 'That's our guy's handiwork,' continued Fabel. 'Is there any reason at all why we should be looking more closely at Klugmann?'

Buchholz shook his head and looked across to Kolski, who gave a dismissive shrug of his vast shoulders. 'No, I know Klugmann of old. He's a cop that went crooked . . . and Ulugbay does use his muscle sometimes, but I don't see Klugmann doing anything like this. He's a thug, not a psycho.'

'I understand Klugmann worked for LKA7, in the Mobiles Einsatz Kommando attached to your drugs unit, before he was dismissed . . .'

'That is correct . . . unfortunately . . .' answered Buchholz. 'We had a few ops go wrong. It was as if the targets had inside information, but we never for a moment considered that one of our own was the source. Then, of course, it came out that Klugmann was exchanging information for drugs. If we hadn't sprung him when we did, who knows what damage he could have done . . .'

'How did you catch him out?'

'We searched his locker,' answered Kolski. He folded his arms and the thick cables of muscle strained against the fabric of his shirt. 'We found an unregistered automatic, a pile of cash and some cocaine . . .'

'What, here in the Präsidium?'

'Yes.'

'Didn't that strike you as a bit . . . well, odd? Convenient, even?'

'Yes, it did, as a matter of fact,' said Buchholz. 'The other thing was that we had been tipped off by an anonymous call, otherwise we never would have caught him. But Klugmann confessed almost immediately that he was using drugs and claimed he had thought the Präsidium was the safest possible hiding place. After all, who would think of searching for illegal drugs here?'

'But we're talking about a tiny amount of drugs, aren't we?'

'Yes, a few grams. But enough.' Buchholz leaned forward. 'As you say, it was all a bit too easy, but we have a theory about that.'

'Oh?'

'Ulugbay has quite a pull on Klugmann. We were never able to prove that Klugmann had been supplying information about our operations to the Turks. If we had, then Klugmann would still be behind bars. As it happens all we could get him on was possession of a tiny amount of drugs and the illegal firearm. He even got to keep the cash: we couldn't prove that it was dirty. It was all enough to get him kicked off the force but not enough to have him put away.'

Kolski picked up the thread. 'But Ulugbay could, at any time, hand us the evidence we need – and Klugmann's head on a plate.'

Fabel nodded. 'So Klugmann had no choice but to work for Ulugbay . . .'

'Exactly,' said Buchholz.

'Do you think that Ulugbay was behind the anonymous tip-off?'

'Possible, but highly unlikely. Klugmann is very valuable to Ulugbay now – as a source of information and a highly trained heavy – but he was a hell of a lot more valuable when he was a serving police officer in a special-operations unit.'

'So who ratted on Klugmann? Any ideas?'

'Your guess is as good as mine,' Buchholz said. 'It was highly valuable information – something we would have paid an informant well for. It was very strange that we were handed it free of charge and anonymously.'

'Maybe someone in the Ulugbay organisation had his own agenda?'

'Again possible – and again highly unlikely. These bloody Turks are tight. Informing isn't just against the code, it's punishable by death – a very unpleasant death – and having your face carved off.'

'And, even if you aren't afraid of what will happen to you,' picked up Kolski, 'there's always the possibility of retribution against your family . . . either here in Germany or back home in Turkey.'

Fabel nodded thoughtfully for a moment, then tapped the scene-of-crime photograph. 'Could this fall into that category? Could it be some kind of punishment? Some kind of ritualised warning – you know, a gang thing . . .'

Buchholz smiled, a little patronisingly thought Fabel, and glanced at Kolski. 'No, Herr Fabel, this isn't a "gang thing". I think you're safer sticking to your serial theory. Having said that, I don't like the idea of any link with Ulugbay . . .' Buchholz turned to Kolski. 'Check it out, would you, Lothar?'

'Sure, *Chef*.'

Buchholz turned back to Fabel. 'If Ulugbay had wanted this girl killed then she would have simply disappeared. We would maybe never have got involved. If, on the other hand, Ulugbay had wanted to make an example of her – if she'd cheated him or informed – she would have been found with a bullet through the head. Or at worst, if he really wanted to make a statement, she would have been garrotted. Anyway, Ulugbay is trying to keep a low profile at the moment . . .'

'Oh?'

'Ulugbay has a cousin, Mehmet Yilmaz,' Kolski explained. 'Most of Ulugbay's success has been through Yilmaz's efforts. Yilmaz has been legitimising large parts of the Ulugbay operation and is reckoned to be the brains behind the more profitable elements of the criminal activity. Yilmaz is boss in all but name. Ulugbay can be a real *Arschloch*. He's temperamental, unpredictable and incredibly violent. The times we have come close to nailing the bastard is when he has gone berserk over some insult or threat to his organisation. He doesn't think – just steams in and starts littering the place with bodies. Yilmaz, on the other hand, is our real target. He keeps a lid on Ulugbay, and makes it difficult for us to get decent evidence. And, although he has been trying to legitimise the business, he is a hard son of a bitch. When Yilmaz kills, it's planned like a military operation . . . it's cold, effective and without evidential traces. His security is unbreakable. Anyway, Yilmaz has been trying to keep a lid on things and keep the organisation's profile low, so as not to compromise his legitimisation programme.'

'So you don't think that they would be involved in anything like this?'

'Certainly not,' answered Buchholz. 'This is not their style at any time but especially not now. Anyway, this guy has killed before, hasn't he?'

'Yes. Once that we know about.'

'And the previous victims had no association with the Ulugbay organisation?'

'No. Not that we know of.'

Buchholz shrugged and held his palms upwards. After a moment he pointed vaguely at the file in Fabel's hand. 'Do you have a copy of the file for us?'

Fabel handed the copy he had brought to Buchholz. 'This is for you, Herr Hauptkommissar.'

Buchholz pointedly handed it on to Kolski. 'We'll keep in touch, Herr Fabel. And, naturally, we would appreciate being notified before you carry out any enquiries directly with anyone in the Ulugbay organisation.'

'That's why I'm here, Herr Hauptkommissar.'

'And I appreciate it,' said Buchholz. 'Naturally we can't ask to be directly involved with your inquiry, but we can avoid stepping on each other's toes.'

'I would hope that we could be of help to each other, Herr Buchholz.'

Wednesday 4 June, 4.30 p.m. Pöseldorf, Hamburg.

It was mid-afternoon before Fabel turned the key of the door to his apartment. He picked up his mail and sifted through it, using his elbow to slam the door behind him. Fabel tossed the mail and the files he had brought home with him down onto the coffee table and walked through to the kitchen area, a bright alcove of steel and marble off the main living space. He filled the coffee machine and switched it on, then went into the bathroom and stripped, stuffing his shirt and underwear into the washing machine that sat in a recess next to the bathroom. Fabel shaved before stepping into the shower. He stood motionless, simply tilting his head back to allow the high-pressure spray to dig into the flesh of his face and letting the water run in rivulets down his body. The water was slightly too hot, but he didn't adjust it, letting it sting away the pollution of the night.

Fabel thought over the last eleven hours. He tried to focus on the facts, on the picture he was piecing together in his mind, but he couldn't erase the image that seared through his brain every few seconds: the image of the girl's body. Christ, he had ripped out her lungs . . . what kind of monster would do that? If it was a sexual thing, what unspeakable mutation of human sexuality could derive gratification from

such an act? Fabel thought about Klugmann, about how
someone so corrupted by greed, drugs and violence had
distanced himself with such clarity and ease from such an
unspeakable deed. Fabel and Klugmann each represented
everything the other was not. They were two extremes of
humanity who had become united in the face of a barbarity
that denied humanity in any form.

Standing naked in the shower, enveloped in a sheath of
too-hot water, Fabel still felt a chill deep in his being: a
permafrost that bound his guts in an icy grasp. It was a chill
that radiated out from a single fact he had locked deep inside:
as sure as the sun would rise tomorrow, this killer would
strike again.

After his shower Fabel pulled on a black cashmere roll-
neck, clipped his automatic to the black leather belt he had
looped through his pale chinos, and slipped into his Jaeger
sports jacket. He poured himself a black coffee and carried
it over to the picture windows. Fabel's apartment was in
Pöseldorf, in the Rotherbaum district of the city. It was on
the attic floor of a substantial turn-of-the-century building
that sat in assured but austere confidence, as did its neighbours, one block from the Milchstrasse. The conversion of
the building into apartments had included, in Fabel's flat,
the installation of almost floor-to-ceiling picture windows
that looked over the roofs of Magdalenenstrasse and out
onto the park-fringed Aussenalster. From his windows Fabel
could watch the red and white ferries zigzag their way across
the Alster, picking up passengers – tourists, commuters,
lovers – from one shore and dropping them on the other;
picking up, dropping, picking up, dropping, with a cheerful
regularity that gave a rhythm to the city's life. When the
sun was at a certain angle, he could see the faint turquoise
glitter of the Iranian mosque on the Schöne Aussicht across
on the distant shore of the Alster. Every time Fabel devoured

the view he blessed the unknown architect who had speci-
fied these windows.

Fabel had been here for years. He loved it. His apartment
lay where the student quarter – the university was within
walking distance – collided with rich and trendy Pöseldorf.
In one direction Fabel could browse through the countless
book and record stores on the Grindelhof, or catch an
obscure, late-night foreign film at the Abaton Kino; in the
other direction he could sink into the chic affluence of the
Milchstrasse, with its wine bars, jazz clubs, boutiques and
restaurants.

The clouds had finally surrendered the sky to the sun. Fabel
stared blankly at the view; a dull nauseating anxiety gnawing
at his gut. He looked out over the Aussenalster again, hungrily
trying to absorb its calm. The scenic Hamburg that opened
itself before the apartment's picture windows seemed neither
scenic nor open. Fabel scanned the horizon, then swept his
gaze like a searchlight over the familiar view: the vast mirror
of the Aussenalster reflecting a steely sky, the expanses of
green that fringed it and punctuated the city, and the orderly
residences and offices that sat like temperate, self-assured
burghers supervising the progress of the day. Today the view
did not calm Fabel. Today it was not 'another' Hamburg,
removed from the city of his work. Today, as he scrutinised
the view, he was aware of the fusion between the city he
loved and the city he policed. Out there, somewhere, was
something monstrous. Something evil. Something so violent
and malevolent it was difficult to imagine it as being human.

Fabel went back into the kitchen and refilled his coffee
cup. He stabbed the replay button as he passed his answering
machine. The sterile electronic voice announced that there
were three messages. The first was from the *Hamburger
Morgenpost*, asking for a comment on the latest killing. How
the hell did these people get his home number? Anyway, they
should know better; wait for the official statement. The last

two messages were from another journalist, Angelika Blüm. The name Maria had mentioned earlier. Her tone was strange, insistent. Instead of asking Fabel for some kind of comment, she had said, in her last message: 'It's vital that we talk . . .' A new approach. Ignore it.

He drained the last of his coffee and made his way across to the phone. He made two calls. The first was to Werner at the office: he was on the other line and Fabel left a message that he was on his way back in. For the second call, Fabel hugged the handset between shoulder and ear while he flicked through his pocket diary for the number. The phone rang for a long time before it was answered.

'Yeah?'

'Mahmoot? It's Fabel. I want a meet . . .'

'When?'

'The Rundfahrt ferry. Seven-thirty . . .'

'Okay.'

Fabel replaced the receiver, slipped his diary back into his jacket pocket and reset his answering machine. He was about to leave the apartment when he turned back and played the messages once more. He listened to Angelika Blüm's telephone number again; it began with 040: a Hamburg number. This time he noted it down on the pad that sat next to the phone. Just in case.

Fabel's footsteps in the echoing hall of the stairwell had hardly faded when the phone rang. After two rings the answering machine clicked on, delivering Fabel's recorded instructions to leave a message after the tone. The voice was that of a woman who said '*Scheisse!*' in genuine frustration and hung up.

Wednesday 4 June, 4.30 p.m. Hotel Altona Krone, Hamburg.

His arrival in the hotel reception was almost presidential. Centred in an envelope of burly, black-leather-jacketed bodyguards, a tall, lean man in his late seventies, dressed in a pale grey raincoat and darker grey business suit. His posture and movements were those of a man twenty years younger and his angular features, hooked nose and a plume of thick, ivory-coloured hair gave him an aristocratic, arrogant look.

His entry into the reception hall had been heralded by a fusillade of camera flashes. Some photographers, seeking a closer vantage, had been bounced off the picket of muscle and leather; one had been sent sprawling on the marble floor.

As it reached the reception desk, the envelope opened, allowing the tall older man to approach the counter. The hotel desk clerk, who had seen it all before – rock groups, politicians, film stars, billionaires with egos to match their bank balances – did not look up from his desk until the group was immediately before the counter. Then, with a polite yet tired smile he asked:

'Yes, mein Herr. May I help you?'

'I have a reservation here . . .' The tall man's voice was resonant and authoritative. The desk clerk continued to project a monumental apathy.

'And your name, sir?' he asked, although he knew very well.

The tall man jutted his jaw, tilting his head back and imperiously peering down his aquiline nose at the clerk, as if he were a morsel of prey.

'Eitel,' he answered, 'Wolfgang Eitel.'

A journalist pushed forward, an untidy man of about forty whose scalp gleamed through a web of carelessly combed strands of blond hair. 'Herr Eitel, do you really thing that your son has *any* chance of becoming Bürgermeister? After all, Hamburg has a tradition of liberalism and social democracy . . .'

Eitel's eyes projected a laser of disdain and contempt.

'It is what the people of Hamburg *really* think that matters – not what people like you tell them they should think.' Eitel bent his face close to the reporter's with a predatory swoop. 'The people of Hamburg buy my son's magazine . . . *SCHAU MAL!* has become the voice of the ordinary man on the street. The people of Hamburg want to be heard – they *deserve* to be heard. My son will make sure they are heard – through the pages of *SCHAU MAL!* and through him, as their Senator and ultimately their Erste Bürgermeister.'

'And what message, exactly, will he bear on their behalf?' A second journalist spoke: an attractive woman of about forty-five with short, styled auburn hair, expensively dressed in a black Chanel suit, the skirt of which was short enough to show off her still-firm and shapely legs. Extending an arm which held a Dictaphone, she leaned in past a bodyguard who placed a beefy restraining hand on her shoulder.

'Lose the hand, *Schätzchen,* or I'll have you for assault.' Her husky voice held calm and menace in perfect equilibrium. The hand was removed. Eitel turned in her direction. Like him, she had a southern accent. He clicked his heels and made a brief, bow-like nod with his head.

'Gnädige Frau . . . allow me to answer your question. The message my son bears – the message of the Hamburg people – is simple. It is that Hamburg has had enough; enough of mass immigration, enough of drug pushers poisoning our children, enough of burgeoning criminality, enough of foreigners taking our jobs, subverting our culture and turning Hamburg – and our other fine German cities – into cesspools of crime, prostitution and drugs.'

'So you're placing the blame on foreigners?'

'What I am saying, gnädige Frau, is that the experiment in "multiculturalism" so vaunted by the Sozis' – Eitel used the pejorative abbreviation of the Social Democratic Party – 'has failed. Unfortunately we are now having to live with this failure.' Eitel straightened his back and turned slightly into the reception, looking over the heads of his bodyguards and turning his answer into a semi-public address. 'How much more of this unremitting assault on the lives of decent German people can we take? The whole fabric of our society is being unravelled. No one feels safe or secure . . .'

Eitel turned back to the woman journalist and smiled. Beneath the thick sweep of her auburn hair was a powerfully carved face, large, penetrating green eyes, a wide mouth accentuated in vermilion lipstick and a strong jawline. She did not return his smile.

'Herr Eitel, your son's magazine *SCHAU MAL!* has a reputation for being sensationalist and, on several occasions – how can I put this – a little *one-dimensional* in its approach to complex political issues. Is that a good summation of the political perspective of the Bund Deutschland-für-Deutsche?'

Each question crashed against the sea-wall of Eitel's goodwill, eroding it swiftly and steadily. The smile remained, but the thin top lip tightened with something other than congeniality.

'There *are* complex issues, and there are simple ones. The destruction of our society by extrinsic elements is a simple one. And there is a simple solution.'

'By that you mean repatriation? Or by "simple" solution do you mean "final" solution?' The other journalist leaned in to ask the question. Eitel ignored him, keeping his laser gaze on the woman.

'A good question, Herr Eitel. Would you care to answer it?' The woman journalist paused, but not long enough for him to answer. 'Or would you prefer to explain why, when both you and your son feel so strongly about foreigners, that the Eitel Group is negotiating property deals here in Hamburg with eastern-European interests?'

Eitel looked taken aback for a sliver of one second. Then something dark and malevolent mustered behind the eyes.

At that moment a second entourage entered. Smaller. More dignified. Less muscle and more business. Eitel turned in its direction without answering the question.

'Papa!' A stocky man, no taller than about one metre seventy-two, with a shock of thick dark hair and a handsome face creased by a broad smile, approached Eitel. He grasped his hand in an enthusiastic handshake, reaching up to place his other hand on the taller man's shoulder.

'And this, gnädige Frau, is my son. Norbert Eitel – the next Erste Bürgermeister of Hamburg!' More camera flashes.

The woman journalist smiled, more in amusement at the unlikely disparity of physical types between father and son than in greeting.

'Of course, I know Norbert already . . .' She smiled and extended a hand to the shorter, younger Eitel. He smiled and kissed her hand.

The older Eitel spoke: 'If you'll excuse us, I'm afraid we have matters of great importance to discuss.' Both men nodded a brief bow. The elder extended his hand.

'You still haven't answered my question, Herr Eitel,' she responded, flatly.

'Perhaps some other time. It has been a pleasure, gnädige Frau . . .'

As she walked away, the woman journalist smiled. *Gnädige Frau* . . . it was an address she would reserve for some stern, aristocratic grandmother.

As Eitel father and son watched her make her way across the reception towards the door, Wolfgang Eitel's smile had been washed away by a more predatory expression. He spoke without turning to his son.

'Who was that, Norbert?'

'Her? Oh she's a freelancer – well respected, done work for *Der Spiegel* and *Stern* . . .'

'Her name . . .' It was a command, not a question.

'Blüm . . . that's Angelika Blüm.'

* * *

Wednesday 4 June, 6.45 p.m. B73, Hamburg–Cuxhaven.
Fear ran through him like an electric current. A delicious fear
that tingled his scalp and tightened his chest. This was his
selected duty and he never resented being the one who had
to take all the risks.

He took his hands from the steering wheel, first one, then
the other, and wiped the sweat from his palms and concen-
trated on the road. All it would take would be a routine
police road check, or a minor accident, or a flat tyre and a
helpful autobahn patrol. Then it would be all over. He angled
the rear-view mirror so that he could see her. She was slumped
in the back seat. Her sonorous breathing was deep but ir-
regular, with a scratchy stridor. Fuck. Maybe he had used
too much. 'Just stay alive,' he muttered, knowing she was
far beyond hearing anything. 'Just stay alive for a couple of
hours more, you stupid bitch.'

Wednesday 4 June, 7.40 p.m. Aussenalster, Hamburg.
The 7.30 Rundfahrt ferry gleamed golden in the evening sun
that had at last triumphed against the rain. Fabel stood on
deck, leaning with his forearms resting on the rail. The ferry
was not particularly busy and the only passengers on deck
were an elderly couple, sitting together and in silence on one
of the benches. They simply stared out over the Aussenalster,
not speaking, not touching, not looking at each other. To Fabel
it seemed that all they had left to share was solitude, and he
reflected for a moment on how, since his divorce, his solitude
had been total. Indivisible and unshared. There had been more
than a few women, yet with each new liaison came a deep
ache that was something like guilt, and the relationships had
never lasted. Fabel had sought something solid in each new
involvement, something on which to anchor some sense of
meaning, but he had never found it. He had grown up among
the tight-knit, Lutheran communities of Ost-Friesland where

people married for life. For better and, quite often, for worse. He had never considered that he would be anything other than a full-time, full-term husband and father. It was a constant in his life, an anchor point, like being a policeman. Then Renate, his wife, had removed the landmark of his marriage from his life and Fabel had been lost for a long, long time. And now, five years after his divorce, each time he shared the bed of another woman felt like a small adultery; an infidelity to a marriage that had died long ago.

The ferry glided on. Fabel had boarded at the Fährdamm quay in the Alsterpark, and now they were moving out from the sweep of green and gold that seemed to glow in the evening sun. Fabel had just looked at his watch – 7.40 p.m. – when he became aware of a figure leaning on the rail next to him. He turned to face a tall Turk, about thirty-five, with a longish handsome face and a shock of black hair. The Turk grinned broadly and the smile lines that were already around his eyes deepened further.

'Hi, Herr Kriminalhauptkommissar. How's the fight against crime?'

Fabel laughed. 'What can I tell you? Just like your business, you're always assured custom. How is the world of porn?'

The Turk laughed so loudly that the elderly couple looked across momentarily, still expressionless, before simultaneously and wordlessly turning their blank gaze back to the horizon.

'Don't do that any more. Technology, you see – video, DVD and CD-ROMs are the thing now.' He sighed with an exaggerated wistfulness. 'No one wants the good old traditional dirty photograph any more. It's enough to force you into a respectable business.'

'Somehow I don't think there's much danger of that.' Fabel paused. 'It's good to see you again, Mahmoot. How are things, seriously?'

'Okay. I've been selling the odd paparazzo shot to the tabloid press. I just cashed a cheque for two thousand euros from *SCHAU MAL!* for a pic of one of our dedicated and earnest city senators on his way out of a stripclub.'

'*SCHAU MAL!*?' Fabel looked puzzled.

Mahmoot laughed. 'Oh they don't mind dealing with a Turk if they get something that sells copies.'

'And I dare say that the senator in question was a Social Democrat?' Fabel asked.

'Got it in one.'

'I can't understand why you would choose to deal with them. After all, they're just a bunch of racist bastards.'

Mahmoot shrugged. 'Listen. I was born and raised in this country. I'm as German as anyone. But because my parents came here as Turkish Gastarbeiters, I spent most of my life, in fact right up until the Schroeder government came in, not entitled to a German passport or nationality.' The half smile faded from his face. 'I've decided that whatever I can get out of this country I'll take.'

Fabel stared out over the water. The ferry had touched the east side of the Alster at Uhlenhorst and was now heading south. 'I can't blame you, Mahmoot. It's just that I think you're really talented. Some of those photographs you took of immigrant families were brilliant . . . I hate seeing that talent going to waste.'

'Listen, Jan. I was proud of that work, but no one wanted to buy it. So I take cheap shots for crappy tabloids and when that dries up I have to do porn shoots. I hate it, as you know, but I have to do it to earn a living.'

'Yeah, I know.'

'Anyway,' the smile returned to Mahmoot's face, 'you didn't call for a meet to discuss the state of my soul. What can I do for you?'

'Couple of things. First of all . . .' Fabel reached into his inside jacket pocket and pulled out a photograph. It was the face of the murdered girl. It had been taken in the morgue and the face had been washed clean of blood and the hair brushed back; death and the sterile lighting had bleached the face into a spiritless mask. 'I'm afraid that's all we've got, other than an old fuzzy photograph of her as a teenager. Do you recognise her?'

Mahmoot shook his head. 'Nah.'

'Take a good look. I think she was a hooker. Maybe worked in the porn business.'

'Not with me. But she's . . . well she's not exactly looking her best in this photograph. Difficult to tell.' Mahmoot went to hand the photograph back.

'Keep it,' Fabel said, 'ask about a bit. It's important.'

'What was her name?'

'That's the thing, Mahmoot. Other than "Monique", which we think is just some kind of professional name, she doesn't have a name, a permanent address or even a history before the night she was killed. Except for one thing: she had a bullet wound on her upper right thigh. We reckon she got it some-time between five and ten years ago. Does that ring a bell?'

'Sorry, Jan . . . but let me sniff around and see what I can find out. How was she killed?'

'Someone decided to carry out an anatomy lesson on her. Sliced her open and scooped out her lungs.'

'Fuck!' Mahmoot's shock was genuine. Fabel could never understand how Mahmoot managed to retain his intelligence and humanity, given the work he was involved in. 'Is this the big case the papers have been going on about?'

''Fraid so,' said Fabel. 'This guy is our number-one priority. This has got serial written all over it. I've got to get to him before his appetite returns.'

'I'll do what I can. But you know I've got to be careful. My social circle isn't exactly renowned for its civic-minded-ness. If they thought I was working for the cops I'd end up on a morgue slab myself.'

'I know – and I want you to be extra careful with this one . . .'

'Why?'

'There's a lot going on in the background I don't like. The BND is sniffing about all of a sudden . . . and the guy who owned the flat was ex-Mobiles Einsatz Kommando.'

Mahmoot gave a start. 'Hans Klugmann?'

Fabel was surprised that Mahmoot knew the name. 'You know him?'

'Vaguely. Our paths have crossed, so to speak.' Mahmoot straightened his frame and took a step back from Fabel. 'Oh no . . . hold on a minute . . . Klugmann is tied up with Ersin Ulugbay and Mehmet Yilmaz, isn't he?'

'We believe so.'

'Listen Jan, I help you out whenever I can. I owe you, after all – but this is different. No way am I sniffing around Ulugbay. He's not just the biggest Turkish Mafia godfather in Hamburg, he's a total fucking headcase.'

'Okay, okay, take it easy!' Fabel held up his hands as if to stem the vehemence of Mahmoot's refusal. 'I don't want you to do anything dodgy, just keep an ear to the ground. See if you can dig up anything on Klugmann. What do you know about him, anyway?'

'Just that he's a part-time heavy for Ersin Ulugbay and a part-time pimp for himself. He's strictly small time, but a nasty piece of work, by all accounts. He has a girlfriend . . . Sonja Brun, a dancer at the Paradies-Tanzbar. Used to be a hooker, working for Klugmann, but he took her off the streets. Love before business apparently.'

'How do you know her?'

'*Elixir* – you know, the hardcore magazine – they got me to do a couple of shoots about six months ago. Sonja was one of the girls. Nice kid . . . turned my stomach to see her do the kind of things I had to photograph. Anyway, Klugmann picked her up after the shoot. He was not a happy man –

got a bit heavy with Sonja on the way out. It was after that that she came off the streets and stopped doing porn shoots.'

'What about the Paradies-Tanzbar?'

'Basically Klugmann's the house heavy. The Paradies is an all-up-front, no-back-room operation. It makes money the usual way: fat, drunk businessmen up from Frankfurt or Stuttgart watching the acts on stage, too pissed to realise they're being charged thirty euros for each glass of cheap wine. But there's no screwing on the premises. Ulugbay bought the Paradies about a year ago, at a knock-down price, apparently. Then he moved Hoffknecht in to run it for him – which was like putting a vegetarian in charge of a butcher's shop. Hoffknecht can be trusted to leave the girls alone. Apparently his taste runs more to eighteen-year-old boys. From what I can gather, Klugmann's job is to keep trouble-makers out and if any of the "patrons" kick up a fuss about paying extortionate prices, he helps explain the bill to them, if you know what I mean.' Mahmoot paused, shook his head and gave a wry laugh. Then his face broke into its habitual broad smile. 'Okay . . . I'll sniff about and talk to Sonja. I'll even chat up that old faggot, Arno Hoffknecht. I'll see what I can turn up. No promises though.'

Fabel smiled. 'Fair enough. Thanks, Mahmoot. Here's the usual to cover expenses . . .' Fabel took a swollen envelope from his inside pocket and handed it to Mahmoot who quickly slipped it into the pocket of his leather jacket.

'There's one other thing about the Ulugbay mob you should know if you don't already . . .'

'Oh, what?'

'They're under a bit of pressure. A lot of pressure in fact. There's talk of a new Ukrainian outfit in town . . .'

'I thought there was an ongoing turf war between the Turks and the Ukrainians anyway . . .'

'Not any more. This new outfit has taken total control of all the existing Ukrainian gangs. The old gangs still exist and they still have their old bosses, but they pay "taxes" to the new outfit and they're not allowed to fight among themselves or with the Turks. The rumour is that Yilmaz, Ulugbay's cousin, has been forced to strike a deal with the new lot. There's talk that Yilmaz is under pressure to speed up his plan to legitimise the Ulugbay business . . . retire, as it were, from illegal business. Apparently Ulugbay himself is very pissed off about it all.'

'So who runs this new outfit?'

'That's the thing. This new Ukrainian unit is supposed to only have about ten or twelve men with some kind of mega-bad-ass in charge.'

Fabel gazed out over the water, weighing up what Mahmoot had told him. Why the hell hadn't Buchholz or Kolski told him all of this? Admittedly it wasn't central to his investigation, but it could have a bearing. He turned to Mahmoot. 'What I don't understand is, if this new gang is so small, why don't the other Ukrainians – or the Turks – just squash them flat?'

'You haven't heard the way the Ukrainians talk – or rather, don't talk – about these guys. I mean, you know Yari Varasouv, don't you?' Fabel nodded: Varasouv was a gargantuan Ukrainian thug suspected of a string of gangland killings. He reputedly specialised in beating his victims to death with his massive, bare hands. The Polizei Hamburg had never been able to gather sufficient evidence to convict him. 'Well, even Varasouv fucking *whispers* when he talks about these guys. Apparently he's taken up early retirement at the behest of his new masters. I tell you, this new outfit scares him shitless. I mean, the Ukrainians are tough cookies – it's almost as if it's something more than the threat of death that is scaring them.'

'I still don't get what it is that is so special about these new faces.'

'The rumour is that they are ex-Spetznaz . . .'

'So what? I know that makes them extremely dangerous, but half of the Russian, Ukrainian and Baltic Mafias in Europe employ former Soviet-special-forces thugs . . .'

Mahmoot shook his head impatiently. 'No, no. These guys are different. They belonged to a special field-police unit. Soviet Interior Ministry or some shit like that. Veterans of Afghanistan and Chechnya. I don't know what they did out there, but my guess is whatever it was is scaring the crap out of everybody.'

The loudspeaker announced that the ferry was pulling in to the St Georg quay. Mahmoot grasped Fabel's hand in a warm handshake, making sure first that no one would witness this act of friendship between himself and the policeman. 'This is my stop. I'll find out what I can about this girl and Klugmann. Take care of yourself, my friend.'

'And you, Mahmoot.'

Fabel watched Mahmoot disembark. As the ferry pulled out again, Fabel noticed a pretty girl with short blonde hair who had just got off the ferry; the dying sun turned her hair an iridescent gold. He felt a pang as he gazed at her radiant youth. He turned and walked over to the other side of the ferry, and did not notice that the girl made off in the same direction as Mahmoot, twenty or so metres behind.

Wednesday 4 June, 8.45 p.m. Alsterpavilion, Hamburg.
The tiredness that had taken hold on Fabel in the afternoon now tightened its grip. When he got off the ferry he felt crumpled and grimy. The evening had defied the earlier gloom of the day and the low-slung sun now splashed the city red and copper-gold. He disembarked at the southern end of the Binnenalster and walked the short distance to the Alsterarkaden in the heart of the city. He took a table under the colonnades of the arcade and ordered a Matjes salad and a Jever beer with which to wash the herring down. The arcade

ran along the side of the Alsterfleet and Fabel let his tired gaze drift idly over the water that sparkled in the evening light while swans glided effortlessly over its surface. On the other side of the Fleet lay the city's main square from which the Rathaus jutted authoritatively up into the sky, the burnished copper clocks of its tower gleaming bright in the evening sun.

Fabel didn't know how long she had been standing there and got a start when he heard her soft Munich accent. 'May I?'

'Yes . . . yes . . . of course, Frau Doktor . . .' Fabel floundered for a moment with his napkin as he got to his feet and pulled out a chair.

'I hope I'm not intruding . . .' said Susanne Eckhardt.

'No . . . not at all.' He beckoned to the waitress and turned back to Susanne. 'Can I get you something?'

Susanne turned to the waitress and ordered a glass of white wine. Fabel asked her if she wanted something to eat but she shook her head. 'I grabbed something at the office. But please, don't let me interrupt you.'

Fabel took another mouthful of herring. He felt strangely vulnerable, eating while she watched. She tilted her head back to let the sun warm her face; Fabel found himself again in awe of her beauty.

'I was doing some shopping in the Arcade' – she nodded towards the bags she had set down next to her – 'when I saw you sitting here. You look exhausted. It's been a long day, hasn't it?'

'It certainly has. Unfortunately, long days and sleepless nights tend to go with the job.'

Her wine arrived. She raised her glass. '*Zum Wohl!* Here's to long days and sleepless nights.'

'*Cheers.*' Fabel habitually used the English expression.

Susanne laughed. 'Oh yes – *der englische Kommissar* . . . I forgot they called you that . . .'

Fabel smiled back. 'I'm half Scottish. My mother was a Scot and I was very nearly christened "Iain". Jan was a compromise. Anyway, a lot of people in Hamburg feel at least a little British. They do call it the most easterly suburb of London . . . I'm sure as a southerner you know what I mean . . .'

Susanne put down her glass. 'Oh yes . . . I didn't expect to experience culture shock without leaving Germany, but when I moved up from Munich I have to admit I felt as if I were emigrating to a strange land. The people here can be a little . . .'

'Anglo-Saxon?'

'I was going to say reserved . . . but yes, now that I've lived here, I can see why they say that about Hamburg people . . .' She took another sip of her wine. 'I love it though. It's a great city.'

'Yes.' Fabel looked out over the water. 'Yes, it is. How long have you been here?'

'Two years . . . no, it's nearer three now. I'm really quite settled here.'

'What brought you here? Was it your job or is your husband from here?'

She laughed at the obviousness of Fabel's question. He laughed too. 'No, Herr Fabel . . . I'm not married . . . nor am I otherwise involved. I moved up here because of the position I was offered at the Institut für Rechtsmedizin. And through the Institut I was offered the consultative post with the Polizei Hamburg.' She leaned forward, resting her elbows on the table and supporting her chin on a bridge of interlaced fingers. 'And how does *Frau* Fabel deal with the long hours you have to put in?'

Fabel laughed at the reflection of his own clumsiness. 'There is no Frau Fabel. Or at least, there isn't now; I've been divorced for about five years.'

'I'm sorry . . . I didn't mean . . .'

Fabel held up his hands. 'No need. I've got used to it. It's difficult for a partner to put up with this life . . . and my wife got involved with someone . . . well, someone who was there when I wasn't.'

'I really am sorry.'

'Like I said, don't be. I have a beautiful daughter who spends all the time she can with me.'

A silence fell between them. The conversation had taken a suddenly and awkwardly intimate turn and neither seemed to be able to find the way back. Susanne looked out over the water of the Alsterfleet towards the Rathaus square while Fabel pushed a piece of herring around his plate with his fork. After a few seconds of silence they both started to speak at once.

Susanne laughed. 'You first . . .'

'I was just going to ask you . . .' Fabel started, aware his too-tentative tone. He repeated himself, this time more assertively: 'I was just going to ask you, seeing as you don't have time just now, if you would perhaps like to have dinner with me sometime . . .'

Susanne smiled broadly. 'I would enjoy that. How about next week? Phone me at the office and we'll arrange it.' She looked at her watch. 'God, it's time I was somewhere else . . . thanks for the wine, Herr Fabel . . .'

'Call me Jan, please . . .'

'Thanks for the wine, Jan . . . I'll hear from you next week?'

Fabel rose from his chair and shook her hand. 'You may count on it . . .'

He watched her as she walked back through the Arcade and the alternating bands of shadow and golden sunlight cast by the colonnades. The beer and his tiredness mingled to give him a sense of unreality. Had she really said yes?

* * *

Wednesday 4 June, 9.00 p.m. Aussendeich, near Cuxhaven.

It was as if she were disconnected from her body, from her immediate environment, from the world. There was a thick viscous coating around her consciousness. Sometimes it thinned and she perceived things more normally, then it would cloud over her again and obfuscate the reality around her. It made her angry, yet even this raw emotion was attenuated by the sludge that enveloped every thought, every sensation, every movement. She fell again. She felt damp leaves clinging to her face; the taste of foetid mulch in her mouth. There were trees all around her. She knew she should know what to call a place like this, but the word 'forest' was too distant, required too immense an intellectual effort to recall. She lay for a moment and then staggered to her feet, took a few more steps and fell again. The slime slugged around her consciousness once more, thick and dark this time, and she slipped back into unconsciousness.

When she awoke, it had become darker. An instinct too powerful to be dulled by the drug seized her and she clambered to her feet. There were lights ahead. Moving lights flickering through the silhouette trunks of the trees. It was her instinct that reached through to pull her towards the lights, not any full recognition that ahead lay a road, help, rescue. She stumbled a couple of times more, but now she was being pulled towards the lights as if she was on the end of a tugged line. The ground underfoot became more even, with fewer snagging roots or branches to trip her. The lights grew bigger. Brighter.

Clarity came to her just before the truck hit her. She heard the scream of tyres and gazed, with wide but undazzled eyes, into the headlights as they hurtled towards her. Her overwhelming feeling was one of surprise: she could not understand why, knowing that she was going to die, she was so totally free of fear.

Wednesday 4 June, 11.50 p.m. Altona, Hamburg.
With most of the office workers and shoppers long gone, the basement Parkhaus was almost empty of cars. The tyres of the Saab yielded a restrained screech as it took the steep sharp turn from the down ramp onto the pillared square of parking places. Instead of parking, it stopped on the main through-way; the headlamps dimmed to side lights.

A Mercedes, which had been concealed in a parking place behind a pillar, pulled out suddenly and drove up to the Saab, stopping when the two cars were almost nose to nose. Neither could now make a quick exit. The Turks got out first, from the Mercedes. Three; heavily built. Two stood on either side of the car, leaving the doors open and resting their arms on them, using them as shields before their bodies.

The third Turk, older and more expensively dressed than the other two, walked up to the Saab, leant down and tapped with his knuckles on the driver's window. There was the buzz and clunk of an opening electric window.

Then a sound like a loud pop.

The two Turks standing by the Mercedes saw an explosive plume of blood spurt from the back of the older man's head as the bullet, fired from inside the Saab, exited his skull. Before they could react there was a series of more loud pops, in rapid succession like hailstones hitting off a roof, this time from behind them.

Like the older Turk, they too were dead before they hit the ground.

Two tall men, both blond, emerged from the shadows behind the Turks' Mercedes. As one methodically picked up the spent shells from the Parkhaus floor, the other calmly walked across to the bodies of the three Turks, firing a single conclusive shot into the head of each; again picking up the spent shells and placing them in the pocket of his thigh-length leather coat. Both men then made their way towards the Saab, simultaneously unscrewing the silencers from their Heckler and Koch semi-automatics. They casually stepped over the bodies, and climbed into the rear passenger seats of the Saab, which carefully reversed into a parking place to complete a three-point turn before driving towards the up ramp.

Thursday 5 June, 10.00 a.m. Pöseldorf, Hamburg.
There was now a solid, dreamless wedge of sleep between Fabel and the events of the day before; yet when he woke, a bone-aching tiredness clung to him. He dragged himself through the routine of a shave and a shower and dressing. A *Hamburger Morgenpost* lay on his doormat; he placed it on the hall table without opening it.

He drank his coffee over by the picture windows, gazing blankly out over Hamburg. A steel sky clamped down on the city, sucking the colour from the water, the parks and the buildings, but a hint of rose bloom behind the clouds promised something better for later in the day. You're somewhere out there, he thought, you're under the same sky and you're waiting to do it again. You can't wait to do it again. And we can't wait for you to make a mistake. The thought clenched in his belly like a fist.

As Fabel stood watching the sky and sipping his coffee, he went over in his mind what they had got so far. He had the jigsaw pieces that were all supposed to fit: a corrupt ex-cop, a prostitute murdered horrifically, a previous victim, four months before, with no shared history or other connection with the second murdered girl, and an egomaniacal sociopath claiming responsibility for the murders by e-mail. But whenever Fabel tried to put the pieces together they snagged on each other. All of it made sense at front of mind, but in some dark, small room at the back of Fabel's brain, where it was being run through a deeper wash, a little red warning light was flashing brightly.

Fabel drained his coffee cup. He took a long deep breath,

drawing in both air and the view across the Alster, then turned, picked up his jacket and his keys, and left for his office.

From the moment he arrived in the wide foyer of the Präsidium, Fabel was aware of frenetic activity. A dozen MEK officers, grey and black wraiths clutching their goggles and helmets, trotted past him and headed out to the front where an armoured transport awaited them. He passed Buchholz and Kolski, both of whom were engaged in a conversation with one of the Schutzpolizei's Ersten Hauptkommisars, who held a blue tactical clipboard. They both looked in Fabel's direction and nodded briefly and grimly. Fabel nodded back; although he was desperate to know what was going on, he recognised the stern determination on their faces and decided to leave them to it. Gerd Volker, the BND man, came out of the elevator with four hard-looking men as Fabel was about to get in. Volker smiled perfunctorily, wished Fabel a good morning and swept past him before he had a chance to speak.

When Fabel left the elevator, he met Werner in the hall of the Mordkommission.

'What the hell's going on?'

Werner pushed a copy of the *Morgenpost*, open at the appropriate page, into Fabel's hands. 'Ersin Ulugbay is dead. A real professional job.'

Fabel gave a low whistle. The image in the *Morgenpost* showed a man in an expensive coat sprawled on the blood- and oil-stained concrete. There was nothing in the article to indicate a motive, but it stated that one of the three victims was Ersin Ulugbay, 'a well-known figure in the Hamburg underworld'. The two other victims, both male and believed to be of Turkish origin, were yet to be identified. Fabel wasn't surprised that he had encountered so much grim-faced activity downstairs.

'Shit. There's going to be one hell of a war out there.'

'That's what they're all preparing for,' Maria Klee had come alongside Fabel, a cup of coffee in her hand. She lifted the cup. 'Want one?' Fabel shook his head. 'The whole Präsidium is crawling with LKA7 and BND . . .' Maria gave a laugh. 'If it wears a black leather jacket and it goes by initials, it's here and it's got a bee up its ass.'

'I don't know why they bother,' shrugged Werner. 'Let the bastards kill each other. Save us all a lot of time and hassle.'

'Unfortunately there's such a thing as crossfire, Werner –' Fabel handed the paper back to him – 'and crossfire and innocent passers-by seem always to come together.'

'That's as maybe, but I for one won't be shedding any tears over this piece of shit.'

Fabel moved towards his office. 'Do you both have a minute?'

Fabel settled behind his desk and motioned for Maria and Werner to sit down. 'Do we have anything more on our victim from yesterday?'

'Nothing,' Maria answered. 'I've done a full check, both with Hamburg and with the Bundeskriminalamt. She didn't have any kind of criminal record. And still nothing on the bullet wound. We can't tie her into any shootings involving women in Hamburg over the last fifteen years.'

'Then widen the net.'

'I'm already on it, *Chef*.'

'Anna and Paul are managing the surveillance on Klugmann,' said Werner. 'So far he went straight home and has stayed in bed. Last report was the curtains were still drawn and there was no sign of life.'

'Did we get anything more from any of the residents around the flat where the girl was found? Anyone mention seeing an older Slavic-looking guy?'

'Who are we talking about?' asked Maria.

'Jan saw someone hanging around with the ghouls when we arrived at the murder scene,' answered Werner.

'A shortish guy, sixty, maybe older . . . looked foreign?'

Both Werner and Fabel stared at Maria.

'You saw him?'

'I arrived on the scene about fifteen minutes before you, remember? A small crowd had already gathered and he would have been a hundred metres from it, coming from the St Pauli direction. I noticed this older guy . . . The way I would describe him is looking a bit like Khrushchev . . . you know, the old Soviet president or whatever they called him . . . in the sixties.'

'That's the guy,' said Fabel.

'Sorry, I didn't think much about it at the time. It wasn't as if he was fleeing the scene or anything, and the crime scene had been populated for at least an hour, so I didn't even think of a possible perpetrator . . . You think he's the killer?'

'No . . .' Fabel frowned. 'I don't know . . . he just seemed to stand out. It's probably nothing. But he doesn't belong to the area and you saw him arriving at the locus. I want to find him for elimination.'

'I'll ask around some more,' said Werner.

'I also want you to try to find out if any of the neighbours saw a policeman in the area prior to the killing. But for God's sake be careful . . . I don't want anyone to think we suspect one of our own.'

'Of course,' said Maria, 'it could be that he isn't in uniform. Maybe he's simply got hold of a Kriminalpolizei ID or shield.'

'I know . . . as you say, that's even if he is impersonating a policeman at all. But a uniform would get him unquestioned entry, probably. It's worth a try.'

After Werner and Maria left his office, Fabel tried to get Mahmoot on his cell phone. A full-scale gang war was about to erupt and Fabel had sent Mahmoot out unarmed into the front line. The phone rang out until, eventually, Mahmoot's answering service cut in.

'It's me. Phone me. And forget all about that favour I asked.' Fabel hung up.

Thursday 5 June, 10.00 a.m. Stadtkrankenhaus Cuxhaven.
Max Sülberg's uniform didn't fit him very well. In fact, in
his twenty-five-year service with the Polizei Niedersachsen,
most of which had been spent at the Polizeiinspektion
Cuxhaven, no uniform had ever fitted him that well. He had,
in that time, slowly metamorphosed from skinny and scruffy
to paunchy and scruffy. Now, his mustard-yellow short-
sleeved service shirt was stretched taut around the belt line
and wrinkled across the chest and back, and his uniform
trousers looked as if they had had only a passing and none
too recent acquaintance with an iron. He was the kind of
scruffy policeman that would normally be hauled up before
the boss – were it not for the two gold pips on his green and
white shoulder flashes, that showed that Max was, in fact,
the boss.

He was a short, balding man with an amiable face that
was well lived-in and almost always on the verge of a smile.
It was a familiar and trusted face among those who lived on
the low, flat lands contained by the sandy arc of the Cuxhaven
coastline that swept from Berensch-Arensch to Altenbruch.

Now, Max's ready smile was absent, bleached from his face
by the mortuary's stark lighting. Next to him stood Dr Franz
Stern, a lean, handsome physician with a thick mane of black
hair who towered immaculately above the crumpled SchuPo
officer. Before them, on the cold steel of a mortuary trolley,
lay the smashed body of Petra Heyne, a nineteen-year-old
student from Hemmoor. Max Sülberg had been a policeman
for a long time and that meant, even in Cuxhaven, he had
seen his fair share of death and violence. But, as he looked
down at the lifeless face of a girl barely a year older than his
own daughter, he felt an overpowering instinct to find a
pillow, something, anything, to put beneath her head. And
to say something to her. To comfort her. But she was beyond
comfort. He shook his head heavily.

'What a waste.'

Stern sighed. 'What on earth was she doing wandering about on the road, miles from anywhere?'

'I can only guess. We'll have to wait for the autopsy, but my guess is she was on some kind of drugs. The driver of the truck said she seemed totally out of it when she stepped out in front of him. There was clearly nothing he could do to avoid hitting her, but he's having a hard time accepting that. Poor swine.'

'Have the parents been notified?' asked Stern.

'They're on their way in. She had no bag or her ID card on her, but she was wearing a medimergency bracelet.'

Without thinking, Stern glanced at the girl's wrist. Silly, of course, the bracelet had been taken away and stored by the police; but something caught his eye and he frowned, his black eyebrows forming a straight ridge and hooding his eyes. He leaned forward.

'What is it?' asked Sülberg.

Stern didn't answer but turned the girl's forearm, scrutinising the wrist. He turned his attention to her right ankle, then her left ankle before finally examining the left wrist with as much intensity.

Sülberg gave an impatient sigh. 'What *is* it, Herr Doktor Stern?'

Stern held the girl's wrist up.

Sülberg shrugged. 'What am I supposed to be looking at. I don't see . . .'

'Look closer.'

Sülberg slipped his reading glasses from his uniform shirt pocket and put them on. As he leaned in to examine the girl's wrist, his stomach lurched from the smell of the freshly dead. Then his attention was caught. There were scrapes on the skin and a very faint redness across the plain of the wrist.

'It's the same on the ankles . . .' said Stern.

'Shit . . .' Sülberg removed his glasses. 'She's been tied up.'

'She's been tied up all right,' said Stern, 'but she hasn't

struggled much against her bonds. My guess is that she has been semi- or unconscious whilst bound. That would explain her being out of it and walking right into the path of that truck.'

Somehow the muscles in Sülberg's face tautened and gave it a harder look. 'I don't want to wait for the full autopsy, Dr Stern. I want you to draw some blood now for analysis.'

Thursday 5 June, 12.00 p.m. Polizeipräsidium, Hamburg.
Fabel knew from the fire in Werner's eyes that it was something important.

Werner had a methodical and painstaking approach to policework that contrasted with Fabel's own, more intuitive style. Werner was all detail: Fabel was all big picture. It was this contrast that made them such a good team. The only thing that frustrated Fabel was Werner's reluctance to open up to Maria Klee's complementary analytical skills. And now Werner had that look that told Fabel he had been sniffing around in some small corner of the investigation and had found a scent to follow.

'What've you got, Werner?'

Werner sat down opposite Fabel and gave a small laugh at being so easy to read. 'Two things. First, difficult though it is to believe, our pal Klugmann has been less than straight with us.'

'You do surprise me.'

Werner showed Fabel a print-out that looked like a phone bill without the costs, just numbers dialled and durations. 'I got the details of Klugmann's cell phone account . . .' Werner read Fabel's raised eyebrows. 'It wasn't easy.' He tapped the beefy tip of his forefinger on an entry. 'Look at this . . . he phoned this number at two-thirty-five a.m. . . . it's the number for the local police. Just like he said and just like the station logged.' Werner slid his finger down the page. 'Now look at this. Two-twenty-two a.m. . . . .'

Fabel looked up from the entry and held Werner's eyes. 'The bastard.'

'Exactly. He was on the phone for twelve minutes to that number. He must have hung up and then dialled the local police. Now who the hell do you phone before the police when you've just found a so-called friend sliced up like butcher-meat? Pizza delivery?'

'So who is it? Whose number is it?'

Werner leaned his broad back against the chair and tilted it slightly. 'That's the other thing. I have checked and double-checked through every relevant federal department, Deutsche Telekom, the cell phone operators . . . this number –' he let his chair slam forward again and stabbed his finger at the entry – 'does not exist.'

'It has to exist.'

'It clearly does, because Klugmann was talking to it for twelve minutes, but it is not recorded anywhere. We're left with only one thing to do.'

'You haven't already tried?'

'I thought I'd leave the honours to you, *Chef*.'

Fabel picked up his cell phone and dialled. It was answered after the second ring, but no one spoke.

Fabel waited a moment before speaking. 'Hello?'

Silence.

'Hello?' Fabel thought he heard the sound of a breath at the other end. He was pretty sure he was connected to a cell phone. After a couple of seconds he spoke again. 'Hello . . . it's me . . .' The line went dead. Fabel redialled the number. He let it ring for several minutes before hanging up. He turned to Werner. 'Okay . . . do Anna and Paul still have Klugmann under surveillance?'

Werner nodded.

'Let's bring him in.'

* * *

It was more of an alley than a street. Because it was so narrow and ran east–west, and because the red sandstone buildings that lined it were never less than three storeys high, it was also gloomy. Parking was permitted only on one side of the street and Anna Wolff and Paul Lindemann's BMW was parked halfway along. There were no other spaces available, so Fabel, with Werner in the passenger seat, had to pull in around the corner.

Sonja Brun appeared around the corner, carrying two Aldi carrier bags, heavy with groceries. She was tall, slim, with long, bronzed legs. Her hair was dark and long, pushed back from her face by the improvised hairband of her sunglasses, which were shoved up onto the top of her head. She looked lithe and fit. Fabel thought of the comments Möller, the pathologist, had made about the second victim's levels of fitness. Sonja was a pole-dancer at the Paradies-Tanzbar, among other things. Maybe 'Monique' had been a whore, after all.

Sonja passed Fabel's parked car, on the other side of the narrow street, and Fabel got a better look at her. She was dressed cheaply in a cropped white T-shirt that strained against her breasts and exposed her tanned midriff, a faded denim miniskirt and canvas sandals with straps that wrapped around her shapely calves. Fabel saw her face only in profile, but he could tell that she was pretty. Given different clothes she would have had a touch of class about her. She crossed the street two car lengths in front of Fabel's car and turned into the alley. Fabel used his radio to let Anna and Paul know she was on her way.

'We'll follow her up. I've got clearance from the Staatsanwaltschaft prosecutor's office to enter and arrest. When she opens the door, we go.' He slipped his Walther from its holster and slid back the carriage to put a round in the firing chamber. He checked the red, raised safety button before reholstering. He turned to Werner. 'Best to be careful with this one. I'm sure Klugmann won't give us any trouble, but if he does, he'll know how to give it.'

Werner checked his own sidearm. 'He won't get the fucking chance.'

They got out of the car and followed Sonja on foot. As they passed the parked BMW, Anna and Paul got out and fell in behind them. Sonja, still lugging her grocery bags, swung round and pushed her back against the heavy street door. As she did so, she glanced in the direction of the advancing party without seeming to notice them. They followed her into the cobbled Hof, and Fabel could hear her sandals clicking rapidly as she trotted up the stone steps towards her apartment. As quietly as they could, they followed on. Sonja was at the door, her grocery bags at her feet, fumbling with her keys. It was then she saw them.

'Hans!' Her scream rang around the courtyard.

Fabel was shocked to see the terror on Sonja's face. He realised that she thought they were someone else. He held up his hand in a gesture that would have been more placatory were it not for the clumpy black Walther sub-compact automatic he held in his other hand.

'Sonja . . . keep calm. We're police and we only want to talk to Hans . . .'

Her terror was now mingled with uncertainty. Fabel and the others ran up the stairs and petite Anna Wolff pushed Sonja backwards so severely that she nearly lost her footing. Anna pinned Sonja against the wall, out of the potential line of fire. Fabel and Paul flattened themselves against the wall on either side of the door. Fabel called out:

'Polizei Hamburg!' and nodded to Werner who kicked the door just below the lock.

Fabel, Werner and Paul swept through the apartment, taking turns of two providing cover while the third scanned a room, swinging outstretched arms from side to side as if their guns were flashlights. A kitchen, a living room, a bathroom and two bedrooms all fed off a short hall. The apartment was clean, bright and tidy but cheaply furnished. It was also empty. Fabel slipped his automatic back into the holster under his arm and nodded to Anna Wolff, who smiled at Sonja and led her gently into the apartment. Fabel told Paul to pick up her grocery bags and put them in the kitchen. Solicitously, Anna led Sonja into the living room and sat her down on the couch. Sonja was shaking and looked close to tears. Fabel crouched down before her.

'Sonja, where's Hans?'

Sonja shrugged and tears welled up in her nut-brown eyes. 'I don't know. He was here when I left this morning. He didn't say he was going anywhere. He hasn't been out since that girl got killed. He's very upset about it.' The eyes went hard behind the tears. 'Is that why you're here?'

'We're not accusing him of anything. We just need to ask him some questions.'

The nut-brown eyes still glittered with a mixture of fear and anger.

'Sonja, could you excuse us for a moment.' Fabel turned to his officers. 'Anna, Paul . . . a word. Outside.'

Once they were out on the landing, Anna Wolff's and Paul Lindemann's expressions showed they knew what this was about. Anna Wolff decided to pre-empt Fabel and held up her hands.

'I'm sorry, *Chef* . . . there's no way he could have got past us. We were on him tight.'

'Not tight enough apparently.' Fabel was struggling to keep a lid on his frustration. 'Klugmann is the only lead we've got, and you've let him get away.' He jabbed a finger at them. 'You lost him. You find him.'

'Yes *Chef*,' they said in unison.

'And start by seeing if any of the neighbours are in.'

Fabel went back into the living room. He sat down next to Sonja on the couch, leaning his elbows on his knees.

'Are you feeling better now?'

'Fuck you.'

'Who did you think we were?'

Sonja turned to Fabel and blinked. 'What? What do you mean?' In that instant he knew she was hiding something.

'I know it's very alarming to have armed police barge into your home, but you thought we were someone else, didn't you?'

Sonja gazed down at her knees.

'Look, Sonja, is Hans in trouble? If he's in danger, we can help him. Help us find him. As far as we know he hasn't done anything wrong other than keep information from us. But we need to talk to him.'

She broke down. Great racking sobs. Fabel put his arm around her shoulders.

'I don't know where he is . . .' She pointed to a cell phone on the coffee table. 'That's his phone . . . he never goes anywhere without that.'

She turned to Fabel, her eyes large and round. Fabel remembered what Mahmoot had said about her: nice kid. He picked up the phone and pressed the last-number redial. It was the same number Klugmann had called after he had discovered Monique's body. He turned the display to Werner who read it and gave Fabel a meaningful look. Fabel slipped the cell phone into his jacket pocket and turned back to Sonja.

'Sonja, who did you think we were?'

'Hans has been doing some business. Foreigners. Russians or Ukrainians, I think. He tried to keep me out of it, but I know these people are dangerous. I think things maybe didn't go so good with them. For the last couple of days he told me not to answer the door, he would go if anyone came.' She let out a sob. 'I thought that's maybe who you were . . .'

'You're safe now, Sonja. There's going to be a police officer watching the flat from now on . . . until Hans comes back or until we find him.'

Ukrainians. Fabel recalled what Mahmoot had said about

the new outfit in town. They must be in the frame for the hit on Ulugbay. And Klugmann worked for Ulugbay. But Klugmann was small-fry in what was shaping up to be a big gang war. He smiled reassuringly at Sonja.

'Where do you think he could be? Maybe he just nipped out somewhere?'

Sonja shrugged again but her expression was one of deep anxiety. 'He would have told me if he was going out this morning. He knew I was getting lunch . . .' She looked over at the shopping bags across the room in the kitchen area. Her bottom lip quivered.

'Don't worry, love,' said Fabel, 'we'll find him.' He hoped to God he was right.

It was all going to hell and he knew his nerves were getting too edgy. He had to focus and stay sharp. Sharp was good; jumpy got you killed. There was a slide bolt on the front door of the flat – he had fucked up the main lock in his haste to get in – and he slipped the bolt over, hoping that they wouldn't look too closely at the lock when they came to the door, which they inevitably would.

Klugmann had just made it and no more. He had been worried about Sonja: she had been late back from her shopping and he had been watching for her, angling his body by the window so that the two KriPo detectives – a man and a woman – in the tan BMW wouldn't see him. Seeing Sonja's jaunty walk, he had smiled to himself: she was a good kid and he had tried to keep her out of it all. Then he had spotted the two cops who'd interviewed him, Fabel and Meyer, following her. As she passed the BMW, the other two cops had got out too and fallen in behind. It was a bust. He didn't know what they had got on him, but now was not the time to be hauled in for protracted questioning. He was too close. It had cost too much – in time, in effort, in a life – for him to be taken out of circulation right at the last minute. He had dashed across the room, grabbing his jacket and stuffing his gun into the pocket. He had closed the door behind him swiftly but not hard enough to slam and taken the stairs two at a time. The landlord had used the same doors on each of the apartments. Security depended on the outer door that opened out onto the street and not the doors to the apartments, which technically should really only have been used as interior doors. He had opened his clasp knife and pushed against the lock, leaning in hard with his shoulder. It was a precise craft: enough force to open the door without splintering the flimsy wood. He had heard the piano-string creak of the spring on the main street door downstairs: Sonja was coming in and they would be just a few paces behind her. The door had yielded and he had half fallen into the apartment, closing the door gently behind him. Then he had heard Sonja's scream, Fabel's shouts and the sound of movements and voices from the apartment above. He had closed his eyes, leaned the back of his head against the door and mouthed the word 'Fuck'. His cell phone. He had left his cell phone behind. And that meant he had left his life-line behind. He'd have to get to a phone and quick.

But now all he could do was wait.

The owner of this apartment was a Yugoslav aged about sixty. Klugmann had assumed he was probably an illegal, but had since found out that he worked for the city as a gardener over at the Sternschanzen-Park, manicuring the flower beds and picking up the used syringes. He was on a permanent day shift that started at eleven. It would be after eight p.m. before the Yugoslav got back. Klugmann had until then to make a break for it.

There would be a cop on the street all the time now. That would make getting out difficult. The main advantage he had was that they thought he was already out of the building and would be watching for him coming back, not leaving. He sat with his back pressed against the door and scanned the room.

Maybe there was something in here he could wear. Make himself look older. The plod outside wouldn't make the connection. He'd be too busy looking for a young man going in, not an old guy going out. He heard voices in the hall: Fabel was chewing out the surveillance team for having lost him. Klugmann allowed himself a smile. He heard footsteps and pressed himself hard against the door. Knocking: the flat-fisted knock of a policeman. Klugmann breathed slow and even. Another knock.

'Police. Anyone at home?'

It seemed like an age before he heard their feet scuff on the landing and then make their way echoingly down the stone steps. They knocked on the door downstairs. Klugmann knew that apartment would be empty just now as well. He heard a woman say 'Shit', and then the sound of the main door's spring. Two outside and Fabel and Meyer upstairs. He scanned the apartment again for anything to help him disguise his departure later. And waited.

Thursday 5 June, 2.45 p.m. Vierlande, outside Hamburg.
The traffic had been heavy in the city and Fabel was glad he'd allowed himself extra time to negotiate the B5 through the centre and down towards Billbrook. Now the city no longer clung to the roadside and the landscape rolled out like the flat, smooth baize of a billiard table. Fabel had left Klugmann's cell phone with Maria Klee to have Technical Section get as much information as possible out of it. Anna Wolff and Paul Lindemann were probably still knocking on doors trying to heat up Klugmann's cold trail. They were good officers, both of them. Klugmann must have pulled a fast one to get past them.

Just after Bergedorf, Fabel turned south towards Neuengamme. It could have been Holland: a landscape so flat it was as if nature had steam-ironed it, smoothing out every wrinkle. Any potential monotony in the scenery was dispelled by the dense clumps of trees, the red-roofed churches, Dutch-style windmills and meticulously restored and maintained Fachwerk houses with their exposed beams and groomed thatched roofs. The low, green expanse of land was threaded through by the network of dykes and canals that stitched it into a patchwork.

As he approached Neuengamme, he felt the weak flutter of a dull and imprecise anxiety. For Fabel, this was a land laden with the past. This is where so much good and bad came together for him. It was an intimate thing. For Fabel, all kinds of history merged in this unlikely bump in the Elbe: personal, professional, national.

As all German children of his generation had had to, Fabel had taken on the burden of his nation's history when he was about ten: a loss of innocence and a coming to terms. He had asked his father about the things he had heard. About Germany. About themselves. About the Jews. Fabel recalled the sorrow in his father's eyes as he had struggled to frame for a ten-year-old boy the monumental monstrosity of what had been done in the name of Germany. It had been shortly after that that his father had made the long journey here. To this place with its pretty half-timbered houses and gentle landscape. To Neuengamme.

More than 55,000 prisoners had been worked to death here, in a camp improvised from a disused brick factory. The British had liberated it, as they had Bergen-Belsen, and with typical Anglo-Saxon efficiency and practicality had handed it back to the German people in 1948, suggesting it would make a good prison. And that's what it had become. Until 1989, a Holocaust memorial and Vierlande Prison had shared the same site. Eventually, the Hamburg Senat saw the bizarre and bitter irony of continuing to confine human beings on the site of such atrocities in the name of the state, and the Vierlande facility was moved outside the former camp.

And now Fabel had come to Vierlande to face, for the first time in over a decade, a part of his personal history that he thought he had long since buried.

The prison officer led Fabel to Dorn's study. It was a bright, airy room with large colourful posters of German historical landmarks on the wall: Lübeck city gates, Trier's Porta Nigra, Cologne cathedral. The room was lined with bookshelves and Fabel felt it had more the look of a school library than that of Dorn's old study at the Universität Hamburg. When Fabel entered, Dorn and a younger man were bent over a reference book. The younger man towered above Dorn and his T-shirt exposed heavily muscled and tattooed arms. His brutish appearance sat incongruously with the intense concentration he was applying to the text. Dorn looked up and saw Fabel, made an excuse to the scholarly thug, who left with the volume and his notebook under his arm.

'Jan . . .' Dorn extended his hand. 'I'm glad you could come. Please, sit down.'

Time had flecked more white through the trimmed moustache and goatee, and had drawn more deeply around the eyes, but apart from that Mathias Dorn was pretty much as Fabel remembered him back when he had been Fabel's European History tutor: a small, neat, compact man with porcelain-blue eyes and features that were a little too fine. Fabel took the frail hand.

'It's good to see you again, Herr Professor,' Fabel lied. For Fabel, Dorn, and the feelings he awoke, belonged in the past. Fabel wished he had stayed there. He sat across the desk from Dorn. There was a photograph on the desk: a young woman of about twenty, with a similar porcelain delicacy to her features. Fabel was involuntarily drawn to the picture, amazed at how unfamiliar the face now seemed.

'I was surprised to find you were here,' said Fabel.

'Just two days a week.' Dorn smiled. 'Enough for me to

qualify as "historian in residence". It's a strange concept, having a historian in a prison. But there again this prison has a special history of its own. I divide my time between here and the Neuengamme memorial.'

'I meant that I'm surprised that you wanted to work with offenders after . . .' Fabel found he had started a sentence he didn't want, or need, to finish. Dorn read his meaning and smiled.

'It's actually very rewarding. Some of the inmates have developed a real hunger for history. In a strange way it helps them make sense of their own histories. But I take your meaning. I suppose I did have my own agenda when I applied for the post. I needed to understand, to be around men who kill, I suppose. To . . . well, to make some kind of sense of what happened.'

'And has it?'

'Has becoming a policeman helped you?'

'I don't know if that was the reason I became a policeman.' Again, Fabel lied. They both knew it was the personal history they shared that had led a gifted historian like Fabel to become a murder detective.

Dorn let it go. 'I wanted to talk to you about this murder you're investigating,' he said.

'Murders,' corrected Fabel. 'There's been another one. The same form of killing as the Kastner girl.'

'My God, that's awful. It confirms what I thought. That's why I wanted to see you.'

'Go on. Please, Professor.'

Dorn picked up a recent copy of *Hamburger Morgenpost*. It was open at an article on the Kastner murder.

'Like you,' continued Dorn, 'I have been, well, forced into taking an interest in the psychotic mind. I hate to say it, but, despite its innate destructiveness, there can sometimes be a form of twisted creativity in it.' He stabbed a finger at the article. 'I think you have someone very creative as well as

very dangerous at work here, Jan. This fellow's psychosis is
certainly very well . . . *informed*, I suppose would be the best
way of putting it.'

'What do you mean?'

Dorn laid the paper back on his desk. He held up his hand
in a gesture that suggested Fabel should slow down and wait
for him to unfold his thesis. It was a gesture with which Fabel
had been so accustomed as an eager student.

'Who are we?' Dorn asked. 'What are we? The Germans,
I mean.'

Fabel frowned. 'I don't understand . . .'

'The concept of German identity . . . what is it?'

Fabel shrugged. 'I don't know,' he said. 'And I don't care.
It's a question that has caused Germany – caused the world
– more grief and destruction than any other.'

'Quite so,' said Dorn. 'The concept of German identity is
a myth. A myth that our little Austrian house-painter amplified into a false history until Germany believed it. One of
the most important lessons I have learned as a historian is
that only the present exists. Only the present has an
immutable, uncompromising form; the past is what we
choose to make of it. History is shaped by our present, not
the other way around. We have spent the last two centuries
reinventing our past: reshaping our identity when all along
we don't have one. The fact is there is no German race. We
are a rag-tag of Scandian and Slav, Celt, Italic and Alpine
. . . a mishmash united by a language and a culture, not by
ethnicity.'

'What's your point? What has this to do with these killings?'

Dorn smiled. 'Do you believe that the god Tuisto was born
from Germany's soil? And through his three sons fathered
the three pure tribes of Germans?'

'Of course not. That's pure myth.'

'Do you believe in the god Wotan? Or the Norse pantheon
of gods, headed by Wotan's equivalent, Odin?'

'No,' answered Fabel. 'Again that's just mythology. Look, I don't see that this has anything to do with . . .'

Again Dorn held up his hand to stop Fabel. 'They *are* myths. Falsehoods. But, as you have already pointed out, believing in myths can be powerful and destructive.' Dorn swiftly picked up the paper and threw it across to Fabel. 'And *he* believes them.'

'What?' Fabel's confusion was genuine. 'Who?'

'Your killer. Every time he kills in this manner he is making a reference . . .' Dorn looked towards the ceiling, but his mind was clearly somewhere else. 'He has spanned a thousand years . . . he has reached into the darkness of the past to pull out a fragment that makes sense of his present. It would be remarkable if it weren't so obscene.' Dorn snapped out of his reverie and looked again at Fabel.

'Are you saying that there is some kind of mythological or historical link to these killings?' Fabel asked.

'The Blood Eagle.' Dorn held Fabel's gaze.

'The what?'

'The Blood Eagle. Your killer is not sexually motivated. He is religiously motivated. He is making sacrifices.'

'Sacrifices? Blood Eagle? I'm sorry, Herr Professor, but what the hell are you talking about?'

'As you know this part of northern Germany was the homeland of the Scandians. It was the Saxons who first founded the village of Hamm. The Franks and the Slavic Obertriten conquered it and made it Hammaburg. And then came the Vikings of Denmark. Look at Altona – right at the heart of modern Hamburg – that was a Danish city until the eighteenth century. Ours is the blood of Vikings . . . among others, of course. The gods worshipped here were Freya, Balder, Thor, Loki . . . Odin. These Norse gods were far from perfect. They were moody, petulant, envious, greedy . . . angry. Wise Odin, father of the gods, the Nordic Zeus, was no exception. It was his favour above all that our ancestors craved.'

Dorn paused. He reached over to the desk and picked up two volumes. 'Odin demanded sacrifice. Like all the gods. But the greater the god, the greater the sacrifice. For example, Adam of Bremen wrote in his chronicle about, well, I suppose you could call it a "festival" at Ubsola – or Uppsala, as it's known today. This festival was held every nine years and lasted nine days. Everyone – king, chieftain or commoner – had to send offerings. In fact, one Christianised Viking king – King Inge the Elder – was deposed for not taking part. On each of the nine days of the festival, nine of all living male things – cattle, fowl and humans – had their throats cut and were hung upside down in the grove beside the temple. Amazing. All because the number nine had some significance in the worship of Odin. Well, my point is that Odin demanded human sacrifice. And one form that that sacrifice often took was that of the Blood Eagle.'

'Which was?' Fabel could feel the adrenalin course through his system.

'It was an offering that made its own way to Odin's lair. A human being given the wings of an eagle.'

'And how did that work exactly?' Fabel asked, although he already knew the answer.

Dorn looked Fabel directly and unblinkingly in the eye. 'You would take a prisoner. Perhaps a woman brought back from one of your Viking raids. You would strip her and tie her down, spread-eagled. Then the Priest of Odin would take a broadsword and slash open her abdomen . . .'

Fabel felt his heart begin to pound as Dorn spoke.

'These priests had the skill of a surgeon. Their blows would slice the victim open, supposedly without damaging essential organs and killing her. Then they would tear the lungs out of the sacrifice and throw them over the shoulders. The wings of the Blood Eagle, do you see? Wings with which they could fly to Odin.'

Fabel sat and stared at Dorn. He felt as if he were standing at the heart of a silent explosion: in a street where a thousand alarm bells had started to ring. 'This is a documented historical fact?'

'Documented, yes. Historical, yes. But how much of documented history is fact depends on the perspective of the chronicler. The Vikings were feared above all other raiders. Portrayed as demons in the chronicles of the time.' Dorn flicked through the pages of one of the volumes. 'Yes, here we are. Victims could be of either sex. For example, here's an account of an English prince taken prisoner and held for ransom by the Vikings. The ransom wasn't paid so he was sacrificed to Odin as a Blood Eagle. There are a number of other documented incidents.' He stopped at another page. 'This is an account of a bishop on one of the Scottish isles.'

'And our killer is emulating these?' Fabel's voice was still full of disbelief.

'Oh yes. I read some of the details in the paper. I could see that you tried to keep as many secret as possible, but from what was said about the dismemberment, I guessed the rest.'

'I can't believe it. It's obscene.'

'To us, yes,' said Dorn. 'But to the killer it's noble. A crusade. He believes he is serving the ancient gods. He has the highest moral authority on his side. He is a proselytiser, a missionary returning Germany to its true faith.' Dorn put the book down. 'You are dealing with the darkest forces imaginable, Jan. This killer is a true believer. And what he believes in is truly apocalyptic, in a way the Christian mind cannot comprehend. The Vikings had their Judgement Day too. Ragnarok. But biblical apocalypses pale into nothing compared to Ragnarok. A time when Odin and the Aesir join battle against Loki and the Vanir. A time of fire and blood and ice when earth and heaven and all living things are consumed. This "Blood Eagle" believes in all of that. His mission is to see the heavens fall and the oceans to fill with blood.'

Fabel sat, holding the newspaper limply in his hands and gazed, unseeing, at the headline. His mind raced.

'How can you be so sure about him? We've got a criminal psychologist who profiles . . .'

'I'm no psychologist, you're right,' Dorn's voice revealed something close to anger. 'But I have spent much of the last twenty years trying to understand minds like this maniac's. Trying to make sense of what drives a human being to become a hunter, torturer and killer of other human beings . . .' Dorn broke off. There was genuine pain in his eyes.

Fabel sat motionless, still stunned. When he did eventually speak, it was as much to himself as to Dorn. 'I just can't believe it. He is out there living out some obscene fantasy, believing he has a mission to fulfil. If what you say is true, that is.'

'What I am telling you is part of the historical record. Whether it really happened as recorded or not, or whether it was exaggerated to demonise the Vikings by those who documented it, doesn't matter. It's there. And your killer believes it.'

'And if it is a mission,' continued Fabel, 'then he is going to go on and on killing. Until we stop him.'

For some reason Fabel did not want to make the call from the visitors' car park outside Vierlande Prison. Instead he drove out to the Neuengammer Hausdeich dyke. He stopped the car and climbed the steep bank of the dyke. From here he could see the Neuengamme Concentration Camp with its symmetrically laid-out buildings and blocks. Most of the prisoners here had been women. The prisoners of Neuengamme and its satellite camps had been used as slave labour to build temporary housing for the people of Hamburg who had been bombed out of their homes. When he had been brought here by his father, the ten-year-old Fabel had learned a new phrase, *Vernichtung durch Arbeit*: extermination through labour. The prisoners had been worked to death.

He sat down on the grass and watched as an empty sun played with cloud shadows across the flat landscape, across the camp. He could just make out the memorial block before which, he knew, was the sculpture of *The Dying Prisoner*: an emaciated figure lying buckled and tangle-limbed on the cobbles.

Fabel looked down at a place where women had been murdered in the name of some sick idea of German identity and thought about what Dorn had told him: about how there was an individual with a perverted sense of history and ethnology and faith who was using it as a justification for satisfying his basest instincts and his psychotic hunger for blood.

Fabel needed time to gather his thoughts before phoning the office. He tried to get Mahmoot, but again reached his voice mail. Fabel cursed silently and flipped shut his cell phone. He didn't like this. He didn't like it at all. He just hoped Mahmoot had had the sense to drop out of it when he heard about the hit on Ulugbay. He sat for a few more minutes, his arms wrapped around his knees and watched sun and shadow dance across the land; then he phoned Werner and outlined Dorn's theory.

'I'll be back in an hour. We'll have a meeting in the conference room. Better get Paul and Anna back in for it. Have they found anything on Klugmann?'

'Nope.'

'I didn't expect they would. Could you contact Van Heiden and see if he's free for the conference. He's going to love this.'

Part Two
Friday 13 June to
Tuesday 17 June

Friday 13 June, 1.50 a.m. St Pauli, Hamburg.

The bass thumped relentlessly. The lights strobed across 400 sweat-sheathed bodies that writhed like a single creature with every pulse of the music's beat. She clung to him as if they were both adrift in this ocean of humanity. His tongue probed her mouth and his hands explored her body. She took her mouth from his and placed it to his ear, shouting something into it that was all but drowned by the deafening music. He smiled and nodded vigorously, indicating the way out with a couple of jerks of his head. He backed away from her, still holding her hands and still smiling, guiding her through the crowd towards the club's exit. God, he was good-looking. And sexy. His T-shirt was soaked with sweat and showed the hard lines of his muscles. He was tall and slim; his hair was dark and sleek and his eyes the most incredible colour of green. She wanted him badly.

Hitting the air outside the club was like diving into a plunge pool. The doormen did not even glance in their direction as they spilled out, still entangled. The street was quiet except for the muffled thumping from the club, and for a moment she paused, the cool air and the decrescent effect of the E she had taken making her suddenly more wary. After all, she didn't even know his name. He sensed the resistance in her body and moved towards her. He beamed a handsome grin at her, revealing perfect teeth that glittered like porcelain in the street lights.

'Hey baby, what's up?' For the first time she heard his voice clearly. There was a hint of some kind of accent.

'I'm thirsty. I took some E earlier. I don't want to get dehydrated.'

'Then let's go to my place to chill. I've got some mineral water in my car. It's just around the corner. Come on.' He took her firmly by the arm.

His car was a sleek, new silver Porsche and they fell against it, becoming entwined again. She pulled away. 'I'm really thirsty . . . maybe we should go back . . .'

He beeped off the alarm and leaned into the car, pulling out two half-litre Evian bottles. He twisted the cap off of one and handed it to her, drinking from the second himself. She took the water and gulped greedily.

'It tastes salty,' she said.

He ran his tongue up her neck, from the shoulder strap of her top to the lobe of her ear. 'So do you.'

She felt suddenly dizzy and slumped against the car. He moved swiftly and caught her, his hands under her arms. 'Easy . . .' he said solicitously. 'You'd better sit down.' He guided her towards the open door of the car. She looked up and down the empty street and then into his eyes. They had changed: they were still the same amazing green, but now they glittered cold and empty.

But she was not afraid.

Friday 13 June, 11.50 a.m. Alsterarkaden, Hamburg.
Fabel had left the Präsidium immediately after the case conference. They had reviewed the progress made over the last week: none. Klugmann was still on the loose, and as an ex-policeman, he would know how to stay on the loose; the leads from the last murder had run cold and they still did not have an identity for the dead girl; even Fabel's green-eyed Slav seemed to have walked from the murder scene and

evaporated into the night. Other than the fact that Dorn had given a name and provenance to the ritualism of this killer's barbarity, they were no closer to nailing him. Fabel was also deeply concerned about Mahmoot, with whom he had still not made contact. Mahmoot was notoriously difficult to reach, but he would have known that not returning Fabel's calls would set alarm bells ringing.

Fabel was not the only wrong-footed cop in Hamburg. Almost every law-enforcement officer in the city had been unnerved by the failure of a gang war to erupt. There had been no retaliations for Ulugbay's murder. In fact, there seemed to have been no intergang violence at all, which in itself was very strange. The Präsidium still buzzed with BND and LKA7 personnel, but the adrenalin-charged intensity had dissolved into an uneasy, frustrated readiness.

This case had begun to suck the light from Fabel's life. It wasn't the first to do so and Fabel knew it wouldn't be the last. It was like hacking his way into dense jungle, slicing a swathe through the clinging undergrowth, only to find that it had closed in behind him, shutting off the way back to the open, to his own life and world, populated by the people he loved. The only way was to press on, cutting a path forward and out into the light.

Fabel had phoned Gabi, his daughter. She had planned to stay the weekend with Fabel, but he explained that he'd have to work at least part of the weekend. He hated having to give up his precious time with Gabi, but, as usual, she had understood. Renate, Fabel's ex-wife, had responded less positively, her tone on the phone laced with an acid resignation.

Instead of taking his car, Fabel had hailed a taxi to take him up to the covered Arcade on the Alster. The sun was shining and the lack of a breeze – unusual in Hamburg – meant that it felt pleasantly warm outside. As always, the Arcade was packed with shoppers and Fabel weaved his way through the crowds with an unhurried purposefulness. His goal was the Jensen Buchhandlung, a bookshop run by a university friend of Fabel's, Otto Jensen.

Fabel loved this bookshop. Otto had invested in the most stylish minimalist interior design – clean, straight beechwood shelves and tables and bright lighting – most probably at the behest of his infinitely more organised and style-conscious wife, Else. Otto, on the other hand, was a moving focus of chaos: a gangling, one-metre-ninety tangle of arms and legs who continually seemed to be knocking things over or spilling a cascade of books and papers from overfull arms. Books were stacked on every surface, magazines heaped on the floor or piled on the counter. But the range of titles was stunning, and the disorder simply turned every visit into a voyage of discovery. In some strange way the disarray was the purest language of the bibliophile. It was a language Fabel spoke.

As Fabel entered, he saw Otto sitting behind the counter. He had a book on his lap, elbows on his knees and head in his hands. It was a pose that Fabel had associated with Otto since their university days: a posture that made Fabel think that Otto was drawing in his gangly limbs to form a cage, cocooning himself from the outside world and committing himself exclusively to the universe that existed between the covers of whatever book he was reading.

Fabel walked over to the counter and leaned both elbows on a pile of books. It took a couple of seconds for Otto to realise someone was there.

'Sorry . . . can I help y—' The question broke into a broad smile. 'Well, well, well . . . if it isn't the powers of law enforcement . . .'

Fabel grinned. 'Hello Otto, you old dope.'

'Hello Jan. How are you?'

'Not bad. You?'

'Crap. I have a store full of people who browse until they see something they like, and then go home and find it second-

hand on the Internet. And the rent on this place is astro-
nomical. The price of a trendy location, Else says.'

'How is Else?' asked Fabel. 'Still not realised she's far too
good for you?'

'Oh no, she tells me that all the time. Apparently, I should
be eternally thankful that she took pity on me.' Otto smiled
his gormless smile.

'She has a point. Have you got my order in?'

'Oh yes.' Otto ducked behind the counter and fumbled for
a moment. There was the sound of books tumbling onto the
floor. 'Just a minute . . .' Otto called. Fabel smiled. Good
old Otto: never changes.

Otto reappeared dramatically and thumped a block of
books onto the counter. 'Here we are!' He tore a yellow order
slip from under an elastic band wrapped around the volumes.
'All English authors . . . all in their original English versions.'
Otto looked across to Fabel. 'A little light reading, huh? How
could I forget you were such an Anglophile . . . your mother's
English of course, isn't she?'

'Scottish . . .' Fabel corrected him.

'That explains it!' Otto slapped his forehead in a dramatic
gesture.

'What?'

'Why you never pay for lunch!'

Fabel laughed. 'That's not because I'm half Scottish . . .
it's because I'm a Frisian. Anyway, it's your turn to pay. I
paid last time.'

'Such a fine mind,' mused Otto, 'such a lousy memory . . .
Oh, by the way, I've got a present for you.' More fumbling
beneath the counter. He added a reference book to the pile.
'Someone from the university ordered it and never collected
it. It's a dictionary of British surnames. I thought what kind
of dull no-life would take this off my hands . . . and I thought
of you.'

'Thanks, Otto . . . I think! What do I owe you?'

'Like I said, it's a gift. Enjoy!'

Fabel thanked Otto again. 'Otto, do you have anything on old Norse religion?'

'Sure. Believe it or not there is quite a demand.'

'Really?' Fabel said disbelievingly.

'Yep. Odinists mainly.'

'Odinists? You mean people still practise this religion?' A faint electric current ran across Fabel's skin.

'Asatru . . . I think they call it. Or just Odinism. Harmless lot, I suppose. Just a bit sad, really.'

'I had no idea,' said Fabel. 'You say you get many in here?'

'The odd one or two. And I do mean odd. Although there's one guy who has been in once or twice who doesn't have the oddball or hippy look.'

Someone increased the current across Fabel's skin. 'When was the last time he was in?'

Otto laughed. 'Am I being interrogated by the police?'

'Please Otto, it could be important.'

Otto recognised the seriousness on his friend's face. 'About a month ago, I think. He may have been in since, but I haven't served him.'

'What did he buy?'

Otto's acre of forehead creased in concentration. Fabel knew that, for all Otto's outward disorder, his mind was a supercomputer of book titles, authors and publishers. The frown evaporated, the data-processing was complete.

'I'll show you. We have another copy in stock.'

Fabel followed Otto across to the New Age and Occult section of the store. Otto slipped a thick volume from the shelf and handed it to Fabel. It was titled *Runecast: Rites and Rituals of the Viking*. It was clearly no academic tome, but intended for a more general audience. Fabel opened the book at the back and scanned down the index. There was an entry for Blood Eagle. A glance through the text showed a page and a half was devoted to the ritual.

'Otto, I need a name for this customer. Or at least a description.'

'That's easy. I don't think I have an address or anything: he's never actually ordered a title. I can look back and see if I can get a credit-card slip or something. But, like I say, remembering the name is easy. He spoke perfect German with only the slightest hint of an accent, but he had a British or American name: John MacSwain.'

Friday 13 June, 3.45 p.m. Rotherbaum, Hamburg.

He had, at least, had the courtesy to inform Kolski at LKA7 Abteilung Organisierte Kriminalität of his intention. Fabel could tell that Kolski was not happy about it, but information had not exactly been flowing from the Organised Crime Division and as a result he felt entitled to pursue his inquiry across boundaries.

Fabel was aware that he was looking at three million euros' worth of property. Mehmet Yilmaz's three-storey Rotherbaum house was, ironically, only ten minutes' walk from Fabel's flat. Its Jugendstil Art Nouveau façade presented a convinced elegance to the tree-lined street. It was one of a row of five houses, each equally vast in scale, each equally solid in presence, each totally different in style: Bauhaus sat next to Art Deco next to Neo-Gothic.

Fabel had expected the door to be answered by a broom-moustached Turkish heavy. It wasn't: an attractive young housekeeper with short but lustrous golden blonde hair politely asked who was calling and for whom, and guided Fabel through a hallway of polished stone to a large round reception room. This was the centre of the house; the room was the full height of the house and capped with a cupola whose central, circular, stained-glass skylight dappled the floor with splashes of colour. From some far corner of the house Fabel could hear halting piano-playing and the sound of children laughing.

There were a couple of piles of leather-bound books on the vast circular walnut table that sat in the centre of the reception room. Fabel had just picked one up, a second edition of Goethe's *The Sorrows of Young Werther*, when a tall, slim and clean shaven man of about fifty entered. His hair was mid-brown and greying at the temples.

'We spoke on the phone, Herr Kriminalhauptkommissar. You wanted to speak to me?' asked Mehmet Yilmaz, without a hint of a Turkish accent.

Fabel became aware that he was still holding the Goethe in his hand. 'Oh, I'm sorry . . .' He put the book down. 'Wonderful condition. Do you collect?'

'As a matter of fact I do,' answered Yilmaz. 'German romantics, Sturm und Drang, that kind of thing. Whenever I can – whenever I can afford – I like to pick up first editions.'

Fabel suppressed a smile: in these surroundings it was difficult to imagine Yilmaz struggling to pay for anything. The Turk walked over to the table and picked up another, smaller volume in a rich burgundy binding.

'Theodor Storm, *Der Schimmelreiter* – a first edition and my latest acquisition.' He handed the book to Fabel. The burgundy leather was soft and yielding. Almost warm. It was as if its age were palpable: as if Fabel's fingertips were brushing against all the other fingertips that had handled the book over the past century.

'Beautiful,' said Fabel sincerely. He handed the volume back. 'I'm sorry to disturb you at home, Herr Yilmaz, and thank you for seeing me at such short notice. I just felt that it was a little less formal . . . I would like to ask you some questions about a case I'm working on.'

'Yes, you said on the phone. Are you sure this shouldn't be done more formally. Specifically, with my lawyer present?'

'That, of course, is up to you, Herr Yilmaz. But I want to make it clear that I am speaking to you not as a suspect but simply as someone who can perhaps provide some helpful information. By the way, Herr Yilmaz, before we go any further, my condolences on the death of your cousin.'

Yilmaz moved over towards a coffee table and two leather armchairs by the wall. 'Please, Herr Fabel, sit down.' The blonde housekeeper came in with a cafetière. She poured two cups and left.

'Thank you, Herr Fabel. It's not often that a Hamburg policeman addresses me so . . . politely. It is sad, but Ersin was always so . . . *impetuous*, shall we say. Anyway, ask your questions and I'll do what I can to help. What is this case? You said on the phone you wanted to talk to me about Hans Klugmann? I've already spoken to your colleagues Herr Buchholz and Herr Kolski about him. I've told them, I have no idea where he is.'

Fabel understood Kolski's annoyance about this visit to Yilmaz: what were LKA7 doing looking for Klugmann?

'Yes. But that's not the case I'm investigating. I'm looking into the murder of a young prostitute who rented an apartment from Klugmann. We know her only as "Monique".'

Yilmaz sipped his coffee without taking his eyes off Fabel. There was no reaction to the name. Not a flicker in the eye. Nothing.

'Was Monique working for you?' Fabel asked. 'Even indirectly, through Klugmann?'

'No, Herr Fabel, she was not.'

'Listen, Herr Yilmaz, I have no interest in your business or other activities. All I am trying to do is to catch a serial killer before he strikes again. What you tell me here is off the record.'

'I appreciate that, Herr Fabel, and I reiterate: this girl was not working for me directly or indirectly. Whatever I may be involved in, I do not run cheap back-street prostitutes . . .'

'Could Klugmann have been running her as a private venture?'

'Possibly. I really wouldn't know. Klugmann is not one of

my people, even if your colleagues from LKA7 Organised
Crime insist that he is.'

'You have to admit that someone with his . . . employ-
ment history would be very useful to your organisation.'

'Herr Hauptkommissar, we have been frank with each other
thus far. In the same spirit of candour I'll tell you this much
– and as you say, off the record. Klugmann is someone on
the fringes. You're right, his particular background makes
him very useful, but he has never been fully trusted by anyone
on our side of the fence. There's always a lingering doubt
about ex-policemen.' Yilmaz took a sip from his coffee cup.
'My cousin Ersin used Klugmann as a freelance resource, but
that's as far as it went.'

'So how does he make a living?'

'My organisation is not the only game in town, Herr Fabel.
Besides, he worked regularly as an assistant manager at one
of our clubs, the Paradies-Tanzbar. All quite legitimate.'
Yilmaz gave a half smile and took another sip of coffee. 'Well,
almost.'

'We believe there was a video camera hidden in the girl's
apartment. It's missing along with any tapes. You've said
you're not into back-street hookers. Well, I wouldn't place
this girl in that category. She was high-end. What about blackmail? Is that a business you're into?'

Yilmaz's posture in the leather chair tautened.

'This is getting a little tiresome, Herr Fabel. I already told
you that I didn't know about the existence of this girl, far
less any schemes she and Klugmann may have been involved
in.' He paused, sat back and let the tension ease from his
pose. 'Look, let me explain something to you. I have lived
in this country for more than half of my life. When I arrived
here I found out very quickly that only certain doors were
open to Gastarbeiter Turks. The door that was open to me
was that of Ersin, my cousin. I worked for twenty years
within or attached to his organisation. For the last ten of

those years I have steadily legitimised those elements under my control. Now that Ersin is dead, the entire operation is in my control and I am legitimising that.'

'But let's be honest, you're still responsible for a huge slice of Hamburg's drug business . . .'

'I hope you're not looking for confessions.' Yilmaz smiled coldly. 'I know that Buchholz sees me as a Turkish Al Capone – and I admit freely that I have broken and continue to break the law – but I am a criminal more by accident than by design. Believe it or not I am a very moral man, but to me the law can be a very different thing from right and justice. Sometimes I think that what most irritates Hauptkommissar Buchholz is that I, a Turk and a crook in his eyes, may do at a stroke what he's been trying to achieve for years: wipe out the Ulugbay criminal organisation. I admit that Ersin would have been up for a bit of blackmail, particularly if it could lever influence as well as money out of the victim. But not me.'

Yilmaz stood up suddenly and walked across to the ornate marble fireplace. He lifted a silver-framed photograph and brought it over to Fabel. It was a picture of a smiling boy, about fourteen. Already the childlike softness was evaporating from the face to expose the same strong jawline as Yilmaz's.

'Your son?'

'Yes. Johann. A German name for a German future. He speaks only a little Turkish and even that with a thick German accent. His identity has to lie in this country, Herr Fabel. I'm making sure that when he takes over the family business it will be a clean business. A legal business. A German business.'

Fabel handed back the photograph. 'I believe you, Herr Yilmaz. But in the meantime you continue to sell drugs to kids and fight street wars with the Ukrainians.'

Yilmaz's face hardened. 'There is no war with the Ukrainians. All that is over.'

'I would have thought they would be the prime suspects in your cousin's killing?'

Something like a smile broke across Yilmaz's face, but his dark eyes remained fixed on Fabel. 'Herr Fabel, shall I tell you what I think of you?'

Fabel was taken aback slightly, but shrugged. 'Okay. Go ahead.'

'You are a policeman; I believe, an honest and straight-forward policeman. You are obviously an intelligent man, but your view of your function is simplistic. In fact, you wouldn't call it a function, you'd call it a duty. You see it as your job to protect the innocent and to catch those who would do them harm. People like me. Or psychopaths or other damaged people who transcend simple good or bad. And, for you, the law is everything. It is your shield, the shield with which you protect others.'

'And somehow this is misguided?'

'Simplistic, is how I described it. It is a moral colour-blind-ness. For you, the forces of law are the forces of good, while people like me are evil. Some of your colleagues, however, are more aware of the shades between. Sometimes they *are* the shades between.'

'Are you saying police officers had something to do with Ulugbay's death?'

'Herr Fabel, what I'm saying is that there is a lot going on out there that someone like you cannot begin to understand. And, with the greatest respect, I think you should stay out of it.' Yilmaz rose to his feet. 'I'm sorry I can't help you with your inquiry.'

Fabel placed his coffee cup on the antique side table. 'Herr Yilmaz, there is a monster out there. He is, literally, tearing the lungs from women's bodies. I need all the help I can get to stop him. If there is anything you can tell me . . .'

'Lying to the police is a skill that I have had to hone over the years. But in this instance, I assure you I am telling you the truth. I really have no knowledge of this girl or of Klugmann's arrangement with her.' Yilmaz paused, as if weighing something up. 'I'll tell you what, I'll have some of my own people look into it. They perhaps have access to sources that would not talk to the police. And, of course, we can be more . . . well, *direct* in our approach. I promise you that if we find out anything I will let you know.'

Yilmaz showed Fabel to the door himself. As he was leaving, Fabel turned to Yilmaz.

'What I don't understand is, if you are so keen to legitimise your business, why don't you just cease all illegal activities now, instead of phasing them out?'

Yilmaz laughed. 'Ask any business consultant: diversification has to be funded and supported by a strong core business base. Once the turnover of my diversified operations – particularly the building and property side – has equalled that of the core business, I will have the security I need to legitimise the business totally.'

He stepped out through the front door with Fabel, turned and looked up at his house.

'Do you like my home, Herr Fabel?'

'Yes. It's very impressive.'

'It was built in the 1920s. The architect who designed it was responsible for a number of properties in Rotherbaum. A German architect with a reputation above all others and one of the most successful architectural practices in Germany. A rich, respected and successful man in his own right.' Yilmaz turned to Fabel. 'He was also a Jew. He died in Dachau Concentration Camp. As I say, Herr Fabel, I distinguish between what is legal and what is moral, and there is a limit to how firmly I grasp the concept of Germanness. While I have hopes for my son, I know that I will always be an outsider. And that is why there remains an "alternative" element to my business activities. Goodbye, Herr Fabel. And good luck in your hunt.'

* * *

Fabel called the Mordkommission from his car. He had put Maria on tracing John MacSwain – a name as distinctive as that wouldn't be hard to find in Hamburg and Maria would be quicker than waiting for Otto to search through his accounts. Fabel got through to Werner who told him they had an address for John MacSwain in Harvestehude, but there was no other information on him yet.

'I've got another strange one for you, *Chef*,' said Werner. 'I've had a call from a Hauptkommissar Sülberg in Cuxhaven. He'd like you to call him urgently. He has a couple of cases of ritualised multiple rape. He thought they may be connected to our serial. Oh, and that journalist, Angelika Blüm, has been trying to get you again.'

'Okay, I'll be right back.' Fabel snapped shut his cell phone and slipped it into his pocket. As he started the car, he caught sight of a pretty girl in his side mirror. She was getting into a car further down the street. She had thick, short hair of iridescent blonde and exuded a lithe youthfulness. He couldn't quite place where he had seen her before.

The voice on the other end of the phone was warm and rich, with a hint behind the standard German of the same Plattdeutsch tones Fabel had grown up with. They had not got far into the conversation when Fabel realised that there was an acute intellect behind the cosy provincial tones.

'And you think there might be a link between these attacks and the murders I'm investigating. What do you base that on, Hauptkommissar Sülberg?' Fabel asked.

'I could be vague and say it's a hunch. But it's an educated hunch. I've got two young women in the Stadtkrankenhaus here, one being treated, the other in the morgue.'

'Murdered?'

'No . . . or at least not directly. But I'm treating it as culpable homicide. Both the dead girl and the one we have in hospital had a hypno-hallucinogenic unknowingly administered.'

'Date-rape drugs?'

'That's what the tests say. Both girls were bound by the wrists and ankles and abused in some kind of ritual. I read the details of your two murders in the Bundeskriminalamt's briefing and saw parallels. This second victim was staying with her cousin in Hamburg last night. She met a guy in a St Pauli nightclub and she thinks he doped her with a spiked mineral-water bottle. So that places the primary scene of commission in your jurisdiction.'

Fabel smiled. This hick cop knew his business. 'What makes you think there's a ritualistic element to all of this?'

'As you know, these drugs cause serious amnesia, but between the gaps the victim has vague recollections of being tied to some kind of altar. She says she thinks there was a statue of some kind as well.'

'Thanks for the call, Herr Sülberg. I think that it's certainly worth having a look at. I have a forensic psychiatrist working with me on this case, a Dr Eckhardt. Would you mind if I brought her along?'

Sülberg indicated that he had no objections and they arranged a time for the next day.

Friday 13 June, 7.30 p.m. Harvestehude, Hamburg.

For Fabel, there were critical moments during the interrogation of suspects or questioning of witnesses: split-seconds where people's reactions were raw and natural; when even the most rehearsed cover story did not have time to kick in. One such time being when the police turn up at the door unannounced. Official contact with the police is the exception in the lives of the average citizen, and when a police officer turns up at the door, the average citizen responds in a set number of ways. Alarm is the most common: the police visit seen as the delivery of bad news, usually the death of a relative. At the very least, a police officer on the doorstep is seen as the sign of something wrong, a crime or an accident, and the reaction tends to be a wide-eyed combination of disquiet and querulousness.

John MacSwain had got it all wrong. When Fabel and Werner had held out their oval shields, MacSwain had smiled his most casual smile, stood to one side and invited them in.

For the second time in a day Fabel found himself in a home that was way out of his price bracket. MacSwain's apartment was vast and very expensively decorated and furnished. The taste was flawless. MacSwain himself was a tall, dark-haired and casually but expensively dressed man in his late twenties. He had the muscular, masculine good looks of a film actor. Fabel noticed his most striking feature was his eyes, that were a light emerald and not unlike those of the Slav he had seen that night outside the murder scene. The architecture of the face, however, was totally different.

MacSwain led them into a huge open-plan living area that was floored in highly polished beech. A few steps took them down into a sunken seating area where MacSwain dropped back elegantly onto one of the two huge hide couches. He indicated the other couch with a wave of his hand.

'What can I do for you gentlemen?' MacSwain's German was perfect and almost totally unaccented.

Fabel smiled and spoke in English. 'I take it you are not German. You're English? Or maybe American?'

MacSwain looked surprised. 'Actually I'm Scottish . . . your English is exceptional, Herr . . .'

'Fabel. Kriminalhauptkommissar Fabel. Actually I am half Scottish myself. I was partly educated in England.'

'Amazing.' MacSwain's green eyes seemed to search for something in Fabel. 'What can I do for you, Herr Fabel?'

'We are investigating a case – a murder case – that involves a highly ritualised form of killing. The ritual, we believe, may be related to Norse mythology, to Odinism or . . . As . . .'

Fabel searched for the name Otto had mentioned.

MacSwain helped Fabel out. 'Asatru. It means belief in the Aesir. Or, if you want to be truly correct and authentic, *Forn Siar*, which means the "Ancient Way".'

'Thank you, yes, Asatru. It came to our attention that you are something of an expert in this area, so we wondered if you could help us with some background to these beliefs.'

MacSwain kept his green gaze on Fabel, silently, for a moment before answering. 'Herr Fabel, I am an information-technology consultant, not an Odinist high priest.'

'But you are interested in the subject?'

'I'm interested in a lot of subjects. The occult is one of them. I am not a member of any Asatru group, or anything. Anyway, wouldn't you be better getting your information from a more authoritative source. The medieval-history department of the university, for example.'

'We are looking into that. In the meantime we need all the help we can get.'

Werner gave a loud and artificial cough. Fabel got the message: the conversation had taken place entirely in English up until now.

'I'm sorry –' Fabel reverted to German, 'I think we should speak German for Oberkommissar Meyer's benefit.'

'Of course. You say this is a murder inquiry?'

'Yes. The victims have been murdered in a way that is almost identical to the Viking "Blood Eagle" ritual.' Fabel watched MacSwain's face. The only emotion that registered was interest.

'Has he been tearing their lungs out, or carving the outline of an eagle on their backs?'

'I didn't realise there were two forms.'

MacSwain stood up and walked over to a large floor-to-ceiling bookcase that was made out of the same beech as the floor, but unpolished. It acted as a sort of divider in the open-plan space. He removed two books: one was the book Fabel had seen in Otto's shop. MacSwain was either playing it very cool or he had nothing to hide.

MacSwain flicked through the other volume until he found what he was looking for. 'Actually, there's a possibility that neither form of ritual ever took place.'

'Oh?'

'Some historians believe that the whole Blood Eagle story was negative propaganda invented by the victims of Viking raids. Examples are cited in the historical record, but they tend to conflict . . . some say the victim was eviscerated while others state that an eagle was cut out of the flesh of their backs. And just because they are there in the record doesn't mean to say that the accounts are true.'

'What about Asatru? I can't imagine it has a big following.'

MacSwain smiled a perfect smile. 'Then you'd be wrong, Herr Fabel. Asatru is very popular these days. The Americans are big on it. Officially it's classed as a neo-Paganist religion. It's all very sanitised now, but Hitler incorporated a lot of its mythology and symbolism into Nazism. To be honest it's been chucked into the New Age stew along with Buddhism, Native American Shamanism, Wicca and the rest.'

'Do you know of any cults operating in Hamburg?'

MacSwain rubbed his chin. 'You suspect Asatru worshippers of these murders? They tend to be harmless New Age types who focus on Balder.' MacSwain read Fabel's questioning expression. 'A Christ-like figure in the Aesir pantheon. A politically correct Viking deity. To answer your question: yes, I do. They call themselves the Temple of Asatru. They meet in an old warehouse in Billstedt, from what I've heard.'

'Thanks for your help, Mr MacSwain,' Fabel said in English and rose from the couch.

Fabel gazed blankly at the doors of the elevator that took them back down to the lobby of MacSwain's building.

'There's something about that guy that doesn't smell right.

He may not have anything to do with these killings, but he didn't seem at all surprised to have the Hamburg KriPo knocking at his door.'

'Sometimes I think half the population of Hamburg has something to hide,' said Werner.

'I want MacSwain watched. And I want a full background worked up on him.'

'Can we justify the manpower to watch him round the clock? All you have is a hunch . . . Although I agree with it. He was too cool by half.'

'Just organise it, Werner. I'll clear it with Van Heiden.'

Friday 13 June, 11.00 p.m. Hamburg-Harburg, Hamburg.
The waterless swimming pool was illuminated by the bright disc of the moon which sat framed in the large roof window; the only window that, because of its inaccessibility, had not been smashed by vandals. The beam of the flashlight swept across the pool's cracked tiles and along the walls. The swimming pool had not been used for years. What had been intended as a cheery mural, depicting bright blue dolphins and children with water wings splashing together in water, was only just discernible on the walls beneath the built-up grime and graffiti. All the windows along the far poolside had been broken and the basin of the pool itself, long emptied of water, was scattered with litter and filth. There were discarded syringes everywhere. Someone had even defecated in the corner.

'This used to be a decent working-class neighbourhood.' It was the man who stood at the far side of the pool, looking out through the broken glazing who spoke. He shone a flashlight in the direction of a double doorway that now housed only one door. 'Check there's no one around . . .'

The younger man of the two made his way over to the doorway and shone his light into what had once been changing rooms.

'Nothing here.'

The older man resumed his reverie. 'I used to go out with a girl who lived just a block away. I even took her swimming here.' As he spoke, it was as if he were reconstructing the past, trying to see everything as it had been, not how it was now. He pulled himself back into the present. He looked across to the younger man who was now holding the gun to the head, covered in a rough sack, of a figure who knelt at the edge of the pool with his hands bound behind his back. The older man took a deep breath. When he spoke, he did so without anger, without malice, without excitement: 'Kill him.'

The kneeling figure's scream of 'No!' was extinguished in mid-flow by the thud of the silenced automatic. He toppled over and fell into the pool.

'A decent neighbourhood . . .' the older man said as he walked towards the door.

Saturday 14 June, 11.00 a.m. Cuxhaven.

It took nearly two hours to reach Cuxhaven, but the drive had been pleasant: it was a bright, gently warm day and the time in the car gave Fabel a chance to talk with Susanne, who had leapt at the chance of a change of scenery. It had also given him a chance to finalise their dinner date. They had become more relaxed in each other's company and there was now an unspoken intimacy between them.

Fabel made only one stop on the way, pulling over at the Aussendeich rest station about which Sülberg had given details over the phone. There was a dense wedge of trees screening the rest station from the road and from the wind that sliced across the flatlands all around. It was from these trees that the dead girl had staggered out into the path of the truck. Fabel swept his gaze across the parking area. His BMW was the only car there, and he could imagine it was an even lonelier spot at night. The other girl had been dumped on the same road, but about twenty kilometres back in the direction of Hamburg.

The seven-storey hospital building of the Stadtkrankenhaus Cuxhaven lay in a verdant square of grass and trees off the Altenwalder Chaussee. Fabel and Susanne were conducted to a bright waiting room with large windows that looked out onto immaculately arranged flower beds and a small square of lawn. They had been waiting about ten minutes when the door opened and a short, crumpled-looking SchuPo came in. His entire face seemed arranged around a broad, genuine smile.

'Hauptkommissar Fabel? Frau Doktor Eckhardt? I'm Hauptkommissar Sülberg.' Sülberg shook hands with them both and apologised that Dr Stern would not be available for another twenty minutes, so he suggested they went straight up to interview the girl.

Michaela Palmer was tall and long-limbed. Fabel knew from the report he had received from Sülberg that she was twenty-three. Her hair was a buttery blonde that looked natural. She would have been beautiful had her nose not been a touch too long, disrupting the otherwise perfect balance of her features. Her skin was tanned golden; not, Fabel reckoned, by the north-German sun and not, from what he had gathered about her, from frequent trips to sunnier climes. It was a sun-salon tan that gave her an exaggerated look of health and contrasted with the pad of white gauze taped to her forehead. It was only beneath the blue eyes that the unnatural tan failed to hide the dark shadows of what had happened to her over the last forty-eight hours. Her room was on the third floor of the Stadtkrankenhaus Cuxhaven, and Fabel could not help thinking how lucky she was that she had not ended up in the basement. In the morgue.

Fabel gestured towards the bed and made an expression

that asked permission. Michaela nodded and moved across the bed slightly. Her white towelling bathrobe slipped to expose a bronzed plain of thigh. She re-covered it with a swift movement. Her actions, particularly the way she moved her eyes, seemed fox-like, hunted; as if she were on the edge of flight. Fabel smiled as reassuring a smile as he could muster.

'I'm a Kriminalhauptkommissar of the Hamburg Polizei.' Fabel was careful to omit that he was from the Mord-kommission for fear of blowing Michaela's already fragile defences to pieces. He had to handle this questioning care-fully, or his witness would simply implode. 'And this is Dr Eckhardt. She is a psychologist who knows a lot about the type of drug you were given. I'd like to ask you a few ques-tions. Is that okay?'

Michaela nodded. 'What do you want to know? I can't remember much. That's the thing . . .' Her brow furrowed. 'I can't remember anything much at all. And it's not just the kidnapping I can't remember – there are chunks missing from the days before.' She looked searchingly at Fabel and her bottom lip quivered. 'Why is that? That was before I was drugged. Why can't I remember what happened before?'

Fabel turned to Susanne.

'The type of drug you were given damages the memory centre of your brain,' she explained. 'You'll find that there are a few things from before the drugging that seem to have been erased from your memory. Those things will generally come back to you, at least in part. But the things you can't remember about what happened to you while you were drugged . . . they won't come back. Which is probably a good thing.' Susanne drew closer. 'Listen, Michaela, I have to warn you that, unfortunately, you will get extremely vivid flashbacks of the things you do remember about the attack.'

Michaela sucked back a sob. 'I don't want to remember anything.' She looked directly into Fabel's eyes. 'Please don't make me remember.'

'No one can make you remember, Michaela,' said Susanne, pushing back a stray tendril of Michaela's blonde hair, as if comforting a child who had awoken from a nightmare. 'What isn't there isn't there. But what you can remember may help us catch this monster.'

'There was more than one.' Michaela lowered her eyes and plucked at her towelling bathrobe. 'There was more than one of them who did it to me. I thought at first there was just one, because the face was the same. But the bodies were different.'

'I'm sorry, Michaela, I don't understand,' Fabel said. 'What do you mean they had the same face but different bodies?'

'Just that. I'm sorry, I know it doesn't make sense, but I know that one of them was fat and older and one was young and slim. But they all had the same horrible face.'

Shit, thought Fabel. Sorry as he felt for the girl, this had been a wasted trip: they would get nothing useful from her. 'Can you describe the face you saw? The face you say they all had?'

Michaela shuddered. 'It was horrible. Expressionless. I couldn't see it too clearly but I'm sure he had a beard . . . and he had only one eye.'

'What?'

Michaela shook her head as if trying to shake free of something. 'Yes. Only one eye. It was like the other eye was just a socket . . . all black and . . .' She broke down.

'It's okay, Michaela,' said Fabel. 'Just take it easy.'

Susanne put an arm around the girl's shaking shoulders. They sat in silence for a while until Michaela gathered her composure.

'How many do you think there were?' Fabel asked eventually.

'I don't know. I only remember flashes. I think three. At least three . . .'

Fabel placed his hand on Michaela's. She pulled away as

if stung. Then she focused on Fabel's retracted hand, frowning.

'There was something. One of them had a scar on the back of his hand. Left hand. It was actually more like two scars running together. It made a wishbone shape.'

'Are you sure?' asked Fabel.

Michaela gave a bitter laugh. 'It's one of the few things I remember clearly.' She looked up pleadingly again. 'It makes no sense. Why should I remember that?'

'I don't know, Michaela.' Fabel smiled as reassuringly as he could. 'But it could be useful. Very useful.' He took out his notebook and lay it on the bed, placing his pen on top of it. 'Could you draw what it looked like?'

She picked up the pen and notebook, frowned for a moment, and then drew two swift, determined lines. It was indeed the shape of a wishbone, but with a slight distortion in each leg.

'That's it,' she said resolutely.

'Thanks,' said Fabel and stood up. 'I'm so sorry about what happened to you, Michaela. I promise you we'll do everything we can to find out who did it.'

Michaela nodded without looking up. Then she seemed to be gripped by something. Her eyes began darting again and her brow creased by the effort of intense concentration. 'Wait . . . there's something else . . . I was at a club . . . I . . . I can't remember the name. There was a man. He gave me some water . . . it tasted salty . . .'

'We know, Michaela, you already told Herr Sülberg. Can you describe him? Anything?'

'His eyes . . . his eyes were green. Cold, bright. And they were green . . .'

On the way out, Fabel and Susanne stopped off at Dr Stern's office. Stern's tall frame was bent over a desk covered in files, charts and yellow notelets that were strewn in layers like windfallen leaves. Fabel considered his own over-orderly nature; that everything had its place in his office, in his home, in his life. Whenever things stacked up he had to sort them all out or he would grind to a halt. Fabel recognised it as a weakness in himself: something that threw a fence around his otherwise intuitive nature. And it was more than a little anally retentive.

Stern stood up and his strong, handsome face broke into a wide and genial smile. 'Hauptkommissar Fabel? Frau Doktor Eckhardt?'

Fabel extended his hand. 'Herr Doktor Stern. Thanks for your time.'

'No problem.' Stern reached into the chaos on his desk and pulled out a file. 'I made you a copy of the report I drew up for the local police.' Stern nodded in the direction of Sülberg, who had entered the office.

'Thanks.' Fabel took the file but did not examine it right away. 'Would I be right in assuming that the girl was drugged with Rohypnol?'

'Drugged, yes. Rohypnol, yes. But not on its own. As I've stated in the report there are only very faint traces of Rohypnol in her blood. Rohypnol metabolises slowly . . . it tends to hang around in the bloodstream for several hours after ingestion.'

'Could it be that the dose was enough to daze her but light enough to have all but disappeared by now?'

It was Susanne who answered. 'No. Even after it has disappeared from the bloodstream it can be traced as a metabolite in urine for more than seventy-two hours.' She turned to Stern. 'I presume you checked urine samples?'

Stern nodded. 'We checked for seven-aminoflunitrezapam in her urine. Very faint residual traces. As Frau Doktor Eckhardt pointed out, if Michaela had been heavily drugged with Rohypnol within the last three days then we would have found more significant traces.'

'But she was drugged?' Fabel asked.

'Absolutely. Michaela had faint chemical burns – and I mean very faint, more of a dermal inflammation in her mouth and throat. And when I asked her about the windows of clarity she had during her altered state, she talked about how unafraid she had felt.'

'Of course,' said Susanne. 'Some kind of cocktail that included gammahydroxybutyrate?'

'Probably . . .' Stern shrugged. 'But gammahydroxybutyrate metabolises so fast that I have no traces to prove it . . .'

'Gamma what?' The conversation was going too fast and getting too technical for Fabel.

'Sorry.' Stern made an apologetic gesture. 'Gammahydroxy-butyrate, GHB. Otherwise known as Gook or Zonked.'

Again Susanne picked up the thread. 'A particularly nasty central-nervous-system depressant. It does the same job as Rohypnol but is potentially much more dangerous. It was, believe it or not, sold until recently in health-food shops as a body-building aid. It really has little medical application, so the majority of production takes place illegally.'

'And because it is made in illicit labs with no controls,' continued Stern, 'there are wild variations in purity. Often the chemicals used to synthesise and stabilise it are highly toxic.'

'And you think it was the toxic chemicals that caused the burns in her mouth?' Susanne asked.

'Yes . . . and GHB can also have very strange side effects. Even light doses can cause nausea, vomiting, delusions, hallu-cinations, seizures and, of course, loss of consciousness. One side effect can be a feeling of fearlessness, such as Michaela says she felt. If she was given a cocktail of either flunitrazepam or clonazepam with gammahydroxybutyrate, the risks of general anaesthesia, respiratory depression and even coma would have been very high indeed. Michaela is lucky that she isn't on a respirator. As Frau Doktor Eckhardt says, GHB is a particularly nasty little product. Whoever did this used it in combination with other drugs that would have a synergistic effect on each other. They may not have been trying to kill their victims, but they didn't particularly care if they survived the experience.'

'And GHB is illegally produced just to be used as a date-rape drug?' Fabel asked.

'No. Actually, it is very popular on the clubbing and rave circuit. It is used a lot as a downer to bring people down from Ecstasy and cocaine highs. I'm sure your own drugs squad will have had a lot of experience of it in the Hamburg club scene.'

'How would it be ingested? Is it flavourless, like Rohypnol?'

'Almost. When diluted, it has a slightly salty taste. In fact, one of the street names for it is Salty Water. Apart from that, it would be pretty easy to administer it in an alcoholic drink, which would synergise its effectiveness, or as a powder hidden in food.'

'Michaela just told us she was at a club and some guy gave her water to drink and she thought it tasted salty.'

'That would probably be it.'

Fabel looked down at Stern's report. 'What about the rape? Did we get any forensics?'

'All we can say is that she was vaginally raped over a period of two to four hours . . . perhaps by more than one man. No sodomy. No forced oral sex. And, unfortunately, no semen for DNA analysis. He – or they – must have used condoms. She was not beaten or otherwise abused. The only other injuries were the ligature marks on her ankles and feet . . .' Stern nodded towards the file in Fabel's hands. 'The pictures are in there.'

Fabel opened the report. The photographs showed the marks on her wrists and ankles. She had been spread-eagled, like the murder victims. But Michaela was alive. There was another photograph, of a woman's forehead with the blonde hair pushed back to reveal a faint but discernible red mark.

'What's this?'

Stern smiled. 'That, Herr Kommissar, is a clue the rapist or rapists didn't intend you to see. Michaela has highly sensitive skin, she has an eczematous condition. That's one of the reasons for her tan – UV therapy.' So much for my sun-salon theory, thought Fabel. 'Anyway,' continued Stern, 'whoever did this to her made some kind of mark on her forehead. They have obviously tried to clean it off, but Michaela's sensitive skin reacted to the paint or whatever it was they used. I thought it was very significant so I included it in the standard rape-kit evidence photographs, even though it isn't much of an injury.'

'And I'm very glad you did, Herr Doktor,' said Fabel. 'This could be of enormous significance evidentially.'

'It looks like an X to me,' said Stern. 'Any ideas what it could mean?'

Fabel looked at the mark and frowned. 'As a matter of fact I do . . . I think that it is a Futhark symbol.'

Stern shrugged his incomprehension.

Susanne moved over to Fabel, who angled the image towards her. 'A Viking rune?'

Fabel nodded and slipped the photograph back into the file.

Saturday 14 June, 3.50 p.m. Övelgönne, Hamburg.
Susanne leaned over and kissed Fabel, stroking his cheek before getting out of the car.

'We still on for tonight?'

Fabel grinned. 'You bet.'

'I'll meet you there at eight.'

He watched her walk up the steps to the lobby of her apartment building, admiring the sleek curves of her body.

She turned and waved at the door and he waved back. He sat for a moment after the door closed behind her, then took out his cell phone and called Werner at home. When Werner answered, Fabel thought he could hear children in the background. Werner's eldest daughter, Nadja, had made Werner a grandfather twice over. Fabel apologised for disturbing him on a Saturday.

'No problem. What's up, Jan?'

Fabel told Werner about his interview with Michaela Palmer. He included the description she had given of the eyes of the man at the club. Fabel deliberately did not stress this element: he wanted to see if Werner's reaction matched his own. When Werner fell silent for a moment, Fabel guessed that he was indeed thinking the same.

'Our guy from last night? Mr Anglo-Saxon cool?'

'Could be. Maybe we should go back and see him.'

'Careful, Jan,' said Werner, 'you don't want to spook him. MacSwain's under round-the-clock close surveillance. If he puts a foot wrong we'll have him. But the fact that he buys books and has green eyes is flimsy stuff to re-examine him on. We were on pretty thin ice before. If he went to his lawyer and complained about harassment, I don't think that our evidential trail would stand up to scrutiny.'

'You're right, Werner,' said Fabel. 'But phone around the team . . . and send Van Heiden an e-mail . . . I'd like a case conference first thing Monday.'

'What about Dr Eckhardt? Shall I contact her as well?'

'That's okay, Werner, I've got that covered.'

Werner laughed at the other end of the phone. 'I bet you have, *Chef*. I bet you have.'

Fabel shaved, showered and dressed in an English sea-island cotton shirt and a pale grey single-breasted suit. He had an hour before he was due to meet Susanne, so he went through the file he had brought back from Cuxhaven. Fabel saw himself as anything but a social conservative, and he did his best to embrace the new; but sometimes he wondered what the hell was happening to the world. Of course, rape was nothing new, but now there were young men out there who routinely set out to stupefy women with drugs that could permanently damage the brain, in order to have sex with them. The thought left Fabel bemused, and filled with dread for the future. But this guy was different. He was part of a group. And the acts they carried out clearly had some ritualistic meaning or purpose. He was using a drug cocktail to obtain victims for others as well as himself. Perhaps not for himself at all. He slipped out the piece of paper onto which he had traced the outline from the photograph of the inflamed mark on Michaela's forehead. Was he putting too much importance on it? It could, after all, be some random sequence of lines rather than a rendering of a runic mark. But that didn't make sense. They had marked her, branded her, with something of symbolic significance. Fabel was pretty certain it was the rune Gebu which was the Viking equivalent of the letter G, but he also knew that Futhark runes had more than a phonetic meaning, that each one had a symbolism that related to the Norse gods or myths. Fabel went over to his bookcase and pulled out a couple of heavy reference books, one of which was the same as the book MacSwain had bought; Otto had let him borrow it. He scanned through it, and finally he found what he was looking for. Fabel frowned as he read the entry, writing the key points down on the same piece of paper. Gebu was a rune that related to sacrifices to and gifts from the gods. Sacrifice. It also was the seventh rune. The number seven: Fabel remembered Dorn talking about the significance of numbers in the Viking belief system. Gebu was the rune most associated with the *Blot* or ritual of sacrifice.

Could there be a connection between these attacks and the two murders? Not only was Michaela Palmer marked with a ritualistic sign, it was a rune associated with sacrifice. But if she and the other girl were intended to be sacrificed, then why did they let them go? A real effort had been made to remove traces of the mark, and both girls had been heavily drugged so that they would remember next to nothing about their attackers. At the first briefing after the murder in St Pauli, Susanne had suggested that there may have been dry runs for the main event; but somehow that no longer seemed to fit with the kind of killer Fabel instinctively felt he was pursuing. Anyway, these attacks weren't dry runs. There was no escalation here: both girls had been attacked after the murders. Fabel dropped the book onto the couch beside him and looked out of the window of his apartment across the Alster. He checked his watch: 7.30. He had better head off: he didn't want Susanne to be there first and have to wait for him.

If it hadn't been for his almost obsessive tidiness he wouldn't have noticed it. He rose from the couch to put the two reference books back on their shelf. Just before he put the one from Otto's store back, he flicked through it absent-mindedly, letting the pages flutter through his fingers. There it was. A full-page colour plate of a wood-carved represen-tation of Odin. The dark wood was crudely but strikingly fashioned into the bearded face and screaming, bared-teeth snarl of a berserker. It was the face of all-wise Odin. And the price Odin had had to pay to drink from the well of wisdom was to lose an eye.

That's why they all had the same face when they raped you, Michaela, thought Fabel. They all wore a mask. The same mask. The mask of one-eyed Odin.

Saturday 14 June, 8.00 p.m. Pöseldorf, Hamburg.
Fabel didn't need to look around to know that she had entered the bar. The barman facing him gazed blankly over Fabel's

shoulder and the motion of his hands stopped in the middle of polishing a glass. Fabel also heard the conversation of the two men to his right trail into silence as they moved aside to make way for her. He felt her presence as she leaned on the bar next to him, and the subtle sensuality of her perfume reached him. Fabel smiled and without turning his head said: 'Good evening, Frau Doktor Eckhardt.'

'Good evening, Herr Kriminalhauptkommissar.'

Fabel turned. Susanne was dressed in a simple sleeveless black dress and her raven hair was loosely tied up. Fabel somehow remembered to take a breath.

'I'm glad you could make it,' he said.

'So am I.'

Fabel ordered drinks and they made their way over to a table by the window. Milchstrasse was full of people strolling or sitting out in the pavement cafés and enjoying the embers of the day.

'I'm determined that we won't talk shop this evening,' said Fabel, 'but would you be free for a case conference on Monday morning at ten?'

'No problem,' Susanne said. 'This case has really got to you, hasn't it?'

Fabel smiled weakly. 'They all do. But yes, this one in particular. There are so many things that don't fit and so many things that fit too well.' Fabel outlined his theory about the Odin masks.

'I just don't know, Jan,' Susanne said, rotating her wine glass by turning the stem between her fingers, 'I still think that this is a single killer. And I still think that you're off-base with your theory about ulterior motives. I think that this is a solo sicko getting off by butchering young women at random.'

'That sounded a less than professional summary, Frau Doktor.'

Susanne laughed. 'Sometimes I feel less than professional.

I am still a human being, an ordinary person, and occasionally I can't help reacting to all this horror at an emotional level. There must be times you feel the same?'

Fabel laughed. 'Most of the time, in fact. But if you feel like that why do you do it?'

'Why do you?'

'Why am I a policeman? Because someone has to do it. Someone has to stand in the way, I suppose . . . between the ordinary man, woman or child and those that would harm them.' Fabel stopped abruptly, realising he had more or less repeated Yilmaz's analysis of him. 'Anyway,' he went on, 'you're a doctor . . . there's a hundred different ways in which you could help people. Why do you do this?'

'I suppose I drifted into it. After qualifying in general medicine I studied psychiatry. Then psychology. Then criminal and forensic psychology. Before I knew it I had become uniquely qualified for this line of work.'

Fabel smiled broadly. 'Well I'm glad that you did. Otherwise you wouldn't have drifted in my direction. Now that's enough shop talk . . .' Fabel beckoned to a waiter.

Saturday 14 June, 8.50 p.m. Uhlenhorst, Hamburg.
Angelika Blüm cleared the clutter from the broad coffee table and spread out a large, detailed map of Middle and Eastern Europe. On top of this she laid out the photographs, the press cuttings, the company details and the pieces of paper she had cut out, each with a handwritten name on it: Klimenko, Kastner, Schreiber, Von Berg, Eitel (Jnr), Eitel (Snr). In the middle of the map she laid the last name. Whereas all the others were written in black, this name was in handwritten red felt-pen capitals: VITRENKO.

It was all there. But the connections that held her theory together were too fragile to withstand the pressure of jurisprudential scrutiny. All she could do was write it up and expose those involved to the attentions of investigators with greater resources than she had. Why hadn't that bloody policeman got in touch? She knew Fabel was investigating Ursula's murder and what she had to say would cast more light on it. Angelika had read about the second murder: the girl whose photograph they had published in an attempt to establish her identity. She did not recognise the woman nor could she see any connection with Ursula or the other elements in her investigation. Either this second murder was a copycat or there was some link that still lay beyond Angelika's investigative horizon.

She rested her elbows on her knees and cradled the bowl of her coffee cup in her hands as she scanned the scattered pieces. They were like components of a machine waiting to be assembled, but she didn't know how the machine worked, what its ultimate function was. Certainly, if all of these components could be put together it would make one hell of a story: a Hamburg Stadtsenator, the office of the Erste Bürgermeister, neo-Nazis, a leading media company and, right at the centre of it all, a faceless Ukrainian special-forces commander whose appetite for atrocity had made him a name others barely dared to speak: Vasyl Vitrenko.

She took a sip of her coffee and tried to disengage her mind from the puzzle for a moment. Sometimes you had to look away before you could refocus and see what had been in front of you all the time. The door buzzer made her jump. She sighed and placed her coffee down on top of the spread-out map and walked over to her entryphone.

'Who is it?'

'Frau Blüm? This is Kriminalhauptkommissar Fabel of the Polizei Hamburg. You've been trying to get in touch with me. May I come up?'

Angelika looked down at her bathrobe and slippers and swore under her breath. She sighed and pushed the button to speak. 'Of course, Herr Fabel. Come on up.' She pressed the button to release the door and moments later heard his footsteps echoing in the hall. She opened the door but kept it on the chain. The man in the hall held up his oval KriPo shield and Angelika smiled and slipped the chain from the door.

'Please excuse me, Herr Fabel. I wasn't expecting anyone.' She stood to one side to let him in.

Saturday 14 June, 11.30 p.m. Pöseldorf, Hamburg.
The moonlight through the deep windows cut geometric shapes across the floor and walls of Fabel's bedroom and accented the sweeps and curves of Susanne's body as she lowered herself onto him. It cast her moving shadow on the wall as the initial gentle, quiet, rhythm of their lovemaking grew in intensity.

Afterwards they lay together: Susanne on her back, Fabel on his side, resting his head on an elbow and studying the moonlight-etched profile of his lover. He raised himself up onto one elbow and looked down at her. Tenderly, he pushed back a strand of hair from her brow.

'Will you stay the night?'

Susanne gave a cosy moan. 'I'm too comfortable here to get up and get dressed.' She turned to him and smiled wickedly. 'But I'm not tired enough to sleep.'

Fabel was about to answer when the phone rang. He gave Susanne a resigned smile and said: 'Hold that thought. I'll be right back.'

Fabel rose and walked naked to the phone. It was Karl Zimmer, the duty Kommissar at the Mordkommission.

'I'm sorry to disturb you, sir,' Zimmer said, 'but something's come up that you ought to know about.'

'What?'

'We've received another e-mail from Son of Sven.'

B L O O D   E A G L E

Polizei Hamburg Mordkommission

From   SON OF SVEN
To   ERSTER KRIMINALHAUPTKOMMISSAR JAN FABEL
Sent   14 June 2003, 23.00
Subject WORDS

I AM, AS YOU WILL HAVE GATHERED, A MAN OF FEW WORDS. MY
VICTIM, HOWEVER, WAS A WOMAN OF MANY.

I DO NOT CARE FOR WOMEN WHO DO NOT FULFIL THEIR PRIMARY
FUNCTION, BUT CHOOSE THE SELFISHNESS OF A CAREER OVER THE
NATURAL IMPERATIVE TO BREED. THIS ONE WAS WORSE THAN
MOST. SHE SAW IT AS HER CALLING TO DEFAME THOSE WHOSE
NOBILITY SHE COULD NEVER ASPIRE TO: SOLDIERS WHO FOUGHT
AGAINST ANARCHY AND CHAOS.

I HAVE ADDED A TWIST THIS TIME. SHE THOUGHT I WAS YOU, HERR
FABEL. IT WAS TO YOU SHE BEGGED FOR HER LIFE. IT WAS YOUR
NAME THAT BURNED IN HER BRAIN AS SHE DIED.

SHE HAS SPREAD HER WINGS.

SON OF SVEN

Sunday 15 June, 1.30 a.m. Polizeipräsidium, Hamburg.
'I'm sorry to have pulled you all in at such an ungodly hour,' said Fabel, but his businesslike expression suggested the apology was a formality. The figures around the table all had the puffy-eyed look of unwelcome awakening, but no one complained; everyone realised the importance of the arrival of a new e-mail. 'But this new e-mail has some unpleasant twists to it, to say the least.'

Werner, Maria, Anna and Paul nodded bleakly. Susanne also sat at the table and there had been an exchange of knowing looks between the others when she arrived with Fabel.

'So what does this e-mail tell us?' Fabel's gesture invited a response from everyone.

It was Maria who spoke first. 'Well, it rather unpleasantly confirms he is masquerading as a policeman. In this case, specifically you.'

'I'm not a uniformed officer. So he can't be dressed up in a Schutzpolizei uniform.'

'It looks like he's got his hands on a KriPo shield or ID warrant . . . or both,' suggested Werner.

'What about his victim?' said Fabel. Mentioning her reminded him of what he had said in the e-mail: that she died thinking that he, Fabel, had killed her. The thought stabbed nauseatingly in his chest. 'He described her as "a woman of many words" . . .'

'A politician?' ventured Maria. 'An actress . . . or a writer or journalist?'

'Possible,' said Susanne, 'but remember he is a psychopath with a distorted view of the world. She might simply be someone he thinks talks too much.'

'But what about her defaming soldiers, as he put it? Sounds like she's someone with a public audience,' said Paul Lindemann.

'What about the e-mail itself?' asked Fabel. 'I take it we've got a fake IP address?'

'Technical Section are pursuing it,' Maria said. 'I got the section head out of bed to check it out. He is not a happy camper.'

Werner stood up suddenly, his face clouded with anger and frustration. He walked over to the obsidian sheet of window that reflected the room in on itself. 'All we can do is wait until her body is discovered. He's leaving us nothing to go on.'

'You're right, Werner,' said Fabel. He looked at his watch. 'I think we should all try to catch up on some sleep. Let's reconvene here at, say, ten a.m.'

They were all rising wearily from the table when the conference-room phone rang. Anna Wolff was nearest so she lifted the receiver. The weariness was suddenly swept from her face. She held up her free hand to stop the others leaving the room.

'That was Technical Section,' she said. 'We've got a genuine IP address from the provider. It belongs to an Angelika Blüm. And we've got an address in Uhlenhorst.'

'Oh my God,' Fabel said. 'She's the journalist who's been trying to reach me.'

'A journalist?' asked Maria.

'Yes,' said Fabel, 'a woman of many words.'

Sunday 15 June, 2.15 a.m. Uhlenhorst, Hamburg.

The apartment building met all of the criteria of Hamburg chic. It had been built in the 1920s and it looked as if it had been comprehensively refurbished reasonably recently. Fabel, who knew a thing or two about Modernist architecture, reckoned it had been designed by Karl Schneider, or at least one of his school. There were no hard edges to it: the whitewashed walls met in elegant curves, rather than corners, and the windows of the serviced apartments were high and wide. Uhlenhorst had never quite achieved the same prestige of Rotherbaum, but it was still an affluent and trendy neighbourhood.

There were two Schutzpolizei cars, which Fabel guessed were from the Uhlenhorst Polizeikommissariat, parked immediately before the bronze and glass doors that gave entry to the brightly lit marble lobby. A uniformed SchuPo stood guard at the door while a second listened as a tall man in his sixties talked animatedly to him. Fabel parked behind the police cars and he, Maria and Werner got out, just as Paul and Anna pulled up. Fabel strode over to the uniformed policeman who was listening patiently to the older man. The policeman's epaulettes told Fabel that he was a Polizeikommissar. Fabel flashed his KriPo shield and the policeman nodded acknowledgement. The taller, older civilian, who had the dishevelled look and red-rimmed eyes of someone disturbed from a deep sleep opened his mouth to speak. Fabel cut him off by speaking directly to the Polizeikommissar.

'No one's tried to gain entry yet?'

'No, sir. I thought it best to hang on until you got here. I've two men on the door of Frau Blüm's apartment and there's no sound from within.'

Fabel looked in the direction of the civilian.

'This is the caretaker,' the SchuPo answered Fabel's unspoken question.

Fabel turned to the caretaker and held out his hand. 'Give me the master key for Frau Blüm's apartment.'

The caretaker had the supercilious, semi-aristocratic look of an English butler. 'Certainly not. This is an exclusive residence and our occupiers are entitled to—'

Again Fabel cut him off. 'Fair enough.' He turned to Werner. 'Get the door-ram from the trunk of the car, would you please, Werner?'

'You can't do that . . .' fumed the caretaker. 'You need a warrant . . .'

Fabel didn't even look in the caretaker's direction. 'We don't need a warrant. We are investigating a murder and we have reason to believe the occupant is in danger.' He jerked his head in the direction of the car. 'Werner . . . door-ram?'

The caretaker spluttered apoplectically. 'No . . . No . . . I'll get the keys.'

The elevator doors slid open onto the third-floor corridor, a wide, immaculate expanse, brightly illuminated by down-lighters that splashed pools of light on the pristine marble. Fabel gestured with his hand for the caretaker to lead the way. They followed a slow sweep in the hall and came upon two officers, one on either side of an apartment door. Fabel placed a restraining hand on the caretaker's shoulder and moved forward, indicating to Werner and Maria that they should come with him. With a silent motion of his hand he gestured that Anna and Paul should move to the other side of the door, next to the second SchuPo. All eyes were on Fabel. He gestured to the caretaker by holding a finger to his lips and whispered: 'Which key?'

The caretaker fumbled for the appropriate key. Fabel took the keys, smiled and nodded to the caretaker, miming a pushing movement with the palm of his hand to indicate that the caretaker should now back off. The mime act continued: he pointed to himself and to Werner, then held up a single finger followed by two fingers to indicate that he and Werner would take the lead. Fabel and Werner drew their weapons and Fabel pressed the door buzzer. They heard the electronic rasping of the buzzer inside the apartment. Then nothing. Fabel nodded to Werner and put the key in the lock. He turned the key and swung the door open in a single fluid movement. The lights in the apartment were on. Werner slipped through the door followed immediately by Fabel.

'Frau Blüm?' Fabel's call was answered by silence. He scanned what he could see of the apartment. Next to the door was a chair and an occasional table. An expensive-looking woman's coat was thrown carelessly onto the chair and an Italian leather handbag had been discarded on the table. Fabel's grip eased on his Walther. He knew there was no one in the apartment. No one alive, at any rate.

The walls of the entrance hallway were a very pale blue and punctuated with large, original canvases: abstract studies in deep, tonal violets and reds that smouldered against the coolness of the walls.

As Fabel made his way down the hall he glanced to the left through the open, glazed double doors that led into the large living area. The room was empty. Again a tasteful coolness set the background for expensive furnishings and the occasional original work of art. In his quick survey of the room, Fabel thought he saw the stretched lines of a Giacometti sculpture. A small one, but it looked like an original. He walked on. To the right the bathroom. Empty. Next right the bedroom. Empty. The last door in the hall was closed and when he swung it open the room was in darkness. He reached in and slid a hand down the wall next to the door until he found the switch. The room flooded with light from a series of angled wall lights.

Horror.

Fabel couldn't understand why he hadn't been prepared for it. He had known she would be lying, dead, inside the apartment, and instinct had told him, when he saw this door closed and this room in darkness, that this is where she would be. But he still felt as if a truck had slammed into him.

'Oh Jesus . . .' It was as if the breath had been sucked out of Fabel's chest. Nausea surged upwards. 'Sweet Jesus . . .'

The room had been intended as a bedroom but had been redesigned as an office. There was shelving, stacked with books and files, on three of the walls. The fourth wall accommodated the window that ran almost the full length of the room and which was now concealed by closed vertical blinds. A wide beech desk with a laptop computer faced the window. As with the rest of the apartment the decor was restrained, tasteful and elegant.

In the centre of the room was an explosion of flesh, blood and bone. A woman's body. Face down. The back had been sliced open by slashes that ran parallel to the spine. The ribs had been prised apart, exposing the raw interior of the abdomen, and the lungs excavated and thrown outwards.

She was naked apart from a pair of towelling slippers with corded soles. A towelling bathrobe, which matched the slippers, had been thrown into one corner of the room. Other than these items there were no clothes in the room.

Fabel noticed that as well as the devastation to the torso, there was a large plume of blood, issuing from the head, that spread across the pine flooring. The back of her skull was a matted mass of blood and auburn hair.

'Oh fuck . . .' Werner was now beside Fabel and spoke between nausea-suppressing gasps. 'Oh fuck.'

Maria and Anna Wolff entered too. Anna suppressed a gagging sound and ran back along the hall. Fabel could hear her vomitting into the toilet bowl in Blüm's bathroom. The Tatort scene-of-crime team would love that: contamination of a primary scene in a murder. Fabel couldn't blame tough little Anna, though. He himself had to close his eyes for a moment and tried to wipe the image from his retina until he regained his composure. The thought of whether Anna was finished in the toilet flashed through his mind. He took a long, slow breath. He did not move closer to the body, again mindful of the need to preserve the primary locus, and when others started to crowd the doorway he ordered them back and out of the apartment.

Within an hour, the entire building was thronging with people. Fabel had asked the Uhlenhorst Polizeikommissar to order up more uniforms to carry out door-to-door enquiries. The Tatort team had arrived, headed up by Holger Brauner, along with Dr Möller, the pathologist. Fabel knew Brauner from previous investigations and regarded him highly. The only problem was that that arrogant asshole Möller always seemed to feel he was in competition with Brauner. The truth was, much as Fabel hated to admit it, that Möller was also an excellent pathologist and had a scalpel-sharp mind.

Fabel had secured the scene of crime and handed it over to the Tatort team. The protocol was that Brauner examined the scene first, without the body being disturbed, and only once he and his team were finished could Möller move in to do his examination. As a result Möller stood at the threshold of the apartment, fuming. For Fabel, it was the only high spot in the day.

Brauner emerged eventually. Ignoring Möller, he asked Fabel to come back inside. 'There's something you should see before we bag it for examination back at the lab.'

Brauner led him into the murder scene. Fabel had to pass the body, squeezing past two overalled Tatort scene-of-crime technicians. The team's photographer was packing up his equipment and it was a tight squeeze in the room. Brauner led Fabel over to the desk and indicated the laptop computer. There was a recently sent e-mail open on the screen. It was the one the Präsidium had received just after eleven p.m. and which had led them here. Not only had the killer sent it from Angelika Blüm's own computer, he had left it open and waiting for them to arrive.

'The bastard!' Fabel felt a black fury surge up from somewhere deep inside. He always prided himself on keeping calm, staying in control, but this guy had burrowed so far under his skin that all his usual defences had been totally overwhelmed. 'The bastard's taunting us. This is what he wanted, this is the precise scene he had in his head . . . me in this room with her body reading this fucking e-mail for the second time!' Fabel turned to Brauner. 'So he was here about eleven?'

'Not necessarily. The e-mail was on a timed send. But there's more.' Brauner, carefully using a single latex-gloved finger, selected 'hide application' and the laptop's desktop was exposed. Brauner clicked on a sequence of folders. They were all empty.

'This is weird,' said Brauner. 'What kind of serial killer goes in and wipes all his victim's computer records?'

'Can I take the laptop in and let Technical Section have a look at it?'

'No, not yet. We've dusted for prints but I want to open this up. Computer keyboards are as much cracks as buttons . . . all kinds of stuff gets trapped under the keys. With a bit of luck we might get a hair or some epithelials from our killer.'

'I doubt it very much,' said Fabel, dispiritedly. 'This guy doesn't make mistakes. Despite the messiness of the method of killing, it's almost as if he kills in a forensic cleanroom. He leaves nothing of himself behind.'

'It's still worth a try,' said Brauner, trying, but failing, to sound encouraging. 'Maybe we'll get lucky.'

'I doubt it. Can I tell Möller he can come in now?'

Brauner smiled. 'I suppose so.'

On the way out to the corridor, Fabel checked on Anna Wolff, who was looking yellow-pale under her spiky black hair and the trademark mascara and flame-red lipstick.

'I'm okay, *Chef* . . . Sorry. It just got to me this time . . .'

Fabel smiled reassuringly, 'There's no need to apologise Anna, it happens to us all. Anyway, your penance will be bad enough: Brauner and the Tatort team are never going to let you live it down.'

Werner tapped Fabel on the shoulder. 'You're not going to believe this, Jan . . . we've got a time of arrival and a witness.'

'Do we have a description?'

'Not a great one, but yes we do.'

Fabel made an impatient face.

'There's a girl who lives on the floor below,' Werner continued. 'She's about thirty and works for an advertising agency or something equally worthwhile and meaningful.

Anyway, she's got this new boyfriend. They had been to a health club for a workout and got back here before nine p.m. I get the impression the boyfriend was planning on another workout with her, the horizontal kind, but he's not been around long enough to have been invited up. Anyway, he parked across the street about eight-thirty. They were sitting in his car with the engine off – he was obviously doing his best to persuade her to let him come up. It was then that they saw this guy arrive on foot. They didn't notice a car, so if he had one he must have parked it some way away. They paid attention to this guy because, just before he pressed the entry button for one of the apartments, he made sure he had a good long look up and down the street. She said he even checked out the lobby through the glass doors.'

'So she got a good look at him?'

'As good as it could be at that distance.' Werner flipped open his notebook to check his notes. 'Tall and well built. She made a point about him having broad shoulders. He didn't look out of place in this neighbourhood and was well dressed in a dark grey suit.'

Not my short, squat Slav with the green eyes, thought Fabel.

'His hair was blond and cut fairly short,' Werner continued. 'But here's the thing . . . she says he was carrying a pale grey raincoat that was draped over a large sports bag.'

'The tools of his trade,' said Fabel in a low, bitter voice.

'The girl says she's never seen him before tonight and the caretaker had only one suggestion for a possible tenant, but the girl knows that guy by sight and swears it wasn't him. Anyway, the girl saw our man pressing one of the apartment buttons, so he's unlikely to be one of the occupiers. We've still got a few apartments to check out, some of which are empty, but so far everyone denies having received a visitor fitting the description.'

'Did anyone see him leave?'

'No. And no one heard any sounds of a struggle or cries for help. It's a pretty robust building, but you would have thought someone would have heard something.'

'Don't let the mess in there fool you, Werner. This guy is cool and has everything worked out to the last letter. We'll wait for the full autopsy, but from the state of the back of her head, I reckon she was dead or close to it before she hit the floor. The bastard obviously introduces himself as a policeman, probably me, and lets her lead the way. While she's got her back to him, wham – he's smashed the back of her skull in. That leaves him all the time in the world to unpack his little kit and set to work.'

Werner stroked the bristle on his scalp. 'This guy's scary, Jan. He never seems to slip up. Except tonight he did. He didn't check the street well enough. But other than a brief sighting from a distance, he's left us nothing.'

'We'll see what Brauner and Möller have to say.' Fabel slapped an encouraging hand on Werner's meaty shoulders. 'Maybe this has been his off-day.'

Back in the apartment, Fabel found Möller, the pathologist, was still standing beside the body, writing notes onto a clipboard. He turned to the two overalled Tatort technicians.

'If the photographer's through, you can take the body back to the morgue.' As he spoke, Möller noticed Fabel and nodded. His usual brusque manner seemed to have left him and there was an almost doleful look in his eyes. This guy's beginning to get to everybody, thought Fabel.

'I don't suppose you need my professional opinion to tell you that this is the same modus as the last two.'

'No,' said Fabel. 'He sent me an e-mail from that computer over there.'

Möller shook his head. 'Anyway, for the record, I'll tell you that there's absolutely no doubt in my mind that this is the work of the same person or persons. Obviously I'll give you a full report once I've done a complete autopsy. Take a look at this . . .' The pathologist bent down and pointed with his ballpoint pen to the edge of where the flesh had been sliced and the ribs pulled back. Fabel bent closer to look. It was like something from a butcher's shop. Focus, he kept telling himself, focus, don't look at the person, look at the detail. Concentrate. But he still had to fight back the nausea.

'See where our chum has made a bit of a mistake?' With his pen Möller followed the line of a deep serration that ran off at an angle from the main slash. 'You can see the shape of the blade. It's a broad blade of a heavy gauge: more like a short sword or a very heavy hunting knife. I'll get some shots of it during the autopsy.'

Fabel breathed in slowly before speaking. 'Is that the only deviation from the main cuts?'

Möller scratched his grizzled beard. 'Yes . . . That's the thing. This has been no frenzied attack. He took his time.' He pointed to the back of the head of Angelika Blüm's body. 'Again the fatal or near-fatal trauma to the back of the skull; again with a very heavy instrument with some kind of ball-shaped impact; and again the dissections to access the lungs and achieve this . . . well, trademark, I suppose.'

'A hell of a trademark,' said Fabel.

Möller didn't reply immediately. He had been squatting down and now stood up with a groan. He gazed down at the body; it was as if he wasn't seeing it, but looking beyond it. 'This man's physical strength must be considerable to say the least. Surgically, opening a body usually needs a sternal saw and mechanical rib-spreaders. This man slashes at his victims with amazing precision and then prises their ribs apart. He is very strong indeed.'

Maria entered the room and beckoned to Fabel. '*Chef?*'

He followed her into the living area. Holger Brauner was in the room with his team. 'Look at this,' he said to Fabel, indicating the coffee table with his gloved hand. 'What do you see?'

Fabel stared at a large rectangle of pale wood. It looked solid and expensive. He shrugged. 'Apart from a coffee table, nothing.'

'Exactly,' said Brauner. 'No ornaments. No ashtrays, no ceramics, no books.' He lifted one of the forensic team's high-powered hand lamps. It flooded the table top with a cold, white, bleaching light. 'Look here . . .' Brauner leaned forward and drew a square on the tabletop. 'There's been something here. And here. His finger swept a circle at the other side of the table. Here too. He switched off the lamp and turned to the window, which was concealed behind closed blinds. 'These windows are fantastic, don't you think? I checked with a compass: this room faces as near as damn it due south. This room will be filled with the best of the day's light. It makes for a bright, cheerful living environment.'

'Are you changing careers and taking up real-estate agency, Holger?' asked Fabel.

Brauner laughed. 'The pay would be a hell of a lot better, that's for sure. But no . . . it's just that light bleaches furnishings. Including wood. These slightly darker areas are where she's had books or ornaments on the coffee table . . . items that were there almost all the time.'

'But they're not now.'

'Exactly. And I don't think our perpetrator cleared it.' Brauner moved over to the stone plinth that surrounded the gas-flame fireplace. He lifted three books that sat stacked on top of each other and placed them on the table. The bottom book matched the slightly darker area he had indicated. From a high table behind Fabel he lifted a circular piece of contemporary ceramic. It too matched its shadow on the table. 'Our guy is so thorough that he would make absolutely certain that he put everything back the way he found it. My guess is that Angelika Blüm cleared this table to spread stuff out on it. Papers or something. Whatever it was she had there, our killer has taken it away. And when he'd done so, he didn't know what should go back onto the table.'

'So you're saying you think that he is stealing items for a trophy?'

'No, Jan,' Brauner's voice was suddenly tighter. 'I don't think that this guy is a random psychopathic serial killer. Most serial-offending psychopaths take trophies, anything from a personal item to an internal organ. This guy's trophies are all documentary. Remember you asked me if we had found a diary or appointment book in the second girl's apartment? And the thing that really doesn't fit is, why did he wipe all of her files from her computer? I'll bet if we keep looking, we'll find even less. She was a journalist, wasn't she?'

Fabel nodded.

'She was freelance, right? And worked from the office in the next room?'

'I guess so,' said Fabel.

'Then I suggest you go through her files. My guess is there'll be stuff missing there as well.'

Fabel looked from Brauner to Maria and then Werner, who had entered the room and had caught the main part of Brauner's theory.

'You're saying that there is an ulterior, objective motive here? Surely this guy is a psycho . . .'

Brauner shrugged. 'That's up to your criminal psychologist to determine, but yes, I agree, the killer is psychotic. However, that doesn't mean he falls into the serial pattern. You've heard of Ivan the Terrible?'

'Of course I have.'

'Ivan the Terrible united Russia. He was the father of the nation. He turned it from a loose collection of feuding principalities and fiefdoms into a cohesive nation. *That* was his motive. But as well as being a monarch and general, Ivan fitted all the criteria of a psychotic murderer. In fact, in many ways, he fitted the profile of the classic serial offender – a shy, quiet, sensitive child who was abused from a very early age. As a result, while still a child, he tortured and killed small animals. Then he killed his first man when he was thirteen. After that he committed countless rapes, murders, acts of obscene torture . . . including frying, boiling, impaling or feeding his victims to wild animals. We're talking thousands of rapes and hundreds of murders committed personally by Ivan.' Brauner nodded in the direction of the next room. 'He even had a similar taste for rituals. He had a personal bodyguard, the *oprichniki*. He formed them almost like a holy order with himself as the abbot. They raped, tortured and mutilated victims in parodies of the Russian Orthodox Mass.'

'What's your point, Holger?'

'Just that Ivan was clearly a psychopath. A sociopath, in fact, totally devoid of any empathy with his victims. But he was also an extremely intelligent man and the worst of his crimes were committed within a structured context. He used his psychopathy as a tool to instil terror and to consolidate his control of state and people. My point is that Ivan's sociopathic behaviour was not an end in itself, it was a means to an end. He channelled his psychopathy to further his strategies and achieve his objectives.'

'And you think this guy is the same, but on a smaller scale?' Fabel asked. Everything that Brauner was saying fitted with what he had started to believe after the second murder.

'Yes, but what's more I think your killer here is flaunting his psychopathy. He wants you to believe that these are random acts to conceal whatever it is he's up to.'

'So what is he up to?' Maria was frowning at the coffee table's surface as if to see that which was already gone. 'He kills a journalist and, we think, steals some of her papers.'

'Papers that relate to a story she was working on, if she had them laid out on the table to look over,' Werner added.

'Kill the journalist and kill the story?' Maria looked up and towards Fabel.

'Could be. But it doesn't fit with the other killings. A prostitute and a civic lawyer.'

'Maybe it does,' said Werner, 'but we just haven't seen the connection yet. After all, we know next to nothing about the dead prostitute. Maybe she had something to do with Angelika Blüm's story. A sex scandal, maybe?'

'Angelika Blüm wasn't a tabloid journalist, but if it were a sex scandal that involved politics or something else, then perhaps.' Fabel rubbed his chin frustratedly, as if the action would stimulate brain activity. 'We simply have to find out who Monique was. And we need to go back to the Kastner case. We have to take a closer look at her personal paperwork. And we didn't get into her professional life because we thought it was a random killing. We've got to go back over it all again. Maria . . . could you start that? I know you're looking into the second victim's identity, but I'd like you to take this on as well.'

'Sure, *Chef*.' Maria answered without much enthusiasm. Fabel had expected Werner to look relieved that he had not landed the job. He didn't. Fabel knew that Werner resented Maria being given so much responsibility, but Fabel didn't have time for good man-management practice just now.

'Werner, I need you to follow up on Angelika Blüm's professional contacts, see if you can find out what she was working on. In the meantime, let's find out if anyone else here caught a glimpse of our mystery visitor.'

Brauner spoke again. 'By the way, Jan, we have picked up a second set of prints.'

'Oh?' Fabel raised his eyebrows.

'Don't get too excited. They're all over the place, some new, some quite old and difficult to lift, but I reckon they're the same person. Someone who has been, well, intimately acquainted with Frau Blüm's apartment for some time. Unlikely to be our guy.'

Fabel suddenly felt leaden and dull, as if the adrenalin had worn off and a sluggish tiredness had reclaimed him, body and mind. He made his way back through to Blüm's home office.

Fabel looked down at the devastated carcass that had once been Angelika Blüm. The pathology technicians had laid out a body bag and were preparing to move the corpse onto it. He watched as they zipped up the remains of a woman who had tried several times to get in touch with him. Calls he had deemed too unimportant to return because he had a major murder inquiry to conduct. Now she was a part of that inquiry. He knew the lead that sat in his chest was guilt. He spoke to a woman who was now beyond hearing him.

'Well, Frau Blüm, I'd better find out just what the hell it was that you wanted to tell me.'

Sunday 15 June, 9.45 a.m. Harburg, Hamburg.

Hansi Kraus was more whippet than man: a small, jangling conjunction of bones held together by grey, leathery skin. His eyes, set deep in a pinched, rodential face, had been pale blue in childhood but had since been dulled to a lifeless bluish grey by fifteen years of absorbing prodigious amounts of heroin. Hansi lay on a stained mattress that fumed a stale, unclean odour into the bedroom of the squat; a smell that went unnoticed by Hansi, mainly because he carried it around with him all of the time. He lay with one arm hooked, the hand supporting his head, while the other hand held the cigarette to his thin lips.

Hansi needed to get happy. And soon. He knew that the bud of an ache he felt in his meagre frame would soon bloom into a body-wracking gnaw. To get happy meant money, and Hansi didn't have any. And, despite the volume and regularity of his custom, his suppliers were unlikely to extend Hansi any form of credit. Fucking Turks. But Hansi's bargaining position had been given an unexpected boost. He swung his legs around and sat up on the edge of the bed. Screwing his eyes tight against the smoke from his cigarette, he reached under the bed with both hands. It was still there. He held this pose for a few seconds, listening, screw-eyed, to the sounds from elsewhere in the squat: a tubercular-sounding cough downstairs, a radio in the next bedroom. Hansi pulled out a small bundle wrapped in a couple of soiled rags and laid it on the mattress. Carefully folding back the cloth, he revealed a glittering nine-millimetre automatic pistol. Hansi didn't know anything about guns but he could tell this one was special. It looked expensive. Its flank was ornately tooled with decorative motifs that looked as if they had been inlaid with gold. The maker's mark was foreign; in Cyrillic capitals – Russian or some shit like that, thought Hansi – followed by the number twelve in numerals. Hansi folded the cloth back over, taking care not to touch the gun itself: there was no way he wanted to be tied into what had happened to that poor fuck in the swimming pool.

It had been the night before last. Hansi had been buying some stuff from the Turk. The disused swimming pool was a regular venue for Hansi's deals. Whenever he had enough cash he would buy a surplus of heroin and sell some of it on. The Turks didn't mind so long as he didn't trade widely or stray onto their patch. Hansi hadn't had cash to spare on Friday and could only just afford to buy enough to keep himself going. The Turk had just left to resume his rounds when Hansi had felt the urgent need to defecate. He was used to the alternating bouts of gut-stabbing constipation and diarrhoea that went with a long-standing addiction. He had just finished emptying his bowels onto the floor when he heard the car pull up. There had been no warning sweep of headlights; the car had obviously driven up with its lights off. Years of street living had given Hansi a sixth sense about when to make himself invisible, and, hastily pulling his jeans up, he had dodged behind the door that at one time had led bathers to the changing area.

His instinct had been right. Three men had entered the swimming pool: an older man, a young guy who looked like a bodybuilder and some poor bastard with a canvas bag over his head and his hands tied behind his back. At that moment Hansi knew that three men had come in, but only two would be going out. He had watched them through the semi-circular window of the surviving half of what had been double doors. The younger guy, a gun in one gloved hand and a flashlight in the other, had made his way over to the door. Hansi had only just made it, skipping back, carefully making sure he didn't stumble or make a noise on the rubbish-strewn floor, and ducking into the remnants of a cubicle. The younger man swept the changing area with his flashlight, making sure it was clear. Hansi exhaled slowly. He heard the older guy talking and he made his way carefully back to the door. They had made the hooded guy kneel at the pool's edge and Hansi heard him scream, 'No!' Then there had been a flash and a resonant thump from the gun. Hansi would have expected a brighter flash and a bigger noise, and had noticed the lengthened barrel of the gun. A silencer. There was the ringing tinkle as the discharged cartridge fell onto the cracked tiles.

The two men had seemed in no hurry as they left. It was then that Hansi had seen them do the strangest thing. On the way out they had lifted the lid from an old waste bin by the door and the younger man had dropped the gun into it. They certainly had not been worried about the murder weapon being found. A few hundred metres away was a canal that had probably already served as the depository for dozens of pieces of evidence. Dumping the gun here was inviting it to be found. And, after they left, Hansi had been only too willing to oblige.

Now Hansi had something to offer in lieu of cash. He knew the Turk's cell phone number by heart and knew that this was the best time to catch him. Hansi stood up from the bed and donned the old ex-army coat that he wore rain or shine, summer or winter. He picked up the carefully rewrapped bundle and slipped it into one of the coat's capacious pockets. He didn't like the idea of carrying the gun around with him, but he knew that anything left lying around in the squat had the habit of vanishing.

Hansi went out onto the landing, down the rickety stairs and out onto the street, trying to think where the nearest unvandalised public phone would be.

Monday 16 June, 10.05 a.m. Polizeipräsidium, Hamburg.
Fabel stood at the conference room's cherrywood table, waiting for the others to take their places. He turned round to the incident board behind him. The board was the physical presence of the inquiry – its shape – and now it was growing in substance. There was a map of Hamburg and surrounding area, on which flag pins marked the two primary murder scenes in Hamburg and the secondary scene where Ursula Kastner's body had been found.

The forensic photographs of Angelika Blüm's devastated body now hung alongside those of the two previous victims. Photocopies of pages from academic books on Viking ritual were pasted next to copies of the e-mails from the killer. Fabel had written the names of the three victims, with the second identified as simply 'Monique?', in the centre of the whiteboard panel. Above the names he had written the name 'Son of Sven' and the words 'Blood Eagle'. Over to the right, the name 'Hans Klugmann' was linked with an upward arrow to 'Arno Hoffknecht' which in turn had an arrow connecting it to 'Ulugbay/Yilmaz'. Next to this, punctuated with a question mark, he had written 'Ukrainians'. On the other side he had written the names of the two known date-rape-drug abduction victims. This was linked to the words 'Blood Eagle' by a line broken by the words 'Odinist cult?'

On the table in front of Fabel sat the case file to which had been added his report of what Professor Dorn had told him and the preliminary forensic and pathology reports on the Blüm murder. They had recovered Klugmann's cell phone from Sonia's apartment and it now sat in a plastic evidence bag, on top of the file. The entire principal Mordkommission team, except Maria Klee, was now gathered around the cherrywood table: Fabel, Werner Meyer, Anna Wolff and Paul Lindemann. Fabel was annoyed that Maria wasn't there.

'She's tying something up,' explained Werner. 'She said she won't be long.'

In addition to the core Mordkommission team, there were half a dozen other KriPo detectives who had been drafted in by Van Heiden to support Fabel's inquiry. Fabel had phoned Susanne Eckhardt, and she had joined the meeting. At the end of the table, Van Heiden sat impassive, as Fabel outlined his conversation with Dorn. When Fabel finished, Susanne Eckhardt was the first to speak.

'I can see that Herr Professor Dorn has been able to draw on his expertise as a historian, but why is he so involved in, well, to be frank, amateur psychology? He has identified the modus as being reminiscent of this sacrificial rite, but he seems to have extrapolated a profile of the killer as well.'

'Professor Dorn has worked for many years with offenders,' said Fabel.

'But that hardly qualifies . . .'

Fabel turned and locked eyes with Susanne. There was a cold steel edge to his voice. 'Dorn was my European History tutor at university. His daughter, Hanna, was abducted, tortured, raped and murdered. About twenty years ago. She was twenty-two. I think Professor Dorn has a more . . .' he sought the right word – '*intimate* understanding of murder than we do.'

What Fabel omitted to say was that Hanna Dorn had been his girlfriend at the time. That he had gone out with her for only a couple of weeks. That they were only just on that threshold between awkwardness and intimacy when an unre-markable thirty-year-old hospital orderly called Lutger Voss snatched her from the street as she made her way home from a date with Fabel. The police had questioned Fabel as to why he hadn't walked her home. He had asked himself the same question over and over again and having an assignment to complete had never seemed a substantial enough answer. Fabel had graduated before the trial. Immediately after the trial he had joined the Polizei Hamburg.

Van Heiden broke the awkward silence.

'How likely is all of this, Frau Doktor? Do you think this psychopath believes this "Blood Eagle" nonsense?'

'It's possible. It's definitely possible. And it does explain the religiosity of the e-mail. But if it is true, then we are dealing with a much more sophisticated and structured psychopathy. I would imagine that he plans everything in great detail and well in advance. That means he'll leave as little as possible to chance.'

Fabel had been turning a pencil around between his fingers. He sighed and threw it down onto the table. 'And that means he's less likely to slip up and give us a lead. And a religious motive means, as we already suspected, he could be on some kind of crusade . . . unless it is all a smokescreen. Or at least a partial smokescreen . . .'

'What do you mean?' asked Susanne.

'I don't entirely know what I mean. I've no doubt that our guy believes this crap, but maybe it isn't what drives him. Maybe he's hiding another motive in all of this. Why did he erase everything from Blüm's computer? And why did he steal files? And I'm not the only one who's flagged up the possibility.' Fabel then gave a brief summary of what Brauner had had to say.

'Frau Doktor?' Van Heiden invited a response to Fabel's statement.

Susanne frowned. 'It is possible. People with a motive to murder have often "dressed it up" to fit with some other psychological agenda.' She turned back to Fabel. 'You're saying that there may be a division between motive and method? That there is a need to kill other than for the pleasure or psychotic fulfilment that he derives from the act?

'Exactly.'

'Possible. I can't say it's likely, but it's possible.'

The door of the conference room opened. Maria Klee, clutching a thick file, came in and apologised for being late, although she seemed less than contrite and looked more than a little pleased with herself. Fabel paused for a second before continuing.

'The only way we can be sure,' Fabel continued, 'is to establish more facts. We've got to probe deeper. We must find Klugmann and find out what it is he's withholding from us. If there's a link between the victims we've got to find it. Are we any closer to finding him?'

Anna Wolff answered. 'No, *Chef*. Sorry. Klugmann obviously knows how to stay lost. We've kept a close watch on his girlfriend, Sonja, but there's been no attempt at contact.'

Fabel worried at his chin with a thumb and forefinger. 'I want us to take a closer look at the Odinist connection. I have a name, the Temple of Asatru, that needs checking out. Werner, I'd like you to pay Mr MacSwain a return visit as well and ask him where he was when Angelika Blüm was being murdered.'

'You think he's a possible?'

'Well we didn't have the time to fix a surveillance on him and he could, just about, fit the description we got from the girl outside Blüm's apartment. Although if it's accurate,

MacSwain's hair is too dark.' Fabel paused. His mind had moved on and there was a bitter irritation in his expression. 'There's no way we can build a fact trail between all three victims if we don't have an identity for one of them. We absolutely must crack the identity of Monique. That is our number-one priority. Someone, somewhere, must know who she is.'

Maria Klee slapped the file she had brought in down on the conference table. Everyone looked in her direction: she was grinning broadly, something she was not normally wont to do.

'I do.'

'What?' Van Heiden and Fabel spoke at the same time.

'I know the identity of "Monique". And I have to tell you that this is dynamite, *Chef*.' Maria turned defiantly to Van Heiden. 'And someone, somewhere has been withholding key information from this inquiry.'

'For God's sake, Maria, just tell us who she is.' Fabel's voice was stretched taut and thin. This was the biggest break in the inquiry so far.

'The victim is Tina Kramer. She was twenty-seven.' Maria's simple statement seemed to electrify the stale conference-room air. 'The good news is that I've discovered her identity. The bad news is how I discovered it.'

'Get to the point, Maria,' said Fabel.

'As you know, I did all the usual checks against our own and the Bundeskriminalamt's records. Criminal records, that is. It revealed nothing. So I ran a wider search.' Maria paused, as if allowing the others to brace themselves. 'I widened the search to include police officers.'

Maria flipped open the file and removed a letter-sized, head-and-shoulders photograph. She walked around the table and behind Fabel and secured the image to the board with a pin, next to where Fabel had written 'Monique'. Maria slapped the photograph with the palm of her hand as if to

stamp it indelibly on the inquiry board. She took the cloth
and wiped the name 'Monique' off the board and picked up
a broad-tipped red felt pen, writing 'TINA KRAMER' in large
capitals. Fabel stood up and looked at the face in the photograph: the same face as in the mortuary picture next to it.
The hair was darker than Fabel had remembered it, scraped
severely back. She was wearing a dull mustard service-uniform
shirt with green epaulettes. Behind him, Fabel heard the elec-
trified silence in the room explode into a buzz of excited talk.
Eventually he turned to Maria.

'Shit, I don't believe this . . . She's one of ours?'

'Yes. Or at least partially. She is . . .' Maria corrected herself
– 'she *was* Polizei Niedersachsen, based at Hanover. She was
a Schutzpolizei Kommissarin. From what I've been able to
gather, she was originally from Hamburg and – get this – she
was seconded to the Bundeskriminalamt; specifically to the
BAO here in Hamburg.' Maria scanned down a report in
the file. 'And this is no admin screw-up with records. In 1995,
she was serving with a Polizei Niedersachsen special-weapons
Sonder Einsatz Kommando based in Hanover. There was a
robbery on a security truck and there was a firefight between
the robbers and the unit. She was hit in the leg. Right thigh.
She's our girl all right.'

'She was seconded to the BAO?' Fabel turned to Van
Heiden. His voice was flat and cold.

'No way, Fabel.' Van Heiden made a face and gestured as
if pushing the accusation away. 'No way did I know about
this! The Besondere Aufbau Organisation has a pretty
autonomous structure . . . but by God I'm going to find out
who authorised this without my knowledge or consent.'

'I just want to be clear on this,' Susanne interjected. 'The
BAO is the special unit set up to fight international terrorism?'

'Yes,' Maria answered. 'It is a cooperation between
ourselves, the Bundeskriminalamt, the BND secret service and
the American FBI. Its principal aim is intelligence-gathering.'

'And,' added Fabel, 'they probably run covert operations.'
He turned to Maria. 'Is she still seconded to the BAO?'

'Yes. And her secondment started just over a year ago.'

Van Heiden and Fabel exchanged looks. But it was Werner
who expressed what they all were thinking. 'Just before
Klugmann was discharged from the service. This victim . . .'
he looked at Maria.

'Tina Kramer.'

'This victim, Tina Kramer,' Werner continued, 'is a serving
officer with the BAO, a highly secretive criminal and counter-
terrorism intelligence unit, and she's also ex-SEK. Klugmann
is an ex-Mobiles Einsatz Kommando member.'

Maria Klee returned to her place at the table, leaned back
in her chair and ran her hands through her short blonde hair.
'Added to which is the fact that we have a hidden video
camera and whatever it recorded missing from the scene. All
of this at a time when one of the top organised-crime god-
fathers is assassinated.' She leaned forward, clasping her
hands with interlocking fingers and resting her weight on her
elbows. 'Do you remember I thought I recognised Klugmann?'

'Yes . . . God, that's right,' said Fabel. 'You couldn't place
him though.'

'It's been bothering me. I couldn't place him anywhere. But
when I found out who Tina Kramer was, I thought I'd check
out Klugmann's files at the Bundeskriminalamt. And guess
what, his records stored at Federal Records and his service
record at the Polizei Hamburg don't match. The dates are all
over the place. Specifically his discharge from the army. He
got out six months earlier than his records show here, and
they place him somewhere very interesting indeed.'

'Where?'

'Weingarten.'

Fabel's face was split by a bitter, knowing smile. 'Of course.
I might have known. The NATO Long-Range Reconnaissance
School?'

'Exactly.'

Van Heiden said: 'Fabel?' and made a gesture of impatient confusion.

'We've got the whole bloody lot of them in here now. If it goes by initials then it's involved.' He slumped back into his chair and threw his pencil onto the table. 'The Long-Range Reconnaissance School at Weingarten is where GSG9 is trained. An elite counter-terrorism unit that's officially made up of policemen and is part of the Federal Border Police. But, nevertheless, our British cousins send over their SAS to train GSG9.'

'As soon as I saw that, it all clicked,' said Maria. 'I met Klugmann at a seminar at Weingarten, when I was attached to a Mobiles Einsatz Kommando myself. I can only have said a couple of words to him and I didn't know his name. He was shaven-headed then and a lot slimmer. But I'd bet a month's pay it was Klugmann.' Her mouth tightened into a grim straight line. 'This is an undercover operation. Klugmann is the deep-cover guy, using as much of his real history as possible to give him credibility. Tina Kramer is his control. She has a fake identity but she's not deep cover.'

Fabel drew a deep breath. 'That's it! Damn it. That is exactly where I've been heading with this whole bloody thing. Our so-called random serial killer has taken out an undercover federal agent. That is one hell of a coincidence. Now we have to go back to the first murder, the civic lawyer, and see if there is a fact trail between her and this policewoman. And we have to check them both out against Angelika Blüm.' He turned to Van Heiden. 'We have some serious ass-kicking to do here, Herr Kriminaldirektor. We are up to our necks in dismembered women and these idiots are playing James Bond. We should have been advised about this girl's identity as soon as she was killed.'

'And that,' interrupted Werner, 'is what that twelve-minute telephone call to a non-existent number was all about.'

Fabel slammed his hand onto the table. 'God . . . you're

right! That must have been Klugmann calling in to get instructions. The poor bastard really was in shock that night. He comes across his contact sliced up like butcher meat and he calls his control to find out what to do. They tell him to phone the police but to stay out in the field and under cover. Bastards!' He turned back to Van Heiden. 'This is obstruction and suppression of evidence. I want people behind bars for this. Do I have your support?'

Fabel had expected Van Heiden to be put out by being asked such a question in front of the whole team. Instead Van Heiden's face was drawn tight and hard and determined. 'Whatever you need, Herr Kriminalhauptkommissar, I'll make sure you get it.'

Fabel nodded his thanks. Whatever else he was, Van Heiden was a straight, honest policeman. Fabel turned to his two lieutenants. 'Good work, Maria, bloody good work. And you too, Werner . . . on the phone link.'

'Speaking of which . . .' said Van Heiden picking up the conference-room phone and pressing the button for his secretary. 'Get me Hauptkommissar Wallenstein at BAO . . .'

Fabel signalled urgently for his boss to stop. Van Heiden cancelled the call and replaced the receiver.

'What is it you have in mind, Fabel?'

Fabel slipped Klugmann's cell phone from the evidence bag. He looked questioningly at Van Heiden who gave a curt and serious nod. Fabel switched on the phone and looked at the last number dialled, then keyed it into the conference room phone. The phone at the other end rang three times. Again there was no voice when it was answered.

'This is Kriminalhauptkommissar Fabel of the Polizei Hamburg Mordkommission. I want you to listen very, very carefully and pass this information on to whoever is in charge. Your operation is totally compromised. We know about Tina Kramer and your other operative.' Fabel was careful not to mention Klugmann's name: he was still out there in the field and if Fabel's hunch about who was on the other end of the phone was wrong, it could be a lethal mistake. 'I am sitting with Kriminaldirektor Van Heiden of the Polizei Hamburg and we will be making a full report to the Erste Bürgermeister and to the Bundeskriminalamt.' Fabel paused again. Still no one spoke but he remained connected. Fabel's voice now developed a harder, sharper edge. 'Your operative is in danger and his cover is blown. Whatever you hoped to achieve with this operation is now unachievable. All you are doing now is obstructing a major murder inquiry. If you do not co-operate with our investigation with full transparency, I promise you I will make sure criminal charges are brought against those behind this operation.'

There was an eternity of silence and then a female voice answered.

'Do you have our operative in custody?'

Fabel looked at those gathered around the table with an expression approaching triumph. 'No. He's still at large. We're looking for him. To whom am I speaking?'

She ignored the question. 'We have lost contact with our operative. Please let us know if you locate him. On this number. Someone will call you back shortly, Kriminal-hauptkommissar.' The phone went dead. Fabel gave a bitter laugh.

'I always thought Klugmann was all wrong. I just never thought he'd be wrong in the right way, if you know what I mean.'

'He's still in the job, isn't he?' asked Werner.

'Yep. I don't know for sure for whom, but I've got a pretty damned good idea. Anyway, we'll find out soon enough . . .'

Nobody spoke. No one seemed to notice how bizarre the situation was: a room full of police officers sitting and standing in silence, the tension almost palpable in the air, and every pair of eyes focused on the missing undercover agent's cell phone. Several minutes passed. Then the room seemed to fill with the urgent electronic trilling of the phone. Everybody gave a small jump when it rang.

It was Fabel's turn to remain silent when he picked up the phone and clicked the answer button with his thumb.

'Hauptkommissar Fabel?'

Fabel instantly recognised the tentative voice at the other end, but he was too pissed off for pleasantries. 'Be in my office within the hour, Herr Oberst Volker.'

Fabel hung up.

It had taken Fabel only twenty minutes to wind up the briefing in the conference room, allocating investigative and follow-up tasks to his team. Fabel waited in his office. He put his phone on voice mail and told Werner and Maria he needed a few minutes to gather himself before Volker arrived. He needed to muster the windblown thoughts, facts and theories that had been scattered by the impact on the case of the second victim's revealed identity. He gazed out of his window and looked out across Winterhuder Stadtpark and the city beyond. But he didn't take anything in. Fabel's mind was in the dark-lands: that grey half world Yilmaz had described, where the space occupied by law enforcers lies somewhere between the legal and the expedient and is shadowed and clouded.

It is not easy to be German. You carry the excess baggage of recent history while other Europeans travel comparatively light. Ten centuries of culture and achievement had been eclipsed by twelve years in the mid-twentieth century, twelve years in which the most exceptional evil had become the commonplace. Those twelve years had defined for the world what it was to be German; they had defined for most Germans what it was to be German. Now, they were not trusted. And they could never again trust themselves.

For each German, this distrust had its own focus, an aspect of German life that had a discordant, unsettling resonance. For some, it was geographical: northern Germans mistrusting southerners for their fascistic parochialism; or West Germans, the *Wessis*, mistrusting the *Ossis*, the East Germans, fearing that Nazism had been cryogenically preserved in the deep freeze of Communism and was now beginning to thaw out. For others it was generational: the protestors of 1968 and '69 who rebelled against the war generation and traditional German conservativeness; the new generation who addressed each other with *Du* instead of *Sie*, de-formalising and liberalising the German language itself.

For Fabel, the focus of his mistrust was the hidden machinery of the state: the deep, internal organs of a new democracy that had been transplanted from a dying dictatorship. And right at the centre of that focus, in the spotlight of Fabel's distrust, was the BND.

The Bundesnachrichtendienst had been set up in 1956. It was part of the machinery of the Cold War, the counter to the East German Stasi, or Staatssicherheitsdienst. The first director of the BND had been General Gehlen. The truth was that the BND had been operating since the end of the Second World War as the Organisation Gehlen. Gehlen had been a general in the Abwehr, the Nazi intelligence service, which had planted spies in the United Kingdom, the United States and around the world. The Abwehr had also operated as a counter-espionage unit, tracking down resistance agents and allied spies in occupied Europe. In its duties it had displayed a slightly smaller appetite for torture than the Gestapo or the SS. After the war, the Americans faced a new threat, Soviet Communism, and found themselves naked of any meaningful east-facing intelligence network. But they knew people who had such a network: the Germans. So the 'South German Economic Development Agency' was set up in Pullach, near Munich, and Gehlen was put in charge and told by the Allies he could have access to any personnel he needed.

Gehlen toured the internment camps and liberated dozens

of SS men to join the new intelligence network. And he did so with the full cooperation and consent of the Allies. Now was not the time, apparently, to get sentimental over a few million Jews.

The Organisation Gehlen, and the BND that succeeded it, had been far from successful. The East German Stasi had infiltrated the organisation from the earliest days and there had been a number of spectacular and very public failures. After the reunification of Germany, the BND found itself without its original *raison d'être*, and started to seek a new role. The fight against terrorism, in which it had been engaged since the late 1960s, became a more central function. But now there were emergent Rechtsradikale neo-Nazi groups as well as the established left-wing brands like the Rote-Armee-Fraktion to contend with. In the mid-nineties it had been decided that the BND should become involved in the fight against organised crime, something that Fabel and other career policemen had viewed with profound scepticism. Fabel was aware that the evil machineries of state that the Nazis had emplaced cast long and dark shadows. And for Fabel, the BND lay half hidden in those shadows. Fabel did not trust the BND. Volker was BND.

A few clouds scudded across an otherwise bright sky. Fabel's gaze through the window and across the city remained unfixed, as if he were looking beyond the visible. From Volker to Klugmann. From the BND to GSG9.

Fabel had Klugmann's adulterated personnel file on his desk. He turned from the window and looked again at the photograph. Klugmann's position within the investigation had shifted. The face in the file was the same face, but now Fabel saw it anew, read the features differently. He was pretty certain that Klugmann was an agent of GSG9, which, technically, kept his status as a policeman. GSG9 – Grenzschutzgruppe Neun – was officially part of the Federal German Border Police, but its agents had nothing to do with checking passports or looking under fruit trucks for asylum seekers. GSG9 was, ironically, born out of Germany's mistrust of itself.

The decision to hold the 1972 Olympic Games in Munich had been a turning point in German history. The mental image that came from putting together the concepts of Germany and the Olympian tradition would no longer begin and end with swastikas billowing above the 1936 Games in Berlin.

It was still dark at four-thirty in the morning of 5 September 1972. A small group, dressed like athletes and carrying sports bags, made their way silently through the Olympic village in Munich. Their destination was 31 Connollystrasse. The Israeli team's quarters. Sixteen hours later, the tarmac of Fürsten-feldbruck military airbase, fifteen miles west of the Olympic village, was scattered with the twisted metal of an exploded helicopter, the bodies of five dead Black September terrorists, one policeman and nine Israeli hostages. Two other Israeli athletes had been murdered in the village earlier in the day.

With the atrocities of the SS so vivid in the national memory, Germany had denied itself, under law, the right to create an elite military counter-terrorist unit, such as the British SAS or the American Delta Force. The result of Germany's lack of preparedness had been a disastrous, extemporised rescue attempt by untrained marksmen. The result had also been seventeen dead under the unblinking gaze of the world's media. Within six months GSG9 was in business, masterminded and led by Ulrich Wegener, a forty-three-year-old officer from a patrician, East German family. Wegener had been a thorn in the side of the East German authorities and was imprisoned by the East German Stasi for two years for pro-democracy and pro-reunification campaigning. After his release, Wegener had escaped to the West and had joined the West German security services.

The premise of the new unit was simple: no member of

the armed forces could serve in GSG9, only policemen. Instead of being part of the Bundeswehr army, GSG9 was a 350-strong unit within the Federal Border Police. In 1977, Wegener was to become the hero of GSG9's most successful operation. The unit, supported by two British SAS 'special observers', stormed a hijacked Lufthansa Boeing 707 in Mogadishu after terrorists, demanding the release of Baader-Meinhof members held in Germany, murdered the captain. Wegener himself led the assault and shot dead one of the terrorists. It was GSG9's shining hour.

Then the gleam tarnished. In June 1993, GSG9 tried to arrest Wolfgang Grams, a member of the Rote-Armee-Fraktion in a rail station in Bad Kleinen in eastern Germany. The operation was botched and Grams killed one policeman and wounded another. The official report, borne out by forensic evidence, stated that Grams then shot himself. Civilian witnesses, however, claimed that they saw the GSG9 operatives hold Grams down and shoot him in the head at point-blank range.

The ensuing scandal resulted in careers lost at cabinet level. And GSG9 sank back into the shadows.

Fabel was no fan of GSG9. Or of the Mobile and Sonder Einsatz Kommando units, styled on American SWAT teams, that had sprung up in almost all of Germany's police forces. The line between policeman and soldier was becoming ever less distinct and it went against every instinct Fabel had. Fabel's view on these paramilitary units won him no friends on the upper levels of the Präsidium, particularly when he pointed to the Royal Canadian Mounted Police as an example. The Mounties had set up a unit similar to GSG9. They had called it SERT – the Special Emergency Response Team – and it was a highly efficient counter-terrorist unit. And it had disbanded. The Canadian officers within SERT could not reconcile the imperative to kill imposed by counter-terrorist operations with their natural instincts as police officers to preserve and protect life. Those, Fabel had always thought, were the kind of cops he'd like to serve with.

He focused on Klugmann's face in the service photograph. It was a leaner face than the one that had been opposite him in the whitewashed interview room in the Davidwache station. It was a taut face, the skin pegged tightly to the heavy skull by guy-rope muscles and ligaments. It was the kind of face that told you that the unseen body to which it belonged was powerful and fit. The photograph wasn't that old; Klugmann must have worked at making himself look that little bit run down for his undercover role.

What Fabel couldn't fully understand was why a GSG9 agent was being used to go undercover. GSG9's stealth was a tactical, operational tool, not an intelligence-gathering one. Fabel had no doubt that if Maria was convinced she had encountered Klugmann before at Weingarten then that's exactly where she had seen him. And the two locations GSG9 used for training were Hangelar and Weingarten. There was no doubt, with so many special agencies involved, that whatever the focus of the operation, the objective was a major one. Volker was BND; Klugmann was GSG9. Fabel's guess was that the dead girl, Tina Kramer, had really been BND too. Only the Polizei Hamburg itself seemed to have been excluded. And Fabel had no reason to doubt Van Heiden's word that he knew nothing whatsoever about the operation. So why was the principal law-enforcement agency for Hamburg kept out of the loop?

There was a knock on Fabel's door that was neither tentative nor assured. Volker stepped into Fabel's office without waiting to be invited. Something had bulldozed across Volker's face and swept with it any vestige of geniality. There was no hostility in Volker's expression, neither was there any other recognisable emotion. This, realised Fabel, was Volker behind the affable mask. The dark eyes were empty and the mouth a straight, determined line. Volker had a thick green file tucked under one arm. Fabel gestured towards a chair.

'What is it you want to know, Fabel? I'll tell you what I can.'

When Fabel spoke, there was a steel cord in his voice. 'No, Volker . . . you won't just tell me what you can . . .' Fabel beckoned to Werner, who came in, closed the door very deliberately behind him and leaned his heavy frame against it, folding his meaty arms across his chest. 'You'll tell me *everything* I want to know. And if you don't, I promise you I will put you in a cell, charge you with obstructing a murder inquiry and leak the story to the press before your pals in Pullach can weasel you out of it.'

'We've had a very good reason for playing this close to the chest, Fabel. We are still on the same side, you know.' Volker's face remained expressionless.

'Are we? I'm trying to solve a series of vicious murders and you have been withholding information – key information – from me. I have had people wasting their time all over Hamburg trying to find out who the second victim was while you saunter in and out of the Präsidium with her identity in your pocket. In the meantime a third victim is killed. You fuck about playing secret agents and some poor woman pays with her life.'

'There is no connection between Tina Kramer and either of the other victims.'

'How can you be sure?'

Volker half threw the heavy green file onto the desk. 'It's all there, Fabel. Everything we have on our operation. We were going to share it with you anyway, we just needed Klugmann to come in from the field. We've cross-checked your other two victims with Tina Kramer and there is no link. Tina just happened to be in the wrong place at the wrong time. Your killer must have picked her at random, like the other victims.'

'That's a pile of crap, Volker. Coincidences like that just don't happen.'

'They do, and in this case they did. Agent Kramer wasn't our main undercover operative. That's Klugmann. Kramer ran the apartment as a meeting venue where Klugmann could talk with his underworld contacts. We've set Klugmann up as a corrupt ex-cop, specifically an ex-special-forces police officer, with a grudge against the police. It's all in there . . .' Volker pointed to the file. 'The story was that Kramer rented the apartment from Klugmann as "Monique" with the suggestion she was a hooker. Their arrangement was supposed to be that Klugmann still used the apartment for secret meetings.'

'Meetings with whom? What was the objective of the operation?'

'It was an observation point. Klugmann was placed on the fringes of organised criminal activity without any clear loyalty. He was employed by Hoffknecht, who was in turn employed by Ulugbay, but he wasn't tied in to the Ulugbay organisation. He's been making noises to the effect that he wants to get involved in some serious action.'

'That doesn't answer my question. Who was the target and what were the objectives of the operation?'

'It was an intelligence-gathering op. The specific target was a powerful new Ukrainian outfit that has moved into town. We suspect that they killed Ulugbay.'

Fabel recalled what Mahmoot had told him. He let Volker continue.

'We instigated the operation because no one will talk to us about them. All our usual contacts are too scared. With good reason. Remember I told you we had a very good reason for playing this close to the chest?'

Fabel nodded curtly.

'Well I'm afraid you're not going to like it. Nobody is prepared to talk about this new outfit because they are unbelievably efficient and ruthless in dealing with informers, competitors or simply anyone who gets in their way. What's more, they've made it clear that they have contacts inside the Polizei Hamburg and that they will find out if anyone talks.'

'They've got insiders here? I don't believe it,' Fabel protested.

'That's what our intelligence suggests. We don't know for sure where, but it would have to be at a pretty senior level. That's why the Polizei Hamburg was kept out of the loop. It was a joint BND and BAO operation, and we recruited Klugmann from GSG9. Sorry, but that's how it had to be.'

'What about Buchholz and the Organised Crime Division?'

Volker shook his head. 'No one in the Polizei Hamburg has any knowledge of the operation. The rumour is, believe it or not, that these Ukrainians were previously policemen and Soviet Interior Ministry special forces. They are supposed to have set up contacts with police officers serving in Germany. That's why we gave Klugmann the background he had – we reckoned he'd fit in more easily. And because he had a genuine special-forces background, his cover would stand up to scrutiny. But we couldn't risk a leak, so no one here knows a thing.'

'Presumably that's why you changed Klugmann's records here, and why his federal records don't match up?'

Volker nodded.

'Who heads up this Ukrainian unit?' Werner spoke without moving from the door. Volker did not turn to answer, but spoke to Fabel, as if he had asked the question.

'That was one of the prime objectives of the operation. We don't know. He is totally faceless and nameless at the moment . . .'

Just like our second murder victim was, thought Fabel.

Volker continued. 'Klugmann has made contact, through a member of Yari Varasouv's outfit – or at least the outfit that used to be run by Varasouv – with one of the new

Ukrainian mob. Klugmann only knows his contact as "Vadim" . . . he reckons that his contact is the real deal, but quite low in the pecking order, otherwise he wouldn't be exposed. That said, we believe there's only ten to a dozen in the main group – we call them the Top Team – each of whom is running half a dozen existing "captains" from the old gangs. The way this new outfit operates puts the "organised" in organised crime. The Top Team works almost like the command structure of an occupying army. They have, in effect, removed the governments of each of the top Hamburg gangs, eliminating the gang bosses. That leaves them with a body without a head which they then control. They started with the Ukrainian, Russian and other east-European gangs, then they turned their attention to the Ulugbay organisation. They were taking the structure out from under Ulugbay. And then, of course, they took Ulugbay out of the structure.'

'Why would they talk to someone as small-time as Klugmann's cover suggests he is?'

Volker hesitated. 'We gave Klugmann something to bargain with . . .'

'What?'

'You've got to understand, Fabel, that we are playing against highly dangerous opponents. People who are often unpredictable. It means that sometimes we have to take risks . . .' Fabel didn't know what was coming, but he already knew he wouldn't like it. Volker sighed. 'We gave them the details of the drugs meet where Ulugbay was killed.'

Fabel stared incredulously at Volker. 'You used a law-enforcement operation to help set up a hit on a major under-world figure? Christ, is there nothing you people won't do?'

'Of course we didn't set up the hit!' Volker's indignation was unconvincing. His eyes settled on a spot on Fabel's desk. 'It all turned to shit. Unlike what we've got on this new crowd, our intelligence on Ulugbay is excellent. We gave Klugmann details of a major drugs deal that was set to make

Ulugbay millions. But we didn't expect Ulugbay to turn up in person. Klugmann had details of the initial meeting, the names and details of the Colombians involved, the quantities, et cetera. Klugmann was able to claim that he had got the information through a contact he had some leverage on in the Drugs MEK unit. It was enough to flush out one of the Top Team. Vadim is obviously low down in the Team, but that's all relative when you think of how much power each of them has. Anyway, all we wanted was to give Klugmann credibility. It was not an easy decision to make. We threw away a major drugs bust in the process, but we thought it was worth it to crack the Top Team. We reckoned that the Ukrainians would move in on the deal. We were right. We were more right than we wanted to be. Before we knew it, the Colombians were back on the plane to Bogota and Ulugbay had his brains splattered across an underground Parkhaus.'

'Ulugbay thought he was meeting with the Colombians?'

'Yes. But instead he met with a bullet. Like I say, he was not supposed to be there. We thought that the Ukrainians would muscle in on the deal or at the most heist the drugs.'

'Christ, Volker, you really couldn't have made much more of a mess of things, could you?'

Volker gave Fabel a defiant stare. 'You don't have a clue what we're up against here, Fabel. We have ten or twelve ultra-hard Spetznaz-trained Ukrainians who are all, except one, totally faceless and nameless. Even the rumour trickle has dried up. They're like ghosts, but they have almost all of Hamburg's underworld in their grasp. Only Yilmaz and what's left of the Ulugbay organisation lies outside their control, but not for long. This Ukrainian unit represents the greatest criminal threat to Hamburg ever. We have to take radical measures to stop them.'

Fabel gazed blankly at Volker as he absorbed the information. He could not believe that Volker did not know much more than Mahmoot had already been able to tell him.

'What about the leader? I can't believe you have nothing at all on him.'

'We don't have anything. All we know is that the Top Team is headed up by a former senior officer in the Ukrainian Interior Ministry. We don't have a name, description or even an age, although we suspect that he has served in Chechnya. And he is rumoured to use unspeakable brutality to achieve his aims.'

'Or even make a point? How can you be sure that it wasn't this guy who is behind Tina Kramer's murder?'

'Because it doesn't make any sense. Klugmann's cover has not been blown, except now, by you, and we're going to have to pull him in. But there's nothing to link our operation with your other two victims. And without Klugmann's cover being blown, the Ukrainians have no motive to kill Kramer.'

'What did Klugmann say when he called in to you that night . . . just before he reported the murder to us?'

'He was in a hell of a state. He told us what had happened to Kramer and we recognised it as the same modus as the psycho who killed the first girl. Like I said, we couldn't see a connection, but I had to make an operational decision in the heat of the moment. I ordered Klugmann to come in, to abort the mission. For all we knew it could have been that his cover was blown. I told Klugmann that once we had him safe we would contact the Polizei Hamburg and report the murder.'

'So why didn't that happen?'

'Klugmann is one of the best officers I've ever worked with. He told me to leave him out in the field, to let him handle it, to check out if his cover had been blown and to report the murder to the police.'

Fabel thought back to the Davidwache interview. Klugmann must have enormous internal resources to draw on. He had sat there and taken Werner's insults, Fabel's questioning and absorbed the shock of his partner's horrific murder. He hadn't let the mask slip once. Fabel had had his suspicions, but not this. Over by the door, Werner gave voice to the same thoughts.

'Son of a bitch! He has balls, I'll give you that. Is he safe?'

'We don't know. We've lost contact. You grabbed his secure cell phone, so we can't reach him on that. And he hasn't called in to us. We're very concerned.'

It was at that point that Maria Klee rapped on the door. Maria's face had a hard, determined look on it and she gestured for Werner to step out of the office.

Volker turned back to the Kriminalhauptkommissar. 'You have to believe me, Fabel, if we had thought there was any connection between Kramer's death and the operation, I would have come straight to you. In any case, we were only holding out until we located Klugmann.'

Fabel was about to say something when Werner came back in, his face like stone.

'It doesn't look like you need to worry about Klugmann any more,' he said. 'The Harburg Polizeidirektion have just found a body in a disused swimming pool. And the rough description matches your boy.'

Monday 16 June, 11.50 a.m. Hamburg-Harburg, Hamburg.

Fabel, Werner and Maria Klee stood at the chipped edge of a swimming pool that had not seen water in years. Volker had come along, but Fabel had made him wait at the cordon. 'The fewer people at the crime scene the better . . . at least until the forensic guys have done their stuff,' Fabel had explained half-heartedly to Volker. The truth was he was finding it increasingly difficult to stomach Volker's presence. Volker was part of a half world, the domain of greys and shadows that Yilmaz had described, and Fabel wanted as little as possible to do with him or his world.

Despite it being nearly noon and despite the absence of all but the occasional shard of glass in the windows that ran the length of one wall, the swimming pool had a gloom to it, as if the grime from the walls and floor had pervaded the air and dulled the light. Now the filth of the swimming pool was accentuated by the stark arc lights that the Tatort forensic team had set up. There were used syringes, condoms, litter and, in one corner, what looked like human excrement. Fabel couldn't imagine a seedier place to die.

A six-strong Tatort team, clad in white forensic overalls were sifting through the filth. Brauner, the head of the team, squatted down beside the body. Klugmann's hands had been tied behind his back and a sack placed over his head. Brauner had carefully cut away the sacking, which had half stiffened with blood that had caked and dried. He looked up and nodded when he realised Fabel was behind him, standing at the pool edge.

'He was shot while kneeling where you are,' said Brauner. 'Execution style and straight through the brain stem. A really professional job. He would have been dead before he hit the bottom. The bullet exited above the mouth.'

'How long has he been dead?'

'You'll have to ask Möller when he examines the body, but from the temperature, the post-mortem lividity and the easing of rigor, I'd say at least a couple of days. Maybe three.'

One of the team called out from the corner of the pool. 'Herr Brauner. Over here!'

Fabel followed Brauner up to where the forensic technican had called.

'Here . . .' The technician pointed to a small metal cylinder that glittered among the dust and debris on the floor. Brauner squatted down on his heels and carefully picked up the object.

'A nine-millimetre cartridge.' Brauner carefully picked up the casing between latex sheathed thumb and forefinger.

'And lying in clear sight of the shooter,' said Fabel. 'A piece of evidence he could easily have denied us just by casting a quick eye around him. An amateurish mistake for such a professional killer to make.'

Brauner shrugged. 'Maybe it was dark. Or maybe he thought he was about to be discovered and made a quicker exit than he'd planned.'

'Could be . . .' Fabel was far from convinced. He could see from the creases on Brauner's brow that something was troubling him. 'What is it?'

'This cartridge is a nine-millimetre all right, but it's not from a common automatic. What is it you carry? A SIG-Sauer P6?'

'A Walther P99.'

'This wouldn't fit either. Most nine-mils are based on either the Smith and Wesson or the Walther configurations. I suspect this is a nine-by-nine-by-seventeen. It's non-standard ammo for a non-standard firearm.'

'Any idea what?'

'Not at this stage. We'll be able to narrow it down to a few makes, but it'll take time.'

Möller, the pathologist, arrived. Fabel nodded an acknowledgement.

'He's been dead a couple of days,' Fabel told Möller as he made his way to the door out of the pool. He smiled at Möller's indignation and made his way out into the fresh air. Volker was half leaning, half sitting on the wing of one of the green and white Schutzpolizei cars.

'Is it Klugmann?'

'Looks like. But we'll have to wait until Möller turns him over and we can see his face.'

A silent minute passed before Werner and Maria emerged, followed by the body, sheathed in a black body bag and on a wheeled trolley between two pathology technicians.

'It's Klugmann all right,' said Werner, grimly.

Volker stepped forward and stopped the technicians with

a gesture of his hand. He sniffed a lungful of air as if preparing himself and then nodded curtly towards the body bag. One of the technicians pulled on a long tab; the zipper peeled open with a resonant rasp to expose the empurpled face of Hans Klugmann. Much of what had been between his teeth and his nose had been blasted into the crater of an exit wound. Volker made a face and nodded again to the technician who re-zipped Klugmann into his vinyl cocoon. He turned to Fabel; the dark eyes glittered with something between pain and anger.

'He was a brave man. And a good and honest policeman. You can understand that, Fabel.' Volker paused and watched the body being loaded into the mortuary wagon. 'I recruited him myself, Fabel. I sent him on this operation and I didn't insist he came in when the girl was killed. It's my fault he's dead.'

'I rather think it is,' said Fabel, without a hint of maliciousness.

Monday 16 June, 2.00 p.m. Altona, Hamburg.
Sonja Brun's pretty face had the sore, inflamed look that only comes with an hour of constant crying. Even now, although the effort had dulled the pain in her red-rimmed eyes, she somehow found the energy to rack her body with intermittent, deep sobs. Fabel had made it clear to a furious Volker that this was now a Mordkommission case and he would treat any intervention by Volker as obstruction. Volker had no choice but to take it on the chin, and had accepted the scrap of being allowed to tag along when Fabel and Werner interviewed Sonja. He had winced when Fabel had revealed to Sonja that Klugmann had been working as an undercover federal agent. She had not been able to accept it and Fabel saw her eyes working through every moment, every word she had shared with Klugmann.

'But he said we were going to get married . . . that we would get out of Hamburg and start over somewhere else, once he had this big deal done . . . was that all a lie?' Her eyes searched Fabel's pleadingly.

'No, Sonja. I honestly don't believe it was. He cared about you. I'm sure he did . . .'

They questioned Sonja about the Ukrainians, the big deal Klugmann had talked about, when he had gone out, who she had seen him with. Fabel tried to keep the pace slow and easy, allowing her a moment between each answer. No, she had never seen 'Vadim'. No, Klugmann had never mentioned him. Yes, he would often go out late when he was off work to meet with people about his 'big deal'.

They got nowhere. Sonja started to sob again, apologising for not being able to help. Fabel suggested they leave it there and crossed the living area to the kitchen and made a cup of green tea from a pack he found on the counter top. He placed the cup in Sonja's hands.

'Just one more question, Sonja. Did Hans own a video camera?'

Sonja frowned above the red-rimmed eyes and shook her head.

'Did he ever bring one home? Or did you ever see a tape cartridge from a video camera?'

Again a puzzled look, a shrug and a shake of the head.

They left Sonja alone in the apartment she had shared with a man she thought she had known, but who had really been a *Bulle* living a lie with her as a stage prop. There was no one to sit with her: no relatives, no friends. She was just a pretty girl left on an empty stage. A girl who just a couple of days before had swung her shopping bags as she strolled back to her flat and her lover, her head filled with dreams of a new life in a new place. Now she would no doubt sink back into the life of prostitution and porno films. Fabel had no idea if Klugmann had really loved Sonja or had ever intended to marry her, but he knew that he had cared enough to seek to liberate her from a degrading way of life.

As he closed the apartment door behind him, Fabel made a silent promise to a dead policeman.

Monday 16 June, 10.50 p.m. Pöseldorf, Hamburg.

It was nearly eleven by the time Fabel got home. He had re-gathered the team to go through everything that had happened. They now knew that 'Monique' was Tina Kramer, a BAO operative. Klugmann was dead. Volker claimed no connection between his investigation and the ritualistic murder of Tina Kramer. MacSwain was now officially under surveillance. Fabel had negotiated with Van Heiden and agreed on a team of six, which had to include two team leaders from the Mordkommission. Van Heiden didn't like hunches. More specifically he didn't like committing a Polizei Hamburg budget on a hunch, but he let Fabel have his way. Fabel had put Paul and Anna in charge of the surveillance, knowing that they needed a display of confidence from Fabel after they had lost Klugmann only for him to turn up dead.

They had also gone over Angelika Blüm's murder again. Brauner, the forensic team leader, had reported back that no physical evidence had been found on Blüm's laptop. According to Technical Section, whoever had wiped the files from the computer's hard drive had done so thoroughly, prob-ably using an external device to do so. It was the work of an expert with sophisticated kit at his disposal. Möller's preliminary autopsy report confirmed his initial observations. Maria Klee had produced something new but, she admitted, pretty tangential. She had placed an exhibition programme on the table. It was for an exhibition of works, in Bremen, by Marlies Menzel. It was not so much that the name was familiar to Fabel as that it stabbed into the memory centre of his brain. Marlies Menzel had only recently been released from Stuttgart-Stammheim Prison. She was a former member of Svensson's Radikale Aktionsgruppe and had taken part in the robbery in which Fabel had been wounded. The day he put two bullets into the face of a seventeen-year-old girl.

The exhibition was called *Germany Crucified*. Fabel had felt a fluttering in his chest as he looked at the photographic plates of the paintings. Each canvas comprised of vivid splashes and smears of blood red, black and an orangey yellow: the colours of the German flag. Each canvas was slightly different, but all used the same colours and all displayed an indistinct figure, crucified and screaming. Fabel understood instantly why Maria had brought the programme to his attention: there was something vaguely but disturbingly reminiscent of the Blood Eagle murder scenes. He had nodded to Maria and had suggested they pay Frau Menzel a visit.

After the meeting, Fabel had spoken to Kolski and Buchholz at LKA7 Organised Crime and had told them about the BND operation and about Klugmann's execution at the swimming pool. Fabel had watched them both as he spoke: their anger seemed genuine, but not as deep as he would have expected; perhaps when you're in the business of dealing with organised crime, you become inured to deceit. At any rate, Fabel had no reason to doubt that Buchholz, just as Volker had claimed, had known nothing about the operation.

Fabel had been dog tired when he got home. He poured himself a glass of wine and slumped into the leather sofa without putting on his living-room lights. Through the picture windows of his apartment the city's lights glittered on the mirror of the Alster. He tried not to think about Angelika Blüm's voice on the phone, about her ripped-apart body, about Klugmann lying in the filth of a disused swimming pool, about a drugged girl staggering into the path of a truck. But the images danced randomly inside his head like bees trapped in a jar. He sipped the white wine and found it acid in his mouth. He placed the glass on the side table and resolved to make the gargantuan effort that would be involved in getting into bed. Before he got off the sofa the lead in his eyelids succumbed to gravity and Fabel drifted into a deep sleep.

He woke up with a start at one-thirty a.m. from a dream in which he'd been forced to watch the snuff movie he had seen as part of an earlier murder investigation. This time it was Sonja Brun's face that had blackened and twisted in terror and instead of PVC bondage masks the men in the video wore masks of one-eyed Odin. Fabel stripped and went to bed, but found that his exhaustion was unable to drag his racing mind to a halt. After an hour of tossing and turning in his bed he rose and dressed again. He grabbed his car keys and went out into the night.

Fabel stopped by the Präsidium to pick up Blüm's apartment keys. He didn't know what he expected to find there, but he felt the need to be surrounded by her things, to walk through what had been her life. At the very least it was as good a place as any to think.

It was a quarter past three when he pulled up outside the apartment block. Fabel parked just about where the girl from the apartment had said her male companion had pulled up. The lights of the lobby still burned brightly and anyone approaching the glass doors would be clearly illuminated. But, at this distance, any description would have had to be as general as the girl had given. A tall, well-dressed, blond man with broad shoulders. But was he the killer?

Fabel took the elevator to the third floor. He stood for a moment before opening the door to the apartment. He stared as if he could see through the wood of the door and into the darkness of the apartment. He found himself remembering the last time he had unlocked this door and opened up a gate to hell and how yet another image of grotesque death had been branded into the matter of his brain. He shook such thoughts free from his head and turned the key. Having

switched on the hall's downlighters, he made his way towards
Blüm's office. Again he found himself unconsciously bracing
before switching on the lights. Once more the sudden illumination revealed an unexpected scene; not one of horror
this time, but one of surprise. Blüm's office had been very
professionally ransacked. Drawers had been carefully
removed from the desk and cabinets and books and files from
the shelves that lined the wall; the furniture had been turned
over so the undersides could be checked. The room could
not be described as being in chaos; it was far too systematic
for that. And Fabel knew that Brauner's team had not left it
in this state. Someone else had been here.

The thought sparked only for a millisecond before a sudden
feeling ruffled the hairs on Fabel's neck. Someone else *was*
there.

Fabel became a statue. He listened to the stillness of the
apartment with such intensity that it amplified the surge of
blood in his ears and the sound of metal sliding against the
stiff leather of his holster as he drew his Walther. He had his
back to the office door and felt exposed. Turning swiftly and
silently, he slipped back into the hall. Silence. He stood
unmoving for half a minute, straining to hear any sounds
from the other rooms. Still nothing. The tension eased, but
only slightly, from his body and he moved silently along the
corridor. Back against the wall, gun raised in his right hand,
he pushed the door of the bedroom as wide open as it would
go. He swung round into the frame and scanned the room
along his gun sight. He took one hand from his gun and
fumbled for the light switch. The room was empty. Fabel
gave a small laugh: he was being an idiot. He led the gun
hang by his side and turned back into the corridor.

The first thought Fabel registered was surprise. How had
the man moved so silently and quickly? He must have been
in the main living room, waiting to strike. Fabel's gun arm
shot up but he looked down in disbelief as it stopped dead

in mid-arc. His attacker had a solid, unyielding grip and Fabel felt as if the bones of his wrist were being crushed into splinters. The pressure seemed to force his hand into an open palm and his Walther clattered onto the wooden flooring. The man was close now and Fabel tried to swing his other fist upwards, but his attacker fastened his free hand around Fabel's throat. In the adrenalin-slowed time of the attack, Fabel realised that his airway was not blocked, but that his assailant was applying intense pressure to his neck, just below the angle of his jaw. Fabel tried to call out but found himself mute. As the world around him started to cloud into blackness, all Fabel could do was wonder if this was what it was to die, and gaze, fearful and helpless, into the cold, glittering green eyes of the man he had seen outside the Tina Kramer murder scene.

Tuesday 17 June, 5.20 a.m. Uhlenhorst, Hamburg.
The first thing Fabel became aware of was pain: a pain that exceeded all definition of a headache, that surpassed any hangover: a buzz-saw that seared through his skull. Then the sound of birds, heralding the breaking day with their chorus. Fabel lifted his head slightly and was rewarded with a cold dagger of pain that sliced through him. He let his head fall back again. He had no idea where he was or how he had got there or even what day of the week it was. It took almost a minute for his full consciousness to boot up. The Slavic guy. He sat bolt upright and was shocked with another, even greater jolt, this time with an accompanying surge of vertigo and nausea. He lunged over the side of the bed and vomited. The surging ache in his head did not abate, but he embraced it. Pain meant he was alive. He flopped back onto the bed and fumbled in his pocket for his cell phone. It was gone. So was the gun from his holster. He eased himself up slowly so that he could look around the room. He was on Angelika

Blüm's bed. The Slav must have put him there. The pain in Fabel's head wrapped a shroud around every thought. In the pale grey light he could see that his cell phone, his handgun and his wallet were carefully laid out on the dresser. It took him another five minutes to ease himself off the bed and stagger over to the dresser. He dragged his cell phone across the maple dresser top and stabbed the preset number for the Präsidium.

By lunchtime, every policeman, uniform and KriPo, had a description of the short, powerfully built Slav who had attacked Fabel. The doctor at the Krankenhaus St Georg who examined Fabel could not conceal how impressed he was with the professionalism of the attack. The Slav had very efficiently cut off the blood supply to Fabel's brain, rendering him unconscious. There had been little permanent damage done, although the pain Fabel was experiencing was the result of brain cells dying, starved of oxygen. The hospital staff insisted on keeping Fabel in overnight for observation and Fabel felt too exhausted and sore to argue. He yielded to a peaceful, dreamless sleep.

Fabel woke shortly after two p.m. The nurse fetched Werner and Maria Klee, who had been waiting patiently outside for Fabel to awake. Maria, with an uncharacteristic informality, sat on the edge of Fabel's bed. Werner stood, awkwardly. It was as if he felt uncomfortable seeing his boss so vulnerable. He dragged a chair from the corner and sat down only when Fabel insisted that he do so.

'You sure it was the guy you saw outside the second murder scene?' Werner asked.

'No doubt about it. I was looking straight into his eyes.'

Werner's face hardened. 'So he's our guy. He's "Son of Sven" . . .'

Fabel frowned. 'I don't know. If he is, why didn't he kill me?'

'He had a bloody good try,' said Maria.

'No . . . I don't think he did. The doctor here says it was very professional . . . that he knew how to render me unconscious. If he wanted to kill me he could have finished me off, silently and with no fuss, instead of laying me out on Blüm's bed.'

'But we've sighted him at two murder locations. That more than makes him a suspect,' protested Werner.

'But why was he there *after* the murder? And why choose now to turn over her apartment, instead of when he was there committing the murder?'

'Maybe he thought he'd left something behind,' Maria suggested.

'We all know this killer doesn't leave anything behind. Anyway, Brauner's team went through that apartment at a microscopic level. They wouldn't miss anything, and our guy would know that. The other thing is, the guy who attacked me doesn't fit the description the girl from the apartment building gave us.' Fabel paused. The sunlight through the tall, narrow hospital window sliced a bright triangle across the floor of Fabel's room and glittered coldly on the porcelain and the stainless-steel pipes and taps of the washstand by the door. His head ached and he closed his eyes and leaned back against the pillow. He spoke without opening his eyes. 'What is really bothering me is the strength of that old guy, and the way he was able to put me out so professionally. That takes training.'

Werner stretched his legs out, resting his feet on the steel bars beneath Fabel's hospital bed. 'Well, both you and Maria say he looks foreign. Like a Russian. If he is so handy, could he be one of the "Top Team" – the Ukrainian outfit Volker was talking about?'

'Could be, I suppose.' Fabel still didn't open his eyes. 'Everything about him says special forces. But again, why didn't he finish the job?'

'It's a big thing to kill a Hamburg policeman,' said Werner. 'Klugmann is one thing, but murder a Mordkommission Hauptkommissar and you'd have nowhere to hide.'

'Whoever he was and whatever he was doing there,' said Maria, 'we've got the whole of Hamburg out there looking for him.'

Fabel slowly eased himself up, the effort stretching his voice. 'I'm not so sure he's going to be that easy to find, Maria. What about MacSwain? Have we got him under close watch?'

'Paul and Anna are on him tight,' said Werner. 'They're there most of the time, even when we've got others on shift. I think they're afraid of another screw-up like the Klugmann surveillance.'

'Good. I'll be out of here tomorrow and we can go over everything. In the meantime, if anything comes up, let me know.'

'Okay, *Chef*,' said Werner. Fabel closed his eyes again and rested his head on the pillow. Werner looked across to Maria and jutted his chin in the direction of the door. Maria nodded and rose from the bed.

'We'll see you later, *Chef*,' she said.

The day passed between gazing out of the window, flicking through the daytime TV stations in the vain search for anything worth watching, and sleeping. As the day went on, Fabel became aware of a growing stiffness in his neck and a tenderness below the angle of his jaw, where the Slav's thumb had squeezed off the blood supply to his brain.

Susanne breezed in mid-afternoon and immediately started to examine Fabel, holding his eyelids back with her thumb and checking each of his eyes in turn and rotating his head with her hands to assess the mobility of his neck.

'If this is your idea of foreplay,' grinned Fabel, 'I have to tell you it isn't doing it for me.'

Susanne was not in the mood for jokes. Fabel saw that she was genuinely upset and it touched him. She sat on the bed and held his hand for a couple of hours, sometimes talking, sometimes in silence, while Fabel dozed. When a nurse came in to usher her out, Fabel was amazed at the fierce authority with which Susanne dismissed her. Susanne stayed until after six and then came back for an hour in the evening. By nine-thirty, Fabel had abandoned himself to a deep, impenetrable, dreamless sleep.

Tuesday 17 June, 8.30 p.m. Harvestehude, Hamburg.
Anna Wolff could have been a secretary, a hairdresser, a kindergarten teacher. She was petite and vibrant, with a pretty round face that was continually full of energy and habitually made up with dark eye-shadow, mascara and fire-truck-red lipstick. Her short hair was raven black and either sleeked flat or waxed spiky. One of the things that threw observers off of any track that would lead them to conclude that she was, in fact, a Kriminalkommissarin, was her youthfulness. Anna was twenty-seven but could have passed for someone in her late teens.

Paul Lindemann, on the other hand, couldn't have been anything other than a policeman. Lindemann's father, like Werner Meyer's father, had been a Wasserschutz policeman, patrolling by boat Hamburg's circulatory system of water-ways, canals, harbours and quaysides. Paul was one of those northern Germans whom Fabel described as 'scrubbed Lutherans', clean, groomed, austere people who often found it difficult to bend to change. Paul Lindemann looked today pretty much as he would have done if he had been the same age in the 1950s or '60s.

Fabel habitually teamed up Anna and Paul. They were chalk and cheese, and Fabel had always believed in putting together teams of individuals who viewed things totally differently: if you came at the same object from opposing angles, you were likely to see more of the whole. Anna and Paul made an odd couple and for months the imposed partnership had sat ill with both of them. Now they worked together with deep mutual respect and regard for their respective, different but complementary talents. It was the kind of success Fabel had hoped to achieve with Maria and Werner, whose potential as a team had yet to be realised.

Tonight, both Anna and Paul felt edgy. Fabel was more than a boss. He had been mentor to both of them and had, by selecting them for his Mordkommission team, set the sights higher for their future careers. To both, Fabel had seemed invulnerable. Now he was lying in a hospital bed in the Krankenhaus St Georg. They would have given anything to have been out searching for Fabel's attacker, rather than keeping tabs on some British yuppie.

There was a newspaper and tobacco stall on the corner of MacSwain's street. A coffee machine sat behind the counter and outside there was the usual brushed aluminium elbow-high tables for customers to stand and drink their coffee. Anna stood at one of the four tables, from which she had a clear view of the crossroads and MacSwain's apartment block as well as the exit from the Tiefgarage underneath. If anyone came out, on foot or by car, Anna would be able to track the direction they took and radio to Paul, who was parked further down the block with a view from the other direction. It was dark now and Anna was on her third coffee, which she was trying to make last. Any more would mean a jittery, sleepless night. The sullen, overweight stallholder barely acknowledged her existence, but when three skinheads in their uniform of field-green jerkins came up to buy some cigarettes, he muttered something to them and nodded in her direction. The fat stallholder and the skinheads burst into crude laughter. Anna kept her gaze firmly on the apartment building. The three skinheads came up to Anna's table, one on one side and two on the other. One of the skins, a tall, bull-necked youth with bad skin, leaned into Anna.

'What's up darlin', you been stood up?'

Anna neither answered nor looked in their direction.

The bull-necked skinhead leered at his comrades and laughed. 'I'd get all stood up for you, babe . . .'

'What, all ten centimetres of you?' said Anna with a sigh and still without looking in the skinhead's direction.

Bull-Neck's two companions exploded into laughter, pointing at him derisively. His face clouded and he pulled close to Anna, slipping his hand under her leather jacket and closing it around her breast.

'Maybe we'll see how much of me you can take . . .'

It all happened too fast for Bull-Neck to register. Anna spun around away from the skinhead and then back to face him, throwing his hand away as if with centrifugal force. As she came around to face him again, her hands moved in two swift movements. Her left hand reached down and grabbed the skinhead's groin while her right elbow slammed into his cheek and then, in a seamless movement, her right hand slipped under her jacket, bringing her SIG-Sauer automatic up and into his face. Hard. She pushed him back, not allowing him to get purchase with his scrabbling feet until he slammed into the stall's counter. She bent his nose out of shape with the muzzle of the gun, twisting it as she spoke.

'You wanna fuck with Anna?' she said in a coquettish voice, tilting her head from side to side and pouting her lips.

Bull-Neck stared at her with terror in his eyes, searching her face as if to assess the extent of her madness and the consequent extent of his danger. Anna swung the gun around at the other two skinheads, stretching her arm out, bolt stiff.

'What about you boys? You wanna fuck with Anna?'

Bull-Neck's companions held up their hands and backed away for a few paces before breaking into a run. Anna turned back to Bull-Neck and rammed the muzzle back into his nose, twisting and rotating it as if toying with it. His face started to smear with the blood that had begun to trickle from his nose. Anna made a girlish, disappointed face.

'They don't want to fuck with Anna . . .' She dropped the cute voice. 'What about you, dickless? You wanna play?'

The skinhead shook his head vigorously. Anna's eyes narrowed and darkened.

'If I ever hear you've laid hands on a woman like that again, I'll come after you personally. Where's your ID?'

He scrabbled in the pockets of his jerkin and took out his identification card. Anna released his crushed testicles and examined the card.

'Okay Markus, now I know where you live. Maybe I'll come visit and we can play some more.' She leaned forward into his face and hissed. 'Now fuck off!' She threw his ID onto the ground so that he had to stoop to pick it up, clutching his bruised groin, before running off in the opposite direction to that taken by his companions. Anna holstered her sidearm and turned to the stallholder.

'Is there a problem, tubby?' she said, smiling her sweetest schoolgirl smile.

The stallholder shook his head and held up his hands. 'No problem at all, Fräulein.'

'Then give me another coffee, fatboy.' Anna turned back to look at the apartment block. MacSwain's lights had gone out. She scanned the exits and the street outside. Nothing. She slipped her radio out from her jacket pocket.

'Paul . . . I think MacSwain is moving . . . you see him come out?'

'No. You?'

'No. Got tied up.' She released the button on her radio and depressed it immediately again when she saw a silver Porsche angle up and out of the exit of the Tiefgarage. 'We're on the move. Pick me up, Paul, and *zack, zack!*'

In a matter of seconds, Paul pulled up in the battered old

Mercedes used for surveillance. Battered on the outside, tuned to peak performance under the hood.

The muscles of Paul's usually expressionless face were struggling with a wry grin as Anna climbed into the car. With her spiky hair, her meticulous make-up and her oversized leather jacket, she looked like a schoolgirl not yet accustomed to the subtleties of cosmetics, going out on her first night clubbing.

'What's so funny, *Schlaks*?' she asked, using the north-German dialect word for 'lanky'.

'You've been playing again, haven't you?'

'I don't know what you mean,' Anna said, keeping focused on the silver Porsche, two cars ahead.

'While I was parked down the road, two skinheads came running past as if they'd seen the Devil. That wouldn't be you, would it?'

'I have absolutely no idea what you mean.'

They pulled up behind a queue at a set of traffic lights. Paul craned his long neck to check if the Porsche had already gone through. It hadn't. He turned to look at Anna and saw, through the passenger side window, a thickset skinhead, bent over, hands on knees, trying to catch his breath. His face was smeared with blood. He was looking back down the road as if to check he was not being pursued. His eyes came round and met Paul's. Then he saw Anna. She blew him a long, sensual kiss with her full, fire-truck-red lips, punctuating it with a smacking sound. The skinhead froze with terror, then looked around for an escape route. The lights changed and the Mercedes started to move. Anna crinkled her nose at him and waggled her fingers in a cute 'bye-bye'.

'Absolutely no idea at all,' said Anna, her face an expression of exaggerated innocence. Paul checked his rear-view mirror. The skinhead was standing in sag-shouldered relief, gazing blankly after the car.

'Anna, just be careful. One of these days you're going to end up biting off more than you can chew.'

'I can handle myself.'

'And one of these days you're going to end up with a harassment or brutality claim against you.'

Anna barked a laugh. She gestured with her hand for Paul to take the next left: the Porsche's indicator was blinking. 'No self-respecting neo-Nazi skinhead fuckwit is going to admit to having his ass kicked by a one-metre-fifty-eight Jüdin. And if they did, it would be laughed out of court.'

Paul shook his head. Anna, he knew, came from a survivor family: Hamburg Jews who had been hidden by a sympathetic family until the British and the Canadians took Hamburg. She had grown up spiked with defences; defences that had been honed by martial-arts training and three years' service in the Israeli army.

The sky had turned a velvet blue. Paul focused on the silver Porsche; MacSwain led them out onto Hallerstrasse. The municipal high-rise flats of the Grindelhochhäuser loomed into the darkness. They could have been in an estate in London, Birmingham or Glasgow. The flats had, in fact, been built after the war to hold the families of the soldiers of the British occupying forces. When the British moved out, they handed the flats over to the Hamburg authorities. Now the Grindelhochhäuser, shunned by the population of Hamburg, were occupied mainly by immigrant families. Ukrainian gangs were rumoured to hold sway in this imported concrete jungle.

MacSwain crossed into Beim Schlump and passed Sternschanzen-Park. He turned into Schanzenstrasse.

'He's heading towards St Pauli,' said Anna.

'Where the second victim was found.' Paul gave Anna a quick look. 'But he's probably just off for a night out . . .'

It is almost as if St Pauli lies dormant during the day, absorbing the sun's energy. At night it explodes into supercharged life. As well as the sex trade and musical shows, it has one of the most vibrant club scenes in Europe with venues like The Academy, PAT, Location One and Cult attracting clubbers from all over the city and beyond. Even on a Tuesday night, one of the least pleasure-focused days in the north-German psyche, the party goes on until dawn.

MacSwain parked in the Spielbudenplatz Parkhaus. Paul dropped Anna at the entrance to watch for MacSwain coming out and parked further down the street. He then took up a position opposite the entrance, in front of Schmidt's Tivoli. MacSwain emerged from the Parkhaus. He was dressed casually but expensively and moved with a relaxed assurance. He didn't notice Anna, who turned away and crossed the road before making a U-turn to follow on behind. In the meantime, Paul had picked up MacSwain and was walking about three metres behind him, but on the opposite side of the road.

MacSwain led them out of Spielbudenplatz, diagonally crossed Davidstrasse in front of the Davidwache police station and into Friedrichstrasse. Anna caught up with Paul and linked her arm through his, a simple gesture of intimacy that instantly transformed them into a couple. They passed the Albers-Eck, with its landmark corner doorway. Somewhere, one of the pubs was having a *Schlager* night, and the enthusiastic blandness of German middle-of-the-road music spilled out into the street. MacSwain crossed Hans-Albers-Platz and walked into a dance club, receiving a nod of acknowledgement from one of two doormen who looked as if between them they kept the German steroid industry in business.

'Shit,' said Anna. 'What do you reckon?'

Paul drew air in through his teeth. 'Don't know . . . it's going to be heaving in there. If we go in he could come out before we even lay eyes on him. And if we hang around out here, we're going to stick out like a sore thumb.' He quickly surveyed the square. 'We could get some back-up to park themselves out here, but we're exposed while we wait . . . Let's go in and see if we can find him. If we can't, we meet back at the door in fifteen minutes. Okay?'

Anna nodded her assent. She led the way up the steps to the nightclub. One of the huge doormen looked at Anna's leather jacket and laughed derisively. As she passed him he placed a restraining hand on her left shoulder. Anna's right hand shot diagonally across her body and grabbed the bouncer's beefy thumb. The doorman tilted sideways, singing an 'ahhhh' song as he stared at his thumb, amazed that it could bend that far.

'No touchie!' said Anna sweetly.

The other hulk moved forward. Paul stepped in his way, holding his Kriminalpolizei shield in the doorman's face. The heavy stepped back and swung the door open for Anna to enter. She let the doorman's thumb go and he cradled it in his other hand.

'She's taking anger-management classes . . .' Paul said to the swollen-thumbed doorman, and chuckled at his own witticism.

The dull bass throbbing they had heard outside the club exploded into an ear-splitting blast of dance music as they swung open the doors from the hall into the main dance area itself. Strobe lighting and lasers pulsed with the music. There were hundreds of clubbers on the dance floor, which was sunk lower than the walkways that circled it. The seething mass of bodies was not as impenetrable as it would be later in the week. Still, it was a daunting task to find one person in this throng.

Anna turned to Paul and shrugged the too-big shoulders of her leather jacket.

'What's the first thing you do when you come into a club?'

'Get a drink?'

Paul nodded, scanning the periphery of the dance floor. There was a wide, sweeping bar slightly elevated at the far side. They split up and made their separate ways on either side of the dance floor, each scanning it for any sign of MacSwain. They arrived simultaneously at opposite ends of the horseshoe bar. There is an art to sweeping a space for a suspect without drawing attention to yourself: Paul didn't have it. Nature and northern-German genetics had conspired to make him look as if his natural attire should be a SchuPo uniform. Here, surrounded by trendily and often scantily attired clubbers, Paul knew his best bet was to shrink as far back as possible into the undergrowth the environment provided. He squeezed his way to the bar and ordered a beer.

From his vantage point, Paul could see Anna. She was a master at this. She managed to make it appear that her attention was focused on the music and the dance floor, while glancing only occasionally and disinterestedly at the bar. She was coming towards Paul when she spotted MacSwain. The first thing that struck Anna was his looks; she had never seen MacSwain close up before and had used an identity photograph Fabel had secured from immigration as a reference. He had a broad, strong face with a heavily caged jaw and broad, pronounced cheekbones. His eyes were a glittering emerald.

MacSwain was engaged in a conversation with two blondes at the bar, who seemed to hang on his every word, laugh on cue and gaze hypnotised into the green jewel eyes. Anna was aware she had been staring at him a little too long and turned her back to the group. She let her eyes drift slowly across the dance floor until they came to rest on Paul. A subtle movement of her eyes signalled MacSwain's position and Paul nodded acknowledgement. Casually, she turned back to check MacSwain was still there. He was. And his green, penetrating gaze was fixed on her. Anna felt an internal flutter of shock but sealed it tight inside, making sure nothing showed in her face. She looked away from MacSwain, everywhere and anywhere other than at Paul, which would give MacSwain a signpost to his other observer. Her heart thudded in her chest, yet she maintained an outer cool.

She allowed her gaze to return to MacSwain. His eyes were

still fixed on her. The two blondes were engaged in a giggling conversation with each other. Shit, she thought, he's sussed me. The corners of MacSwain's lips curled in a knowing smile. All Anna could hope for was that if she slipped out of the picture, Paul could stay on him while she radioed up a new set of faces. She cursed silently to herself. They'd fucked up another surveillance. Fabel was lying in that hospital bed and when he got back to the Präsidium he'd discover she'd allowed MacSwain to eyeball her. The knowing smile on MacSwain's face grew to a grin. Go on, you smart-assed bastard, thought Anna, rub it in. Then she realised: Shit, he hasn't sussed me at all . . . the bastard's hitting on me!

She smiled back. MacSwain said something to the two blondes and made an apologetic gesture; it was clear that they were not at all pleased and drifted off in search of less evasive prey. MacSwain took a few steps towards Anna and, without looking, she knew that Paul would have set himself on an intercept course. She stepped forward to the bar, wrong-footing MacSwain by passing him and leaning against the counter. She asked the bartender for a rye and dry. MacSwain turned back to the bar and smiled.

'May I get this for you?'

'Why?' Anna responded in a cool, unimpressed tone. Over MacSwain's shoulder she could see Paul approaching. She made the most subtle movement of her eyes which Paul read instantly, turning to conceal himself once again in the foliage of designer clubwear.

'Because I'd like to.'

Anna shrugged and MacSwain paid when the drink arrived. She tried to make her movements relaxed, almost careless, but her brain was running on overload, playing catch-up with the situation. Surveillance had turned into undercover. And she hadn't been prepared for that. All she had for back-up was the tenuous line of sight that Paul maintained on her and, for all she knew, MacSwain could be the madman who was ripping women apart for kicks. Focus, Anna, she told herself. Keep breathing slow and easy. Don't let him spot you're scared. She sipped the bourbon and ginger ale.

'I've never seen you here before,' MacSwain said.

Anna turned to him, her face mocking. 'Is that the best you can do?'

'It was a genuine statement. I make conversation, I don't do chat-up lines.' As he spoke, Anna detected the hint of a foreign accent for the first time. His German was perfect, if a little stiff, and the accent was only just discernible under layers of learning.

'You a foreigner?' she asked bluntly.

MacSwain laughed. 'Does it show that much?'

'Yes, it does,' said Anna, taking another sip of her drink.

You didn't like that, did you? she thought. MacSwain clearly wasn't used to women not hanging on his every word. His expression relaxed into one of resigned politeness.

'Enjoy your drink,' he said, 'I'm sorry to have bothered you.' And he started to walk away.

Shit, thought Anna, what now? If he goes I can't follow him, and I can't stay with him for the rest of the night. Think.

'I'll be here Friday night . . . if you want to buy me another,' she said without turning to face him. 'About eight-thirty.' She turned. Maybe Friday was too long-term for MacSwain's agenda; maybe she should have said tomorrow night. But if Fabel were to go for this spontaneous idea, they would need time to assemble a plan and back-up team.

MacSwain hit her again with a smile. 'I'll be here. But I'm here now . . .'

'Sorry,' said Anna. 'Got things to do tonight.'

'Eight-thirty Friday it is then.'

He didn't show any signs of moving. Anna drained her drink too fast and it burned all the way down. Again she didn't let it register on her face.

'See you then.'

She could feel MacSwain's eyes on her as she walked away, giving Paul a look as she passed. Paul read the signal as 'You're on your own.' He stood up and walked over to the steel rail that bounded the dance floor, passing close to Anna without looking at her and allowing her to palm the car keys he passed to her.

Anna sat cramped in the car for two hours before she saw MacSwain walking back towards the Spielbudenplatz Parkhaus. He had a girl with him, a tall, attractive blonde who leaned into him and giggled or kissed him every few steps.

'Ahhh . . .' Anna said to herself, 'so you're cheating on me already . . .'

She saw Paul some distance behind them. There were quite a few night owls out on Spielbudenplatz and Paul was keeping a few of them between himself and his target. Anna slunk down into her car seat as MacSwain and his trophy passed by on the other side and went into the Parkhaus. Paul dropped into the passenger seat.

'What do you reckon? Should I go in on foot and keep an eye on him?'

'No. We might lose them on the way out. We have to make sure his date makes it home.'

Paul laughed bitterly. 'Well, that all turned to crap. Your cover's blown completely.'

'I wouldn't say it was a complete wash-out,' replied Anna with a self-satisfied smile. 'After all, I got a date out of it . . .'

Wednesday 18 June, 11.00 a.m. Polizeipräsidium, Hamburg.

Fabel's eyes were shadowed and sunken into his skull. The only other evidence of the attack was the bronze and purple bruise on the side of his neck and the stiffness with which he moved his head, tending to shift his shoulders in whichever direction he wanted to look in. After being discharged at eight-thirty that morning, he had gone home to shower off the taint of the hospital and change his clothes. He had spent the last hour reading through the file on Klugmann and Kramer's covert operation.

According to the BND file, the aim had been to gather intelligence on intergang rivalry and, specifically, on the encroachment by the Ukrainians into Ulugbay controlled areas. The file contained warrants from the Justizministerium for a phone tap on the main land line into the apartment. There was no mention of video equipment or bugging inside the apartment itself. Tina Kramer's role had been as a back-up, conveying any materials or cash needed and keeping Klugmann isolated from direct contact with any agency. Her instructions were to stay overnight in the apartment anytime she had contact with Klugmann. That way, anyone watching Klugmann could not then trace Kramer back to BAO or BND. Kramer's own apartment was in Eimsbüttel, far enough away from St Pauli to avoid any suspect accidentally bumping into her while she was buying groceries. Her instructions on counter-surveillance measures were complex. There were four safe houses set up. She would visit at least one of these, for at least an hour, every time she returned to her own apartment after making contact with Klugmann. She could also pick up materials and money at the safe houses. Like Klugmann, Kramer had not seen the inside of a federal-agency building for months. The idea was that, should anyone follow her, they would assume that she was visiting clients. Thereafter she would take a circuitous route to Eimsbüttel, punctuated by counter-surveillance checks and evasive manoeuvres. It would mean a very long journey home.

There was a subtext here. She was really just Klugmann's courier, yet every move she made, every link back from

Klugmann, was ring-fenced with precautions. Klugmann himself, ironically, had less cloak-and-dagger manoeuvring to do. He had one main form of protection: to live the life. He was to become so immersed in his identity as a low-life on the fringes of organised crime, and so totally isolated from his controls, that his cover would be impenetrable. Klugmann had two life-lines: Tina Kramer and his cell phone. These were not just his way of staying in touch, they grounded him; kept him connected with who he really was and what his true objectives were.

There was a lot of detail on the Ulugbay and the Varasouv criminal organisations, as well as other, peripheral criminal interests. But there was not enough on the new outfit, the so-called Top Team, despite Volker himself admitting it was the main focus of the operation. The transcripts of the bugged conversations from the apartment yielded nothing worthwhile either. Something was missing.

Volker had promised him the full story: Volker had lied.

Fabel asked Werner to gather everyone together in the main Mordkommission office for a briefing. As he stepped out of his room he was aware of the eyes of his team on him. He pulled himself as straight as possible and tried to invest his movements with as much vitality as he could muster. There was a low buzz in the office and Paul Lindemann was on the phone. Fabel waited for him to finish his call and clapped his hands together twice, sharply.

'Okay people, what have we got? Maria?'

Maria Klee was sitting on the corner of her desk. She was wearing an expensive pale blue blouse and elegant grey trousers. The heavy black clump of her automatic looked totally incongruous on her hip. She reached over for a clipboard with some notes on it.

'I have tracked down a member of the Temple of Asatru . . . someone called Bjorn Jannsen. He runs a New Age store

of some kind in the Schanzenviertel. He's also behind a
website on Odinism or Asatru or whatever you want to call
it . . .'

'A pile of crap,' volunteered Werner. There was a ripple of
laughter which foundered on the rocks of Maria's businesslike
manner.

'Anyway,' she continued, 'it was through the website that
I found him. When I asked him if he knew about the Temple
of Asatru he freely and openly admitted membership of it –
he's one of its "high priests" apparently. He claims it's all
completely above board and describes Asatru as a "celebra-
tion of life". I've arranged to see him on Friday, ten a.m.'

'I'll come along.' Fabel turned to Werner. 'Anything more
on MacSwain?'

It was Werner's turn to refer to notes. 'John Andreas
MacSwain . . .' Like everyone in the Mordkommission with
the exception of Fabel, Werner could not get his tongue
around the soft Anglo-Saxon 'w' in MacSwain's name. 'Born
1973 in Edinburgh, Scotland. His father is a partner in an
Edinburgh firm of corporate accountants. His mother is
German, from Kassel in Hessen. He was privately educated
at one of those snob schools the British have and has a degree
in computing from . . .' Werner struggled with the name –
'Heriot-Watt University. He also has a degree in advanced
applied computing from the Hamburg-Harburg Technische
Universität here. He is a permanent resident in Germany but
has not sought nationality. MacSwain works for the Eitel
Publishing Group. But he's not an employee. He has a freelance contract as an IT consultant.'

'Perfect for sending encrypted e-mails,' said Anna.

Fabel, sitting on the edge of Werner's desk, absorbed the
thought, allowing his chin to rest on his chest. He raised it
again quickly when a pain jabbed him in the neck, where the
Slav had exerted pressure. 'Go on, Werner.'

'He has no record either here or in the UK. Not even a

speeding ticket.' Werner lowered his notes, making a 'that's it' face.

'Anna, how about the surveillance? Anything to report?'

Anna and Paul exchanged a look. Fabel drew a long, slow, breath.

'Okay Anna . . . let's hear it.'

She related the events of the previous night.

'Okay . . .' Fabel's expression was one of exaggerated astonishment. 'You're telling me that the outcome of your surveillance is that you have arranged to meet the target . . . *for a date?*'

'What can I say? You've either got it or you haven't.'

Fabel straightened himself up. 'I'm glad you find this amusing, Kommissarin Wolff.'

'Listen, *Chef*, this could work. I can pull out of the surveillance team and not keep my date with MacSwain . . . on the other hand, I could keep it and probably find out more about him than we could in a month of observation.'

'And what if he is our guy?' said Paul. 'You could be the next victim.'

Fabel looked at the little-girl face behind the make-up, the small, defiant frame and felt a lurch of unease in his gut. 'I don't like it, Anna. I don't want you in any jeopardy . . . but I'll consider it.'

Paul Lindemann made a sound as if he'd tasted something noxious and threw his pen onto his desk. Fabel ignored him, but decided that, if Anna didn't choose Paul herself, he would insist on him leading the back-up team: Paul would place Anna's safety above his own life.

'I want you to draw up an operational outline and have it on my desk today,' continued Fabel. 'And if it's not watertight, we're not going ahead. And, Anna, I want you to wear a wire. I want the back-up team to know everything that's going on.'

'Aw . . .' Anna made a disappointed face. 'You trying to

cramp my style?' Then, when she saw her joke was not appreciated: 'Anything you say, *Chef*.'

Fabel felt a band tighten around his head. The stark strip lighting in the Mordkommission office seemed to sting his eyes. He checked his watch: it was nearly half past noon; it would be another hour before he could take his next set of painkillers.

'What do we have on Angelika Blüm?' Fabel massaged his temples as he spoke. 'Do we know anything more about her?'

'I've got a full breakdown of her work history,' said Werner. 'There are a couple of interesting things that have been flagged up. You know that exhibition in Bremen?'

Fabel nodded, intrigued at what possible link there could be.

'Well, Marlies Menzel, before she graduated to a career planting bombs in the Alsterarkaden, worked as a journalist and satirical cartoonist on a left-wing magazine called *Zeitgeist*. Angelika Blüm was also on the magazine. Her boyfriend at the time was the editor.'

'Were Menzel and Blüm friends?'

'That I don't know yet. I was hoping you and I could interview Blüm's former boyfriend to find out.'

'You hardly need me along to do that,' said Fabel, puzzled.

'Oh I think I do.' The rugged topography of Werner's features shifted slightly to make room for a wry smile. 'In fact, I wouldn't be surprised if Kriminaldirektor Van Heiden wanted to come along.'

'Why?'

'Angelika Blüm's lover at the time . . . and for four years in total . . . was a young left-wing lawyer and journalist with political ambitions. His name was Hans Schreiber.'

Fabel stared at Werner. 'Not *the* Hans Schreiber. Not the Erste Bürgermeister?'

'One and the same.'

Fabel raised his eyebrows. 'What else have you got?'

'Blüm had a good friend who works for NDR Radio. Erika

Kessler. I talked to her on the phone. A bit prickly but very upset about Blüm's death. She seems to know something, but not much, about what Blüm was working on. I've fixed up a meeting with her too.'

'Anything on the guy who attacked me at Blüm's flat?'

'Nothing, I'm afraid, *Chef* . . . but it hasn't been for the want of looking.'

The rest of the briefing dealt with scheduling in the various interviews and apportioning responsibility for tasks. Fabel was just winding up the meeting when his cell phone rang. He recognised the voice immediately.

'Hold on.' Fabel took the phone from his ear and spoke to his team. 'Okay folks, keep me informed of any developments on all or any line of enquiry.' He went into his office, closed the door behind him and lifted the cell phone back to his ear.

'Mahmoot, where the hell have you been? I've been worried sick. Listen, forget all about asking questions about these Ukrainians or the dead girl. We know who she is and it isn't safe for you to be involved . . .'

'I know, Jan. I think it's a bit late for that. I've been keeping a low profile anyway. This sounds like a line from a bad movie, but I think I'm being followed. I'm going to lie low for a while, but I need you to check out a name.'

'What is it?'

'Vitrenko. Vasyl Vitrenko. I think he may even be known as Colonel Vitrenko.'

'What about him?'

'He's the Devil, Jan.'

Wednesday 18 June, 3.00 p.m. Hamburger Hafen, Hamburg.

Summer had arrived in Hamburg and the temperature had soared. Paul, Werner and Fabel had their jackets off and

Maria sat on a low wall next to the elbow-high tables with her elegantly trousered legs crossed and her interlocked fingers hooked around her knees, the sun's sheen on the pale blue silk of her blouse. They had locked their holsters and sidearms in the boot of Fabel's BMW convertible and, had it not been for Werner's heavy features and Anna's neo-punk chic, they could have been a group of corporate lawyers slumming it at a Schnell-Imbiss down at the docks.

After the ever jolly Dirk had served them each with a chilled beer, Fabel choosing his accustomed Jever, they gathered around two tables away from the couple of dock workers who were the only other customers.

'Our friend Volker is keeping a lot from us, despite his promise to be open,' said Fabel. 'I am getting more information from my unofficial source than I am from the machinery of federal intelligence.' Everybody knew that Fabel had his own, protected informants, as did they all, and knew not to ask who the source of the new information was. 'I have to say that I am unsure as to what direct relevance this has to our investigation, but it is a dangerous element that is at least on the edges of our inquiry. There's a good chance that these people are the ones who killed Klugmann. And it's almost certain that they assassinated Ulugbay to move in on his Colombian drugs connection.'

No one spoke. Fabel took a sip of his Jever, knocking back a couple of codeine with it.

'The "Top Team" as Volker calls them is made up of ex-Spetznaz officers. These are not your usual thugs. According to my informant, they are all Chechnya and Afghanistan veterans, headed by a Colonel Vasyl Vitrenko. This guy has a terrible reputation and the mention of his name is enough to scare the shit out of the other Ukrainian outfits. No one is sure if Vitrenko is even really here, but they do know that the Top Team is comprised of officers who served under him. I have no idea what this guy has done, but his reputation for atrocities means no one dares take the risk of believing that he isn't, in fact, here.'

'Could this Vitrenko be the one behind the Blood Eagle murders?' Maria asked.

'I doubt it. Son of Sven sees himself as some kind of Germanic crusader. Vitrenko is a foreigner. But I do believe that he, or the group that is using his reputation as a terror tool, was the real target of the Klugmann-Kramer operation. The security and anti-detection measures that were put in place suggest they were dealing with a highly organised and professional opponent. If things were different we could bring in Organized Crime Division to run interference for us, but Volker claims this outfit have contacts within the Polizei Hamburg. That's why I'm keeping this information between the five of us.'

'Christ, Jan,' Werner shook his head. 'You don't seriously believe that crap?'

'I'm not prepared to take any risks. According to Volker, these people have some kind of special police background in the Ukraine. And, let's face it, there are elements within the force here who can't decide if they're soldiers or policemen. I can't even ask Volker for help. He was open enough about the Top Team, but he insisted that the top guy was faceless and nameless. If my contact can put a name to him then I'm damned sure the BND can. And anyway, the file Volker gave me has been edited to minimise the importance of the Top Team. I want us to do a special sweep to establish anyone within the Polizei Hamburg who has had official, semi-official or unofficial contact with the Ukrainian security services. Maria, can you and Werner do that between you? I know you're both laden with stuff so don't make it a priority, but make sure it gets done. And for God's sake be discreet.'

Maria nodded.

Werner said, 'Discreet is my middle name,' and all five laughed out loud.

* * *

Wednesday 18 June, 7.00 p.m. Blankenese, Hamburg.

Blankenese lies to the west of Hamburg, on the northern bank of the Elbe. The land banks steeply in stepped terraces from the river and is studded with verdant nuggets of broad-leaved woodland. The area is associated with a mix of quaint fishermen's cottages with large and elegant nineteenth- and early-twentieth-century villas. While the cottages cluster together cosily, the villas avoid any ostentation and maintain their north-German decorum behind modesty screens of trees and vast gardens. Contemporary architecture has made a limited incursion into Blankenese, but in the most selective and tasteful way. For all of these reasons it has become arguably the most desirable suburb of the city. The fishermen and the craftsmen who invested Blankenese with its character and quaintness have long since been displaced by enterpreneurs, media types and the management classes of Hamburg's multinational corporations.

Werner had called Erika Kessler at her office in the NDR Radio studios in Rothenbaumchaussee, but she had asked specifically if the interview could be held that evening at her home in Blankenese. Although steam-hammers continued to pound at Fabel's temples, he told Werner that he wanted to come along. Fabel needed to build an image of Angelika Blüm in his head. He had to understand the impulses that had driven her and where they had taken her. The editors and agents who regularly commissioned work from Blüm had all said the same thing: she never disclosed the nature of her investigation until her article was ready for publication. That left Erika Kessler, who had known Angelika Blüm since university and was the closest thing to a friend she had.

Erika Kessler was a producer at NDR and her husband was a partner in a production company that made television commercials. The three-level contemporary home they shared reflected their combined income and the trendy credibility of their occupations. Kessler's husband, a small, neat, balding

man in Armani slacks, a cashmere V-necked shirt and sandals
that flapped noisily on the terracotta floor tiles of the atrium
as he walked, led them onto a wooden decking balcony that
projected out over a steep garden.

Fabel knew as soon as the view from the balcony opened
out to him that it must have added half a million to the value
of the house. He was aware that Werner, someone not usually
sensitive to the aesthetic, was also silently absorbing the
panorama. The Kessler residence was set on one of the
terraces that stepped back and up from the Blankenese
Strandweg. From the deck, Fabel and Werner had an unin-
terrupted view right across the Elbe: from the broad sands
that outlined the river, over the wooded sickle of Ness-sand
island nature reserve which splits the Elbe into two channels,
and across to the Altes Land on the southern shore of the
river. The Elbe was flecked with the white triangles of a dozen
sailboats. Only a hulking, long container ship provided a
reminder that the river's primary function was not pleasure
but commerce.

In the last week or so, Fabel had seen a lot of impressive
real estate – Yilmaz's mansion, MacSwain's hip loft and
Angelika Blüm's 1920's Modernist apartment – but none had
pricked his envy. This home did: with its relaxed but elegant
style, its location and its amazing view that rivalled his own
apartment's cityscape. But when he shaped a vision of himself
in this home, it was with his ex-wife Renate and their
daughter, Gabi. The thought was the bitter aftertaste to his
envy and he found himself feeling resentful of the Kesslers.
He turned his back on the view.

When Erika Kessler stepped out onto the balcony she
revealed a glacial near-beauty that was let down by a jaw of
nearly masculine strength. There was ice in the pale blue eyes
and her head was angled in a way that suggested arrogance.
The severity of her expression was mitigated by the fine ash-
blonde hair that she wore loose and which framed her face

in soft ringlets. She was dressed in a white cotton scoop-necked top and wide-legged white linen trousers. She gestured towards a set of solid-looking hardwood loungers and sat down. Werner and Fabel took two chairs opposite her. They had flashed their oval shields to Herr Kessler on arrival: Erika Kessler now asked if she could see their identification and studied both cards carefully, looking from photograph to face and back again in each case.

'You wanted to ask me about Angelika?' she asked eventually, handing back their IDs.

'Yes,' said Fabel. 'I know you must be very upset about Frau Blüm's death . . . and the manner of it . . . and I assure you we don't want to cause you further distress, but we do need to know as much as possible about Frau Blüm in order to find her killer.'

'I'll tell you what I can. Angelika was not someone who . . .' Frau Kessler took a moment to search for the right word. '. . . who *shared*. She really did not give of herself much.'

'But you were close friends?' Werner asked.

'We were friends. I knew Angelika at university. We got on well. She was bright and attracted men and those were critical credentials at the time.'

'What was she like?' asked Fabel.

'When we were at university or after?'

'Both.'

'Well, Angelika was never what I would call carefree. She was always serious about her studies and she was very politically aware. We went on holiday together a couple of times. We worked in vineyards in Spain one summer. I remember on the way back we visited the Basque region and ended up in Guernica – you know, the place that Picasso painted the picture about. I remember we were at a memorial there to the people killed in 1937 by the Legion Kondor whom Hitler had ordered to bomb the city as a favour to Franco. This old woman heard us speaking German and started to berate us about what *we* had done to her town. I told her straight that it had nothing to do with me, that I was born a full decade after the war, but Angelika got really upset. I'd go so far as to say that it was a significant event in her political awareness.'

'You say she was political. Presumably left-leaning?'

'Definitely left. But not Marxist or anything like that. She was a liberal at heart. And environmentally conscious. She was involved with Die Grünen at one point. After re-unification, when the Green Party went into alliance with various opposition groups from East Germany and formed Bündnis90/Die Grünen, I believe she even flirted with the idea of standing for election to the Bundestag.'

'Why didn't she stand?'

Frau Kessler swept a stray golden ringlet and tucked it behind her ear. She looked out across the river. 'Angelika was an excellent journalist, and she knew it. She chose to remain an excellent journalist rather than become a mediocre politician. She felt she could do more for social justice and environmental protection through her writing.'

'When was the last time you saw Frau Blüm?' asked Werner.

'I had lunch with her a couple of weeks ago. The fourth, I think.'

'How was she? Did she mention anything unusual?'

'No. No, I don't think so. She was quite upbeat, really. She planned to intercept the arrival of that Nazi asshole Wolfgang Eitel later that afternoon.'

'The father of Norbert Eitel, the publisher?'

'And ex-SS officer and leader of the so-called Bund Deutschland-für-Deutsche.'

'What was Frau Blüm's interest in him?'

She crossed her long legs with a whisper of linen. 'She wasn't specific. As you've probably already gathered, Angelika kept the details of her investigations secret until she was ready to go to press or transmission. She was trying to get me interested in doing a radio documentary with her. All she would tell me at this stage was that she had some dirt on Eitel that would ruin his credibility with his supporters. She did say that it involved property speculation.'

'Was there any suggestion of her investigation placing her in danger?'

Frau Kessler's brow furrowed. 'I don't think it occurred to her. It didn't occur to me, either. You don't suspect Eitel's lot, do you?'

'Not specifically. Was there anything else she was working on?'

'I know she was doing something on BATT101. But I don't think that it was a major project.'

Fabel frowned. Before and during the Second World War, Police Reserve Battalion 101 had been drawn from ordinary, mainly middle-aged and working-class men from Hamburg, considered one of the least Nazified cities in Germany. In 1942, these ordinary men of Police Reserve Battalion 101 massacred nearly 2,000 Jews in Otwock, Poland. By the war's end, BATT101 had exterminated more than 80,000 Jews and other 'undesirables'. Fabel remembered the owl-eyed old woman, Frau Steiner, who lived beneath the apartment where Tina Kramer had been murdered. He remembered the old black-and-white photographs of a man wearing the uniform of a Police Reserve Battalion.

'BATT101? It's hardly current affairs.'

Erika Kessler shrugged. 'I don't know. Maybe she had another angle on it. She said something about comparisons with Soviet police actions in Afghanistan and Chechnya.'

'What about relationships?' asked Fabel. 'Was Frau Blüm involved with anyone?'

There was a pulse beat of a hesitation. 'No . . . I don't think there was anyone special recently. She was involved with another journalist for a while. Paul Thorsten.' Fabel noted the name. 'But they broke up about a year ago. I don't think there's been a significant relationship since then.'

Fabel looked into Erika Kessler's arctic blue eyes. They held his gaze resolutely. She had almost got away with it, but in that split second before answering with the too-natural response and the too-steady gaze, she had revealed to Fabel her first lie. But why would Kessler lie about Blüm's boyfriends?

'Do you know Marlies Menzel?'

'The painter?'

'The terrorist.'

Kessler laughed, but the ice in her eyes frosted and hardened a little more. 'Shall we say the *former* terrorist turned painter? I know *of* her, but no, I don't know her personally.'

'But Angelika Blüm did.'

'I believe they worked together at one time.'

'On *Zeitgeist*, the left-wing magazine. I believe the editor at the time was a young Hans Schreiber. Frau Blüm and he were involved at the time?'

'I believe so. I think they lived together for a while,' said Kessler. Again Fabel detected a defence slide down behind the eyes. The art of the interrogator is to put together not just that which is said, the truth and the lies, but to assemble the silences, the gestures, the directions taken by the eyes. Fabel felt the thrill of a small epiphany as he made a connection. He considered challenging her, but decided to keep his thought locked up tight for the moment.

The rest of the interview yielded nothing of any significance. Fabel thanked Erika Kessler for her time and her nod was somewhere between courtesy and curtness. She led Fabel and Werner to the door, through the tile-floored atrium which was a few palpable degrees cooler than the temperature out on the south-facing deck.

Fabel had some difficulty finding the road back to the city, continually tripping up over Blankenese's elaborate one-way system. Eventually he turned the BMW onto Elbchaussee.

'Well, what did you think?' he asked Werner.

'She's holding something back. I suspect that Blüm was involved with someone and Kessler is trying to keep that someone out of all of this.'

'That's exactly what I think.' Fabel paused for a while. 'Werner, how would you describe Hans Schreiber, the Erste Bürgermeister?'

Werner turned to Fabel with a puzzled frown. All Fabel gave was his profile.

'I don't know . . . tall, I suppose. Expensively dressed. Grey-blond hair. Obviously works out . . . broad shouldered . . . Why?'

Now Fabel turned to Werner. 'Now describe the man your witness saw going into Angelika Blüm's apartment block.'

Part Three
Thursday 19 June to
Sunday 22 June

Thursday 19 June, 10.20 a.m. Hamburg Rathaus, Hamburg.

Kriminaldirektor Van Heiden had reacted almost exactly as Fabel had anticipated. Almost, but not quite. Van Heiden has been shocked by Fabel's revelation that Erste Bürgermeister Schreiber was now a suspect in this most high profile of investigations and Fabel had watched his boss from across the vast desk in Van Heiden's fourth-floor office. Van Heiden had seemed frozen in his leather chair, gazing at the desktop, as if all physical movement had been suspended to divert energy to his racing thought processes. Eventually, and unexpectedly, Van Heiden had looked up with an expression of resignation and asked Fabel what they should do next, as if Fabel were the senior officer and Van Heiden the subordinate.

'Arrange to see him,' Fabel had said. 'If he were anyone else I would haul him in . . . but I do appreciate the need for, um . . . diplomacy, shall we say, in this case.'

'When do you want to do it?'

'Schreiber has been placed at the last murder scene . . . or at least someone very close in appearance to him . . . and he has a . . . *history* . . . with the victim. That would not incline me towards seeking out the next convenient "window of opportunity" in his diary. I need to talk to him now.'

'Leave it with me.'

Van Heiden had made a call to the Rathaus and had

obviously encountered some bureaucratic resistance. The threats that Van Heiden had made to the poor administrator at the other end of the phone had been given added menace by the quiet, restrained and cold voice in which he had delivered them. He had been put through to Schreiber. The conversation had been short and to the point. Schreiber had agreed to meet them in his chambers immediately. Van Heiden had stared at the phone after replacing the receiver.

'It was almost as if he had been expecting the call. I got the feeling he was relieved.'

The Rathaus is Hamburg's city hall, home to the Hamburg state government and one of its most striking buildings. The main entrance to the Hamburg Rathaus sits immediately beneath the clock tower and spire which soar above and dominate the vast Rathaus square.

When Fabel and Van Heiden entered the Rathaus, the huge main hall with its colonnades and multi-vaulted ceiling opened up to them. A few dozen tourists were scattered throughout the hall, clustered around the illuminated glass displays that circle the immense pillars. The Kriminaldirektor was about to say something when a liveried official approached the two policemen.

'I've been asked to meet you gentlemen and take you to meet his honour the Erste Bürgermeister.'

The Bürgermeistersaal, the room used for official and ceremonial functions, is on the second floor of the Rathaus, just off the main tower hall. The working offices of Hamburg's Erster Bürgermeister, however, are on the ground and first floors, set in the south-east corner of the building. It was to the first floor Bürgermeisterzimmer that Fabel and Van Heiden were conducted.

Schreiber stood up when they entered his oak-panelled office. Fabel noticed the cut of Schreiber's suit. Yet more expensive Italian tailoring that hung perfectly from the Erste

Bürgermeister's powerful shoulders. But Fabel sensed that he also bore something that sat less easily than Armani: there was a certain awkwardness in his movements. Schreiber thanked the attendant and asked the two policemen to sit down. Fabel took his notebook out and flipped it open.

'You said this was something to do with Angelika's death?' asked Schreiber.

Fabel paused the couple of seconds that protocol demanded, in case Van Heiden wanted to take the lead. When Van Heiden remained silent, Fabel spoke.

'You expressed considerable concern about these murders, Herr Erste Bürgermeister . . .'

'Naturally . . .'

'And you also made it clear you wanted as swift and successful a conclusion to the investigation as possible . . .'

'Of course . . .'

Fabel decided to play his cards face up. 'Then could you explain to me why you neglected to inform us that you visited Angelika Blüm the night she was killed?'

Schreiber returned Fabel's stare, but there was no hostility, no defensiveness, no strength in the gaze. After a moment, Schreiber sighed. 'Because I didn't want to get caught up in all of this. The scandal. As you can imagine, the press would have a field day . . .' Schreiber looked in Van Heiden's direction, as if he would appreciate the point. Van Heiden gave no indication that he did.

'Herr Doktor Schreiber, you are a lawyer, so you understand your rights under the relevant articles of the Grundgesetz, and that your answers to our questions from now on may be used in evidence.'

Schreiber's broad shoulders sagged. 'Yes, I understand.'

Fabel leaned forward, resting his elbows on the carved lion-claw arm rests of the oak chair. 'And I take it you understand that I – that we – do not give a rat's ass about your concerns about the media. You have withheld potential information about a series of murders. Murders, I have to point out, for which you are fast becoming a prime suspect. There are women being butchered – and I don't mean that metaphorically – and you are worried about your PR?'

'I think the Bürgermeister takes your point, Fabel,' Van Heiden said, quietly and without anger.

'If your answers do not satisfy me, Herr Doktor Schreiber,' Fabel continued, 'then I am going to arrest you here and now. And believe me, I will lead you through the Rathaus in handcuffs. So I think you should exhibit a little more candour than you have thus far.' Fabel leaned back. 'Did you murder Angelika Blüm?'

'Christ . . . no.'

'Then what were you doing at her apartment the night she was murdered?'

'Angelika was an old friend. We saw each other now and again.'

Fabel's face hardened. 'I thought I made myself clear, Herr Schreiber. We can do this here or at the Präsidium. And unless you start being totally honest with us – and I mean about everything – then we'll do it on our ground, not yours. Let's start with the true nature of your relationship with Frau Blüm. How long had you been having an affair?'

Schreiber looked empty. He had been scrabbling around for some scrap to cover at least something of his privacy and Fabel had snatched it away from him.

'A year. Maybe a little longer. As you probably know we had been intimate years ago. I had asked Angelika to marry me at the time but she turned me down. We remained friends throughout the years and then, somehow, something began to spark between us again.'

'Is Frau Schreiber aware of this relationship?' asked Van Heiden.

'No. God, no. Karin has no idea. Neither of us wanted her to get hurt.'

'So you didn't plan to leave your wife?' Fabel asked.

'No. Or at least not now. I had suggested it to start with but Angelika didn't want us to move in together. She wanted her independence and I suppose the arrangement . . . well, suited her. Anyway, like I said, we didn't want Karin or the kids to get hurt.'

'It doesn't sound like a particularly deep relationship.'

Schreiber leaned forward onto the desk. He picked up a pen and fiddled with it, turning it end to end between his fingers. 'That's not true. We cared for each other. It's just that we were being . . .' he paused to find the right word – '*practical*. The other thing was that we always had a sense of unfinished business between us.'

Fabel decided to play another hunch. 'Would I be right in saying that Frau Blüm wanted to end the relationship?'

Schreiber looked stung. 'How did you . . .'

Fabel cut him off. 'Was that why you were up there that evening? Were you trying to talk Frau Blüm out of ending the relationship?'

'No. We had already agreed to stop seeing each other.'

'I take it you had stayed the night on previous occasions?'

Schreiber nodded. 'When circumstances allowed.'

'In other words when you had a credible alibi to offer your wife.'

Schreiber made a small signal of resignation with his shoulders.

'So I assume you had some stuff in Frau Blüm's apartment and you were picking it up that night.'

Schreiber's eyes widened slightly. 'Yes . . . shirts, a spare suit, toiletries, et cetera . . . How on earth did you know that?'

'The sports bag. You were either collecting something or carrying the murder weapon in it.'

It had been the sports bag that had brought Fabel to envision the scene: the end of a relationship; the removal of the last personal belongings from the apartment. Fabel remembered how he himself had used exactly the same kind of bag, Renate standing silent, Gabi asleep in her room, as he had disinvested himself from their family home five years before.

'When did you leave the apartment?'

'About a quarter to nine.'

'You were only there for fifteen minutes?'

'I guess. Angelika had just stepped out of the bath and had some work to get on with that evening, so I just picked up my stuff and went.'

'Was there any kind of argument?'

'No . . . of course not. Our continued friendship was too valuable to throw away. It was all very civilised really.'

'And you didn't see anyone else arriving as you left?'

Schreiber took a moment to think, then shook his head. 'No, I can't say I did.'

'What time did you get home?' asked Fabel.

'About nine-ten, nine-fifteen.'

'And your wife can confirm this?'

'Do you have to bring Karin into this?' There was a hint of pleading in Schreiber's tone.

'I'm afraid we do, if she's the only person who can confirm you were back by nine-fifteen. The autopsy of Frau Blüm states she was murdered sometime around ten p.m.'

Schreiber had the look of a man who had sewn his life together, tight and neat, only to see it come apart at the seams.

'And we'll need your fingerprints, Herr Doktor Schreiber,' added Fabel.

'I think we could arrange for a technician to do that here . . .' said Van Heiden, looking at Fabel as if for approval, 'discreetly.'

Fabel nodded his acceptance. 'Brauner himself is the best guy to send. I'll arrange it.' Fabel turned back to Schreiber. 'I'll probably have more questions for you at some point.'

Schreiber nodded. There was a pause.

'The first victim, Ursula Kastner – I believe she worked for the Hamburg state government. Did you know her?' asked Fabel.

'Of course I knew her. She worked in our environment and property law office. She was involved with projects like Hafen City and the St Pauli regeneration project. I knew her well. She was an excellent lawyer.'

'Did you have any kind of relationship with her, other than a professional one?'

Schreiber straightened his shoulders, as if mustering the scattered remnants of his dignity. The trapezius muscles strained against the sleek fabric of his Armani suit. It was the kind of conformation that only comes from serious weight work in a gym. Fabel could imagine that Schreiber was physically very strong. Powerful enough in a killing frenzy to wrench open a victim's ribs.

'No, Herr Fabel, I didn't have any kind of inappropriate relationship with Frau Kastner. Contrary to the impression you may have of me, I am neither a serial killer nor a serial philanderer. The affair I had with Angelika is the only time I have strayed in my marriage. And the only reason that happened was because Angelika and I had a history. There was no personal dimension to my relationship with Ursula Kastner . . . although it was I who introduced her to Angelika.'

There seemed an eternity of silence. Fabel and Van Heiden exchanged a look. Fabel felt a tingle of electricity. It was Van Heiden who broke the spell.

'Are you telling us that Angelika Blüm and Ursula Kastner knew each other? That there is a connection between them?'

'I assumed you knew . . . with them both being killed by the same person, I mean.'

'The only link we had between them was you, Herr Doktor Schreiber,' said Fabel. 'Now you say they had contact with each other?'

'Yes. It was Ursula who instigated the introduction. She said she needed a "friendly" contact in the media for background information.'

'Is that normal?'

'No. I wasn't too happy about it. I suspected that Ursula had information on something that she wanted leaked to the press. I insisted she tell me if it was anything potentially injurious to the Hamburg state government. She assured me that she had no knowledge of anything that would attract negative attention to the city government. She insisted it was only for advice.'

'Did you believe her?'

'No. I don't think I did. But I had to take her word for it. And anyway, if she was going to blow the whistle on something to do with the city, she would hardly come through me.'

'Angelika Blüm never told you what it was about.'

'No.'

'Did you ask?'

'A couple of times, but I didn't get anywhere. Then I gave up. If you knew Angelika you would understand.'

'How often did they meet?'

'I don't know. I don't even know if they ever met other than at the Neuer Horizont reception where I introduced them. They maybe met regularly or not at all, or dealt with each other by phone or e-mail. I just don't know.'

'Did you invite them both to this function?'

'No, it so happens they were both there . . . on business, as it were. Neuer Horizont is a plan to regenerate areas of the city that have missed out on the big schemes, like Hafen City or the St Pauli regeneration, but which may still qualify for federal, state or EU funding.'

Fabel gazed out through the huge stone arched window that faced out back towards the Alsterfleet and the Alsterarkaden. He tried to keep his mind working logically and methodically, but his thoughts were turbocharged by the thrill of epiphany. Previously unconnected trails were now converging. Colliding and sparking off each other in Fabel's brain. Two out of three victims had been in contact with each other. And both had a connection to property dealings through the city government. He turned back to Schreiber.

'Who is behind the Neuer Horizont initiative?'

'A private consortium. The main shareholder is a subsidiary of the Eitel Group. It was Norbert Eitel who held the reception.' Schreiber shrugged. 'I'm afraid I'm no fan of Eitel, but the city cannot be seen not to support any initiative that offers potential benefits.'

Another connection. Another spark. 'I thought the Eitel Group was exclusively a media business?'

Schreiber shook his head. 'No, the publishing arm is their main business, but Eitel is involved in dozens of other areas. Information technology is one. Property development is another.'

Fabel nodded thoughtfully. 'Was Eitel's father there? Wolfgang Eitel?'

'No. he wasn't. That's where I draw the line . . . I won't share a platform with a Nazi like him, no matter how beneficial the cause. I think that's why he was kept away . . . despite their public shows of solidarity, Norbert Eitel is very much aware of the liability his father represents to his political ambitions.'

'You must have been shocked by Kastner's murder.'

'That's an understatement. It was a terrible shock. You remember Innensenator Hugo Ganz?'

Fabel nodded. He thought of Ganz's scrubbed, fleshy pink face.

'Frau Kastner worked quite closely with Herr Ganz. Specifically to do with environmental and property-development projects. She provided the legal back-up. Innensenator Ganz was

very upset by Frau Kastner's death. That's why I think he was
so . . . *emphatic* when you met him last.'

'Presumably you remember where you were when Frau
Kastner went missing?'

'I was attending an environmental conference in Rome.'
Schreiber spoke without emotion. Then a small hope lit up
his face. 'That's right! I wasn't even in the country when she
was killed. And I have a hundred witnesses. And when was
the second victim killed?'

'The early hours of Wednesday the fourth,' said Fabel.

Schreiber scrabbled though his desk diary. 'I was at home
with my family. They can verify it.'

Fabel didn't look impressed. 'All I am interested in just
now is Frau Blüm's murder. And you were there immediately
before she was killed.'

'But I had nothing to do with it. Nothing at all.' A hint
of defiance was beginning to creep into Schreiber's tone. The
realisation that he had alibis for the other two killings clearly
emboldened him.

Fabel changed tack. 'Did you know that Frau Blüm had
been trying to get in touch with me, personally?'

'No . . . no, I didn't. What on earth for?'

'I don't know. I didn't get a chance to return her calls,'
Fabel lied. It sounded better than saying he hadn't bothered.

'Do you think she thought she was in any kind of danger?
Do you think that's why she was trying to contact you?'
Schreiber didn't wait for an answer. 'Why didn't she tell me?
If she was afraid . . . why didn't she talk to me?'

Fabel stood up. Van Heiden followed his lead. 'I have no
reason to believe that she felt in danger. All I know is she
tried to get in touch with me three or four times before she
died. But she didn't indicate in any of the messages she left
that she was in danger.'

Fabel made for the door without shaking Schreiber's hand.
'Like I say, Herr Doktor Schreiber, I may have more questions

for you. And I'll arrange for our forensics guy to come and take your fingerprints.'

Fabel had opened the heavy oak door when he turned back to face Schreiber. 'One more thing. When was the last time you met or had any contact with Marlies Menzel?'

Schreiber looked at first surprised, then a little worried. 'God . . . I don't know . . . not for years. Not since we worked together on *Zeitgeist* and certainly not since she got involved with terrorism.'

'You haven't been in touch since she was released from Stuttgart-Stammheim?'

'No. Absolutely not.' And Fabel knew he was telling the truth.

The same liveried attendant escorted Fabel and Van Heiden out into the main Rathaus hall. The sun dazzled them both as they stepped through the Gothic arch out into the wide expanse of the Rathaus square.

'What do you think?' asked Van Heiden.

'He's not our man,' said Fabel, taking his sunglasses from his breast pocket and donning them. 'I have to take a trip to Bremen. Can I buy you a coffee in the Alsterarkaden before I head off, Herr Kriminaldirektor?'

Thursday 19 June, 2.20 p.m. Kunstgalerie Nordholt, Bremen.

Fabel had estimated that the journey to Bremen would take about an hour and a half, but halfway there the traffic on the A1 began to thicken and slow. Facing a long stretch of autobahn, he decided to put a CD into the player of his car: Herbert Grönemeyer, *Bleibt alles anders*. He had just turned up the volume when his cell phone rang. It was Maria Klee; they had the autopsy findings on Klugmann. He had been killed by a single bullet that had passed through his cerebrum and pulped his medulla oblongata, exiting, as Brauner had pointed out, above the top lip and below the nose. The estimated time of death was between 6.00 p.m. on Friday the 13th and 6.00 a.m. on Saturday the 14th. Fabel flinched when Maria told him that the autopsy had revealed signs of torture and beating in the period immediately pre-mortem. Tests had also revealed traces of amphetamine in Klugmann's blood. Living the life. The ultimate cover. And it had failed.

Maria also had a ballistics report. Brauner had been right: the bullet casing belonged to a non-standard weapon. Fabel gave Maria a snapshot of his interview with Schreiber and asked that she update Werner.

The traffic eased. Fabel found himself further along the road than he had been aware of driving. He had been on automatic pilot, his mind in some dark, lonely place with an undercover policeman who knew, as he was being tortured, that death was waiting for him with an immediate and ineluctable certainty. For a split second Fabel was able to mentally place himself there and felt a nauseous fluttering in his chest. A feeling he recognised as the pale shadow of an unimaginable terror.

The signs indicated he was approaching Bremen Kreuz and he took the exit from the A1 onto the A27 towards Bremen.

Nordholt art gallery was just off the main Marktplatz in Bremen. It was housed in a fine late-nineteenth-century building with huge bow-fronted windows. When Fabel entered, Marlies Menzel was supervising the hanging of one of her paintings. A woman of about fifty, she wore a long dark skirt and a loose black jacket with padded shoulders. Her dull brown hair was cut short with dyed highlights. She wore a pair of small, square wire-framed glasses. She looked more like a librarian than a recently released terrorist, thought Fabel as he made his way across the gallery. He stopped halfway. The blank white walls of the gallery were punctuated by huge canvases. Fabel had already been aware, having seen them in the exhibition brochure, of the bizarre similarity of the paintings with the Blood Eagle murder scenes. What he had not been prepared for was the powerful visual impact of the artworks. Each canvas was two metres tall by one wide. The paint screamed from the canvas in vivid, visceral colours. The brushwork was forceful and confident. Each painting was violence in two dimensions.

Fabel made his way over to the small group.

'Frau Menzel?'

She turned to Fabel. 'Yes?' A polite smile stretched the thin lips.

'I wonder if I could have a word.' Fabel held out his oval KriPo shield.

The smile was swept away. 'This really is getting tiresome. I have been visited by almost every security service in Germany since my release. This is beginning to look like harassment.'

'This isn't really official . . .'

'Oh? In that case I don't know if I should be talking to you at all.' Menzel turned away.

'Frau Menzel,' Fabel said, 'I'm Kriminalhauptkommissar Jan Fabel. I was the police officer who was involved in the shooting at the pier in 1983 . . .'

Menzel stood with her back to Fabel for a moment. 'You shot Gisela?'

'I had no choice. She'd already shot me once and was going to shoot me again. I begged her to stop, but . . .' Fabel's voice trailed off.

'She was just a child.' Menzel turned to face him.

'She gave me no choice. She had killed my colleague and she had already wounded me,' Fabel said without any hint of bitterness. 'I told her to drop the gun but she aimed at me again.' As Fabel spoke, he saw Gisela Frohm once more, at the end of the pier, the glittering gun hanging at the end of her skinny girl's arm, like a weight on a rope, then swinging up to fire. He had shot her twice. In the face. He remembered her punk-pink hair as her head snapped back and she fell into the harbour. It had been the worst day of his career. Of his life. And he would never forget it.

Marlies Menzel regarded Fabel. There was no hostility in the look. It seemed to Fabel that she was considering his words. She turned to the two assistants who were helping her to hang the painting. 'I'm just going out for a moment. We'll hang the rest later.' Then to Fabel: 'I think we should go somewhere else to talk.'

The café was just off Bremen's Katharinenstrasse. A highly polished counter ran its entire length. The staff behind the counter continuously placed trays with white tea or coffee pots and cups on the polished bar. The air was full of the rich odour of freshly milled coffee. The waiting staff, dressed in black trousers and waistcoats with white aprons tied around the waist, collected the trays and carried them over to the customers' tables. There was a comforting rhythm to the mechanics of service.

Fabel and Marlies Menzel chose a table by the window. Menzel sat with her back to the oak panelling while Fabel sat opposite her, with a view up the street towards the Marktplatz. She pulled out a packet of French cigarettes, and after a moment's thought she offered one to Fabel.

'No thanks. I don't smoke.'

She smiled and lit a cigarette. She inhaled deeply, tilted her head upwards and to one side and blew the smoke into the air, twisting her mouth slightly to make sure it blew away from Fabel.

'It's a habit I picked up in prison,' she said. There was a bitterness in her voice. 'What can I do for you, Herr Fabel?'

A waiter arrived at their table before Fabel had a chance to answer. He ordered a Kännchen of tea and Menzel asked for a black coffee.

'I wanted to ask you about your paintings,' Fabel said, after the waiter had gone.

Menzel smiled. 'An art-loving policeman? Or have I violated some civic ordinance relating to canvas size?'

Fabel told Menzel about the killings and how her canvases were strikingly redolent of the murder scenes. He asked her if she knew of Angelika Blüm's death, which she did. She had read about it in the papers.

'When was the last time you saw Frau Blüm?'

'Not since before I was imprisoned. We used to work together on a magazine in the seventies. It was called *Zeitgeist*. We thought the name clever then, but it seems so predictable when you look back on it. Why do you ask? Am I a suspect because my paintings remind you of . . .' Her brow furrowed as if she had realised the significance of what she had said. 'Poor Angelika . . .'

'No, Frau Menzel, you're not a suspect,' Fabel said, without revealing he had already had Maria check out where Menzel had been on the dates of the murders. She was still incarcerated when Ursula Kastner had been murdered and was at a gallery reception when Blüm was killed. 'It's just that there is a disturbing similarity between what you are painting and the death scenes. It's probably purely coincidental, but there is a chance that the killer has seen your paintings and is emulating them. It is quite common for serial killers to "pose" their victims. In this case we might have a case of life imitating art.'

'Or rather death imitating art.' Menzel took another long pull on her cigarette. Fabel noticed the yellow-brown nicotine staining on her fingers. 'How awful,' she said.

The waiter arrived with the tea and coffee.

'Have you received any . . . well, *odd* correspondence regarding your work? Particularly e-mails?' Fabel asked.

Menzel shrugged. 'Just what you'd expect. A lot of letters telling me that I should still be in prison, that I'll burn in

hell for my crimes, that it's obscene to try to define myself
as a creator of something rather than a destroyer. That sort
of thing. Sentiments you probably have some sympathy with,
Herr Hauptkommissar.'

Fabel ignored the bait. 'But nothing you would describe
as a strange, or even an inappropriate response to the
images?'

Menzel thought for a moment. 'No, not really. Although
there was an unpleasant scene at the gallery a few weeks
back. Wolfgang Eitel turned up with a full press and TV
crowd in tow and started to rant about me having no right
to exhibit work, calling me a murderer and a criminal and
condemning my use of the colours of the national flag. Nazi
swine.'

Fabel absorbed the information. Another mention of Eitel.
'Were you present when this happened?'

'No. I think that kind of undermined his plan. I think he
had it in mind to go toe to toe with me in front of the
cameras.'

Fabel sipped his tea. Menzel turned her head towards the
light and looked out of the window. Fabel noticed that the
candour of daylight revealed a greyish tinge to her skin.

'Why did you do what you did? Why did you follow
Svensson?'

The question surprised Fabel almost as much as it did
Menzel. She looked at him curiously, as if trying to establish
whether there was any malice behind the question. Then she
shrugged.

'It was a different time and a different place. We believed
in something and we believed in someone. Karl-Heinz
Svensson was an incredibly powerful presence. He was also
highly manipulative.'

'Is that why you followed him with such . . . well,
fanaticism?'

'Fanaticism!' Menzel gave a low, bitter laugh. 'Yes, you're

right. We were fanatical. We would have died for him. And most of us did.'

'For him? Not for your beliefs?'

'Oh, in those days we convinced ourselves that we were bringing the world socialist revolution to Germany; that we were soldiers fighting the capitalist inheritors of the Nazi mantle.' She took another long draw on her cigarette. 'The fact is we were all in Karl-Heinz's thrall. Did you never think about how many of our group were women? Young women? After the trials the press called us "Svensson's Harem". The fact is that we had all slept with him. We were all in love with him.'

'A lot of people died for the sake of schoolgirl crushes.' Fabel couldn't keep the bitterness from his voice. He thought of twenty-five-year-old Franz Webern, married, the father of an eighteen-month-old baby, lying dead on the street. He thought too of Gisela Frohm sinking slowly down through the murky waters of the Elbe.

'Christ, don't you think I know that?' retorted Menzel. 'I've had fifteen long years sitting in a cell in Stuttgart-Stammheim to think it over. What you have to understand is the *power* he had over us. He demanded total commitment. That meant cutting ourselves off from our families, from our friends, from every sane and rational influence. His voice was the only one we heard. He was mother, father, brother, comrade, lover . . . everything to us.' The passion seemed partially to rekindle in her and then died. 'He was a manipulative bastard.'

Menzel lit a fresh cigarette from the stub of the last. Fabel noticed again the yellow staining on her fingertips.

'Was Gisela as fanatical as the rest of you?'

Menzel's smile was laden with sadness. 'More than anyone. Karl-Heinz was her first lover. She was besotted with him. What you said earlier was right. You had no choice other than to shoot her. Karl-Heinz had conditioned her to kill.

You were only the instrument of her death: he was the engineer.'

'What I can't understand is why.' Fabel's puzzlement was genuine. 'Why did Svensson – why did you – feel the need to do what you did? What was so terrible about our society that you had to declare war on it?'

Menzel paused before answering. 'It's the German disease. A lack of history. A lack of a clear identity. Trying to work out who the hell we are. It's what led us into Nazism. It's what made us become ersatz Americans after the war: like an errant child trying to make up by imitating its parent. It was that ultra-capitalist, popcorn banality that we despised. We declared war on mediocrity –' she gave a sardonic smile – 'and mediocrity won.'

Fabel sat staring into his tea. He knew what his next question had to be. He already knew the answer, but he had to ask it anyway.

'Is Svensson really dead?'

Svensson was supposed to have died during a firefight at the scene of an attempted assassination of the then Erste Bürgermeister of Hamburg. A police bullet had hit the fuel tank of Svensson's car, which had burst into flames. Svensson had burned to death. The police had not been able to trace the dental records essential to establishing his identity. Svensson, the consummate terrorist, had spent years erasing his existence from official files.

Marlies Menzel didn't answer for a moment. Instead she leaned back and drew on her cigarette, examining Fabel as if appraising him.

'Yes, Herr Fabel. Karl-Heinz died in that car. I can assure you of that.'

Fabel believed her. 'I'd better get back to Hamburg,' he said. 'I'm sorry I disturbed you.'

'Or are you simply sorry you disturbed the past? That's where I belong: in your past. That's where Gisela belongs as well.' She paused. 'Have you got what you came for, Herr Fabel?'

Fabel smiled as he stood up. 'I don't even know what it was I came for. I hope your exhibition goes well.'

'An act of creation. Some kind of atonement for the acts of destruction I was involved in. A fitting end, I think. You see, Herr Fabel, it will be my debut and my finale.' Menzel flicked some more ash into the ashtray on the table.

'I'm sorry?' Fabel's face signalled confusion.

Marlies Menzel held up her cigarette and studied it carefully. 'I have cancer, Herr Fabel.' She smiled bitterly. 'Terminal. That's partly why I was released early. If you came here looking for some kind of justice, that's about all I can offer you.'

'I am sorry,' answered Fabel. 'Goodbye, Frau Menzel.'

'Goodbye, Herr Kriminalhauptkommissar.'

Thursday 19 June, 6.00 p.m. Pöseldorf, Hamburg.

On the way back from Bremen, Fabel phoned in to the Mordkommission. He asked Maria to compile all the information she could on Wolfgang Eitel. There was nothing new to report from the Kommission, so Fabel told her he would not come in until the morning. He hung up and redialled, asking to be put through to Brauner, who told him that Schreiber's fingerprints matched the second set found in Blüm's apartment. For once, the presence of fingerprints exculpated rather than incriminated a suspect. If Schreiber had been the killer, he would have done everything he could to wipe all traces of his presence from the apartment. And Son of Sven had left them nothing at any other scene to go on.

Fabel had a reserved space in an underground parking garage along the street from his apartment. It had just turned eight when he pulled into his space. When he got out of the car he placed his hands in the small of his back and arched his spine, trying to stretch some of the stiffness and tiredness out of it. It was then that he became aware of the presence of two huge men behind him. He spun around and instinctively placed his hand on his gun. Both men smiled and held up their hands in a pacifying gesture. Each was black-haired, one with thick curls, the other with straight hair sleeked back against his scalp. Curly also sported an unfeasibly large and thick moustache. They were clearly Turkish. It was Curly who spoke.

'Please, Herr Fabel . . . we want no trouble and we didn't mean to startle you. Herr Yilmaz has sent us. He would like to talk to you. Now, if it's convenient.'

'And if it isn't?'

Curly shrugged. 'Of course, that is entirely up to you. But Herr Yilmaz told us to tell you that he has something for you that may be of importance to your investigation.'

'Where is he?'

'We are to take you to him . . .' Curly's smile broadened in a way that didn't make Fabel feel any more secure – 'if that is convenient to you.

Fabel smiled and shook his head. 'I'll take my car and follow you.'

The two heavies had a Polo waiting outside and Fabel followed them as they made their way through the city. They led Fabel into the Harburg area. Fabel called the Mordkommission and told Werner that he was being taken to a meeting with an informant, but didn't tell Werner it was Yilmaz. Werner was all for sending out a full back-up team but Fabel told him to hold off and that he would ring him back when he knew where the meeting was to take place.

The Turks' VW pulled into a small estate of unimaginatively designed industrial and commercial buildings. They parked in front of a wide, low-rise warehouse. It had been built at some point in the seventies or eighties and the bright red paint was flaking off the exterior metal pipes that had been the only concession to the architectural fashions of the period. As the two Turks were getting out of their car, Fabel called Werner back and gave him his location.

'Take care, Jan,' Werner said.

'I'll be fine. But if I don't check in in half an hour, send the cavalry.'

Fabel flipped his cell phone shut and got out of his BMW. Curly beamed a searchlight smile from underneath his dense moustache and held open a door which was in as much need of a paint job as the pipework. Fabel indicated that it was okay; the two Turks could precede him.

The warehouse was small but packed with crates of food-stuffs, all of which were labelled in a language that Fabel assumed to be Turkish. A partition wall, as much wire-reinforced glass window as plasterboard, ran along one side of the building: the aspect looking out onto the car park. This division separated the main warehouse from the offices. Through the glass of the main office, Fabel could see Yilmaz sitting with two men. One was a tough-looking Turk; the second was a small, dirty-looking man in a filthy military-style coat. He had the jaundiced skin tone and sunken eyes of a habitual drug user.

Curly held open the door for Fabel, still grinning, but didn't follow Fabel into the office. Yilmaz stood up and smiled, genuinely, and extended a hand which Fabel took.

'Thank you for coming, Herr Fabel. I'm sorry we couldn't conduct our business in more conducive surroundings, but I thought it best not to be too conspicuous. I have . . . or rather my friend here has some important information for you. I have kept my promise, you see, Herr Hauptkommissar.'

Fabel scrutinised the small whippet-like man. Like most users, he was ageless. Fabel knew he might have been in only his late twenties. Equally, he could have been in his late fifties. Fabel noticed that one of the high cheekbones was swollen and even more discoloured than the skin around it. There was a crust of dried blood around one nostril.

'Are you okay?' asked Fabel.

'I fell down some stairs,' the small man replied in a high, throaty voice, giving the tough-looking Turk a resentful look.

'This . . . *gentleman* . . . is Hansi Kraus,' said Yilmaz. 'He has some information . . . indeed some evidence . . . he wishes to share with you.' Yilmaz nodded to the Turk who had been leaning against one of the desks. The Turk reached behind him and picked up a bundle of soiled rags. He carefully unfolded the corners to reveal a glittering gold-coloured nine-millimetre automatic. The flanks of the gun were ornately tooled and the word ΦOPT12 in Cyrillic was engraved into them. Beneath, in the Latin alphabet, were the words MADE IN UKRAINE.

'Herr Kraus wants to hand this over as material evidence in the murder of Hans Klugmann,' said Yilmaz. 'He apologises for the delay . . . he had intended to hand it in, but it completely slipped his mind.'

'Where did you find this?' Fabel asked Hansi Kraus.

Kraus looked from Yilmaz to the other Turk to Fabel. 'In the swimming pool. I was there when that guy got his in the head.'

'You witnessed the murder of Hans Klugmann?'

Kraus nodded.

'Did you see his killers?'

Kraus hesitated. The tough Turk shifted on his desk, creaking the leather of his jacket. Kraus glanced at him and nodded again.

'Could you recognise them again?'

'Yes. An older guy and a younger guy. They both looked fuckin' hard. The younger guy was built like Arnold Schwarzenegger. It was the young guy who popped the dead guy.'

Fabel gestured to the other Turk, who handed him the gun. Fabel kept his hands flat and held the gun as if he were holding a hot roast on an over mitt. MADE IN UKRAINE. 'Were they foreigners? Did you hear them speaking Russian or something like that?'

'No . . . I mean yes, I did hear them, but no, they weren't foreigners. They were German. The older guy was banging on about the area having gone to shit. He said something about having brought a girl to the swimming pool when he was younger. They definitely weren't Ivans.'

'What about the gun? Where did you get that?'

'I saw them dump it in a trash can. When they left I went and got it out.'

'You followed them?'

'No. They dumped the gun in the trash can inside the Schwimmhalle.'

'They didn't make any effort to hide it?'

'Not much. And there's a canal just a few metres from the pool. I guess they didn't care if it was found or not.'

'Or maybe they wanted it found . . .' Yilmaz suggested.

'That's what it looks like,' agreed Fabel. 'German hitmen – a Ukrainian weapon. It would appear they were trying to point us in the wrong direction.' He turned back to Hansi. 'I need you to come down to the Präsidium and make a full statement. And I need you to look at some mug shots; see if you can identify the shooters.'

Hansi Kraus nodded. He looked less than happy about it, but had the doomed air of someone who accepts that shit happens. And usually to him.

Fabel placed a hand on the shoulder of Kraus's grubby military overcoat. 'Listen Hansi, I can't make you do this. And nor can Herr Yilmaz or anyone else . . .' He looked pointedly at the other Turk who returned his gaze disinterestedly. 'Your evidence is only good if you give it freely and honestly.'

Kraus gave a bitter laugh. 'Nice world you live in, Herr Hauptkommissar . . . I'll give you your statement.'

Fabel led Kraus out to his car. Yilmaz walked with them

to the door. 'I appreciate your help on this, Herr Yilmaz,' Fabel said, and meant it.

Yilmaz smiled broadly and gave a dismissive shrug.

'But I take it you understand that this doesn't buy you any favours from me,' said Fabel. 'I owe you for this, but I'll never compromise the law or myself to help you out.'

'That is something I already know.' Yilmaz laughed. 'I didn't expect anything in return. That's the problem with dealing with an honest policeman. The only thing I'd ask is that my part is kept out of Hansi's statement.'

'That's one compromise I can make. Thanks again. Goodbye, Herr Yilmaz.'

All the way back to the Präsidium, Fabel had kept his window open to mitigate the influence Hansi's overcoat was having on his upholstery. When Fabel arrived, he handed Hansi over to Werner and told him to order something from the canteen for their guest to eat. Looking at Kraus, however, led Fabel to believe that they would have to turn him loose reasonably soon: his eyes were becoming increasingly mobile, darting from side to side, like those of a hunted animal. There was also a nervous intensity to his movements. Fabel knew Hansi needed a fix and they had only so long to get information out of him.

Back at his office, Fabel cleared his desk of clutter, heaping files into a pile on the floor and pushing his keyboard and mouse to one side. He found a large layout pad in the bottom drawer of his desk and flipped through it until he found a clean page. As he laid the pad on his desk, an image of Angelika Blüm's apartment came spontaneously to mind. He remembered the cleared coffee table, with objects placed out of the way to allow the unobstructed flow of ideas. He felt another pang of guilt when he thought about a woman he had never met, but whom he now knew so intimately, who had tried so insistently to make contact with him.

Angelika Blüm was the first name he wrote down. Next to her name he wrote that of Ursula Kastner. Then Tina Kramer. He drew a vertical line and divided the page in two, with the three victims' names on one side. On the other he wrote the names of Hans Klugmann and John MacSwain. Another vertical line. Then he wrote the name Mahmoot had mentioned to him, Vasyl Vitrenko.

Half an hour later Fabel had six vertical columns of names, dates and key facts. Each column was headed by one of the six names he had begun with. The column headed with the name of Vasyl Vitrenko was the sparsest. Fabel had plotted out all of the possible connections, coincidences and commonalities. The result was a tighter summary of what was already on the incident board. But there was no redundancy in redrafting the information. For Fabel the activity itself was the goal: refocusing and reordering his thoughts; a chance to map out the journey he had made. One name appeared regularly in half of the columns: Eitel. The first victim, Ursula Kastner was involved, albeit tangentially, with Neuer Horizont, the major shareholder for which was the Eitel Group; there was no known connection with the second victim, Tina Kramer; the third victim, Angelika Blüm, knew Eitel junior and had interviewed Eitel senior and, according to her friend, Erika Kessler, was working on a negative story about one or both of the Eitels; John MacSwain worked for the Eitel Group. Vitrenko's outfit seemed to cast a shadow behind the rows of names and facts. Klugmann had been trying to infiltrate the Ukrainians and a Ukrainian-manufactured handgun had been retrieved from the murder scene. But the shooters had not been Ukrainian. Kraus was absolutely certain about that. Angelika Blüm had been working on a story relating to the actions of former Soviet police and security battalions, probably drawing comparisons with the experiences of Hamburg's BATT101 during the Second World War.

And, of course, Fabel had suffered the ignominy of having

his ass kicked by some kind of Slavic senior citizen. To say his attacker had known how to handle himself would be an immense understatement: he was obviously a highly trained professional. Fabel circled Vitrenko's name. He had no idea how old Vitrenko was. Could the older guy have been Vitrenko himself?

Hans Schreiber, Erster Bürgermeister of the Free and Hanseatic City and State of Hamburg was also a conspicuous presence. He had known two of the victims, one of them intimately. And he had been the last person to see Angelika Blüm alive – except for her killer.

Fabel leaned back in his chair, placed his hands behind his head and looked down onto the page, as if surveying the landscape of his investigation from high ground. He needed to talk to both Eitels, father and son. He wanted to see his hunch about MacSwain played out. Fabel was not convinced that MacSwain was their man, but there was something that didn't smell right about him. He looked at Anna Wolff's proposal for the Friday-night 'date' operation. It was well worked out, but Fabel was still uneasy about placing Anna so close to a possible suspect; and they would have to be very careful to avoid accusations of entrapment.

Fabel had been so involved in navigating the deep channels of his own thoughts that the phone startled him. It was Holger Brauner, the head of the scene-of-crime team.

'Well, Jan, I can honestly say that you make sure life is never dull. That was a very unusual piece of ordnance you brought in.'

'Is it the murder weapon?'

'Yes. It is. And like I say, it's a very, very unusual and interesting piece to turn up in Hamburg.'

'Oh?'

'It's a FORT Twelve, that's what the Cyrillic lettering stands for. It's a nine-millimetre. Basically it has a nine-by-eighteen Makarov chamber, takes twelve rounds and is a double-action, blowback-operated pistol. And here's the interesting bit. It is a Ukrainian police and security-forces weapon.' Fabel absorbed the fact. Another connection. Brauner continued. 'The Soviet security services relied on Makarov PM pistols, but after the break-up of the Communist bloc, Ukrainian special forces and security services demanded something more reliable, so they bought Czech machinery from the Uhersky Brod factory and started producing the FORT Twelve.'

'And it's exclusively non-civilian issue?'

'As far as I'm aware. I got Kapff, our ballistics and firearms guy, to dig up the information. Basically it's a police and security services rather than an army weapon.'

'Thanks, Holger.' Fabel hung up and then redialled Werner in the interview room. There was no answer. He went out into the main Mordkommission office. Maria Klee was the only one there.

'You seen Werner?' Fabel asked. Maria said she hadn't. 'I'm heading home. If you see Werner tell him to give me a buzz. I just wanted to know how he got on with Hansi Kraus.'

'Are you still on for our meeting with the Odinist weirdo. Ten tomorrow morning?'

'I can hardly wait.'

It was about half past eight when Fabel left the Mordkommission. He called Susanne from his car. She had already eaten but agreed to meet him in a bar in the Milchstrasse. After he hung up he put the top down on his car and slipped a Bap album in the car's CD player. *Fortsetzung Folgt*. He turned the volume up and his cell phone off. Tonight he was going to have a night off. *Feierabend*.

Friday 20 June, 10.00 a.m. Schanzenviertel, Hamburg.
The Schanzenviertel is one of the areas of Hamburg that still has a lingering reputation bordering on the seedy and yet is

on the cusp of trendiness. The quarter is packed with a range of restaurants, bars and cafés that reflect the multicultural profile of its population, and there is a rich variety of speciality shops and stores. Yet alongside the cool sit the poor, with sub-standard housing for immigrant families. The large Sternschanzen Park with its monumental Wasserturm attracts families by day and drug dealers by night and has been the scene of anti-drugs protests by the forces of gentrification.

Bjorn Janssen's enterprise was squeezed between an espresso stand and a sushi bar just off Stresemannstrasse. It was a narrow, cramped space from which he sold books, artefacts and artworks, all of which looked second hand and which were all vaguely New Age.

Bjorn Janssen was not exactly what Fabel had in mind whenever he visualised a Viking. Admittedly he had blond hair, but it was a shade or two darker than Fabel's own, and carefully but unsuccessfully arranged to conceal the pink sheen of a balding scalp. Janssen was a short and rather plump man who spoke German perfectly but to the music of a distinct Danish accent. The idea of Janssen as a steel-helmed berserker, leaping from a longboat and swinging a Viking battleaxe, stretched beyond both the comical and the physically feasible.

Janssen was standing behind a cluttered counter and extended his hand across the disorder when the two police officers approached. He had a furtive manner about him and Fabel noticed that the surreptitious glances of his watery blue eyes fell frequently onto Maria's legs and breasts. She caught him at it and her returned gaze very eloquently expressed the word 'creep'.

'Herr Janssen.' Fabel smiled politely. 'Frau Klee here tells me that you belong to an Odinist cult, and that you may be able to offer us some assistance on a case we've been working on.'

Janssen smiled back and shook his head. His expression

was one of weary indulgence. 'No no no, Herr Fabel. I'm not involved in any *cult*. I am the *Gothi* – the High Priest – of the *Blot* of Asatru. I am a practitioner of the original faith system of northern Europe.'

'Whatever. I would like you to tell us something about the system of beliefs you have. We are investigating murders that have a ritualistic element to them. We believe that this element is perhaps influenced by old Norse rituals.'

'I can assure you, Herr Fabel, that Asatru is a faith of peace and harmony.'

'Two values marauding Vikings were particularly renowned for,' Maria said, levering a sneer into her tone.

Janssen smiled at her and continued. 'Asatru was the faith of all northern and western Germanic peoples: the Svear, who became the Swedes, the Dan, who became the Danes, the Angles, who became the English, and the various tribes who became the Germans. Men and women, farmers and warriors, freemen and slaves. It was no more exclusively the religion of the raiders than Christianity was the exclusive religion of the Nazis. Anyway, the etymology of the word "Viking" is obscure. Some say it comes from *Vik* meaning village . . . that the Vikings were merely villagers who went on trading and raiding journeys when harvests didn't meet the needs of a growing population. Their beliefs were more founded in nature than in war.'

'But they made blood sacrifices,' said Fabel.

'Yes. And we still do. The *hlautbowl* is the vessel of the *Blot*. Today we fill it with honey mead and drink from it before offering up the share apportioned to the gods. *Blot* is the old Norse word for "blood". In the olden days the *hlaut-bowl* would be filled with blood from a slaughtered animal. It's a mistake to believe that this was a barbaric or exceptional act. People would slaughter the animal for the *Blot* in much the same way they would do so for a feast to be shared with a visitor. Asatru has a more *immediate* relationship with

its gods and they were treated more like real, living and par-
ticipative elements in ordinary, daily life.'

'And sacrifice no longer plays a part in Asatru?'

'Oh yes . . . very much so. The *Blot* is still a ritual of sacrifice. But in Asatru, the concept of sacrifice is more in the
sense of giving. Sometimes we pour the mead onto the ground,
to honour the Mother Earth. We give to her in return for
what she has given us. Our sacrifices and symbolisms have
been subsumed into Christianity. The Roman Catholic Mass,
for example, or harvest festivals. And Easter is the theft of
the goddess *Eostre*, who turned herself into a hare and hid
golden eggs in the fields. That's why children still go on egg
hunts.'

'Do women have any role in your religion?' asked Maria.

'Indeed they do, Frau Oberkommissarin.' Janssen's smile
stopped just short of a leer. 'Women are the creators of life.
They are revered in Asatru and often it is the *Gythia*, or
priestess, rather than the *Gothi* who presides over the *Blot*.'

Maria looked unimpressed. 'And what is the special "gift"
women are supposed to offer up?'

'I don't understand your question . . .' answered Janssen,
but his expression suggested that he did.

Fabel reached into his inside jacket pocket and produced
a copy of the photograph taken at the Stadtkrankenhaus
Cuxhaven of Michaela Palmer's forehead. 'I believe this to
be the rune *Gebu* . . .'

Janssen shrugged. 'It could also just be a cross. An X.'

'This mark was daubed on the forehead of a victim who
was forced to take part in a Norse-type ritual. She was repeat-
edly raped by men wearing masks of a one-eyed, bearded
figure.'

Janssen winced. 'Wotan . . . or Odin . . .' He thought for
a moment. 'Whoever these people are, Herr Fabel, they are
committing not just a terrible crime but an offence against a
peaceful, gentle faith. Asatru, unlike other faiths, believes in

the freedoms and rights of the individual as being inviolable. I'll help you in any way I can.' Janssen looked more closely at the photograph. 'Yes . . . yes . . . that could be the rune *Gebu*. *Gebu* has a specific relevance to the *Blot*. It is the symbol of giving and of sacrifice. As I said, the two concepts are closely related.'

'You claim none of your devotees would be involved in something like this?'

'Certainly not! This is a corruption of our faith. Much in the way a Black Mass is a corruption of Catholicism.' Janssen paused as if weighing something up.

'What is it, Herr Janssen?'

'There were rumours . . . a couple of years ago.'

'About what?' The impatience was clear in Maria's voice. Fabel gave her a quick look.

'There are a few Asatru groups in and around Hamburg. We all share the same broad beliefs and are opposed to any negative or violent interpretation of them. But like every other religion there can be a darker aspect. A couple of years ago there was talk of some breakaway group. They were supposed to be few in number and I heard that they were very exclusive in their membership.'

'And this group was supposed to be on the black-magic side of all of this . . .' Maria struggled for a word – *'religion?'*

Janssen nodded. 'They were supposed to be focused on *seidhr* . . . that's the shamanic tradition in Odinism. You asked about the role of women in Asatru. Well there is a tradition of women being the main practitioners of *seidhr*. This group, however, were supposed to be mainly or exclusively men.'

'Do you have any idea who was involved in this group?'

'I don't know. Like I say, it was all rumour at the time. But I do know that the word was that this group included very important people. I also heard that there was a foreigner involved with it.'

Fabel and Maria exchanged glances.

'Could ritualised rape play a part in their ceremonies?' asked Fabel

'Not in any traditionally legitimate way. But one element of the *Blot* is the concept of self-sacrifice. Giving oneself. Maybe it's a perverted interpretation of that. Certainly the rune *Gebu* is associated with the "gift" or the sacrifice. It is recited as a *galdr* or ritual chant during a *Blot*. There's also the concept of *ond*. It means ecstasy. It really means "joy", but it's open to perverted interpretation, I suppose. And I won't deny that there were some dark acts committed by the ancient practitioners. An Arab observer witnessed a woman at a Viking chief's funeral having sex with seven different men before boarding the funeral longship and being burned alive with the body of the chieftain.'

'So much for your peaceful, gentle religion,' said Maria.

'And Christians used to burn heretics and so-called witches at the stake,' said Janssen, with a cold smile and a glance at Maria's blouse. 'Like every philosophy or religion, Asatru is open to abuse. I really have no idea whether the rumours about this sect were true, or if indeed they have any connection to the crime you're investigating. I'm just trying to be helpful.'

'And you have been, Herr Janssen,' said Fabel with a meaningful look in Maria's direction. 'Very helpful. Was there any mention of where this "foreigner" might have come from?'

Janssen shook his head. 'Sorry.'

'Or where this group held their meetings?'

'No. I'm afraid not. They were supposed to be very secretive.'

'Thanks again for your help,' Fabel said and extended his hand to Janssen.

Janssen made a big deal of coming around his counter and showing them out. 'Anytime,' he said. He held the door open for them both, his smile reserved exclusively for Maria.

They had taken Maria's car and were parked around the corner. She beeped off the car alarm and Fabel paused, his hand resting on the door handle and looking over the roof at Maria.

'What?' she said, defensively.

Fabel smiled. 'You don't like Herr Janssen very much . . . do you?'

Maria feigned a shudder, grimaced and made an *uurgh* sound.

'Such a pity,' Fabel said getting into the car, 'I rather think he had a thing for you.'

Maria didn't switch on the engine immediately. Her face was thoughtful and her gaze unfocused.

'It's weird, isn't it?'

'What?' asked Fabel.

'The way people are always reaching out for something. And sometimes that something is as scary as hell.'

'You mean the breakaway group Janssen was talking about? The fringe element's fringe element?'

'Yeah. Do you think Janssen really believes all of that Asatru crap? Or the people carrying out these rapes? Do they feel they have some religious justification?'

Fabel pursed his lips. 'I doubt it, Maria. Not on any meaningful level, that is. As for Janssen . . . maybe. As you say, there are so many people clutching at moral straws, trying to give shape and meaning to their lives. It's a dark and lonely universe otherwise.'

Maria started the engine and pulled out into the traffic.

Friday 20 June, 12.00 p.m. Polizeipräsidium, Hamburg.
Norbert Eitel's secretary's sole mission seemed to be to prevent the outside world from having any contact with her boss. She eventually put Fabel's call through, but only after he threatened to arrive unannounced with a team of officers and arrest anyone who obstructed them.

'Yes, Herr Kriminalhauptkommissar . . .' Norbert Eitel sounded distracted, as if he were reading something of much more importance while he spoke to Fabel. 'What is it I can do for you?'

'I would very much like to come and talk to you . . . and to your father, should he be available at the same time.'

'May I ask in regard to what?'

'I understand you knew Angelika Blüm?'

'Oh . . . yes . . . a terrible, terrible thing. But how can we help?' Fabel could tell he now had Eitel's full attention.

'Background mainly.'

'But my father didn't know Angelika. I think they only met once and very briefly . . . I can't see what use he can be.'

'Well I think we're better discussing this when we meet. Could you make time at two-thirty this afternoon?'

'Well . . . I suppose so, but I can't speak for my father. He does not work in this business. He has his own interests.'

'That's fine, Herr Eitel. If your father can't make it, we can arrange for a car to pick him up and bring him down to the Präsidium . . . I wouldn't want to inconvenience him.'

Eitel's voice turned cold and hard in the face of the threat. 'I'll see what I can do,' he said, and hung up.

Fabel arranged lunch for everyone to be delivered to the Mordkommission from the canteen. He was keen for Anna to go through her briefing for the MacSwain operation the following evening. Anna had made only a few changes from her initial proposal. She had asked for two extra officers to work on the surveillance team, boosting its number to ten, not including herself. Fabel approved of the added security and suspected that Paul Lindemann had insisted on it. As Fabel had hoped, Anna had chosen Paul to lead the back-up teams. There would be two officers inside the club; the other eight would be split between five vehicles. The main vehicle would be a panel van that would house two heavily armed

MEK officers, Paul and Maria, as well as the electronic equipment to listen in on Anna's wire. The van would operate as the command centre, monitoring activity and issuing instructions to the rest of the team. There would be two team members on motorcycles, allowing them to match MacSwain's Porsche for speed, and two cars, each with a Mordkommission officer. Altogether, it meant that MacSwain's tail could continually change to avoid suspicion, and if he put a foot wrong, he would be swamped by police officers within seconds. As Van Heiden had already pointed out, it was an expensive operation to launch based on Fabel's hunch and Anna's on-the-spot improvisation. This was as secure an operation as Fabel could justify a budget for.

After the briefing, Fabel called Anna, Paul, Werner and Maria into his office. He told them about the meeting with the Eitels that afternoon and asked if both Maria and Werner would come along.

'I want to outnumber them . . . or at least match their numbers,' said Fabel when asked why. 'There are two of them and I suspect they will have at least one lawyer present. I just want to make our presence felt.'

Fabel had the Klugmann murder weapon and the full report back from Brauner. He updated everyone on the background to the gun and what Hansi Kraus had said about the shooters. Fabel invited opinions.

'Looks to me like we were meant to find the gun,' volunteered Maria, 'and Kraus screwed things up by being there and picking it up first. Someone wanted us to think that it was a Ukrainian hit.'

'But they would have known that it looked contrived,' said Fabel.

'That's only because we have someone who overheard them and can identify that they were German,' said Werner. 'If we didn't have that we could have read the deliberate leaving behind of the gun as some kind of message . . . a claim of responsibility.' He frowned. 'There's something odd going on with Hansi Kraus, *Chef*.

'I got a full statement from him last night and we went through some of the photo files. Then I took him to the canteen for something to eat. I don't know what the hell got into him but all of a sudden he said he had to go. I asked him what the hurry was but he didn't say anything that made any sense. He promised to come back in today, but I said he'd have to stay a little longer to check through some more mug-shots. I sat him down at a table and went up to the counter – when I came back he was gone. That's when you tried to get a hold of me . . . I was running around trying to find him.'

'But you got his statement?' asked Fabel. Werner confirmed that he had. 'I wouldn't worry about him taking off, Werner. He has a habit to feed and, when I last saw him, he was looking particularly ropy. We'll pick him up if he doesn't come in.' Fabel turned to Maria. 'Did you get the information I asked for on the Eitels?'

Maria handed Fabel a folder she had brought with her. 'Eitel senior is not a pleasant piece to research. My notes are all in there, but to summarise . . . Wolfgang Eitel is seventy-nine years old. He is originally from the Passau region of Oberbayern. He was a member of the Hitler Youth until 1942 when he enlisted in the SS. Like most SS swine, he seems to suffer from selective amnesia, but the records, as far as they can be trusted, show that he started as an SS Untersturmführer – a second lieutenant – and was a Hauptsturmführer – a captain – at his time of arrest by the Allies.'

Fabel slipped out a black-and-white photograph of an arrogant young man, no older than twenty-one but trying to affect the look of someone more authoritative. He was wearing an SS uniform. Fabel had expected to see the double-lightning-bolt Ss on the collar. Suddenly Fabel remembered that, had they been there, he would again have been looking at an ancient Germanic rune. The *Sigrunen* – the ancient rune for victory – had been appropriated by the Nazis and used as the double-S insignia of the Schutzstaffel. But they were absent in this photograph. Instead Eitel's right collar patch was of a white lion rampant against a black background. Fabel turned the photograph to Maria. 'What does this insignia mean?'

Maria smiled broadly. 'Now that takes us into interesting territory. I have no doubt that this is coincidental, but that is the insignia of the Fourteenth Waffen-Grenadier Division der SS. Also known as the Division-Galizien – the Galician Division. And as you know, Galicia was the historical region that encompasses part of modern Ukraine. The Galician Division of the SS was made up of Ukrainians who saw it as a way of liberating their country from Stalin.'

'Ukrainian men but mostly German officers.'

'Exactly. And Eitel was one of them. After its defeat at the battle of . . .' Maria paused and consulted her notes – 'Brody, the division made its way back to Austria. It was there that Eitel surrendered to the Allies, desperate to stay out of Soviet hands. After the war he was imprisoned for four years. He began Eitel Importing in Munich in 1956 and was a multi-millionaire by the mid-sixties. His late wife was from Hamburg and he moved his headquarters here in seventy-two. He helped his son set up the Eitel Media Group and sold Eitel Importing to the Group ten years ago. That allowed him to concentrate on his "political" career. He established the BDD – the *Bund Deutschland-für-Deutsche* – in 1979. It didn't make much of a mark until the fall of the Wall and the *Wende*. Even then its support was weak and sporadic. In short, a nasty piece of work.'

Fabel stared at Maria as if studying her would help him to process the information she had supplied. Then he said: 'It's odd the number of times a Ukrainian connection comes up in this case.'

'This time, as I said, it's more than likely just coincidental,' said Maria.

Fabel shrugged. 'I suppose so.' He paused. 'What about the son – Norbert?'

'A tabloid publisher with political ambitions. He studied at Hamburg and Heidelberg and set up *SCHAU MAL!* with his father's support, including financial help. Through acquisition and growth the Eitel Group is involved in all forms of communication media, including the Internet . . .'

'That's why they'll use someone like MacSwain,' Werner interrupted.

Maria continued. 'The Group also has interests in tabloid publishing in the Netherlands, Poland and the Czech Republic. As well as media, there is a property-management business and a small-scale development company. Added to all of that is the import-export business Norbert bought from his father. Politically, his stance is right of centre. Way right of centre. But he stands as an independent. He obviously realises affiliation with the BDD would be a liability. He insists he is no neo-Nazi or extreme-rightist. But his platform is primarily anti-immigration and pro law and order. He is married to some aristo. Martha Von Berg.'

'Any relation to Jürgen Von Berg, the city senator?' asked Fabel.

'Don't know, *Chef*. I do know she's kept her name and he went around for a time calling himself Norbert Von Berg Eitel. But he dropped that. The price of including his wife's aristocratic name meant he was seen as adopting the trendy new custom of more liberal German men of combining their names with their wives'. It didn't fit with the traditionalist image. He also had a reputation for womanising, which he has done much to play down.'

Fabel rubbed his chin. 'Nice people.' He looked at his watch. 'I think it's time we paid them a visit.'

Friday 20 June, 2.30 p.m. Neustadt, Hamburg.
The Eitel Media Group had its offices in a burnished steel
and glass commercial monolith in the heart of the Neustadt's
business district. Fabel had an interest in good architecture;
which meant he had no interest in this building. It was a
soulless, corporate box that was finished with expensive
fittings but had all the character of a hotel lobby. The
uniformed commissionaire, who manned the reception desk
on the ground floor, guided Fabel and his entourage to the
elevators.

The first two floors of the building were occupied by the
editorial offices of *SCHAU MAL!*, the third by *TVEspresso*,
a weekly television guide published by the Eitel Group. The
fourth floor was designated Communications Department.
The floor above was devoted to the Group's corporate and
administrative offices. This was where Norbert Eitel had his
suite.

A middle-aged woman with a severe expression was waiting
as the lift doors opened onto a large open-plan office. Fabel
guessed this was the person with whom he had crossed swords
on the phone. Her face suggested that she was not used to
having her authority outflanked.

'You are here to see Herr Eitel?'

Fabel flashed his oval KriPo disk. 'I'm Hauptkommissar
Fabel.'

She examined the others with a studied and pompous
disdain, which was instantly punctured by Werner's laughter.

'Follow me,' she said grudgingly.

Fabel, Werner and Maria, were shown to a cheerless reception bay at the far side of the office, a shore on which broke
the babble of voices from the sea of desks. After ten minutes
they were summoned into a glass-fronted meeting room by
the stone-faced secretary.

Norbert Eitel entered the room a minute later. Jacketless,
he had his shirt sleeves folded clear of his wrists and his tie

had been loosened. He smiled a polite smile but his body language was one of a man with more important things to do. He held open the door for a tall, lean, aristocratic-looking older man with a crest of thick, ivory hair that had refused to retreat from its hairline of sixty years before. Fabel recognised the older man as the SS officer in the photograph, except now he had fully achieved the authoritative maturity that he had sought so hard to project as an arrogant youth. Eitel senior was followed by a man of middle height in his late thirties.

'Good day, Herr Hauptkommissar Fabel,' said Norbert Eitel. 'This is my father, Wolfgang Eitel.' Eitel senior extended his hand and gave a sharp nod of his head. Fabel almost expected to hear heels clicking. 'And this is Wilfried Waalkes, our head of legal affairs.'

Fabel and Maria exchanged smiles. The lawyer. Fabel introduced Werner and Maria. Fabel studied the lawyer for a moment. Waalkes was a Frisian name, but the lawyer's *'Guten Tag'* was in a geographically indistinct Hochdeutsch.

'What can I do to help you?' said Norbert Eitel, a wave of his hand indicating that they should all take a seat around the oval conference table. Before Fabel could answer he added: 'Can I get you anything? Coffee . . . tea?'

'We're fine, thanks.' Fabel answered for everyone. The lawyer and Eitel senior took their places. 'We would like to ask you about Angelika Blüm. Could you tell me what kind of relationship you had with her, personally and professionally?'

'Personally, not much . . . professionaly none. To be frank, Angelika would look down her nose at our publications. She considered herself to be in a different league.'

'And you don't agree with her assessment?'

Norbert Eitel laughed. 'I had a very high regard for Angelika's abilities. But I also happen to consider our titles as a quality market offering. My main contact with Angelika was through trade events and mutual friends. We were acquainted.'

'And you, Herr Eitel?' Maria addressed Eitel senior. 'What contact did you have with Frau Blüm?'

Wolfgang Eitel tilted his head back and regarded Maria down his aquiline nose. 'None. Well, we met just the once, at the Altona Krone . . . that would be a couple of weeks ago.'

'But I dare say she was not particularly popular with either of you . . .' Maria left the thought hanging.

'I don't understand . . .' Norbert Eitel employed the geniality of his features in a confused smile while his father remained expressionless.

'Frau Blüm was about to publish a story alleging you were engaged in property speculation that involved foreign interests.' Maria kept an even, authoritative tone as she spoke. Fabel stared hard at Norbert Eitel, determined not to show any surprise at Maria's bluff. Eitel's smile showed no sign of shifting and its endurance, in itself, made it seem fake. Maria had hit the mark. But it was Norbert's father who spoke.

'Herr Hauptkommissar Fabel, we were not aware that Frau Blüm intended running any kind of story on either my son or myself. It is true that we have property interests. It is true that we do business with other nations. My own career was based on importing and exporting. If Frau Blüm was about to run a story about us then not only were we totally unaware of it, I can assure you we have no idea what the grounds for such a story would be.'

Fabel changed tack. 'I believe you served in the *Ostfront* during the war. You commanded Ukrainians, didn't you?'

A spark became a flame that became a raging dark fire in Wolfgang Eitel's eyes. But nothing of it leaked out into his voice, his expression, his movements.

'I really don't see what that has to do with anything, Herr Hauptkommissar . . .' Fabel felt as if he were looking in through a metre of lead glass into the heart of a nuclear reactor: witnessing something uniquely powerful and deadly, but contained.

'It's just that the Ukraine has featured so prominently in our investigation.' It was true; but how would Eitel interpret it? Fabel paused, inviting him to comment.

Wolfgang Eitel smoothed the ivory hair at his temples with the heels of both hands. But it was his son who spoke: 'We have business interests across Europe and beyond. We own publications in the Netherlands, in Poland, in Hungary. Our property business involves partners in the United States as well as those in the Ukraine. I don't see that that is, in itself, particularly newsworthy.'

Bull's-eye. Fabel and Maria exchanged a quick, surreptitious look. Fabel fought to keep the exhilaration of discovery from his expression. He again addressed Wolfgang Eitel.

'I think we all know that Frau Blüm's article was based on more than a simple deal with eastern-European business partners, don't we?'

'Then you know more than I, Herr Fabel.'

Waalkes, the lawyer, interrupted. 'I think this has gone quite far enough, Herr Hauptkommissar. We have agreed to this interview because everyone here is horrified by Frau Blüm's murder and we are committed to doing all we can to help catch this monster. But I have to say that your line of questioning seems both impertinent and irrelevant. You seem to be seeking to implicate my clients in some totally unrelated issue.'

'I wasn't aware we had accused anyone of anything,' said Maria. 'We're simply trying to find the connection between the Eitel Group and Frau Blüm.'

'And I think we've dealt with that.' Norbert Eitel stood up to signal the discussion was at an end. None of the police officers followed his lead. Fabel addressed Waalkes.

'I think it would be in everyone's interest if both your

clients supplied us with accounts of their movements on the dates of the murders we're investigating, along with the names of anyone who can corroborate those accounts. And I'd be obliged if this could be done as soon as possible . . .'

'This is outrageous!' Eitel senior's voice thundered as he rose to his feet with a swiftness that belied his age. 'Are you accusing me or my son of involvement in these acts?'

Fabel, remaining in his chair, said, calmly: 'It is a routine enough request, Herr Eitel.' Maria handed Fabel a piece of paper on which she had written the times and dates of each murder. Fabel stood up and turned again to Eitel senior. 'Anyway, Herr Eitel, I should have thought that you have had some experience of answering difficult questions . . .'

This time it was Waalkes who exploded. 'That is quite enough, Herr Fabel! This is intolerable. I intend to notify your superiors about this . . .'

Fabel stood up and handed Waalkes the slip of paper. 'Times, places, witnesses . . . I need a full account for both your clients.' He turned to Norbert and Wolfgang Eitel. Eitel senior's eyes were incandescent beneath the thick white brows. 'Good day, gentlemen,' said Fabel and led Maria and Werner from the room.

They didn't speak until they were back in the elevator. As soon as the doors closed Fabel, Maria and Werner exchanged broad smiles.

'I think we have a lot of digging to do, don't you?' said Fabel.

'I'll get on it right away,' said Maria. 'It was very good of them to point us in the right direction. I'll start by getting a breakdown of all Ukrainian contacts Eitel Importing and the Eitel Group have had.'

'That was an excellent piece of work, Maria,' said Fabel. 'Thanks, *Chef*.'

Werner said nothing.

'By the way,' said Maria as the doors opened onto the

foyer, 'I meant to tell you earlier . . . I've got the details of any contact between currently serving Hamburg police officers and the Ukrainian security services. You're never going to believe the one name that came up.'

'Whose?'

'Yours.'

'What? I've never been to the Ukraine in my life.'

'Remember you wrote a paper for the Europol convention on psychotic serial offending? The one about the Helmut Schmied killings?'

'Yes . . .'

'Apparently it is used as a text at the Forensics and Criminology Centre in Odessa, where the Ukrainian police train to track down serial killers.'

Werner and Maria made their way towards the huge glass and chrome double doors of the street exit. Fabel stood for a moment looking after his colleagues, before following on behind.

Friday 20 June, 7.00 p.m. Polizeipräsidium, Hamburg.
Anna Wolff's colleagues were so accustomed to her customary neo-punk look of the overdone make-up, oversized leather jacket and the skin-tight jeans that they all looked somewhat startled when she walked into the main Mordkommission office. Werner and a couple of the back-up guys gave low whistles of appreciation, Maria complimented Anna on her look and Fabel made a small gesture of applause. Paul Lindemann simply looked worried.

Anna's make-up had been toned down to a subtle emphasis of her strong bone structure and she had softened the style of her short, dark hair. A black halter-neck dress that ended mid-thigh accentuated the curves of her body and exposed her shapely legs. Beneath the dress, tucked uncomfortably into her strapless brassiere, was the mobile transmitter, wire and microphone that Maria had helped her fit. Technical section had already tested that it was working.

'I would say the bait is on the hook,' said Maria with a smile.

'Okay,' said Fabel, 'let's go through it one more time. Anna?'

Anna Wolff went through the operation in detail once more. She saved the most important point until last.

'Remember my panic-button phrase. If you hear me say, "I don't feel too well," that's the signal for you to come in and get me.' Anna had chosen the words carefully. It was something you could say suddenly and in any context. The room buzzed with anticipation, nervousness and adrenalin. 'You sure you don't want to come along, *Chef*?'

'No, Anna . . . this is your gig. But I'll check in with the team to make sure everything is going okay. Good luck.'

'Thanks.'

The team followed Anna out to the car pool, leaving Fabel and Werner alone in the Mordkommission. The room seemed empty and dull, drained of the electricity that had filled it a few seconds before. Fabel and Werner stood in silence for a minute, then Werner turned to Fabel.

'Now?'

Fabel nodded. 'But stay well out of the operational area. Just move with the action and monitor the radio. I don't want Anna and Paul to think that I don't trust them to pull this off themselves. If there is any trouble, I'll have my cell phone on all night.'

'Sure, Jan.'

'And Werner . . .' said Fabel, 'I appreciate you doing this. It sets my mind at rest knowing they've got your expertise and experience just around the corner.'

Werner shrugged his tree-stump frame and grinned. 'It'll be fine,' he said. He gave his car keys a small toss in his hand, turned and made his way out of the office.

Friday 20 June, 8.00 p.m. St Pauli, Hamburg.

A large dark-blue Mercedes Vario panel van, its sides bearing the company logo of 'Ernst Thoms Elektriker' was parked opposite the entrance to the nightclub. Passers-by would have hardly registered its presence: the driver's and passenger's seats were empty and there was no sign of life other than the steady, silent spinning of the roof vent. What most people would also have failed to notice was that the second roof vent didn't spin, but remained open, facing the club.

Anna Wolff smiled to herself as the doorman held open the door, clearly not recognising her as the same woman who had demonstrated so spectacularly the flexibility of his thumb joints. She half turned in the doorway and glanced idly in the direction of the Mercedes van. She tapped her fingers against her chest in an absent-minded gesture then turned and entered the club. She knew that Paul and Maria, sitting in the cavernous rear of the van, watching the image from the roof-vent camera on a monitor, would have seen her tap and should have heard her too. If they hadn't, someone would have been straight over to pull her out. It was a disconcerting feeling, to be deaf but not dumb. Her watchers in the van could hear all that went on around her, every word that she spoke or that was spoken to her, yet she could not hear them. An earpiece would have been easily and quickly detectable. She knew, however, that there were already two members of the team inside the club, both equipped with earpiece radios, who would track her every move.

Anna took a deep breath and swung the door open into the main dance area of the club. The pulsing beat washed over her, but failed to rinse the feeling of unease from deep within her belly.

Friday 20 June, 8.00 p.m. Alsterpark, Hamburg.

Fabel met Susanne for a drink and something to eat in

Pöseldorf. Throughout the meal Fabel had been distracted and he apologised to Susanne.

'I have an officer out in the field,' he explained. 'And I can't say I'm totally happy with the situation.'

'Is it to do with the Son of Sven case?'

Fabel nodded. 'At least, it could be. I've let a young woman officer allow herself to be used as bait.'

'For Son of Sven?' Susanne was genuinely shocked. 'We're dealing with a highly dangerous, unpredictable and intelligent psychotic. You're right to be worried, Jan. I have to say I think it's bordering on the irresponsible.'

'Thanks for that,' Fabel said, gloomily. 'That makes me feel a lot better. But I'm not at all sure that this is our guy. Although he could well have something to do with the date-rape abductions.'

'All I can say is I hope your officer can take care of herself.'

'It's Anna Wolff. She's a hell of a lot tougher than she looks. In fact, she's a hell of a lot tougher than most of us. And she's got a full team backing her up.'

Susanne looked unconvinced. Her concerns spurred Fabel to phone Werner, who was monitoring radio traffic from the surveillance team. Nothing to report as yet. This was Fabel's third call and Werner's tone was that of a babysitter reassuring an overanxious parent. He told Fabel that Anna was in place and waiting for MacSwain to show, and reassured him once more that if there was anything significant happening then he would let Fabel know right away.

After their meal, Fabel and Susanne walked through the park and town to the waterfront and sat on one of the benches that looked out over the water. The sun was setting behind them and stretched their shadows out before them.

'I'm sorry I'm not much company.' He smiled weakly at Susanne, who leaned across and kissed him softly on the lips.

'I know. It's this case.' She kissed him again. 'Let's go back to your place and get a little drunk.'

Fabel smiled. 'Okay.'

They had just stood up when Fabel's cell phone rang. Fabel snapped it open, expecting to hear Werner's voice.

'Jan . . . it's Mahmoot.'

'Christ, Mahmoot, where have you been? I was getting—'

Mahmoot cut Fabel off. 'Jan, I need you to meet up with me now. It's important and I don't want to talk on the phone.'

'Okay.' Fabel looked at his watch and then at Susanne, making an apologetic gesture. 'Where are you?'

Mahmoot gave an address in the Speicherstadt.

'What on earth are you doing there?' Fabel laughed. 'Stocking up on coffee?'

Mahmoot's usual good humour seemed to have deserted him. 'Just get over here. Now.'

'Okay, I'll be there in ten minutes.'

'And, Jan . . .'

'Yes?'

'Come alone.'

The line went dead. Fabel snapped his cell phone shut and stared at it. In all their dealings Fabel had never once compromised Mahmoot's vital anonymity by bringing another officer along. Mahmoot could not have thought of a more redundant thing to say. The only way it made sense was if someone had told Mahmoot to say it: someone who wanted to make sure they got Fabel alone. He turned to Susanne.

'I'm really sorry. I have to go . . .'

'Is it to do with Son of Sven?'

'No . . . I think a friend might be in trouble.'

'You want me to come along?'

'No.' Fabel smiled and handed her the keys to his apartment. 'But keep the bed warm for me.'

'Is this dangerous? Shouldn't you get help?'

Fabel stroked Susanne's cheek. 'It's okay. Like I say, just something a friend needs help with. I need to pick up my car. Let's see if we can get a taxi . . .'

Friday 20 June, 9.00 p.m. St Pauli, Hamburg.
Anna had, at first, been polite and apologetic; but by the time the fifth guy in rapid succession had tried to pick her up, her responses had distilled to the sharp and bitter. When she heard yet another bar-room Romeo say 'Hi!' she spun round with her teeth bared.

MacSwain backed away with his hands raised.

'I'm sorry . . .' said Anna, sheepishly. 'I thought it was someone else . . . well, anyone else, I suppose . . .'

'I'm flattered.'

'Don't be. The competition's lousy.' Anna eyed him up and down. 'I was beginning to think you weren't going to show up.'

'I got held up at work. Sorry.' He held out his hand. 'I'm John MacSwain . . .' and then in English: 'it's nice to meet you . . .'

'Sara Klemmer . . .' said Anna, using the name of a former schoolfriend. 'Are you English?'

'Almost,' replied MacSwain. 'You hungry?'

Anna shrugged non-committally.

'Let's get out of here . . .'

From the command post within the parked van, Paul Lindemann alerted the officers inside the club. 'Get ready . . . we're on the move.' He turned to the MEK officer dressed in electrician's overalls. 'We go when the two lead cars are in position.'

Friday 20 June, 9.00 p.m. Speicherstadt, Hamburg.
Speicherstadt means 'warehouse city'. The Speicherstadt is one of the most striking cityscapes in Europe. The Gothic architecture of the vast, seven-storey, red brick warehouses, capped with verdigris-covered copper turrets, thrusts out of the harbour with an overwhelming confidence. The monumental

warehouses are interlaced with tight narrow streets and canals, and galleries span from one building to another, often at fourth-storey level.

Speicherstadt is also the biggest bonded warehouse on the planet: millions of tons of coffee, tea, tobacco and spices are stored in ten square miles, along with more modern commodities like computers, pharmaceuticals and furnishings. In recent years, there had been an influx of antique dealers who had set up next to the offices of maritime and trading businesses, and some of the coffee companies had opened up cafés for the public. But this was still very much an active part of Hamburg's life as one of the world's most important port cities.

Fabel parked in Deichstrasse, outside the customs-controlled Speicherstadt itself. He unholstered his Walther P99, checked the magazine and snapped it back with the heel of his hand before reholstering. He left his car and walked, the spires of the St Katharinenkirche and the St-Nikolai-Kirche piercing the sky behind him, across the Kornhaus-brücke that spanned the narrow Zollkanal. As he crossed the bridge he looked along the canal, hemmed in by the red brick cliff face of the looming warehouses. The sun was lower now and infused the rich red brickwork with a deeper red. Something more than unease fluttered in Fabel's chest. He walked past the customs point and found his way to St Annenufer. A couple of turns took him into the narrow cobbled street Mahmoot had mentioned on the phone.

It was darker in the Speicherstadt than in the city beyond. The sun now sat lower in the sky and it could not squeeze past the hulking Victorian cathedrals of commerce. There were no offices or coffee bars at ground level in this street; the windows of the warehouses lay dark and blank. Fabel was aware of his footsteps echoing in the empty street. He almost passed the number Mahmoot had given him. A small sign indicated that the warehouse was occupied by Klimenko

International. There was a large arched double doorway and no window at street level. Fabel turned the iron-ring handle and pushed: it was unlocked. He stepped through into a vast, open warehouse space, punctuated by the rows of brick and iron pillars that bore the weight of the floors above. The floor-to-ceiling height would have been almost nine metres and Fabel estimated there would be more than 400 square metres of floor area. The entire space was empty, except for a modular office cabin that sat elevated at the far end of the warehouse. It was dark. Only one of the many suspended striplights was switched on; at the far end of the warehouse the windows, more like glazed archways, were thick with grime and reduced the summer evening outside to a dim, orange bloom. The door swung shut behind Fabel, giving him a start and echoing in the vastness of the warehouse. If there was anyone here, Fabel had successfully announced his arrival.

He drew his Walther and snapped back the carriage. He scanned the warehouse, checking the pillars for any hint of movement, although they were quite narrow and a man would have difficulty in concealing himself behind them. If there was anyone here, they were in the Portakabin or behind it. Fabel moved across to his right, hugging the wall to limit his exposure and, bracing his right hand with his left, extended his gun, keeping it in eye line. He inched up the wall until he was parallel to the office cabin. He took a swift decisive sidestep, braced to fire, so he could see behind the cabin. There was no one there. He relaxed the tension in his arms slightly and moved swiftly across to the cabin. Fabel rested his back against the wall. The brickwork upon which the cabin was elevated came to Fabel's waist, so he reckoned that his head was just above floor level. He turned into the wall but could hear nothing. Fabel carefully made his way around to the steps and slowly climbed them, keeping his automatic trained on the door. There was still no sound from inside.

He had just placed his hand on the door handle when he felt it: the cold, hard disc of a gun muzzle pressed hard against the nape of his neck.

'Please, Herr Fabel. No trouble . . .' The voice was a woman's and she spoke in thickly accented German. 'Remove your index finger from the trigger and hold your weapon above your head.' Fabel complied and felt his Walther being snatched away from him in a fast, fluid action. He stared at the flaking green paint of the office cabin's door and wondered if it would be the last image his brain would register. His mind raced, desperately trying to recall the strategies for negotiation in a situation like this that he had learned in training seminars. Then the door to the cabin opened. Before him stood a short, stocky man in his late sixties. Fabel recognised the Slavic architecture of his face. But most of all he recognised the piercing, almost luminous green eyes of the man who had attacked him in Angelika Blüm's apartment.

Friday 20 June, 9.10 p.m. St Pauli, Hamburg.
As MacSwain held the passenger door of the silver Porsche open for her, Anna swept her eyes casually back along the street. The battered yellow Mercedes surveillance car was parked about twenty metres back and she caught sight of a faint movement behind the windscreen. They were in position and ready. She smiled at MacSwain and climbed into his car. Anna glanced into the cramped rear seat of the Porsche and saw a large wicker basket sitting on the leather upholstery. MacSwain took his place behind the steering wheel and caught her quizzical look.

'Oh that?' He smiled knowingly. 'I thought we'd have a picnic.'

Anna's smile suggested that she was intrigued and relaxed, but a knot tightened deep in her gut: a picnic basket suggested a remote location. And the more remote the location the more difficult it would be for back-up to follow without being spotted. It took all her will-power not to glance into MacSwain's wing mirror to check that her support was behind them.

'So . . .' she began in an intrigued tone, 'where are we going?'

'It's a surprise,' said MacSwain with a smile, but without taking his eyes from the road.

Anna sat half turned in her seat, watching MacSwain's profile. Her posture was one of relaxation and ease, despite the stretched steel tension she felt in every minute movement.

Anna repeated the phrase I *don't feel too well* over and over in her mind, as if placing it within instant reach.

They drove out of St Pauli. East and then south.

I *don't feel too well*: Anna turned the phrase over once more and closed her mind around it like a grasping hand.

Friday 20 June, 9.05 p.m. Speicherstadt, Hamburg.
Fabel had been right: there had not been enough room behind the pillars for a man to conceal himself. But there had been enough room for a slim, lithe woman, with iridescent gold hair and an aura of youthfulness; strategically placed so that a few swift, silent steps would take her up behind anyone trying to reach the cabin door.

Fabel's fear subsided slightly when the pressure of the gun muzzle was removed from his neck as soon as he had been disarmed. Looking past the Slav in the doorway, Fabel could see Mahmoot sitting at the far end of the office. He looked less than relaxed and there was a bruise on the right side of his forehead. Apart from that he looked okay. The Slav stood to one side to allow Fabel to enter. If Fabel was going to make a move, it would have to be now. But there was no move to be made.

It was as if the Slav had read Fabel's mind. 'Please do not do anything rash, Herr Fabel.' The accent fitted with the face. Fabel wondered if this was one of the Ukrainian Top Team; if he was looking at the face of Vasyl Vitrenko. 'We do not intend you, or your friend here any harm.'

'It's okay, Jan,' Mahmoot called from the far end of the office. 'They're cops . . . kind of. I wouldn't have got you to come here if I thought there was a real danger.'

The Slav indicated a second chair, next to Mahmoot. 'Please, Herr Fabel. Sit down.' When Fabel complied he turned to the girl and spoke in German. 'Martina, please give the Hauptkommissar his weapon back.'

The girl expertly slipped the magazine out from the grip of Fabel's gun and handed them to him separately. Fabel holstered the Walther and put the magazine into his pocket. As he did so, he noticed that the girl carried the same model of automatic as Hansi Kraus had picked up in the disused Schwimmhalle. The only difference was that this gun was not decorated with the presentational inlays and tooling.

He turned to Mahmoot. 'You okay?'

Mahmoot nodded. 'I'm sorry about this, Jan. But I think you ought to hear what they have to say. They reckon they're after the same guy you are. They've been watching you for some time now – and they tailed me after our meeting on the ferry.'

Fabel turned to the Slav, whose smile did not engage his cold green eyes. 'You're some kind of Russian law enforcement? If so, why didn't you go through the proper channels? I have to tell you that you've broken several German federal laws . . . the city is currently crawling with police hunting you after your attack on me . . .'

Mahmoot turned quickly in his chair and made a move to get up. The blonde girl waved the barrel of her automatic, indicating for him to remain seated.

'You were attacked?'

Fabel nodded. 'Your new friends are not as cuddly as they seem.'

'I'm sorry about that, too, Herr Fabel,' said the Slav. 'But I could not afford the . . . *complication* of being taken into custody at that point. I'm sure you appreciate that I could have done you real, lasting harm had I chosen.'

Fabel ignored the statement. 'Who are you? Who do you work for?'

The Slav's smile again failed to ignite in the cold green eyes. 'My name, at this stage, is unimportant. My colleague –' he nodded in direction of the golden-haired girl – 'and I are officers of the Ukrainian counter-terrorist police. The *Berkut*.'

'Ukrainian secret service?'

'No . . . that would be the SBU – the *Sluzhba Bespeky Ukrayiny* – who, unfortunately, probably have their part to play in this drama.'

'And what have these murders to do with terrorism?'

'Directly? Nothing. Herr Fabel, I will explain everything in due course. I'm afraid there is a great deal to explain and my German has its limits, so I ask you to be patient. The main thing is I believe we would both benefit from an exchange of information.'

Fabel gave the Slav a hard stare. His German seemed pretty solid to him, despite the heavy accent. 'What were you doing in Angelika Blüm's apartment? And what were you doing outside the murder scene in St Pauli?'

'As your friend has indicated, we have an interest in the same case. Prior to her death, Frau Blüm was investigating certain property transactions involving the Eitel group of companies, yes?'

Fabel gave a non-committal shrug.

The Slav smiled. 'These property deals were established to benefit Klimenko International, which is a Kiev-based consortium. These premises we are in have only recently been vacated by Klimenko International.'

'These deals were illegal?' asked Fabel.

The Slav waved his hand dismissively. 'Technically? Probably. They depended on information being passed on to Klimenko from official sources in the Hamburg government, perhaps more *predictively* than the authorities would have liked.'

'Let me guess, the focus of these deals would be the Neuer Horizont partnership?'

'You are perhaps more familiar with the situation than I thought. Yes, Herr Fabel, that is correct. There are pieces of real estate all around Hamburg that are, in themselves, of little commercial value. But once it becomes known that an area is due for regeneration or high-value development, then the value of the ground itself on which each piece of real estate stands appreciates spectacularly.'

'So Klimenko International and Neuer Horizont stand to make a fortune by buying cheap and early.'

'That was the idea. I will tell you something now that I will never again repeat and which you will never be able to prove. Klimenko International is a front for my government. The Ukraine is a poor country, Herr Fabel. It has, however, the potential to become a very wealthy and influential part of Europe. There are those who would use any – and I mean any – tool or weapon at their disposal to ensure that this potential is fulfilled. Klimenko International was one such tool. To answer your question . . . the reason I was at Frau Blüm's apartment was to find out if there was anything there that would incriminate my government or which would aid me in fulfilling my mission here. I will explain the objectives of that mission shortly. I thought there was a chance that your people might have missed some paperwork or information that would not have been immediately associated with the killing but would relate to the Klimenko operation. I underestimated you.'

'That wasn't all down to us. Whoever killed Angelika Blüm

wiped her computer and, we suspect, removed files from her apartment.'

The Slav stared blankly at Fabel and ran his hand across his scalp, palming the coarse white bristle; then he continued in his heavily accented, grammatically perfect German: 'There is a third element at work here. One of which you are already, in part, aware.' He paused for a second, as if punctuating the delivery of the information to emphasise the importance of what was to follow. 'The front man here for the Klimenko operation was Pavlo Klimenko, the putative head of the consortium. Klimenko is, in fact, an officer of the SBU secret service with an impressive service history with the military. Unfortunately for those behind this "enterprise", other interests had already been at work for some time. You know the name Vasyl Vitrenko?'

Fabel nodded. 'He is supposedly the head of a Ukrainian crime gang. A new one that is taking over the activities of all others in the city.'

'Vasyl Vitrenko is – was – a full colonel in the *Berkut*. Vitrenko has a service record that many admire to the point of adulation. Others see him as a monster. As the Devil. In another place, in another time, I was charged with the responsibility of finding and stopping Vitrenko's worst excesses. Vitrenko has gathered around him ten of his former subordinate officers – men who served under him in Chechnya or Afghanistan, or both – each of whom has a record of both outstanding bravery and exceptional cruelty. Each of these officers remains fiercely loyal to Vitrenko. What is more, Vitrenko has promised to make them all millionaires. A promise he is already close to fulfilling. One of these officers was a Major Pavlo Klimenko.'

'So Vitrenko snatched your crooked little scheme away right from under you?' Fabel gave a bitter laugh.

The Slav's green eyes glittered in the bleak artificial light of the Portakabin. 'That is correct, Herr Hauptkommissar.

But before you get too smug, I would point out that your government is capable of underhand dealing too. What was the objective of the operation involving the unfortunate Herr Klugmann?'

'I'm not prepared to discuss that with you.'

'No? All right, Herr Hauptkommissar. Allow me to answer my own question. You believe that Herr Klugmann was carrying out a surveillance and intelligence-gathering operation on the activities of Vasyl Vitrenko and his crew. Correct?'

Fabel shrugged and nodded.

'Not so, Herr Fabel. Herr Klugmann had only one objective: to contact and negotiate with Vasyl Vitrenko. Klugmann was an operative of the BND and he had a deal to offer. Your government, in the full knowledge of Vitrenko's murderous past and his criminal present, is prepared to offer him immunity from prosecution and a lucrative deal.'

'Why on earth would the German federal government do business with an known major criminal?'

'Because of September 11th, 2001.'

'What?'

'Eight of the ten suicide bombers that carried out the attack on the World Trade Center in New York lived in or passed through Hamburg immediately before the attack. It has been a matter of considerable embarrassment both to the city and national governments. In short, you Germans would do anything to help the Americans. And the Americans need all the help they can get. Vasyl Vitrenko is a highly intelligent and educated man; he is also a leading expert on Afghanistan and Islamic terrorism. The CIA have made it clear to BND that they would be greatly obliged if they could land Vitrenko for them. Your colleague, Klugmann, was briefed to begin negotiations; the apartment in which the girl was killed was set up as the venue for those negotiations.'

Fabel looked hard at the Slav, and then at the girl with the blonde hair. It wouldn't be the first time expedience and the imperative of 'the greater good' had bulldozed over the rule of law. The Slav watched Fabel impassively, giving him the time to consider his response. Eventually Fabel said: 'But the only contact Klugmann had with the new Ukrainian outfit was someone called Vadim. Other than that there was no contact.'

'Not so. What you have to ask yourself, Herr Fabel, is who the source of that information was and if they have a vested interest in misleading you. Vadim is indeed one of Vitrenko's men – Vadim Redchenko – and Klugmann will have had contact with him as the principal intermediary. But Klugmann had three separate meetings with Vitrenko. What the final outcome was, I can only guess. But the evidence of Vitrenko's decision is bloodily apparent.'

'You're saying that Vitrenko is committing these horrific murders?'

'I am certain of it, Herr Hauptkommissar.'

Friday 20 June, 9.25 p.m. Altona, Hamburg.
Anna had managed to chat with MacSwain in a relaxed manner, but her occasional casual glances away from his profile and out through the side window or windscreen of the Porsche had been like the casting out of safety lines, each time anchoring on a road sign or a landmark. They were heading towards the Elbe. Where the hell was he taking her?

'I'm intrigued,' Anna said, levering as much calm into her voice as she could muster.

MacSwain smiled knowingly. 'I have something rather special in mind for you, Sara. I promise you this is something you won't forget . . .'

Paul Lindemann winced as if MacSwain's phrase, heard through Anna's wire, had stung him. He turned to Maria who sat next to him in the back of the Mercedes panel van. 'I don't like this at all . . .'

'There's nothing been said or done yet that suggests we should intervene. Anna's looking after herself all right. And we're tight on their tail. Try to relax.'

The blank stare Paul gave Maria did not suggest that he was in any way convinced or reassured by her comments. He lifted the radio mouthpiece to his lips and demanded an update from both close-surveillance vehicles. They both confirmed that they had good and close visual contact.

'The target has just turned into Helgoländer, heading south,' reported the radio voice of the lead surveillance car. 'We seem to be heading towards the Landungsbrücken . . .'

Paul adjusted his hold on the radio, as if a tighter grip would squeeze more satisfactory information from it.

'Kastor four-one to Kastor four-two . . .' the first car called the second, 'I'm going to pull back now. Overtake and take up the lead. Kastor four-four . . .' He now called one of the motorcyclists. 'See if you can get ahead of him and down onto the Landungsbrücken . . .'

Another silence.

'Kastor four to Kastor four-four . . .' Paul's stretched thread of patience snapped once more: 'report . . .'

'We've turned onto the Landungsbrücken . . .' he paused and then added with a puzzled tone: '. . . we seem to be heading towards Baumwall and the Niederhafen . . . or the Hanseboothafen . . . the target is now on Johannisbollwerk.'

Anna felt the knot in her gut pull tighter. MacSwain turned off the main city harbour road and onto the pontoons that separated the bays of the Niederhafen and the Schiff-bauerhafen, which offered berths for exhibitors and visitors to the Hanseboot Boat Show. He parked the Porsche and came round to her side, holding the door open for her to get out. Anna sat still for a moment. She could hear the creaking, tinkling and ringing sounds from the forest of yacht masts around her.

'Come on,' said MacSwain without impatience, 'I've something to show you.'

Anna gave a small involuntary shiver as she stepped out of the car, although the evening was far from chilly. MacSwain missed it, because he was reaching into the back seat to remove the wicker hamper. He closed the door and used the key-ring fob to lock the car and set the alarm. He extended an elbow, the hamper in his other hand, indicating that Anna should take his arm. She smiled and did so. They walked along the pontoon towards Überseebrücke. Suddenly MacSwain stopped beside a small but sleek and expensive-looking motor cruiser.

'Here we are . . . she's small, but she's comfortable and she's fast. Nine point three metres. Three-metre-plus beam.'

Anna stood and stared at the craft. It was pristine white with a single blue line along its bow. In prestige and elegance, it was the water-going equivalent of MacSwain's Porsche.

'Beautiful . . .' Anna's voice was dead and empty. At that moment she didn't have a clue what she would do next.

'Fuck! He's got a boat.' Paul stared wildly at Maria. 'If Anna gets on it and he takes it out of harbour, we'll lose them. Shit. We never thought he'd have a boat. I'm calling in the team to pull her out of there . . .'

Maria Klee frowned. 'But that'll blow the whole operation. We can't arrest him for anything . . . he hasn't done anything wrong. All we'll succeed in doing is blowing Anna's cover and alerting MacSwain to the fact that he is under suspicion. And Anna isn't calling us in yet.'

'Christ, Maria . . . if he gets her out onto the water she is totally unprotected. We can't leave her exposed like that . . .' He grabbed the radio. Maria placed her hand over his.

'Wait, Paul,' said Maria. 'We can get the Wasserschutzpolizei and maybe even a helicopter out here. We're sitting smack bang in the middle between the WSP river police Kommissariat on the Landungsbrücken and the Wache in the Speicherstadt . . . we can get water-borne support out here in minutes. Move the team in but keep them out of sight. If we suspect Anna's in trouble then we can move them in before he clears his berth.' She snapped up her cell phone in a decisive gesture. 'I'll get on to the Wasserschutzpolizei . . .'

Anna's mind raced. This was an element she had not factored into her plan. She simply stared blankly at the sleek lines of the craft as if she were looking at a loaded weapon pointing in her direction. Her guard was down and MacSwain noticed.

'Sara? Is there something wrong? I hoped you'd be impressed . . .'

MacSwain's voice snapped Anna back to the task in hand. She turned to him and smiled weakly. 'I'm sorry. It's just that boats aren't really my thing.'

'What?' MacSwain mimicked shocked surprise. 'You're from Hamburg, aren't you? The sea's in your blood!' He climbed down the small metal ladder, carefully carrying the hamper in his free hand. He placed the hamper on the deck and held his hand out to help Anna down from the quay.

'No . . . honestly, John . . . I have a thing about boats. I get sick. And I get scared . . .'

He smiled broadly and the green eyes glittered in the dim light. 'You'll be fine. Come and try her for size. I won't even start her up. If you don't feel happy, then we'll eat in town . . . I just thought it would be nice to watch the city lights from the water.'

Anna made a decision. 'Okay. But if I don't feel happy about it, then we go somewhere else. Deal?'

'Deal . . .'

Back in the Mercedes command van, Paul turned to Maria with a hard stare and said: 'Phone Fabel.'

Friday 20 June, 9.30 p.m. Speicherstadt, Hamburg.

'I was a major in the Soviet interior-ministry forces. MVD Kondor. The Americans had been supplying the rebel forces with the most highly sophisticated weapons and the war in Afghanistan was fast becoming the Soviet Union's Vietnam. It was a desperate time. We had always prosecuted the war aggressively, but more and more of our boys were coming back in body bags. Worse still, a lot of them were disappearing without trace. It was clear we were not winning the conflict and attitudes were hardening.' The Slav pulled a cigarette packet with Cyrillic writing on it from his coat pocket and offered it first to Fabel and then to Mahmoot. Both shook their heads. He shrugged and pulled an untipped cigarette from the packet and placed it between his slightly fleshy lips. He took a heavy chromium-plated lighter from his pocket; Fabel noticed it carried some kind of crest, featuring an eagle. The strands of tobacco crackled as he lit the cigarette and took a long draw.

'I am not proud of all that happened in those dark days, Herr Fabel. But war is war. War is, unfortunately, fuelled by retribution. In Afghanistan, the retribution became more and more extreme. On both sides.'

The Slav exhaled the smoke in a forceful blow before resuming.

'The sheer number of ground-to-air missiles the Americans had supplied made air support and supply practically impossible. Units became cut off. Often they were simply abandoned to fight their own way out or otherwise fall into the hands of crazed fanatics. One of these units was an MVD Kondor Field Police Spetznaz.'

'Commanded by Vitrenko?'

The Slav thrust the cigarette in Fabel's direction, causing a small cloud of grey ash to drift slowly towards the floor. 'Exactly . . .' He paused. 'I think that now I should tell you something about Colonel Vitrenko's *special* abilities.

Command is a gift. Commanding men in battle is like being their father. You must make them believe that their trust in you is total and unique, that only you can guide them into the light and safety; only you can protect them. And if you cannot protect them and it is their time to die, they must believe that you have chosen the only true and proper place for them to die . . . that survival and life in another place and time would be a betrayal. All of this means that the commander's most important strategies are psychological, not military. Vasyl Vitrenko is a unique commander of men. As a child he was identified as having a special, powerful intellect. Unfortunately, he was also identified as having certain potentially problematic personality traits. He was born into a military family and these *quirks* in his make-up were considered to be best managed in a military career.'

Another long draw on the cigarette.

'He did excel as a soldier, and it was soon recognised that he had a very special ability as a leader. He could make people do things they wouldn't consider themselves capable of . . . exceptional things. What the authorities were less comfortable with was his almost cult-like status. He propagated a philosophy of the "eternal soldier" . . . those under his command saw themselves as the latest in a long line of warriors that stretched back two thousand years.' The Slav leaned forward, resting his elbows on his knees. A curl of smoke cupped his small baby chin and traced its way up his cheek, causing him to narrow the green eyes against its sting. 'Your killer. He has a noble mission, no? He sees himself as a Viking warrior returning his people to the true Nordic faith?'

Fabel felt his chest tighten as he heard an almost perfect repetition of the description Dorn had given him. 'Yes . . . but how . . .'

The Slav cut him short. 'And you are, therefore, looking for a German or Scandinavian?'

'Well, yes . . .'

'You disappoint me, Herr Fabel. You studied medieval history did you not?'

Fabel nodded curtly. 'What's your point?'

'Just that I would have expected you to think more broadly . . . both geographically and historically.'

The point hit home like a heavy blow to Fabel's chest.

'Shit . . .' Fabel's eyes darted around as he processed information retrieved from some deep storage. 'Kievan Rus . . .'

'That's right, Herr Fabel. The Kievan Rus. The founders of Kiev and Novgorod and who gave their name to Russia. But they weren't Slavs.'

Fabel felt the same thrill of epiphany that he had felt when he had sat in Dorn's office. Here it was. The final link. The connection between the Ukrainian element and the rest of the puzzle. 'No . . .' Fabel said. 'No, they weren't. They were Swedes. Swedish Vikings.'

'Exactly. They sailed up the Volga and set up their trading posts and cities at strategic points along the river. Warriors. And it is from this origin that Vitrenko drew inspiration for his quasi-religious philosophy of soldiering. He instilled in his subordinates a belief that they were the inheritors of a warrior code that stretched back to the Viking origins of the Kievan Rus. He made them believe that what they were fighting for did not matter in the least: it was the fighting in itself, the comradeship under arms and the testing of individual and collective courage that mattered . . . nothing else. They could be Soviet troops, mercenaries, even fight for the West . . . Vitrenko invested them with the belief that only the act of war itself was the single inalienable and indissoluble truth. And, I believe, he dressed up this philosophy in the semi-mythical codes of the Viking. The result was something in his men that went beyond all definition of loyalty . . . a total dedication and devotion. He was – he is – quite capable of talking people into committing the most atrocious acts. Even for them to sacrifice their own lives without a thought.' The Slav gazed at the floor before absent-mindedly flicking some ash onto it. Then he looked up into Fabel's eyes with as candid and uncompromising a gaze as Fabel could ever remember encountering. 'I feel my words are inadequate to describe the raw, total power Vitrenko can exert on others . . . or the horror of the acts of which he is capable.' It was as if the Slav had run out of fuel; as if the last reserves of energy that were stored in the heavy, squat shoulders were depleted.

'I can understand why all of this leads you to suspect Vitrenko of these killings, but you said you *knew* he is the killer. How do you know?'

The Slav rose and walked over to one of the wide, shallow windows. Fabel could tell that, although he looked out into the dark void of the warehouse, he was seeing something and somewhere else. Sometime else.

'Like I said, Vitrenko's unit was isolated in rebel territory. And without air support. To say they were cut off would be to use the language of conventional war, and this was anything but a conventional war. To get back to friendly territory, they had to make their way through a rebel-controlled valley. It took them ten days to get from one end to the other, making short, fast runs at night from one cover to the next. Each night men would die . . . and, worse, some were left wounded and were picked up by the rebels. And during each day in that valley, pinned down and unable to move from their cover, the survivors would hear the screams of their captured comrades as the mujahidin tortured them. It was enough to break the spirit of the most dedicated and loyal soldier. But something happened in that valley, between Vitrenko and his men: something unbreakable was forged between them.'

He turned from the window and lifted the cigarette to his lips and snapped open his lighter.

'Out of a hundred-plus-strong force, only about twenty

men made it to the valley's end. Of those, a handful were walking wounded. These were sent back to safe ground, but instead of returning to Soviet territory, Vitrenko and the rest of his men travelled only a short distance from the valley before turning back under cover of darkness. The mujahidin, of course, were not expecting them to return. Vitrenko and his men played the rebels at their own game, taking to the mountains and stalking any small group of fighters they encountered. They would kill all prisoners taken in any engagement except one. This prisoner would be tortured mercilessly for any intelligence he could give and then crucified, left to scream for hours until he died. At first the rebels would try to rescue the victim, but Vitrenko had snipers hidden to pick them off. After the casualties they experienced through these attempted rescues, the mujahidin learned to live with the screams. Vitrenko and his men became like bandits, outlaws, beyond the control of any military management. They also became heroes to the ordinary Soviet soldier in Afghanistan. It was only a matter of time before the GRU – the *Glavnoye Razvedyvatelnoye Upravleniye* – our main field-intelligence service started to become frustrated: they knew that Vitrenko and his men were gathering important intelligence that was not being passed back. Then the stories became more gruesome. Reports of mass murder of anyone in the rebel-held areas; of robbing and raping.'

'I shouldn't have thought that that would have offended Soviet sensibilities at the time,' said Fabel.

The Ukrainian examined Fabel's expression for signs of sarcasm. There was none.

'No. You're right. But by this stage in the war we were suffering from Vietnam syndrome: we were fighting an unequal battle where our superior numbers, resources and technology should have assured us an easy victory, but we were being solidly beaten and we desperately wanted a way out with the minimum of disgrace. That meant that by eighty-seven, eighty-eight, the Soviet authorities were becoming slightly more sensitive to world opinion. And Vitrenko's actions were becoming more and more . . .' he struggled for the word – '*unpleasant*. So the GRU sent me in with two Spetznaz detachments to track down and re-establish control of Vitrenko and his unit.'

'And did you?'

The Ukrainian leaned against the wall and lit the cigarette. Then he signalled to the blonde-haired girl, who handed him a buff-coloured envelope.

'Yes. Eventually. And Vitrenko and his men were commended for exceptional courage behind enemy lines.' He tossed the envelope at Fabel, who made a fumbling catch. 'But the things I encountered on the way . . . I tell you Fabel, I have seen some terrible things in my life, as you can imagine, but it was as if I were on the trail of the Devil himself . . .'

Friday 20 June, 9.40 p.m. Niederhafen, Hamburg.

The two surveillance men could not get close enough to the boat to see what was happening. Paul ordered the two Mobiles Einsatz Kommando officers, clad in their dark body armour, coveralls and helmets, to move in closer. One managed to get into a position advanced enough to get the bead of his Heckler and Koch on MacSwain's torso as he sat in the rear of the boat, handing a glass of Sekt wine to Anna Wolff.

In the command van, Maria received a return phone call from the Wasserschutzpolizei: they had a launch on its way and it would be positioned with a clear view of the exit of the Niederhafen onto the Elbe's main water-traffic lanes. If MacSwain moved out into the river, they could pick him up and follow at a discreet distance. The Wasserschutzpolizei's only concern was that MacSwain's boat was clearly a fast vessel that could give their launch a run for its money. Maria had already placed a request for a helicopter to stand by. None of these precautions cleared the frown from Paul Lindemann's brow. What had added to his concern was that Maria had not been able to raise Fabel on his cell phone, getting his voice mail instead: why had Fabel switched off his phone when he had promised he could be contacted all night?

The late evening air had developed a chilled edge and Anna gave another involuntary shiver as MacSwain handed her the glass of sparkling Sekt.

'Just a moment . . .' MacSwain slid open the two small doors that were sculpted to follow the smooth curve of the facing panel. They opened onto the steps that led to a small but brightly lit cabin area. While MacSwain had his back to her, Anna sniffed at the wine and took a tentative sip. She smelled and tasted nothing but the crispness of German champagne; but she knew that Rohypnol or GHB was almost impossible to detect in any beverage. She took a fuller mouthful and repeated her silent mantra in her head: *I don't feel too well.*

MacSwain reappeared with a dark-blue woollen cardigan which he draped across her shoulders.

'We can go below if you're too cold,' he said. Anna shook her head. MacSwain smiled and handed her a plate of pâté, bread and herring salad. 'Relax for a minute,' he said, 'there's something I want you to see. I know you're not a good sailor, Sara, so I promise to take it slow.' He looked at Anna as if asking permission. Anna, like MacSwain, had not seen the MEK men move into position, but she guessed – she hoped – that they would be there by now, somewhere in the shadows. What she had to gamble on now was whether or not Paul had arranged cover for her should MacSwain take the boat out.

She resisted the temptation to search the pontoons for her

support and kept her eyes resolutely focused on MacSwain.

'Okay . . .' she said and nodded; for her invisible audience, she added, 'I think that'll be fine.'

Paul Lindemann instructed the MEK not to intervene. Maria warned the Wasserschutzpolizei launch, which was now in direct radio contact with the team, that MacSwain was on the move.

MacSwain untethered the boat fore and aft and started the engine. Its deep, throaty rumble disturbed Anna, whose instincts told her that a lot of power and a great deal of speed lay in that rumble. MacSwain, as good as his word, took the boat out from its mooring slowly and gently. Anna noticed the relaxed, almost careless ease with which he manoeuvred the craft. She looked back at the receding mooring and just made out the merest hint of a shadow, moving low and fast towards the land end of the pontoons.

The Elbe stretched out before them, obsidian black and unfathomable, fringed on the far shore by the lights of the shipyard. MacSwain turned the boat so it was parallel to the shore and cut the engine. He hit a button on the console and Anna heard the rapid rattle of a heavy chain as the anchor slipped deep into the dark river. With the engine dead, Anna could hear the sounds of the water around them: she felt as if she were on the back of some vast, living thing whose breath and skin sleeked against the hull of the boat as its endless body rippled past beneath them. MacSwain killed the lights.

'Isn't it magnificent?' he said, a gesture with his champagne flute sweeping along the distant shore.

In any other situation Anna would have been captivated by it: Hamburg glittered in the night and the Elbe held up a mirror to her beauty, animating the city's sparkling reflection.

'Beautiful . . .' said Anna. 'Really. I'm glad you brought me out here . . .'

'I love this city,' said MacSwain. 'This is where I belong. This is where I will always want to be.'

'But you're British, didn't you say? Don't you miss . . .' Anna tried to think of something British to miss – 'the *rain?*' she said with a laugh.

MacSwain laughed too. 'Trust me, Hamburg supplies more than enough rain to quell any homesickness for a damp climate. But no, there's nothing I miss about Britain. Any Britishness I need Hamburg supplies . . . sometimes it really is like living in London's most easterly suburb. There is no other city in the world like Hamburg. I wouldn't leave it for the world.'

Anna shrugged. 'Me . . . I can take it or leave it.'

MacSwain's face became animated. 'I can't understand that. You only have one life. The time we have is too precious to waste. Why would you want to spend it in a place you feel indifferent about?'

'Inertia, I guess. It takes less effort to stay put. I suppose I can't be bothered building up the energy to achieve escape velocity.'

'Well I'm glad you haven't, Sara. Otherwise we wouldn't be here.' He sat down next to her. 'I would love to show you your own city . . . with the eyes of an outsider. I'm sure I could change the way you feel about it. And anyway, it would give me a chance to get to know you better . . .'

He drew closer. Anna could smell the most subtle hint of an expensive cologne. She looked into the sparkling green eyes and scanned the perfectly sculpted features. Anna found herself doubting very seriously that he could have anything to do with the murders they were investigating or even the doping of girls for ritualised sex. MacSwain was classically handsome; through his clothes it was clear that his body was perfectly proportioned and muscular; he was urbane, intelligent and confident. Everything about MacSwain should have pushed Anna's buttons. Yet, when he drew his face close to

Anna's and closed his mouth around hers, she had to fight the nausea that churned in her chest.

The fifteen-metre long, Barthel-built WS25 was the Hamburg harbour police's newest launch, but not its fastest. Kommissar Franz Kassel had ordered all the lights to be dimmed in contravention of the very harbour regulations he enforced daily. Kassel lifted his binoculars and scanned MacSwain's powerboat as it slipped from the quays. He muttered something to himself as he recognised the boat as a Chris Craft 308 or 328 Express Cruiser. Ideal for cruising. Also fast. Much faster, if its owner decided to run for it, than the WS25's 22 kilometres per hour. But not faster than radio waves or radar. If the cruiser made a break for it, Kassel could summon up support from any of the WSP Kommissariats along the river from there to Cuxhaven. All the same, he knew there was a female police officer aboard that cruiser. And, from what Oberkommissarin Klee had told him on the radio, if there was a call for help, the speed of response could be the difference between life and death. Kassel was a wraith of a man: unfeasibly thin and tall, with reddish hair and freckles that seemed to have merged after twenty years' exposure to brackish harbour air, sun and spray. He let the binoculars hang around his neck and took the WSP peaked cap from his head, running bony fingers through his thinning thatch of dry sandy hair.

'Naughty boy . . .' he muttered and reached for the radio.

Anna pulled away from MacSwain, placing her hand on his chest and pushing: not hard, but firmly enough for him to get the message. As their faces parted, Anna made sure she was smiling.

'What's wrong, Sara?' MacSwain's voice suggested a concern that did not show in the cold, green eyes.

'Nothing . . .' said Anna. Then, almost coquettishly, 'I just don't want to rush anything. I hardly know you. I don't know you.'

'What's to know?' He made to kiss her again. Anna pulled back. This time the shunt of her hand's heel into his chest was more businesslike.

Maria Klee turned to Paul Lindemann, still holding the radio handset halfway to her mouth. 'The WSP launch commander says we have a way of ending this now, if we want, without alerting MacSwain to our surveillance.'

Paul's eyes lit up. 'How?'

'MacSwain is doing a little "Hamburg by night" sight-seeing. According to the launch commander, he's switched his nav lights off. That's against the law . . . he's near enough to a main shipping lane to represent a hazard. Fortunately, our WSP guy has done the same. He reckons he can be on MacSwain before he knows it and escort him back to his berth and fine him. Let's say it'll ruin MacSwain's evening . . . and it'll get Anna back on dry land.'

'What do you think?'

'Anna hasn't indicated that she wants out. And we've not picked up any information of any use. I think we should stick with it. But, on the other hand, once he's switched on his navigational lights again our excuse becomes weaker. It's your call, Paul.'

Friday 20 June, 9.40 p.m. Speicherstadt, Hamburg.
The untipped cigarette now burned perilously close to the Ukrainian's lips, and he pinched them tight as he took a final draw. He made a pincer with his forefinger and thumb, retrieved the tiny stub and dropped it onto the floor, crushing it with his heel.

Fabel removed about a dozen photographs from the buff envelope. The first images kick-started a hammering in his chest. Three colour photographs, from different angles, showed the same woman, her abdomen split and ripped open and her lungs cast out from her body. A taste of bile rose in the rear of Fabel's mouth. More horror. Fabel noticed the gold-haired girl turn her head to look out through the small window and into the empty whale belly of the warehouse, as if she were preventing her eyes from falling onto the pictures. The Ukrainian dismissed the images with a wave of his hand.

'I'll come to that case shortly . . .' The Ukrainian indicated that Fabel should move on to the next set of images. The girl turned back from the window. The next images had been taken without extra lighting, instead relying on a camera flash to bleach a pool of intense light and vividity. Strangely, the amateurish flash photography gave each scene an immediacy and a reality lacking in the clinical objectivity of forensic photography. Fabel found himself looking, with each shuffle of horror, at a new image of women, some only girls, ripped apart in the same manner. But in each picture, lurking in the dark fringes of the camera flashes, Fabel could see there were other victims. He turned to the final image.

'Sweet Jesus . . .' Fabel gazed at the image uncomprehendingly, as if the awfulness of what lay before him defied belief. A girl, no older than sixteen or seventeen, had been nailed to the wooden wall. Nails, more like crude iron spikes, had been driven into her hands and the flesh and muscle of her upper arms. She had been sliced open and Blood-Eagled in the same manner as the others, except that the dark and bloody masses of her lungs, too, had been nailed to the wall. Somehow, through the gut-wrenching disgust, some deep, analytical part of Fabel's brain processed the similarity between the photograph in his hands and the canvases he had seen at Marlies Menzel's exhibition. Fabel let the photograph drop from his hands. As it fell, image upwards, onto the floor, he could see the steamed marks where his thumbs had held it. He looked up, almost pleadingly, at the Ukrainian, as if looking for some explanation that would, somehow, make what he had seen less terrible.

'It was the last village we came to before we caught up with Vitrenko. It was well within rebel territory and we'd had a hell of a fight to get as far as we did. We weren't sure if Vitrenko's unit had hit the place or if it was held by rebels. As it turns out, it was just an ordinary non-combatant village. But we had to make sure: so we spent half a day under a relentless sun, continuously scoured by wind-blown dust and sand. Then, just after midday, the wind changed direction and brought with it the stench of death from the village. We knew then that Vitrenko had been there. I sent in a recon squad who signalled for us to come in. When I joined up with the leader, I knew from his face it was bad.'

The Ukrainian paused and nodded towards the image that now lay on the floor between Fabel's feet.

'It was in some kind of barn or storage building for the village. If hell exists, then it must look pretty similar to what we found in that barn. The men had all been shot. There was a great cluster of them just inside the doors. They had been tied hand and foot and forced into a kneeling position before being shot. Then there were the women. All of the women of the village, probably. About twenty of them. All ages . . . from children to the grandmas. Every single one had been ripped apart with their lungs torn out – just like your victims here. A couple had been nailed to the wall of the barn, splayed out like some kind of exhibit . . .' The Ukrainian paused. His eyes searched some invisible scene for details that would allow him to find the right description. 'Like butterfly collectors display their butterflies.'

'Vitrenko did all this?' asked Fabel.

'Not personally. That's the thing: he made others do it for him. He has a talent for that. He created this obscene gallery of exhibits without getting blood on his own hands. It was like some kind of test . . . a proving. It was like a ritual that bound them to their leader.'

'And it was just the women?' Mahmoot, who had been silently listening to the Ukrainian's account, asked.

The Ukrainian nodded his head. 'I remember the head of the recon team said that at least the men had had an easier death. But then we realised that they hadn't. Vitrenko had forced them to witness. He had made them watch the women die before they were killed.'

Fabel and Mahmoot exchanged a long look. There was silence in the small Portakabin. Again Fabel found himself drawn back to the images Marlies Menzel had displayed in her exhibition and imagined himself in an obscene gallery in a stifling, airless barn in some desolate landscape, staring at the devastated corpses of twenty women: the perverted artworks of a psychopathic creativity.

'You caught up with him?'

'Eventually, yes. My orders were to escort him and his men back to Soviet-controlled territory. And that's what we did. But only after a lot of negotiation. When we caught up with them, Vitrenko's men actually took up defensive positions. I had to order my men to take cover. They couldn't understand why their comrades were keeping them in their sights. But these men were no longer Soviet soldiers. They were Vitrenko's. Bandits. Highly trained, highly motivated and highly efficient . . . but bandits just the same. And their allegiance was exclusively to Vitrenko.

'After Afghanistan he was a hero. The details of his atrocities were eclipsed by his popularity among the ordinary men. To be honest, there were few at any level who gave a damn about what happened to a bunch of foreign Muslims, so long as it bore results. Vitrenko soon became acknowledged as an expert on Islamic terrorists. After the break-up of the Soviet Union, he became a valuable member of the new Ukrainian counter-terrorist forces. He joined the *Berkut*, the "Golden

Eagles". Again, he had an exemplary record. Vitrenko is a highly intelligent and educated individual and he studied all forms of criminology, psychology and counter-terrorism. This, combined with his experience in the field, made him a highly respected expert. But then there was the series of brutal rapes and killings in Kiev.' The Ukrainian indicated to the photographs again. 'The first picture you looked at was one of the victims, a young journalist for an independent radio station in Ukraine. We got someone for the killings, a young man in his mid-twenties. He fitted all the criteria of a serial killer and confessed to the killings, but we were pretty certain that he was not acting alone. In fact, Herr Hauptkommissar, I'm not convinced he was the killer at all. There were rumours of some kind of cult behind them and Vitrenko's name was mentioned. We also had our suspicions that a well-placed police or security officer was masterminding organised criminal activity, but Vitrenko was never directly connected to this. Then, about three years ago, he disappeared. Shortly after, one by one, twelve of his former subordinates dropped out of sight . . . or actually deserted their posts in the military of Russia, Belarus and the Ukraine.'

Fabel gave a bitter laugh. 'And so they have moved to Hamburg, where the pickings are better. I suppose these are the people our Organised Crime Division call the "Top Team" . . .'

The Ukrainian shrugged. 'Whatever you call them, Vitrenko's unit has been systematically seizing control of the major underworld activities in your city. You see, to them, your precious Hamburg is no different from Afghanistan or Chechnya or any other theatre of operation. It is simply another landscape. Their loyalty to each other and to their leader, their commitment to achieving their mission objective . . . nothing else matters to them.'

'But Vitrenko is mad,' protested Fabel, aware of the weakness of his own words.

'That is neither here nor there. I, too, believe that he is insane. A psychopath. But his madness has become his greatest asset. He is so stripped of inhibition and, well, moral constraint, that he can use it to terrorise those he would subjugate and mesmerise those he would use as his instruments.'

'Ivan the Terrible . . .' Fabel muttered.

'What?'

'Just something someone said to me recently,' Fabel said. 'Why are you telling me all of this?'

Something seemed to dull the green eyes. Fabel could almost have defined it as sadness. The blonde girl once again interpreted the Ukrainian's silent command and handed him a file from the same desk. He flipped open the file and slipped out another photograph and handed it to Fabel. It was a military-service portrait of a man in his forties. The Ukrainian laughed quietly at Fabel's confusion as he looked from the photograph to the Ukrainian and back again. The face in the photograph had exactly the same architecture and the same green eyes as the old man, but the jaw was wider and stronger and the broad forehead was framed by thick butter-blond hair. For a moment, Fabel wondered if it was a photograph of the Ukrainian when he was younger; but despite the confusing similarities, there were too many fundamental, structural differences in the face. In the space of a couple of seconds, Fabel covered more ground than he had in the whole investigation to date. He leaned back in his chair and looked at the old man with a discernible sympathy.

'Your name is Vitrenko?'

The Ukrainian nodded.

Fabel looked at the face in the photograph again. 'Brother?'

The Ukrainian shook his head slowly as if it were made of lead. 'Son. I am Vasyl Vitrenko's father.'

Friday 20 June, 10.00 p.m. Niederhafen, Hamburg.

The sliding panel door of the command-post Mercedes Van had been opened, now that there was no risk of being spotted by MacSwain. The MEK surveillance men stood outside smoking. Inside, the air was clearer but the atmosphere remained electric. Everyone was listening to the conversation taking place on a darkened boat, somewhere out on the black water. Anna's voice sounded relaxed and confident. Paul Lindemann spread his hands on his knees, rubbing their heels along the material of his trousers and drawing a long slow breath before snapping himself upright in a gesture of decisiveness.

'Tell the WSP launch to stand by. If Anna wanted us to pull her out, she would have given us the signal.'

Maria lifted the radio handset but did not transmit. 'You sure about this, Paul?'

'Tell them to stand by. But I want them to make sure they maintain visual contact, even if there's a risk of being spotted. I don't want Anna to be beyond our reach.'

'I think you're right to let it go, Paul. The boat was a nasty surprise, but now we've got the water police out there we're back in control of the game.' Maria paused for a moment. 'If you wanted, we could get water-borne ourselves . . .'

Paul shook his head. 'No. They'll be coming back to land . . . one way or another. And it makes sense that he'll come back to his berth here. I want to be on his back as soon as he does.

MacSwain hit a button on the broad white dash next to the boat's wheel. The navigational lights and the cockpit courtesy lights came back on. He held out the bottle of Sekt and raised an eyebrow. Anna held out her glass.

'You not having any?' she asked, checking, as far as she could without being obvious, that it was the same bottle that had been opened before the lights had been put out.

MacSwain smiled. 'One glass only when I'm in charge of the vessel . . . but please, you go ahead.'

He filled her glass and replaced the bottle in its ice bucket. Anna took a sip of the wine. Was there something there that wasn't there before? An aftertaste? She felt a cold sweat prickle on her brow and held the wine in her mouth, pushing the analytical capabilities of her palate to the limit. Anna swallowed the wine, bringing her panic-button phrase back again to the front of her mind, like a life preserver to be seized and clung to at the first suggestion of submersion. She smiled weakly at MacSwain, whose expression remained blank and unreadable. The moment passed. There was no dizziness, no foggy feeling.

'How long have you been interested in boats?' It was all Anna could think of to say.

'Oh . . . since I was a kid. My father used to take me out sailing in Scotland. I've always been around boats and the water. I love it.'

'Are you close to your father?'

MacSwain laughed. 'No one is close to my father. He is a cold fish. We never really got on. I was sent away to boarding school and only saw my parents during the holidays. Even then, apart from taking me along with him when he went sailing, or tagging along on holidays abroad, my father didn't have much time for me.' He gave a philosophical shrug. 'My mother's German and I have always had more to do with her side of the family. Would you like something more to eat?'

'No thanks . . . It must be tough . . . for a guy, that is, when you don't have a good relationship with your father.'

MacSwain frosted slightly. 'I'm not a little boy any more.' He forced a smile. 'It's getting chilly out here . . . would you like to come into the cabin for some coffee?'

Anna laughed. 'Is that the best you can do? Or do you have some etchings for me to look at?'

MacSwain held up his hands. 'If coffee is all you want, coffee is all you'll get.'

Anna strained the muscles of her cheeks to maintain her smile. Coffee. Another hiding place for something less innocuous. 'Okay . . .'

The cabin was small but bright and sleek, crafted from white moulded polymer with wood features. There were two oval portholes on either side and three in the ceiling to the deck. To the right there was a small couch moulded into a recess; a compact galley and a cubicle which Anna guessed was the 'head' pressed themselves into the available space on the left. A double bed spanned the bow end. The cabin was filled with a rich aroma from the coffee maker set into the galley wall. MacSwain motioned for Anna to sit on the couch. She watched him pour both coffees from the same pot and was relieved when MacSwain sat on the edge of the bed, instead of forcing intimacy by squeezing into the small space next to her on the couch.

'You say you work for a travel agency?' he asked.

Anna felt a chill in her chest. It was an area of her cover which she did not want to fall too much under MacSwain's scrutiny. She dredged her memory for true emotions that her short spell in Meier Reisen had evoked.

'Yes. It's the most boring job on the planet. Sending the average German family on its two weeks in Tenerife or Gran Canaria and then listening to their complaints that Bratwurst wasn't on the hotel menu . . . Why?'

'Have you never sent someone to a place that they didn't want to return from . . . a place that awoke an instinctive feeling within them. Somewhere they felt they truly belonged?'

Anna shrugged. 'No . . . I can't say I have . . .'

'That's the way I felt the first time I saw Hamburg. And sometimes it's like that with people too.' A fire ignited in MacSwain's eyes. 'Sometimes you meet someone for the first time and it's like you have known each other for an eternity.

Like this is just the latest variation on a theme that has been playing for a thousand years.'

'Sounds romantic . . . is this a line you use on women?'

MacSwain's expression darkened. 'This has nothing to do with women or sex. I'm talking about something a thousand times more significant than . . . well . . . love. I'm talking about a true bond between a person and a place . . . between an individual and others.' MacSwain frowned as if searching for a point of reference, a landmark, that he could indicate to Anna. 'There's a word in German that doesn't translate into English . . .'

'There are quite a few of those . . .'

MacSwain brushed away Anna's comment with a sweep of his hand. '*Heimat*. The concept of a place, a time and a people to which you belong. It lies somewhere between the concepts of home and homeland.'

Anna nodded vaguely. It was a word she associated with parochialism and narrow-mindedness; with the bland, politically bleached and mannered films that had been made in Germany in the period after the Second World War: a time when any sense of Germanness seemed inappropriate or even in bad taste.

'There are relationships that you find and forge in life that give you that inner feeling of *Heimat*, of belonging. Except it is not necessarily anchored in one place. Whenever you meet – wherever in the world you meet again – you are at home.' The intensity melted from MacSwain's eyes. He shrugged and took another sip of his coffee. 'That's why my father is no longer a figure in my landscape, other than as an incidental character. I have learned that there are much more significant bonds between people than mere genetics. Anyway . . . enough about me . . .'

He moved over to the couch. Anna was forced to move to make room for him. He drew close and moved his face towards hers. Once again Anna took in his almost perfectly handsome features and was amazed at the lurch of disgust in her gut as he put his lips to hers. She eased back from him and smiled.

'Time we set sail for shore, skipper,' she said, hoping her jocularity didn't sound as hollow outwardly as it did inwardly.

MacSwain smiled dryly and sighed. 'Sure . . .'

MacSwain had been polite and courteous but perceptibly cool on the return to the jetty. Anna felt a surge of energy and relief as the lights of shore drew closer. She declined MacSwain's invitation of a lift home, claiming her car was parked near the nightclub; he insisted on dropping her there instead. Paul Lindemann and the surveillance team had withdrawn from sight as MacSwain had pulled into his berth, picking up the trail again on the way back to the nightclub.

'Here'll be fine . . .' said Anna as they pulled up outside the nightclub.

Again, MacSwain smiled a polite smile. 'Where's your car?' he asked.

Anna made a vague gesture with her hand. 'Around the corner.' She took a small notepad from her clutch handbag and noted down the number of the cell phone she'd been allocated for the operation. 'Listen . . . I don't think I've been the best company tonight . . . Give me a call and we can arrange something some other time.'

'I was beginning to think you didn't like me, Sara. You seemed . . . well, uneasy or something.'

Anna leaned across and gave MacSwain a lingering kiss on the lips. She withdrew and smiled. 'I told you . . . I'm not good on boats. That's all. Call me.' She opened the Porsche's door and swung her legs out. 'Next time let's make it on solid ground . . .'

* * *

One of the surveillance cars took off at a safe distance behind MacSwain's Porsche. Anna stood on the sidewalk watching after the car as it turned the corner of Albers-Eck. It was only after the surveillance car confirmed that MacSwain was clear of Der Kiez that the Mercedes Vario pulled up next to Anna. Maria was first out and put her arm around Anna in an awkward, unaccustomed gesture of affection.

'You did bloody well, Anna,' she said.

'He gave us a turn when he pulled the boat stunt.' Paul Lindemann was now out of the panel van and standing next to Maria. 'I don't know how you kept so damned cool.'

Anna gave a small, childlike laugh and realised that her legs were shaking. 'Nor do I.'

'We had the Wasserschutzpolizei keeping an eye on you,' explained Paul. 'You were safe all the way through . . . help was only seconds away if you needed it.'

Maria was just about to say something when her cell phone rang. She took a few steps back and answered it.

'I have to say, Anna,' said Paul, 'you did really well. But we didn't get much out of it. He didn't say or do anything to suggest that he's connected to either the abductions or the killings.'

Anna didn't answer, but remained facing in the direction taken by MacSwain's car. Somewhere deep in her gut lurked the phantom of the nausea that had gnawed at her every time MacSwain had touched her

'I have a feeling about MacSwain,' she said, without looking at Paul. 'A real, powerful, physical reaction to him.'

Paul gave a small laugh. 'Female intuition?'

'No,' Anna replied in a small but hard and sharp-edged voice. 'Policeman's instinct.'

'Well,' said Paul, 'it looks like you went through all of that for nothing. I suspect *Mr* MacSwain is nothing more than a womanising yuppie.'

'It would appear you're right.' Maria snapped shut her cell

phone. 'That was Fabel . . . at last. Seems he's had quite an evening of it too. MacSwain's out of the picture. We have a name for our killer. Vasyl Vitrenko.'

Anna now turned back to face her colleagues. Her dark eyes sparkled cold in the neon glitter of the Kiez. 'I don't care what Fabel's turned up. I know that there is something evil about MacSwain. He's our killer. I just know it.'

Saturday 21 June, 1.04 a.m. Harburg, Hamburg.
Despite it being a mild night, Hansi Kraus lay shivering under both his rank, ragged bed linen and the heavy army greatcoat that accompanied him everywhere. His meagre frame convulsed, his teeth chattered and he had the feeling that a rat gnawed endlessly at his gut. He maybe shouldn't have come back to the squat; but he had needed somewhere warm and a place where, perhaps, he could beg, borrow or steal enough to pay for the fix he so badly needed. Unfortunately for Hansi, there had been no opportunity to exploit any of the three means.

He was exposed here, but he had to get sorted out. He would go to the Turk in the morning and tell him what he had seen in the Polizeipräsidium. The Turks would know what to do: they might, for once, even give him a little something on account. He had also written a letter to his mother, the first proof he had given her in five years that he still drew breath. In it he had come as close as he was capable to apologising to her; asking forgiveness for having destroyed her only son and extinguishing every hope and dream she had had for him. It was ironic that, after a decade of fear and threat, and five years in which his mother and sisters had probably assumed him dead, Hansi had come to terms that this was now, probably, his time. It was now that he made amends; it was now that he had left a message that would endure beyond his life.

Hansi was scared. Hansi was always scared, it was his natural state: but now his fear had switched up a gear.

Somewhere, infused into his bones, was some memory of childhood that had not melted away with the flesh that had once given his frame some form. Whenever Hansi had been ill or afraid, his mother had let him sleep with a low light by his bed. The wraith Hansi now reached back to the child Hansi and remembered the soft, warm pool of light, the smell of fresh linen, the sensation of polished skin after his bath and the tickle of joy and cosy security that snuggling down into his bed had brought.

Now, twenty years on, all that was left to Hansi was a naked bulb burning bleakly and ineffectually in the ceiling as a talisman against the chills and the aches and the terrors that wracked his wasted, craving body. He heard footsteps out on the landing. Normally he would have ignored them: there was always activity in the squat, people coming and going, drunk or high, fighting or calling out in their sleep. Unmoving, he strained his ears but the footsteps had stopped.

Not faded away. Stopped.

He had just started to raise himself up on one elbow when the door slowly opened. Hansi actually found the mental time to note that he would have expected them to burst the door open, instead of gently and quietly easing it open the way his mother used to when she checked on him as a child. The older man held the door open and allowed the younger man, the one built like a bodybuilder, to enter and move swiftly and silently across the short distance to Hansi's bed. The cry that started to rise in Hansi's throat was muffled by the younger man's huge, powerful hand as it clamped down hard and immovable onto Hansi's mouth. The older man came in and closed the door. Smiling at Hansi, he produced a metal case from the pocket of his tan leather coat. Still smiling and tilting his head slightly, he held the oblong case up between finger and thumb and rattled it, like a parent teasing a child with the offer of some candy.

'Time to get happy, Hansi,' he said in a voice that could

almost have been kind, as he opened the case, taking out a disposable hypodermic syringe. 'Happy like you've never been happy before . . .'

Hansi tried to scream, but the younger man rammed a foul-tasting cloth into his mouth before forcing his arm out straight and pulling up his sleeve.

In the fraction of a second before the lethally pure heroin hit his system, Hansi's eyes darted from one man's face to the other. The words, *I know who you are . . . I saw you and I know who you are . . .* died on his immobilised tongue under the filthy rag they had stuffed in his mouth. It took only a few seconds for the heroin to invade all that was the meagre presence of Hansi Kraus. As they pulled the rag from his mouth and turned their backs on him, leaving him to die alone, he thought he could smell freshly laundered bedclothes.

Saturday 21 June, 4.00 a.m. Polizeipräsidium, Hamburg.
The atmosphere in the incident room was an odd mix of excitement and exhaustion. In the dead hours before dawn, officers just awoken and those, like Fabel, Maria, Paul and Anna, who had been awake and active all the previous day struggled to shake off the physical tiredness that clung to them, dulling the thrill of closing in on their prey. There was a buzz of voices on telephones, waking disgruntled officials across Europe, from Hamburg to Kiev.

And there, centre stage, enlarged and pinned to the middle of the inquiry board, the cold green eyes of Vasyl Vitrenko, like the malevolently heroic portrait gaze of some eastern-European dictator, stared out defiantly at those who would pursue him. Beside the image of Vitrenko were copies of the images in the barn supplied by his father. When Fabel had first taped the images to the board, a stunned incredulity had temporarily muted the clamour in the room.

Maria, who spoke English reasonably well and a little

Russian, had been pursuing by telephone reluctant police officials in Odessa and Kiev. She had also scanned Europol's and Interpol's databases, finding a scrap here and there to help assemble a person behind the image on the inquiry board.

Fabel took a moment of comparative quiet in the room to call together the majority of the team, who then waited until their colleagues still on phones concluded their calls.

Fabel stood before the incident board and leaned on the table, pressing his knuckles down onto the polished cherry-wood. He took in a sharp breath before starting his debrief of what the Ukrainian had told him. There was a silence in the room, an intense quiet as if the air had been corded and stretched tight, as he repeated the old man's account of pursuing his son through the mountains and half-desert plains of Afghanistan, following a trail of growing atrocity, culminating in the discovery in the barn. He then outlined what he had learned about the killings in Kiev.

'Okay, people. We have a clear prime suspect . . . but, while we have enough to get the Staatsanwaltschaft state prosecutor to grant us a warrant for his arrest and questioning, we have absolutely no solid evidence to nail him with.' Fabel turned and slapped his hand against the blown-up portrait. 'Colonel Vasyl Vitrenko, formerly of the Ukrainian *Berkut*, or Golden Eagle counter-terrorist unit. Forty-five years old. And a tough and heartless son of a bitch. We have our eye-witness account, albeit after the fact, of Vitrenko having orchestrated mass murders using exactly the same modus we have seen here in Hamburg. We also have an identical series of murders in Kiev . . . But again this isn't much good because we cannot tie Vitrenko conclusively to these, particularly as the Ukrainian police believe they already have the perpetrator. But what we do have is a potential motive. It would appear that at least two of our victims had some knowledge, potentially very damaging, about a vast property scam that involves our friends the Eitels and Ukrainian connections. Maria?'

Maria Klee pulled out her notes and flicked through them. She started to speak but tiredness had cast gravel in her throat and she gave a small cough before resuming.

'I've spoken to the Ukrainian police in Kiev, the *Berkut* CT unit and the SBU secret service. Unsurprisingly, the SBU were not very forthcoming, but I did get some information from the police about the Kiev murders. They seem to think we've got a copycat killer, because, as Hauptkommissar Fabel has stated, they swear they got the right man for it.' She checked her notes again. 'A Vladimir Gera . . .' Maria stumbled over the name and took another run at it. 'Vladimir Gerassimenko. Apparently he was a bright underachiever who worked as an administrator for the railways. There were three victims. Two of whom were found to have been, well, sacrificed as part of some kind of rite. It was suspected that there were others involved in the rituals, but Gerassimenko was convicted for the third killing.'

'The journalist?' asked Fabel.

'Yes. And in her own apartment.'

'Just like Angelika Blüm.' Fabel stated the obvious for emphasis, but his voice was dull and tired. 'Is there any chance that we can get someone over to the Ukraine to interview this . . .'

'Gerassinenko . . .' Maria helped Fabel out. 'Not likely. The Ukraine signed a moratorium on the death penalty in 1997 and abolished it in 2000 . . . but Gerassimenko was executed in ninety-six.'

Fabel sighed. 'What else did you find out?'

'Well . . . your guy – Vitrenko's father – he's no longer on active service in any arm of the Ukrainian police. I spoke with someone from the Ministry of Internal Affairs – the only one they were willing to get out of bed – and, according to him, Major Stepan Vitrenko was retired out of the *Berkut* years ago. I was able to squeeze out of the guy I spoke to that Vitrenko senior has made hunting down his son a bit of a one-man crusade. Apparently the Soviets sent him after Vitrenko in Afghanistan, and since that time it has become an obsession with him.'

'I can imagine why,' said Fabel.

'I have to add,' said Maria, 'that the only reason the Ukrainians are giving more weight to Vitrenko's disappearance than a standard missing person is his importance as an anti-terrorism and organised-crime specialist. As far as they're concerned, the only crime he has committed is to desert his post.'

'What about the *Berkut* . . . this counter-terrorist unit to which he belonged?' asked Fabel.

'Basically they're the Ukraine's all-purpose riot-squad and counter-terrorism unit. Concerns about their conduct have been raised by Amnesty International. They are run by the Ukrainian Ministry of the Interior. From what I can gather, Vitrenko's brief went far beyond the *Berkut*'s usual operational parameters. He was a high-flyer with an expertise across the board of civil, political and terrorist crime. The Ukraine has a real problem with organised crime and there are massive tensions between the minority Russian and majority Ukrainian populations. Added to this, they have probably the highest incidence of serial murderers in the world. Which is why they lead the world in tracking down serials.'

Fabel rubbed the twenty-hour-old stubble on his jaw. 'If Vitrenko's father is on a one-man crusade to track him down, who is the girl who is working with him? And why?'

'I think I have an answer for that,' said Maria, again shuffling through her notes to find the relevant fact. 'I suspect she is Lieutenant Martina Onopenko. She was, until recently, an officer in the Kiev police.'

'A detective?'

'No . . . uniform branch. But she has some military experience. It also turns out she is the younger sister of the journalist who was killed. She, apparently, shares the old guy's conviction that it is truly Vitrenko who is guilty of her sister's killing. She resigned from the police force when they refused to reopen the case.'

'It's an unlikely partnership,' mused Fabel. 'The sister of a victim and the father of the chief suspect . . .'

Maria shrugged. 'I'm merely assuming that's who your girl is. They certainly were active together in the Ukraine after Vitrenko's disappearance.' She handed Fabel a head-and-shoulders photograph of a young woman. 'I had this e-mailed to me by our Ukrainian friends . . .'

Fabel examined the photograph. In many ways the girl in the photograph was similar to the old Ukrainian's assistant, but the hair was darker and the face more oval.

'She looks similar, but this isn't her . . .'

'I know. This is the murdered Kiev journalist. Valerie Onopenko.'

'Then this is definitely the sister of the woman with Vitrenko senior. This entire case seems to be about bloody families.'

'Speaking of which –' Werner eased to the front of the gathered team – 'I checked out our friends the Eitels. I know we're not looking at them directly for the murders, but they both have solid alibis for the first killing. The father has a corroborated alibi for the second and Norbert Eitel for the third. I've spoken to some of our financial and corporate crime guys on the second floor, but they say they're not looking at the Eitels for anything at the moment, although they are now taking an active interest in these allegations of property fraud. I've handed over a copy of our file. They were able to give me a full breakdown of the registered companies and interests controlled by the Eitels or in which they have an interest. And, right enough, they are directors of Neuer Horizont.' It was Werner's turn to flick through his notes. 'They also have an interest in Galicia Trading. It is a holding company that seems to be doing on-paper trade with the Eitel Group's property wing. It's this news that has whetted the appetite of the financial and corporate crime squad. I've been able to establish that Galicia Trading is co-directed by Wolfgang Eitel, Norbert Eitel, Pavlo Klimenko and an American businessman called John Sturchak. Galicia Trading has been buying quite a bit of Hamburg real estate recently.'

'And Pavlo Klimenko is one of Vitrenko's men.' Fabel thought for a moment. 'What do we know about this American?'

'Not a lot, but I'm getting an e-mail translated into English for sending to the FBI and Interpol.'

'I think we should have another little chat with the Eitels,' said Fabel. 'And this time I think instead of us enjoying their corporate hospitality, they should enjoy ours.'

Anna Wolff stood up. She still wore the smart dress she had for her date with MacSwain but had donned her trademark leather jacket over it. Her face looked drawn and wan under her make-up.

'What about MacSwain?'

'What about him?'

'Is he still a suspect or not?' Despite her tiredness there was a defiance in her voice.

'Not for these killings . . . no. But we'll keep him under observation anyway. I still think he may have something to do with the abductions, which I now feel are unrelated to this main case. But I've got to be careful, Anna. Kriminaldirektor Van Heiden is becoming uneasy about more than the expenditure: he feels that if MacSwain twigs that we've been watching his every move without substantive evidence to indicate why he's a suspect, we could end up with an embarrassing claim on our hands.'

Anna sat down.

Fabel, still standing, paused before addressing the whole assembly again.

'Now for a history lesson . . .' He had set a box file on the chair next to the one on which he had hung his Jaeger jacket. He flipped open the lid and took out a sheaf of papers. There was impatient shuffling from his audience. He froze them with a cold stare. 'This is necessary. We are dealing with a ritualised method of killing that has a thousand-year history. Our killer – Vitrenko – lives as much in the past as he does in the here and now. We have to understand what perverted sense of history and destiny drives him. I have found out quite a bit that should interest us . . .'

Fabel did not mention that he had woken up Mathias Dorn with a phone call. Professor Dorn had furnished him with the key facts he needed or the directions in which to look. More importantly, Dorn had remembered the name of the Viking king who had replaced King Inge the Elder when he refused to commit the nine-fold sacrifice at Uppsala. Fabel lifted a photocopy from the papers and taped it to the incident board, next to and almost overlapping the image of Vitrenko. The photocopy was of a nineteenth-century copper-plate illustration. It showed an improbably broad-shouldered warrior mounted on a fierce-looking steed. He had long flowing light-haired locks and a huge moustache and a beard that was braided and beaded. He wore a mail tunic and a vast rug of fur sat as a cloak on the unlikely shoulders. His head was topped by an eagle-winged helm.

'This,' said Fabel, 'is Vasyl Vitrenko's true father. Not the Ukrainian who has been tracking him. At least, I suspect that is how Vitrenko sees it.'

Fabel waited for the sudden chatter, including some laughter, to subside.

'Now this is all only my supposition. I will need to run this by Frau Doktor Eckhardt tomorrow . . . I mean, later this morning . . . but this, ladies and gentlemen, is Sven. As in "Son of Sven". His full name is *Blot-Sven*, Bloody Sven or Sven the Sacrificer, depending on how you interpret it.

He was King of Sweden between 1084 and 1087. His half-brother, King Inge the Elder, converted to Christianity and refused to perform pagan rites of sacrifice at the temple of Uppsala. Sven took over the sacrifices and earned his name. Inge fled to Västergötland and *Blot-Sven* became king of Sweden, or *Svealand*, So, you may ask, what is the link between a Ukrainian madman and Sweden?' Fabel taped a second, similarly heroic illustration next to that of *Blot-Sven*. 'This gentleman is Rurik, the first Grand Prince of Kiev. Rurik was supposedly a Viking prince from around this part of Germany, maybe Frisia, or Friesland as we call it now. The warriors he led to conquer Novgorod and Kiev were called the Rus, or the "Rowers", and it is from them that Russia gets its name. Rurik's band included Varangians and other mercenaries. The story, unlikely as it may sound, is that the Slavs of what is now the Ukraine and Russia were living in anarchy and invited Rurik and his brother to come and establish order. It is the same fable that is told about the Saxons in England, in their case the brothers being Hengist and Horsa. Anyway, the point is that Rurik and his men were outsiders subjugating a strange land. Their allegiance was exclusively to each other. And their reward was wealth and success. They would go on to become the elite of this new land and the founders of Russian and Ukrainian aristocracy. Vitrenko and his men are doing the same thing here . . . and Vitrenko has wrapped it all up in his semi-mythical concepts of brotherhood under arms and arcane Viking ritual.'

'But it's all a pile of crap,' Werner said. 'They can't really believe that they are a band of Vikings occupying a new land.'

'Yes they can. And as for it all being a pile of crap, you can say that about any religion or system of belief if you stand on the outside. It isn't *what* you believe in that's important. It's the act of believing that matters. No matter how bizarre or extreme it may seem to others. It's what makes otherwise sane young men fly airliners into buildings full of people.'

Werner shook his head. More in dull, sad puzzlement than in any sense of disagreement. Fabel continued.

'I have no idea if Vitrenko believed any of this stuff to start with,' Fabel went on, 'or whether he used the myth as a cult-like device to manipulate those under his command. But I am pretty convinced that he believes it all now . . .'

Fabel paused for a moment and thought back to the end of his conversation with the old Ukrainian soldier. His powerful shoulders had sagged as he spoke of Vitrenko the child. The pale boy with his father's eyes who was capable of so much and who had revealed an early and vast appetite for cruelty. Tales of other children being manipulated, bullied and cajoled into carrying out acts of torture on small animals. Then on each other. Fabel continued.

'And I am also certain that Vitrenko has been a psychopath for as long as he can remember. But instead of being treated and controlled, he was sent to elite Soviet military academies where his natural abilities, and psychopathy, were honed.' Fabel picked up the papers from the table and they made a cone in his fist. He held them out before him as if they were aflame. A burning torch that he held out to his colleagues. 'Vasyl Vitrenko is the most dangerous individual we have ever had to deal with. He will kill anyone whom he perceives as a threat. And that includes you. And it includes me.'

Fabel couldn't think what to say next. His mind flooded with the images of the victims, of Vitrenko's father's eyes as he had seized Fabel by the throat . . . the same cold, emerald eyes as his son's. A shudder ran through him as he imagined Ursula Kastner, Tina Kramer and Angelika Blüm all locking gazes with those stone-cold, glittering eyes as their lives left them. The rest of the team must have each been in some similar, dark place, because the silence remained crystal whole for a few seconds before Maria Klee's voice shattered it.

'What about Vitrenko's father? Did you bring him in?'

Fabel shook his head.

'But he assaulted a senior police officer. You. We can't let him away with that.'

'I can and I have. It was me he assaulted and I've called off the search for him. He has agreed to contact me whenever we need to share information again. I honestly believe he just wants his son stopped.' As he spoke, the first e-mail echoed in his mind: *You can stop me, but you will never catch me.*

'And what is Vitrenko's father doing in the meantime?' Maria's frown lay somewhere on the edge of a scowl.

'He is doing exactly what we are doing: he is trying to find and stop Vitrenko.'

'And what if he catches our guy first?' Werner picked up Maria's thread.

Fabel remembered asking the old man the same question as they had stepped out of the Portakabin and into the echoing gloom of the warehouse. The Ukrainian had turned to Fabel and said, in a quiet, flat voice: 'Then I will end it.'

Fabel locked eyes with Werner and lied. 'He has given me his word that he will hand Vitrenko and any evidence he finds over to us. That is why I do not want him picked up. I want him treated as a key informant. Okay?' Fabel leaned forward again, knuckles on the table, his face set hard and tight over his tiredness. 'I need things to start happening now. Firstly, I want the Eitels brought in for questioning. Now. If they protest then I want them arrested on suspicion of being accessories to murder. And Werner, get the corporate and financial crime guys to put together the questions they want to ask them. A joint interview would be good.'

Werner nodded his assent.

'Secondly,' continued Fabel, 'I want every Ukrainian informant turned over and worked on. Hard. I want operational locations for Vitrenko's outfit and I want them before

the end of today. And, just to be clear, I do not give a rat's
ass if you step on the toes of our Organised Crime colleagues
over at LKA7. I will be doing a little of that myself, as well
as squeezing our BND colleagues.' Fabel's expression darkened even more. 'No one is telling us what we need to know.
And that ends right now. Oberkommissarin Klee and Oberkommissar Meyer will assign your tasks. Werner, hang around
a moment, I want a word.'

'Sure, *Chef* . . .'

It took a few minutes for the room to clear. Werner
remained seated and Anna Wolff walked round the conference table to face Fabel. Her eyes were shadowed, but something akin to defiance smouldered in them.

'So what do I say if he calls me?'

'Who?'

'MacSwain. I've given him the allocated cell phone number.'

'Cancel the number. I don't want you having close contact
with him again. And I can't justify to Van Heiden any more
expensive undercover ops. We need to check him out more,
but he's a low priority.'

'I think he's our man, *Chef.*'

Fabel frowned. 'Why, Anna? You've seen what we've got
on Vitrenko.'

'MacSwain is a predator. It's in the way he observes you
. . . the way he moves around you. Like you're prey.' She
shook her head slightly, as if irritated by the inadequacy of
her description. Then she fixed Fabel with a bright, hard,
resolute gaze. 'He is a rapist, *Chef.* And, I suspect, a killer.
Our killer.'

Fabel stared silently at his subordinate for a moment. He
could not condemn a junior officer for responding to her
instincts about a case or a suspect: it was how he operated
himself, processing, in some deep part of his brain, the
smallest details of how someone moves or talks or the minu-
tiae of a scene. And from these deep processes would come

forth a conclusion of which, like Anna, he would be certain, although he could not rationalise it with a solid piece of evidence. After all, it was just such a feeling, a judgement on the way MacSwain had reacted to finding two Hamburg policemen on his threshold that had led Fabel to suspect MacSwain.

'Okay, Anna. I trust your judgement, but I can't say I agree with your conclusion.' The stubble rasped under rubbing fingers once more. 'I'll keep someone on MacSwain, just to make sure. But I definitely don't want you seeing him again – especially if your instincts about him are right. Werner and I may pay him an official visit just to check out his whereabouts on the key dates. Of course that'll alert him to the fact that we're watching him.' Fabel sighed. 'But I have to say I think you've got it all wrong, Anna. We may not have a smoking gun, but the circumstantial evidence is pretty conclusive against Vitrenko.'

'I know,' Anna replied. 'I see that. But thanks for keeping an open mind on MacSwain.'

'That's okay.' Fabel took in Anna's face. She looked totally drained. Fabel had never been undercover but knew many officers who had. It was one of the most physically, emotionally and mentally exhausting challenges for a police officer to undertake. The image of Klugmann, sitting opposite him in the interview room at Davidwache, slipped to the front of his mind. He remembered attributing the red-rimmed eyes to drugs. But it had more probably been stress. And the traces of amphetamine found in his autopsy would have probably been Klugmann's way of taking the edge off it. Now Fabel detected the same leaden edginess in Anna's movements, the same red rims and dark shadows around the eyes. 'Listen, Anna. I've made sure you're clear of duties for the next twenty-four. Go home and get some sleep.'

*   *   *

Saturday 21 June, 10.00 a.m. Polizeipräsidium, Hamburg.
At least Fabel felt cleaner. A change of clothes had been like sloughing off a layer of crumpled skin; but the couple of hours' sleep hadn't dispelled the shadow of tiredness that still clung to him, and he had to make an effort to shake it from his movements and thoughts. As promised, Werner had picked up Wolfgang Eitel shortly before eight a.m. and a second team, led by Paul Lindemann, had brought in his son at the same time. Eitel father and son were being kept apart, but their furious threats of litigation against individual officers, the Polizei Hamburg and the state government had been almost identical. Fabel knew that if they didn't turn up something solid on the Eitels, these threats would have to be taken very, very seriously indeed.

To underline the fact, a small cluster of legal types, including Waalkes, were waiting in the main waiting area of the Präsidium when Fabel arrived. Waalkes spotted Fabel just as he was about to step into the elevator and set off full steam towards him. Fabel called out an enthusiastic 'Good morning, Herr Waalkes!' as the elevator doors closed, Waalkes halfway across the reception area and halfway through an infuriated protest.

Fabel called Werner out of interview room one, where he had been stalling Wolfgang Eitel, who was demanding immediate access to counsel.

'There are enough of them downstairs,' said Fabel. 'Tell him he's entitled to one legal representative to be present, but let the Corporate and Financial boys soften him up first. Same deal with Norbert.'

Fabel went to his office and closed the door behind him. He picked up the phone and called Susanne at the Institut für Rechtsmedizin. He had phoned her after he left the Speicherstadt the night before and a strained cord of worry had been stretched through her voice. He had reassured her that he was fine but that he would have to head off to the

Präsidium and that she should sleep. As he had hung up, he felt slightly guilty about the warm glow he experienced from having someone to worry about him again. Now he called her to give her a summary of the evidence he had uncovered and to outline his theory about Vitrenko and his 'spiritual father' *Blot-Sven*.

'It makes some sort of sense, I suppose,' said Susanne, but she sounded less than convinced.

'But?'

'I don't know. Like I say, it all makes sense. And I think you're right. At least in the main part. I have no sound professional grounds for doubting your theory. I just feel uneasy because of the scope of participation.'

'What do you mean, Susanne?'

'He doesn't act alone. He may not even act at all. Remember Charles Manson in America? The mass killings in the Tate and LaBianca homes? Manson wasn't even present at the Tate home and left the LaBianca residence after ordering his followers to murder the tied-up victims, but before the actual killings took place. So Manson didn't actually commit the crimes personally. But they were his crimes. He manipulated others to commit them for him. He engineered a wider scope of participation that not only involved his so-called family, but excluded himself.'

Fabel thought over what Susanne was saying. He had studied the Manson murders in depth: Manson had cemented the bonds in his 'family' by having sex with all of 'Charlie's Girls', the female members of his group. It was the same trick that Svensson had used to ensnare the loyalty of his female acolytes, like Marlies Menzel and Gisela Frohm. Fabel had come to realise that he and Gisela had not stood alone on that pier. Svensson had been there too. Invisible, insidious. His presence evident only to Gisela. Fabel exhaled loudly, as if blowing the ghosts from his skull.

'I don't know, Susanne. I see Vitrenko as a hands-on butcher. And, if I'm right, he sees himself as the natural heir of *Blot-Sven*, the master of the sacrifice . . .'

Fabel could hear her breath at the other end of the line. 'Just be careful, Jan. Be very careful.'

Werner came into Fabel's office just before lunchtime. The Corporate and Financial Crime officers were still with both Wolfgang and Norbert Eitel, two detectives questioning each man separately.

'Markmann from Corporate Crime reckons we're on to something with this property deal, but there's no hard evidence as yet,' Werner said glumly. 'He's setting up teams to raid Galicia Trading and the Eitel Group's offices but the Staatsanwaltschaft is being a bit coy about granting a warrant on such flimsy evidence.'

Fabel nodded. He'd already had a call from Heiner Goetz, the chief state prosecutor, who had made clear his concerns about bringing in such high-profile personages on suspicion. Fabel had known Goetz for years and there was more than a little mutual respect between the two men, but Fabel knew that Goetz was a cautious and methodical prosecutor who didn't like short cuts. Fabel also knew that Goetz would see through any hastily spun screen of bluster, so he had had to admit that he was taking a big chance with the Eitels. It all came down to a judgement call, and Goetz was prepared to allow the Hauptkommissar some latitude. Fabel, however, chose not to enlighten Goetz at this stage about his plan to bring MacSwain in for questioning: Fabel hoped that MacSwain would want to make a show of cooperation.

'Corporate Crime say they're screwed if the Staatsanwaltschaft won't accept that they've established reasonable grounds for seizure,' said Werner. 'And without the paperwork to prove wrongdoing they can't bring a case.'

Fabel's face hardened and he snatched up the handset of his phone and dialled the cell phone number the Ukrainian had given him.

'I was not expecting to hear from you so soon, Herr Fabel,' said Vitrenko senior, in his perfect but accented German.

Fabel explained the situation with the Staatsanwaltschaft state prosecution service. 'I need something, anything, concrete that gives us grounds for detaining the Eitels longer and getting our hands on their files. The Eitels are our only potential link to your son's organisation.'

There was a silence at the other end of the phone. Then the Ukrainian said: 'I don't know if I can help you. There is certainly nothing I can give you right now. But meet me tonight, say eight o'clock, in the warehouse in the Speicherstadt.'

The hard resolve on Fabel's face remained undiluted when he came off the phone. 'Werner, go get Maria. We're going to visit the BAO.'

Maria talked as the trio walked briskly along the corridor that led from the elevator to Volker's office. She handed Fabel three or four pieces of paper stapled together.

'I checked into Vitrenko. This is as close to a background as we're likely to get. From what I can gather the *Berkut* unit is being built into a serious counter-terrorist and anti-organised-crime outfit, although its primary function has until now been basically that of a riot squad. As an operational unit it is similar to GSG9 here in the Bundesrepublik. They are clearly very highly trained. I contacted their headquarters in Kiev – they were cooperative but not overly forthcoming about Vitrenko. It would appear that he was one of their top experts on Islamic terrorism, mainly because of his time in Afghanistan and Chechnya. All I got from them was this résumé of Vitrenko's career. Buried in amongst it all was this . . .' Maria flipped over a couple of the pages Fabel was holding. There was a sheet headed with what Fabel guessed was the crest of the Ukrainian Interior Ministry above a page of Cyrillic text. The next page was the translation into German. 'Look at this: two weeks training at a serial-offenders profiling unit in Odessa.'

Fabel came to a halt. 'And you said my Europol paper on the Helmut Schmied killings was circulated in the Ukraine?'

'Exactly. I've still to get a reply, but I'll bet a month's salary that it featured or was available as part of the course.'

Fabel felt the hunger that comes to the hunter when close to his quarry. 'That's why we've been dealing with a classic textbook case of psychotic serial murder; because it's all based on textbook cases. And he chose me because he happened to read a paper I had published on serial offending.'

Werner gave a bitter laugh. 'So he thought he could pull all of your strings and have you look in the wrong direction.'

'Except you didn't,' added Maria.

Fabel handed the file back to her. 'Let's go,' he said, and Maria and Werner fell in behind him.

The secretary did her best to stop the train of Fabel, Maria and Werner as it steamed past her and into Volker's office. Volker was sitting behind his desk and was talking in English to two shirtsleeved men who sat opposite him. Fabel guessed that the two *Amis* were members of the six-strong FBI team that had been seconded to the Polizei Hamburg following the September 11 attacks. Volker hastily wrapped a smile around his naked annoyance at being disturbed.

'I take it this is a matter of some importance, Herr Hauptkommissar?'

Fabel did not answer but looked pointedly at the Americans.

'I'm sorry, gentlemen,' said Volker in what Fabel recognised as excellent English. 'I wonder if we could conclude our briefing later?'

As they left, the Americans cast glances at Fabel that lay somewhere between curiosity and anger. Volker leaned back in his leather chair and held his hand out, as if inviting Fabel to bring it all on. It was a gesture of arrogant casualness that Fabel realised was intended to push him into anger, and therefore nudge the balance of any exchange in Volker's favour. Having recognised Volker's strategy, Fabel paused before speaking, moving over and taking one of the chairs recently vacated by an American.

'Yes, Oberst Volker, this is a matter of importance. And some urgency. I intend to call a press conference about the murders I'm investigating,' Fabel lied. 'I need to set a few things straight for the public. In fact I intend to render you something of a favour.' Fabel smiled coldly.

'Oh? How so?'

'Well, I have prepared a statement which categorically denies that the BND is protecting the murderer, a former Ukrainian counter-terrorist officer called Vasyl Vitrenko, just because he may be of use as a source of information on al-Qaeda and other Islamic terrorist organisations.'

Fabel could see that Volker was using every ounce of his will-power to keep his face from betraying his emotions.

Fabel continued. 'I am going to make special mention that you, personally, would obviously have no truck with any such cover-up and all rumours to the contrary are false.'

Volker's lips slipped back from his teeth in something that defied description as a smile. 'You wouldn't dare.'

'Wouldn't dare what? Protect your reputation in the face of such scurrilous rumours?'

'There are no rumours . . .'

Fabel looked at his watch. 'No? So it isn't true that an incriminating, anonymous package of information has been received by *Stern* or *Hamburger Morgenpost* . . .' Fabel leaned forward in his chair and almost spat the final word at Volker: 'yet!'

'Like I say, you wouldn't dare . . .' said Volker, but his voice betrayed a shadow of uncertainty.

'Oberst Volker, I would be obliged if you could fulfil our original agreement and share all the information available to you that is relevant to this investigation. Let's start with the Eitels' involvement with a Kiev-based cartel that is somehow profiting illegally from property-redevelopment initiatives in Hamburg. The Corporate and Financial Crime Division is questioning both Eitels as we speak. When I go downstairs after this meeting, Herr Oberst, I intend to hand them a lead substantial enough to allow the Staatsanwaltschaft to grant a search-and-seizure warrant. In addition I want to know where to find former Comrade Vitrenko and his principal officers. Now . . . if this were all to happen, these leaked documents and the press conference I mentioned may not be necessary.'

Volker gave Fabel a long, dark stare. 'I could make life very, very difficult for you, Fabel, you know that, don't you?'

'It's kind of you to remind me, Volker. Particularly in front of two witnesses.'

'Just what do you think we do, Fabel? Do you think we're just some kind of dirty-tricks department?'

Fabel shrugged. 'I'm a policeman. I like to let the facts do the talking. And so far those facts tell me not only that you have been concealing evidence from me, but also that you obviously have your own agenda as far as Vitrenko is concerned.'

Volker gave a bitter laugh. 'For a senior officer investigating serious crimes you seem to have a habit of making the facts fit *your* particular agenda of prejudices.'

'You're denying that you are trying to tie up a deal with Vitrenko?'

'No. I am not denying that. But not to the extent of ignoring these bloody murders, if that's what you mean. And I'm not denying that our American friends are perhaps less squeamish about doing deals with the Devil, if it brings them the heads they're after. But no. If –' Volker emphasised the word and repeated it – '*if* Vitrenko is indeed your killer, then of course we would not consider dealing with him, although we would want to talk to him. And as for us not being forthcoming with information . . . you never thought to ask yourself if there was another possible reason for our reticence?'

'Like what?'

Volker stood up and leaned on his desk. 'Like maybe you can't be trusted. Like maybe one of your precious Polizei Hamburg is on the take. And maybe because of that, Klugmann – someone I recruited personally and a bloody good man – was killed.'

'This is all a smokescreen, Volker.' Fabel also rose to his feet.

'Is it? Klugmann was onto the *real* leak of information from within the Polizei Hamburg. He found out that someone, someone at a high level – perhaps even a Kriminalhauptkommissar – has been selling high-level information to the Ukrainians.'

Fabel took a second before responding. In that second he hastily constructed a web of cables and threw it over the anger that surged within him. 'Are you telling me that that is why you have been withholding information on Vitrenko? I don't believe it.'

'Ask Van Heiden. He knows all about it. Someone either within this Präsidium or in a major city-centre Polizeidirektion is selling Vitrenko information that is helping him to hit his main rivals and take over their operations and hijack their deals – like the Colombian deal where Ulugbay was wiped out.'

'But you said Klugmann gave the Ukrainians the information . . .'

'He did. And that's why we think he's dead. Klugmann sensed his contact, Vadim, was pulling back from him. Of course, deep-cover work makes you hyper-paranoid, but

Klugmann was very concerned that the Ukrainians were becoming suspicious of him.'

Fabel said nothing, but recalled Sonja's fear when Fabel's team had raided the flat in search of Klugmann. And how Klugmann himself had sought deeper refuge somewhere, only to end up lying at the bottom of a filth-strewn swimming pool. Volker could see that Fabel was considering his words, and he eased back into his seat. Fabel did the same. When Volker continued, his tone was markedly less aggressive.

'You may remember, Herr Hauptkommissar, that you were more than critical of the way we supplied information to the Ukrainians, through Klugmann, about the deal where Ulugbay ended up being murdered. Well, we're not as stupid or ruthless as you seem to think we are. We made damned sure that there were crucial gaps in the details Klugmann supplied about Ulugbay's deal with the Colombians. The hit on Ulugbay took more – a lot more – than Klugmann gave them. And whoever really supplied the information must have sussed that Klugmann's mole in the drugs MEK was a fiction.'

'You're saying that it was a police officer who killed Klugmann?' It was Maria Klee who beat Fabel to the question.

Volker shrugged. 'Directly? Perhaps, I don't know. Indirectly? Probably. Whoever has been selling information has been demanding a high price, and I'm pretty sure they would go to great lengths to protect themselves. But they wouldn't necessarily have to get their own hands dirty. If they tipped off Vitrenko's mob that Klugmann was undercover, then the Ukrainians would gladly take on the burden of removing him.'

'*Chef* . . .' Werner, who had been standing behind Fabel, spoke in a low, tight voice.

'Shit . . . of course. We brought our witness into the Präsidium. Damn it, Volker, if we had known all of this before, we wouldn't have exposed him to danger. We never, for a moment, thought that bringing him here would mark him out.' Fabel turned back to Werner. 'Get Hansi into protective custody now.'

'I'm on it, *Chef*,' said Werner and left the office. Maria sat down in the vacant chair next to Fabel.

A look of disbelief invaded Fabel's expression. 'So that, you claim, is why you have been withholding evidence from this investigation?' asked Fabel.

Volker sighed. 'I haven't been withholding anything. If you really believe that Vitrenko is behind these killings, then I'll do all I can to help. In fact, our willingness to deal with Vitrenko died with Klugmann.' Volker considered his next words carefully. 'You don't like me much do you, Fabel?'

'I don't know you. I neither like nor dislike you.'

There was acid in Volker's small laugh. 'Well, let's put it this way, you don't like what I *represent*.'

'I can't say that I do, much.'

'You've made it very clear that in your eyes I'm one step away from the Gestapo while your Polizei Hamburg represents all that's good and pure. Well let me tell you something, Fabel, I'm lucky to be sitting here. If the Polizei Hamburg had had its way my family tree would have been axed in Hamburg Police Prison Fuhlsbüttel.'

Fabel's eyes widened.

'Surprised? My father was a social democrat and trade unionist. A nineteen-year-old idealist. And so, inevitably, there was the knock on the door in the middle of the night. But it wasn't SS or Gestapo who came knocking. It was your precious Polizei Hamburg who took my father off to the police prison at Fuhlsbüttel. It was reclassified soon after, wasn't it Fabel? Konzentrationslager Fuhlsbüttel . . . the Polizei Hamburg's own little concentration camp. Of course you'd like to forget all about that.'

Fabel knew the history well: Fuhlsbüttel Concentration Camp, known as *Kola-Fu*. It was the darkest, most despicable chapter in the history of the Polizei Hamburg. After the Nazis came to power in Hamburg in March 1933, the Polizei Hamburg had been responsible for rounding up Communists and Social Democrat activists. It had been taken over by the SS in September of the same year, but those six months of police control had been enough to tarnish the Polizei Hamburg's history indelibly.

'Okay,' said Fabel at last, 'I take your point. But I don't see its relevance.'

Volker's reply snapped at the tail of Fabel's statement. 'The relevance is that you have a whole lot of theories about why I joined the BND. Well let me tell you the truth. I joined because I wanted to defend the only things that stand between Germany and history repeating itself: democracy and the Grundgesetz. You see yourself as a defender of the law. Well I see myself as a defender of the Basic Law . . . the constitution. I do it because I believe that the only just way to govern is a true liberal democracy.' He leaned back into his leather chair. 'Do you know what I really am, Fabel? I'm a fireman.' He jerked his head towards the window. 'Out there, Fabel . . . out there are all kinds of losers and sad wankers who are playing with matches. Extreme right, extreme left, fundamentalist religious nuts . . . they're all out there playing with fire in the dark. And my job is to kill the sparks before they become flames.'

'Okay, I guess I owe you an apology,' said Fabel. 'But the fact remains that you withheld evidence from us.'

'We owe each other nothing, Fabel, other than a little mutual respect and not to make each other's job more difficult than it is.' Volker picked up his desk phone, stabbed a button and gave an order that the Vitrenko file was to be brought in.

After the file was handed to Volker he flipped it open and removed a single sheet of paper. He handed the sheet to Fabel. It contained several rows of initials and numbers.

He scanned it a couple of times before giving it to Maria.

'It doesn't mean anything to me,' said Fabel. He looked at Maria who shrugged.

'But it will mean a great deal to your Corporate Crime colleagues.' Volker tilted his leather chair back and interlocked his fingers before him. 'These are transaction trackings. They detail movements of funds between accounts – times, dates and amounts.' He let the chair snap forward again and handed Fabel two more sheets from the file. 'This is the key to the accounts. It details who holds each account. There is also a federal court warrant –' Volker smiled, almost maliciously – 'just to prove we obtained the information legally.'

The list of account holders included Galicia Trading, Klimenko International, Eitel Importing and several others Fabel didn't recognise.

'There's enough there for you to get a seizure warrant. If your fraud people prise open the cracks in some of these phoney accounts they'll find a trail that leads straight back to the Eitels. And I mean personally. Not to their businesses. There may be some other surprises for you in there as well.'

Fabel raised an eyebrow.

'Just get your experts to look into it all.' Volker leaned forward, resting the weight of his broad shoulders on his elbows. 'As for Vitrenko . . . I honestly cannot give you any clue about where to find him. It's like he's a phantom. We do, however, have locations for a couple of his lieutenants.' Again he dipped into the file and pulled out a couple of photographs. He placed them both on the desk, turned round for Fabel and Maria to see. They were typical close-surveillance images: taken from a distance through telephoto lenses. Both men were in their late forties; one was lean and wiry; the other heavy set. Both had the dangerous look of seasoned soldiers. Volker tapped the image of the lean man.

'This is Stanislav Solovey. It was he who pointed out the

advantages of retirement to Yari Varasouv. The other is Vadim Redchenko.'

'Klugmann's contact?' asked Maria.

'And possible executioner,' added Volker.

Fabel shook his head. 'Hansi Kraus said the killers spoke unaccented German. And they deliberately left a Ukrainian security-services handgun to be found. I think they were trying to point us in the wrong direction.'

'Well, Redchenko is a killer through and through, whether he took out Klugmann or not. He was based in Reinbek, running a drugs factory and network from a disused mill. We launched a raid in conjunction with the drugs MEK unit a month back.'

'Let me guess,' said Maria, 'no one was home?'

'Exactly. In fact the place burst into flames just as we took up position. Some kind of Soviet mine and strategically placed vats of flammable chemicals did the job. Very professional and very thorough. It destroyed any evidence we might have picked up. Since then we've been unable to track Redchenko to any particular address, although we do have a couple of operations he visits regularly. Every time he does, we put a tail on him, and every time he loses us. These people could not be better trained. Take Vitrenko himself – it's not been easy getting information out of the Ukrainians, but from what we have uncovered he served not just with MDV Kondor and Alpha brigades, but also the *Vysotniki* brigade, as did some of his current group. *Vysotniki* was – and still is – based on the British Special Air Service model, made up of small operational units of eleven men. From what we have been able to squeeze out of our contacts, Vitrenko set up such a unit in Afghanistan and revived it in Chechnya. But instead of eleven it had thirteen men. We think that's how many he has with him here.'

'That fits with our information,' said Maria.

Volker placed his hands behind his head. 'Our operation

with Klugmann and Tina Kramer was intended to gather intelligence on Vitrenko. I never misled you on that count, Fabel. I do admit that our ultimate objective was to offer him some kind of deal – immunity from prosecution for his organised-crime activity on the condition that he cooperate with the *Amis* and, of course, that he give up all illegal activities. But it is difficult to make immunity from prosecution sound very inviting when there seems to be almost no chance of you ever being found, far less arrested and enough evidence scraped together to prosecute you. And, of course, if Vitrenko really is behind these killings, then all bets are off.' He lowered his arms and leaned forward in the chair. 'You do believe that, don't you, Fabel?'

'If you tell me it's the truth, Herr Volker,' said Fabel.

Volker put all the photographs and papers back in the file and pushed it across the table. 'The unedited, unexpurgated version. Make sure you don't lose it.'

An e-mail had arrived from the FBI, addressed to Werner, when Fabel and Maria returned to the Mordkommission. Maria printed it out and brought it through to Fabel's office.

'Listen to this . . .' She sat down across the desk from Fabel. 'John Sturchak – the Eitels' American business associate?'

Fabel nodded.

Maria scanned through the document as she briefed Fabel. 'The FBI are *very* interested in any information we might have on John Sturchak or deals he's involved in. Apparently, Sturchak is the son of Roman Sturchak, who was an officer in the SS Galicia Division at the same time as Wolfgang Eitel. Sturchak was one of the Ukrainians who fought their way back to Austria to surrender to the Americans at the end of the war. If the Red Army had got him he would have been shot. Roman was allowed to emigrate to the US and set up an importing business there. It would appear that this latest enterprise may not be the first collaboration between the Eitel and Sturchak families. The Sturchak business is based in New York and, according to the FBI, Roman Sturchak was suspected of having organised-crime links, but has never been indicted for any offence. John Sturchak took over the Sturchak business empire when his father died in 1992. When the Wall came down there was a flood of Ukrainian immigrants, legal and illegal to the US. According to this information, John Sturchak is suspected of helping some in without the burden of a valid passport or visa. The *Amis* now have a real problem with the Odessa Mafia, which is based at Brighton Beach in Brooklyn, New York.' Maria looked up from the document. 'I've heard about them before – mostly Ukrainian and Russian. They make the Italian Mafia look tame by comparison.' Maria returned to scanning the document. 'John Sturchak is suspected of close involvement with Russian and Ukrainian organised-crime groups.'

Fabel smiled broadly. 'So that's the connection Wolfgang Eitel, upholder of law and order, cannot allow to be exposed. That he does business with the Ukrainian Mafia.'

Maria continued to read through the document. 'Shit. Listen to this. One of the reasons the FBI has been unable to pin anything on Sturchak is the way the Odessa Mafia operates. It's totally different from the Italian Mafia. It's organised into cells headed up by a *Pakhan* or boss. Each cell is made up of four groups who operate separately. No one has direct contact with the *Pakhan* who instead controls them through a so-called "brigadier". Added to that, they have a habit of recruiting teams of "freelancers" who may not even be of Russian or Ukrainian origin and who do one job, get paid, and have no idea who it was they were really working for. So the chance of the FBI ever working their way up to Sturchak is practically zero.'

'And that's why they're so keen to hear if we have any kind of direct link to criminal activity here?'

'Exactly. But there's more. Apparently the Russian and Ukrainian Mafias don't do much narcotics business. They're into financial and high-tech scams. But their main activity is illegal financial transfers, setting up phoney import-export businesses to launder the proceeds of their organised criminal activity in Russia and Ukraine to and from the US, usually via European banks or investing it in property deals.'

'Like the ones here in Hamburg.' Fabel allowed himself a small moment of satisfaction. The pieces were coming together in one small corner of the puzzle. It might only be the Eitels, but at least there was a chance that someone was going to be nailed for their part in all of this mayhem. He stood up suddenly and decisively, snapping up the account-tracking sheet and the key that went with it. 'Let's go talk to our colleagues in Financial and Corporate.'

Saturday 21 June, 1.30 p.m. Polizeipräsidium, Hamburg.
Markmann looked the part: more accountant than policeman. He was a small, neat man whose otherwise immaculate blue suit seemed to seek more substantial shoulders on which to hang. He shook Fabel's hand with an overstated firmness.

'I've had a look through the account details you supplied, Herr Fabel,' Markmann spoke with a faint lisp. 'They certainly raise enough questions to allow us to secure a warrant for seizure of files from each of the principal companies and individuals involved. However, I don't think we can hold either Eitel for much longer without at least beginning to discuss a specific charge. They're beginning to pile on the pressure – or rather, their team of expensive lawyers are beginning to justify their hourly rate. Unless you've got something . . .'

Fabel smiled. 'Only suspicion . . . and bluff. Let's at least see if I can ruffle their feathers a bit. We'll take Eitel senior first.'

*　　*　　*

The scene was what one would expect in an interview room. Four men, two on either side of the interview table. One man was standing, his arms locked and leaning on the table, looking down at his opposite number who, in turn, was defiantly trying to look uncowed by the baiting of the other. But there was something wrong with this picture. It was the police team who sat in the shadow of Wolfgang Eitel. Fabel could see that throughout the interview, the psychological balance had been slowly, skilfully and decisively tipped in Eitel's favour. Fabel realised he had to give the scales a swift kick.

'Sit down!' Fabel said as he entered the room.

Eitel straightened himself up to his full and considerable height and regarded Fabel down his aquiline nose.

'Never mind the aristocratic posturing, Eitel.' Fabel's voice was laced with contempt. 'We all know you're the son of a Bavarian peasant farmer. Turning your nose up at people is easy when you've spent half your childhood knee-deep in pig shit. Now sit down!'

Fabel was surprised to see that Eitel's counsel was Waalkes, the Eitel Group head of legal affairs, whose area of expertise was presumably more commercial than criminal. The lawyer was incandescent and shot to his feet.

'You can't . . . you simply cannot . . .' His words tripped over each other in a rush of outrage. 'This is intolerable. I will not have you talk to my client in that manner. It's abusive . . .'

Eitel smiled knowingly and indicated to Waalkes to sit down, which he did. It was like watching a shepherd silently control his dog. 'It's all right, Wilfried. I think Herr Fabel is deliberately trying to upset us.' With that, Eitel retook his seat. Markmann nodded for the two interrogating officers to leave, and he and Fabel took their places.

'A change of team, I see,' said Eitel. 'I now warrant a more senior level of interrogator.'

'Which, Herr Fabel,' said Waalkes, 'would suggest that you

are becoming increasingly desperate to find some grounds to continue harassing my client.' Another hand gesture from Eitel silenced Waalkes once more.

'I do not intimidate easily,' said Eitel, again tilting his head back and making the most of his superior height, even when seated. 'At the end of the war they all tried their little techniques. The Americans were crude and obvious: they also made much use of insult and threat. The British were altogether more subtle and professional: unfailingly polite but unremitting and relentless. They made you feel respected, even admired, while they tried to get you to give them enough to hang you. As you can see, Fabel, neither succeeded.'

Fabel did not appear to have heard anything Eitel had said. He picked up the phone and dialled Maria's extension number. When she answered, he asked for the FBI and other files to be brought down to the interview room. He then sat in silence. Waalkes opened his mouth to protest.

'Shut up,' said Fabel, quietly and without anger.

'That's it.' Waalkes said and stood up again. 'We're leaving.'

'Sit down!' Eitel barked. 'Don't you see that Herr Fabel is trying to provoke some kind of incident?'

By the time Maria arrived with the files, the atmosphere in the quiet interview room was electric.

'Maria,' said Fabel cheerfully, 'why don't you sit in on this too?'

Maria pulled a chair over from the wall by the door and placed it at the end of the interview table. It was an invasion of neutral territory that made Waalkes tut and edge his chair sideways slightly, towards Eitel. Fabel could see that Waalkes' relinquishment of a centimetre of territory infuriated his client.

'Can we begin now?' said Waalkes. 'Or do you want to invite the rest of your department?'

Fabel ignored him. He took the file from Maria, opened it, and spoke without looking up. 'Herr Eitel . . . you deal with what our American friends call the Odessa Mafia, don't you?'

Waalkes moved to speak. Another hand movement from Eitel.

'I have no contacts whatsoever with any type of Mafia, Herr Fabel.' His voice was quiet and calm, but heavy with menace. 'And I suggest that you be a little more careful in your accusations.'

'You deal with John Sturchak?'

'I do indeed, as I did with his father, and I am proud to do so.'

Fabel looked up from the file. 'But Sturchak is some kind of godfather . . . a sort of chief . . .' He made a show of struggling for the word.

'*Pakhan.*' Maria said, her eyes not moving from Eitel.

'Yes . . . some sort of top *Pakhan.* Isn't that so? Someone who deals in fraud, cloning cell phones, prostitution and drugs . . .'

Eitel's eyes hardened and there were now icicles in his voice. 'That is a slur. That is an unjustified, uncorroborated, unsubstantiated and slanderous slur on a respected businessman.'

Fabel smiled. He was now where he wanted to be: under Eitel's skin. 'Oh come on now. John Sturchak is just another Ruskie crook, just like his father.'

Fire flushed up through Eitel's cheeks, all the way to the temples. 'Roman Sturchak was a brave soldier and a military genius. And, might I add, a true Ukrainian patriot. I will not listen to someone . . .' Eitel sneered: the kind of face someone has when holding something noxious and malodorous from their body – 'someone like *you* malign his memory.'

Fabel shrugged with as much nonchalance as he could muster. 'Oh come off it. Roman Sturchak was a mercenary for the Nazis. He killed his own countrymen at the behest of a bunch of gangsters in Berlin.'

It was as if Eitel were clinging onto a rope, furiously trying to rein in his rising fury. 'Roman Sturchak fought for his country. All he cared about was liberating the Ukraine from Stalin and his henchmen. He was a freedom fighter and a better man than you could ever dream of being.'

'Really? How do you measure that quality? By the number of his own countrymen he murdered? Or by the amount of dirty money he accumulated in the States through theft and corruption? No, you're right . . . I don't think I would ever aspire to be a Roman Sturchak.'

Eitel started to rise from his seat. It was at this point that Waalkes started to earn his money. 'Herr Fabel, you are doing nothing here but antagonising my client. I will not put up with this crude baiting one second more. Unless you have any specific questions that relate to any financial impropriety, this interview is at an end.'

'I believe your client is laundering money for the Russian and Ukrainian Mafia, probably through phoney companies set up with John Sturchak.' As Fabel spoke, he felt Markmann tense beside him. Fabel knew he was showing his hand. And it was not a winning hand. 'But there are other, even more serious offences we need to discuss.'

'Such as?' Eitel had regained his composure. Fabel could see that he was realising just how much of a game of bluff this all was.

'We will return to that soon. In the meantime I'm going to leave you in Herr Markmann's capable hands.' Fabel rose and Maria followed suit. 'I will be back shortly, and you will remain here until I do.'

On the way out Fabel nodded to the two Financial and Corporate Crime detectives who rejoined Markmann in the interview room.

'We're clutching at straws, *Chef*,' said Maria.

'You're right,' Fabel said grimly. 'Let's try Eitel number two.'

This time, when Fabel stepped into the interview room, he did so without speaking, taking a place leaning against the rear wall. Maria stood next to him. The intention was to signal that he was an observer and not a participant in the interview, but also to disquieten Norbert Eitel. After all, why would a murder-squad officer be interested in a fraud inquiry?

Another lawyer and another expensive suit sat next to Norbert Eitel. The two Corporate Crime Kommissars were going through a copy of the transaction sheet. After about ten minutes, Fabel moved over to one of the officers and whispered in his ear. The policeman nodded and they swapped positions with Fabel and Maria.

'Thanks guys . . .' said Fabel. 'This won't take long.'

Norbert made an expression of patient indulgence as Fabel once again asked about the connection with the Sturchaks. This time, however, Fabel failed to ignite anything other than an irritated impatience in Norbert.

'This is getting nowhere,' said Norbert's counsel. And Fabel couldn't help but agree. He had absolutely nothing on either father or son that could lever out information about Vitrenko. Fabel got to his feet and nodded to the two fraud officers that they could resume their questioning. It was at that point that Norbert Eitel smelled victory. He dropped his disinterested tone and stood up, his face contorted with a mixture of hatred and contempt. He jabbed Fabel in the chest with the index finger of his left hand.

'I am going to ruin you, Fabel,' Norbert spoke through tight teeth. 'You are not going to get away with this.'

He jabbed Fabel in the chest again, giving an extra push as if dismissing something worthless. Fabel's hand shot up and seized Norbert's wrist.

'Keep your hands to yourself.'

Norbert tried to wrench his hand away but Fabel held it fast. He looked down at it and was about to throw it back into Norbert's chest. Instead he froze. Fabel stared blankly

at Norbert's now clenched fist and Norbert tried to wrench
it free again. Again it merely wobbled from side to side in a
mini arm-wrestling tussle. Fabel's grip tightened around
Norbert's wrist, turning the captured fist an angry red. Fabel
looked up from the fist and into Norbert's eyes. He smiled.
Coldly and malevolently.

'I've got you,' said Fabel and his voice was filled with a
quiet, bitter triumph. 'Now I've got you.'

Norbert Eitel's eyes searched Fabel's face for some sort of
meaning. Fabel allowed himself one more look. There, on
the back of Norbert Eitel's left hand. A scar. Or more like
two scars that coincided to form a slightly distorted wishbone shape. Just as Michaela Palmer had described it.

Fabel managed to force the grin from his face before he swung
open the door of interview room number one. He didn't enter
but merely leaned in. Wolfgang Eitel, Waalkes and the two
corporate-crime officers stopped their exchange and all turned
to the door, as if caught in the headlights of an oncoming
vehicle.

'Just to let you know that, as far as I am concerned, you
are free to go when these gentlemen are finished with you.'

Wolfgang Eitel's face lit up with a cold, malicious triumph.
Fabel started to leave, then checked himself and leaned back
in, as if some incidental detail had suddenly occurred to him.

'Oh, by the way, your son Norbert has been charged with
rape, attempted murder and suspicion of being an accessory
to murder.'

Fabel closed the door and allowed his smile to return as
he heard the explosion of voices in the interview room.

Fabel was halfway down the hall when Paul Lindemann
came running up to him. '*Chef,* I've just had Werner on the
phone. He wants you to go over to Harburg. He's found
Hansi Kraus. Dead.'

Saturday 21 June, 3.30 p.m. Harburg, Hamburg.
In his twenty years as a policeman, most of which had been
with the Mordkommission, Fabel had visited dozens of death
scenes. It was something you either got used to or you didn't.
Fabel had never become accustomed to intimacy with death.
Each new scene left its own tiny scar somewhere deep within
him. Unlike many of his colleagues, he had never been able
to separate the humanity from the corpse; the spirit from the
meat.

Death is nothing if not imaginative in the variety of its
guises. Each had its especial unpleasantness and Fabel had
seen most of them. There was the horrific: the body fished
from the Elbe after a month with the eels, or the gory tableaux
laid out for him by this latest killer. There was the bizarre:
the sex games gone wrong, or the unusual choice of murder
weapon. There was the surreal, like the drugs trafficker who
had been shot in the back of the head while he sat eating at
the kitchen table, and who, post-mortem, had remained seated
upright, fork still in the hand that rested on the table, as if
pausing between scooping mouthfuls, while the plate before
him had been spattered with fragments of bone, brain and
blood. Then there was the pathetic, where the victims had
sought escape from inevitable death behind a curtain or under
a bed in a desperate attempt to conceal themselves from their
killers; the body coiled into a foetal position, hugging into
itself and making itself small.

Hansi Kraus's demise fell somewhere between the pathetic
and the sordid. The small, filthy room in which he had taken
his leave of the world was as unpleasant as it could have
been. The paintwork, the walls, every surface in the room,
even the single naked light bulb that hung desolately from
the ceiling, was coated in a greasy dust. Despite Werner having
opened the room's only window wide, a stale odour hung in
the air like a malevolent spirit defying exorcism.

Hansi, who was now beyond feeling cold or hot, lay with

his heavy greatcoat partially covering his legs. His eyes were open, sunken balls in the sockets of his skull-like face. Decomposition, thought Fabel bitterly, had had a head start, thanks to Hansi's active participation in wasting his own body to a skeleton. One sleeve of a shirt that had once known a pattern was pulled up to the halfway point on Hansi's meagre left bicep. A rubber-tubing tourniquet remained wrapped but loosened just above the elbow joint and there was a fresh puncture mark in his forearm, just discernible among the hideous track marks, the road map of a decade's journey through hard addiction. A syringe lay empty in the limp grip of Hansi's right hand.

Nice try, thought Fabel. He looked over the whole sordid scene. Really nice try. This was a murder masquerading as a drug death that would slip swiftly and quietly into a statistic. It was the kind of anonymous, unsurprising death that passed by with nothing other than a perfunctory official recording by the police: another junkie succeeds in finally poisoning himself to death. Except this junkie had a story to tell and someone had silenced him before he could tell it.

'You informed the local boys yet?'

Werner shook his head. 'I wanted you to see it first. Very convenient, isn't it?'

'And one hell of a coincidence. I want Holger Brauner's team to do their thing. Inform the local Polizeidirektion, but tell them we are treating this as a suspected murder, and that means it's a Mordkommission case.'

Fabel looked back down at Hansi. Again he couldn't help seeing past the corpse, past the junkie, to someone's son, to a person who must once have had dreams and hopes and ambitions.

'You said that Hansi seemed to get suddenly uneasy at the Präsidium?' he asked Werner. 'In the canteen?'

'Yes, he did. I thought it was really odd the way he suddenly seemed uncomfortable and desperate to get away.'

'And I told you that he was probably just itching for his next fix. But what if that wasn't it? What if, after we make him trudge through mug shot after mug shot, he sees one or both of the killers right there in the Präsidium?'

'He was okay to start with . . . there were a few uniforms in the canteen, some KriPo. The usual mix. He didn't start to get jumpy until we sat at the table. In fact we were sitting there a while before he started . . .' Werner's face emptied of expression and his eyes moved as if the images from his recall were playing out in front of him. 'That's it!' Then the sudden illumination of his expression faded just as quickly. He looked at Fabel grimly. 'Oh shit . . .'

Saturday 21 June, 5.30 p.m. Polizeipräsidium, Hamburg.
Fabel and Werner made their way directly to Van Heiden's office as soon as they got back from the squalor of Hansi Kraus's squat. Even as they were shown into Van Heiden's office, Fabel thought he could still smell a hint of the musty, unclean odour that had lurked heavily in the air, as if it had partially invested itself into the fabric of his jacket. He felt the urge, almost an obsessive compulsion, to get home to shower and change.

Van Heiden was clearly in no mood for chit-chat. 'Are you sure about this, Fabel?' The Kriminaldirektor asked the question almost before the office doors had closed behind him and Werner. Volker, who was already seated in front of Van Heiden's desk didn't rise from his chair but nodded in Fabel's direction when he and Werner entered. Fabel noticed there were two red folders – personnel files – on the desk. 'This is a very serious allegation . . .'

'No, Herr Kriminaldirektor, I'm not sure. All we actually have are a handful of facts of which we can be reasonably certain . . .'

Fabel and Werner now stood before the broad expanse of

Van Heiden's desk. Van Heiden beckoned for them to take the two vacant chairs next to Volker. They both sat down and Fabel continued.

'Herr Volker's intelligence tells us that there is some kind of leak from within the Polizei Hamburg selling information to this new Ukrainian outfit and, for all we know, to other organised-crime outfits. Whoever this leak is, he, she or they have a motive for killing anyone who can identify them. Oberst Volker believes that they identified Klugmann as an undercover federal agent and either exposed him to the Ukrainians or killed him themselves.'

'And it looks like they did their own dirty work,' interjected Werner. 'Hansi Kraus told us that the killers he saw were Germans, not foreigners. And they enjoy their work. According to the forensic pathologist, the bastards tortured Klugmann before they murdered him. And, of course, the Ukrainian-made automatic that Hansi found was left behind to point us in the wrong direction.'

Fabel took up the story again. 'And when Kraus is brought in here to look at mug shots, Werner takes him down to the canteen where something or someone spooks him so badly he can't get out of the place quickly enough. The next thing we know, Kraus is found lying dead in his squat from a beautifully staged overdose.'

Van Heiden had sat grim-faced throughout. Fabel had noticed that Volker's attention had not been focused on the speakers, but on Van Heiden's reaction to what was being said.

'Okay . . . the evidence points to corrupt police officers. But what evidence do we have against these two officers in particular?' said Van Heiden, picking up the red personnel files and throwing them across the wide expanse of his desk so that they came to rest the right way round in front of Fabel.

'We have no hard, objective evidence as yet, Herr

Kriminaldirektor,' answered Fabel. 'But the physical descriptions we got from Hansi match them perfectly. What's more . . .' Fabel flipped open the first file and stabbed a finger at the photograph in the top right-hand corner of the first page – 'when I was in his office, I noticed several boxing trophies, one of which was for junior light-heavyweight in Hamburg-Harburg. That is where he grew up. Hansi Kraus mentioned that the older of the two hitmen was whining about how the area he grew up in was going to the dogs.' Fabel flipped open the second file. 'Kraus also described the second, younger man, the one who pulled the trigger, as looking like some kind of muscleman. I couldn't think of a better description to match this guy.'

'It all seems very flimsy and circumstantial,' said Van Heiden.

'It is,' said Fabel, 'until we get some hard evidence against them. We're starting with a complete forensic exam of the murder scene. The local guys know that this is being treated as a murder, and I'm sure word has already got back to our chums here. But the most compelling piece of, admittedly subjective, evidence is Kraus's reaction in the Präsidium canteen.' Fabel looked over to Werner.

'I tried to pinpoint the exact moment that Hansi started to get jumpy,' said Werner. 'Then I remembered these two,' he pointed at the files, 'coming in and sitting down not far from where we were. It was then that Kraus started to act like he had an electric wire up his ass. He even asked me who the big guy with the muscles was. I told him.'

'You asked me if I'm sure about this. Well, I'm sure these are our guys all right.' Fabel nodded his head in the direction of the open files, with the two faces staring blankly out from the windows of their photographs at their accusers. 'They are in exactly the right position to sell extremely valuable intelligence . . . they're high-enough ranking and they're in the right department.' He fixed Van Heiden with a candid stare. 'Am I sure we can prove it? No. Whether we can get enough evidence to convict them is an entirely different proposition.'

There was another small silence as they all looked down at the photographs of Kriminalhauptkommissar Manfred Buchholz and Kriminalkommissar Lothar Kolski of LKA7.

Saturday 21 June, 8.00 p.m. Speicherstadt, Hamburg.
Fabel parked, as before, on Deichstrasse before crossing over to the Speicherstadt on foot. Again the vast hulks of the warehouses loomed against the darkening sky, the red brickwork seeming to smoulder like dull embers in the failing light. He retraced his steps to the former Klimenko warehouse and swung the heavy door open. It had been dark enough on his last visit; this time, there were no lights on. The vast belly of the warehouse had swallowed the evening whole, with any hint of light from the distant windows or the open door sucked into oblivion. Fabel cursed himself for not having brought a flashlight. He knew there were neon striplights scattered throughout the warehouse, hanging down like trapeze bars from the high ceiling; he guessed that there must be a switch near the door, but he had no idea where.

'Major Vitrenko!' His voice resounded against the walls before being swallowed up by the darkness. He muttered a curse before calling out 'Vitrenko!' once more. Despite his irritation, Fabel could not help seeing the irony in calling out that particular name. It was almost an analogy of his investigation, chasing a monstrous spectre in the dark. There was no reply. Fabel peered into the warehouse, narrowing his eyelids and craning his head forward, as if the action would filter out some of the darkness. He thought he could see a dim oblong glow set deep into the gloom. From memory, Fabel reckoned that the pale light would fit with one of the Portakabin's narrow windows. He called out once more.

Silence. This wasn't right. He checked the luminous dial of his watch. It was after eight and he knew that a man as habituated to military regulation and precision as the Ukrainian must have been would not be late. Fabel reached under his jacket and slipped his Walther from its holster. He cursed his lack of foresight: he had not considered there would be any danger in meeting the Ukrainian again. No one knew Fabel was here. He was alone. He reached out and slapped and slid the palm of his left hand on the wall next to the door, but his exploring hand refused to find the switch.

A sound. Somewhere in the black chasm something made a noise so small and so indistinct that Fabel could not identify it. He froze and extended the Walther out before him in the vague direction of the sound. He strained his ears. Nothing. He took his fix on the insubstantial glow in the window and edged towards it. By occasionally shifting his position sideways he could identify where the pillars stood and as he reached one he would run his left hand around and up it to check for a light switch.

He heard it again. A moan. Or a voice muffled.

'Vitrenko?' He called out again, this time with a tentative tone in his voice, as if unsure which Vitrenko, father or son, might answer him. The answer came in a low, stifled cry, as if from someone gagged. Fabel snapped his head round in the direction of the sound. His ears strained hard, but the silence of the warehouse was already filling with the jackhammer thudding of his own pulse. He tightened his grip on the Walther, aware that his palms, like his face, were now sleeked with sweat.

He was now close to the office cabin. Fabel guessed that the steps were just a few feet from him. He had reached another pillar and laid his free hand flat against it. He felt the ridge of a cable conduit running vertically down the pillar. He swiftly ran his hand down and found the square switch box. Fabel took a long, slow, silent breath and moved himself back and out from the pillar, stretching his arm out straight with the fingers of his left hand resting on the switch. He again loosened and then tightened his grip on his pistol, and readied to fire at whatever awaited him when he hit the lights.

Fabel pressed the light switch and a bank of about a dozen striplights, spanning the mid-section of the warehouse, flickered reluctantly into life and illuminated a scene from hell.

The girl with the golden hair, the girl who had seemed so full of youth and lithe vigour, was pinned, dead, against the side of the Portakabin. Her naked, butchered body, the lungs ripped from the body cavity, had been nailed in the same manner as the victims in the photographs taken two decades ago in a distant land. Blood and viscera glittered like wet paint splashed across the wall of the elevated office cabin. In losing her life she had lost her humanity: Fabel struggled to see the person she once was, instead irresistibly drawn to the feeling that he was looking at the twisted carcass of some grotesque, human-headed bird. He cursed the thought, for it was exactly what the killer had wanted to create. Fabel fought for his next breath and staggered back, coming to rest against a pillar. He so desperately wanted to look away, but found he could not tear his eyes from the tableau of horror before him.

Again, Fabel heard a low, muffled groan. Like a sleep-walker suddenly awoken he spun, gun poised, in the direction of the sound. The old Ukrainian was standing upright against the pillar that faced the horror on the cabin wall. He was bound tight with wire, a loop of which had been fixed above and behind his head, then drawn down and tight under his jawline. The wire had cut deep into the old man's flesh and the front of his shirt was soaked black-red with his blood. His mouth had been sealed with a broad swathe of tape. Fabel could see that the Slav was still alive, his eyes wild and staring. The realisation hit Fabel low in the gut: Vitrenko had made his own father watch. He had repeated his own history and made the poor bastard bear witness as he ripped the breathing lungs from the girl's body. Fabel lunged forward and placed his hands on either side of the old man's head, and the green eyes locked Fabel's in a wild, intense gaze. He was trying to say something.

'Wait . . . wait . . .' said Fabel, hastily examining the lethally tight wire bond, completely at a loss as to where to begin extricating the Slav before he bled to death. 'I'll get you out . . .'

The Ukrainian shook his head violently, causing the wire to slice even deeper into his flesh, and something that should have been a scream struggled behind the tape. Fabel backed away, shocked.

'For Christ's sake, keep still . . .' Fabel holstered his gun and started to ease the tape from the mouth. Again the Ukrainian reacted violently, jerking his head in a sideways and downwards nod. Fabel followed the direction of the green eyes.

Then he saw it.

Strapped to the pillar, next to the old man's ankles, was a large, thick metal disc that Fabel recognised as some type of anti-tank charge. Clamped to the mine was a fist-sized, black electrical box with a flickering green light. Fabel's terror tightened itself around him another notch as he realised that the two thick wires that snaked out from the box were the same wires that bound the Ukrainian to the pillar. His entire body was primed. And the flashing green light on the box suggested there was also some kind of timing device. Once more the bound man started to make urgent gestures with his head and eyes, as if trying to nudge Fabel back in the direction of the warehouse door.

Fabel's voice cracked as he spoke. 'I can't . . . I can't leave you here . . .'

Something approaching calm seemed to settle back into the Ukrainian's green eyes, and with it a quiet, strong resignation.

He closed his eyes and made the slightest nodding movement with his head. It was a gesture of release: he was releasing Fabel from all obligation, from death; he was releasing himself from a troubled life.

'I'll get help . . .' said Fabel, although both men knew that the Ukranian was as far beyond anyone's help as it was possible to be. Fabel backed away from him, holding his gaze for as long as he could before turning and quickening his pace into a run, then a flat sprint across the empty expanse of the warehouse. Towards the door. Towards life.

Fabel burst out onto the narrow pavement outside the warehouse with such force that his headward plunge into the canal beyond was prevented only by the railing he slammed into. His feet slid and scraped on the cobbles as he scrambled along the wall of the neighbouring warehouse. He sat on the cobbles, his back pressed against the red brickwork, braced for what he knew must come. And it did.

There was a thunderous, reverberating whump from deep within the warehouse, as if some giant fist had slammed into the building, and Fabel felt a shockwave pulse through the wall at his back and the ground beneath him. The heavy door of the warehouse was ripped from its frame and the windows at second-storey level burst into a shower of glittering fragments. Fabel fell onto his side and cradled his head in his hands, drawing his knees up to his chest in a foetal position. A billowing wave of white and red flame bloomed through the shattered doorway and windows and then retreated, like an angry animal returning, growling, to its lair. The air was filled with a choking powder of brick dust, smoke and grime. After the earth-shaking violence of the blast, it seemed as if the world had gone still and silent. Then the alarm of every adjacent warehouse began ringing or whining in pale urgency. Fabel pulled himself back upright and sat motionless for what seemed an age. He squeezed his eyes tight closed, but he could not extinguish the fire in the green eyes of a dead old man that burned in his brain. The same eyes that had locked with Fabel's as he had had the consciousness squeezed from him in Angelika Blüm's flat. The same eyes that had released Fabel from any obligation to remain with him. The same, sad father's eyes that, nearly two decades before, had looked upon the horror of the handiwork of his own flesh and blood.

In the distance, he could hear the growing whine of sirens approaching the Speicherstadt. Fabel got to his feet, pressing the palms of his hands against the wall and pushing himself up. Dust had invaded his nose and mouth and he coughed to free his throat of it. He clung to the wall as if moving from it would mean becoming lost in the swirl of dust and darkness, closed his eyes and saw again the horror that Vasyl Vitrenko had painted for him in flesh and blood on the wall in the warehouse; he saw the old man strapped to a pillar and forced to watch the horror and hear the screams of a young woman being dismembered before him. This had been Vitrenko's masterwork. And Fabel had been intended to see it. With that thought came the realisation that Vitrenko had intended Fabel to live. He had arranged and timed it to perfection: allowing Fabel time to witness his masterpiece, to agonise futilely about how to extricate the old man from the ineluctability of his death and then to escape. That way, Vitrenko had placed two indelible images in Fabel's mind to haunt him for the rest of his life: the butchered girl; the old man's resignation to death. And having placed the images safely in Fabel's mind he blasted them into nothing. Expunged them from reality, leaving them to live only in the gallery of Fabel's memory.

He slid back down the wall into a sitting position and felt a sob begin to rise in his throat. He forced it back down and rested his head back against the brickwork and waited for help to come.

* * *

Saturday 21 June, 8.30 p.m. Polizeipräsidium, Hamburg.
The Feuerwehr fire commander's report told Fabel what he
already knew: 'In addition to the explosive charge on the
pillar we found evidence of some kind of accelerant in or
near to the office cabin . . . my guess is petroleum. There
was nothing much left of the cabin after the blast and
whatever was inside it ignited immediately. We found a couple
of open five-litre containers. Anyway, it very efficiently
destroyed all forensic traces from the murder scene.'

Fabel thanked the Feuerwehr captain bleakly and the
fireman left the office. There was a despondent silence that
Maria tried to fill. 'Holger Brauner and his forensics team
are there now,' she said. 'But there's not much for them to
pick through.'

Fabel spoke without looking up at Maria, Werner or Paul.
'He's playing with us. With me. He wanted me to see it and
to live to tell about it. That's why he left those women hanging
like exhibits in that bloody barn in Afghanistan, for others
to bear witness.' Fabel looked up at his colleagues, and, for
the first time, they saw their boss lost and helpless. 'This is
his art. Just like those canvases Marlies Menzel is displaying
in Bremen.'

'What now, *Chef*?' Werner's tone was that of a challenge,
not a question.

'Now I'm going home for a shower.' Fabel had been around
too much death in one day. His hair and skin were dusted
with powder and his mouth and throat felt caked. 'Let's meet
back here at the Präsidium at about ten.'

'Okay, *Chef*. Shall I get the whole team together?'

Fabel smiled. Maria never complained. She just did whatever it took to get the job done.

'Yes, please, Maria . . . but leave Anna out of it. I've given
her twenty-four hours off. I think the whole MacSwain operation exhausted her.'

Maria nodded.

'But would you contact Kriminaldirektor Van Heiden and see if he will come in for the meeting?'

'Yes, *Chef.*'

Saturday 21 June, 9.30 p.m. Pöseldorf, Hamburg.

The three messages on Fabel's answerphone were like life-lines to a world that lay beyond that of violence and murder: the first was from his daughter Gabi. As he listened to her message he heard the tinkle of laughter that had been spun through her voice since she uttered her first words. Hearing Gabi's voice at a time like this was like someone tearing down heavy, dusty curtains in a dark and scary room, flooding it with light from outside. But tonight it was just one room within a mansion of darkness.

Gabi wanted to make up for their missed weekend by staying over next weekend, if that suited. There was a concert she wanted to go to, *Die Fantastischen Vier*. Fabel could never wrap his mind around the concept of rap – a musical form born in the ghettos of New York, Chicago and Los Angeles and anchored in that particular form of street English – being performed in German. But it was Gabi's thing: one of the countless points of divergence that grow in number as a child becomes a personality independent of its parent. He sighed heavily, it was by no means certain that this case's insidious grip on his life would have eased any by the coming weekend.

The second message came from Susanne. She wanted him to give her a ring and let her know how he was. The third was from Fabel's brother, Lex.

Lex was the elder brother chronologically, but Fabel often felt Lex's irrepressibly, defiantly youthful spirit made him seem a decade younger. It wasn't the only stark contrast: Lex was shorter than Fabel and dark-haired with a wickedly Celtic sense of humour that had crinkled the skin around his eyes into permanent creases. Lex ran a restaurant and hotel on Sylt, the North Frisian island that had once been famed only for fishing, but which now netted a much more profitable catch: the rich, the powerful and the famous from Hamburg and Berlin. Lex's restaurant sat on a low ridge behind the dunes, with a spectacular view of a broad scythe of white sand and the changing palette of the North Sea beyond. Fabel had spent a lot of time at Lex's. It had become something of a refuge for him. It had been there that Fabel had recuperated after being shot. It was there he retreated when trying to come to terms with the fact that he was no longer a member of a family. No longer a husband. No longer a full-time father.

Lex had no special reason for calling. It was just brother reaching out to brother: a traffic, Fabel guiltily realised, that tended to be too much one-way. Hearing his brother's voice filled Fabel with an urgent desire to escape Hamburg and spend weeks staring at the ever-changing ocean; to abandon his sharp tailoring and city grooming and loaf around, stubble-jawed, in sun-faded sweatshirt, jeans and deck shoes. The image was clear in his head, to return to his favoured refuge, but this time his imagination painted a companion: Susanne. He made the decision there and then: whenever this hideous case was over, he would ask Susanne to come with him to Sylt.

Before returning any of his calls, Fabel called Mahmoot's cell phone. Mahmoot had been there with Fabel when he first met Vitrenko's father in the Speicherstadt. Two out of the four people who had been present were now dead: Fabel had to reassure himself Mahmoot wasn't the third. He breathed a small sigh of relief when he heard Mahmoot answer. Fabel told Mahmoot what had happened on his return to the warehouse and was surprised to notice that his hands trembled as he related the events to his friend. Mahmoot had been silent for a while.

'Christ, Jan. I thought I lived in a dark world,' he said

eventually, 'but yours scares the shit out of me. I can't believe they're dead. I can't believe he did that to his own father.' Mahmoot paused, as if thinking something through. 'Listen, Jan, I'm going to drop out of sight for a while. Get out of Hamburg. I don't know if this über-Viking sees me as a loose end or not, but I don't want to end up as some kind of Nordic kebab. I'll get in touch when I get back. But Jan, in the meantime, don't look for me.'

'I understand,' said Fabel.

Mahmoot hung up.

He phoned Gabi. It was the usual short, cheerful exchange that he tended to have with his daughter. There was a shorthand between them that squeezed paragraphs of history and meaning into a few words. Fabel was worried that this case would still be consuming nearly all his time, but he wanted her to come. She told him not to worry if he had to work. Fabel's time with Gabi was more precious than gold and he treasured every opportunity to be with her. The same economy they managed with words allowed them to condense a lot of value into a little time.

After he came off the phone, Fabel realised he hadn't eaten. He went into the kitchen and fixed himself a salad and a too-strong black coffee. As he prepared the meal he started to dial Lex's number but hung up before it connected, realising that Lex would probably still be busy in the kitchen or dining room. He phoned Susanne instead. She was horrified to hear about the events in the Speicherstadt and insisted on coming round right away. Fabel put her off, explaining that he was going to have to return to the Präsidium for a case conference. She was clearly upset and worried, but when Fabel mooted his idea of their taking time out together on Sylt, her voice lightened.

'I'd love to, Jan. And I think it would be a good idea for both of us. I'm worried about the psychological price you're going to have to pay for all this horror.'

So am I, thought Fabel.

After talking to Susanne, Fabel ate the salad without enjoyment, poured himself another coffee and made his way through to his living room. He switched on the lights and sat down on the couch, seeing himself reflected in the huge picture window. He took a deep breath and looked at his watch. He needed to ease some of the hawser-tight tension in his neck and shoulders before he went back to the Präsidium.

Fabel reached over to the coffee table and picked up the *Dictionary of English Surnames* that Otto had given him. He let a small laugh slip. Only Otto would know that Fabel could find peace in volumes of German or English etymology. Fabel loved reference books. They were oceans on which you could set sail without a course, first seeking out one piece of knowledge and then becoming diverted to another, totally tangential but equally engrossing track. He began by idly looking up his own name. He knew 'Fabel' was found in the Netherlands and Denmark as well as Germany. He was a little disappointed to find no trace of it among the surnames of the British Isles. He racked his brain for unusual British names that he'd encountered recently. There was one that was front of mind because of the case. He flicked through the pages to find a huge section devoted to the Mc and Mac surnames that predominated in Ireland and Scotland.

He found the entry for MacSwain.

Fabel froze. The coffee cup in his hand was suspended between saucer and lips. There was a quiet beyond silence. He felt locked in that moment between heartbeats, his blood still in his veins. Then the spell was broken. He slammed the cup back in its saucer, spilling a swirl of black, viscous liquid. He was on his feet and across the room before realising he was no longer sitting. The book was still in his left hand, open, and his eyes remained locked on the entry. His right hand found the cordless phone and hit the single button to retrieve the Mordkommission's number.

'Shit . . . oh, shit . . .' muttered Fabel as the ringing tone seemed to go on endlessly.

It was Maria who answered. Fabel didn't even announce himself.

'Anna was right, Maria . . . Christ, we've got this one all wrong. It's MacSwain. MacSwain is Son of Sven . . .'

Maria sounded confused and unconvinced, but Fabel washed her incredulity away with a torrent of words. 'He's been telling us who he is all along. And we missed it. He's been flaunting it in every e-mail. Do we still have a surveillance team on MacSwain?'

'Yes. Or at least one guy just now. He's outside MacSwain's apartment.'

'Get someone else over there right now! Tell them to wait until we get there, unless MacSwain tries to leave, in which case I want him arrested on suspicion of murder. Get everyone together in the incident room. And tell Eitel's lawyer I'm going to talk to Norbert in ten minutes' time, whether he's present or not. I'll see you and the others in the conference room in fifteen minutes.'

Saturday 21 June, 9.00 p.m. Eimsbüttel, Hamburg.

Anna had soaked herself in a deep, dark and warm lake of dreamless sleep. When she had returned to her apartment from the Präsidum she had not expected to sleep: she felt overtired and scenes from her evening with MacSwain re-ran themselves out of sequence through her mind, like randomly switching TV channels. A thick-fingered, lead-limbed tiredness had slowed all Anna's movements as she had carried out the tasks that lay like an obstacle course between her and sleep. She had fed Mausi, her ragged tiger-stripe cat, wiped the make-up from her face and stripped for bed.

It was nearly five p.m. before she awoke, Mausi sitting at

the foot of the bed, watching her with an arrogant detachment. The lead had melted from her limbs, but a band of pain had tightened itself around her head while she had slept. She rose and took two codeine before immersing herself in a tepid bath. She lay unmoving, a soaked facecloth over her eyes, and allowed the bathwater around her to cool and chill her skin to goosebumps. There was an almost perfect silence in the bathroom, broken only by the echoing sound of the water when she moved and, once, by her calling out 'Mausi!' in as stern a voice as she could muster and without removing the cloth from her face, when she heard sounds from the kitchen.

Anna examined her pruned and whitened fingertips and reluctantly rose from her bath. She towelled her hair and body dry and made her way through to the kitchen, where Mausi sat in a corner, looking uncharacteristically sheepish.

'What have you done, *Spitzbube*?' Anna cast her eyes around the kitchen to check for evidence of feline felony. She swung open the kitchen window that allowed Mausi access to the apartment's small balcony and he darted out. Anna shrugged and took some chilled water from the fridge, taking several refreshing gulps. She moved back through to the bedroom and had just finished dressing when she heard a knock at her door. It would have to be one of the neighbours, because visitors to the apartments used the electronic entry system. Anna knew, before she opened the door, that it would be Frau Kreuzer, the old woman who lived immediately above. Frau Kreuzer, aware of the nature of Anna's occupation, would often come to her door with stories of suspicious characters she had seen at the Mini-Markt supermarket, in the library or hanging around in the street outside the apartment building. Anna always listened patiently, offering the old woman a cup of green tea and allowing her to drift from her supposed motive of good citizenship and towards general gossip and chit-chat. Anna was well aware that her elderly neighbour's concerns were a ruse to create an oasis of companionship in the lonely desert of her day, but she didn't mind. Tonight, however, she could do without the distraction. In fact, despite her long sleep, Anna felt decidedly dizzy as she made her way to the door.

'Good evening, Frau Kreuz . . .' Anna started as she opened the door. It seemed as if her heart stopped at the same time as her voice, as she looked into the cold, green fire of John MacSwain's eyes.

'Hello, Anna,' said MacSwain.

Anna looked confused. As if in answer, MacSwain held up his index finger and dangled her door keys from it. Anna spun around. The movement of her head made her senses swirl and fog. She searched for her service SIG-Sauer nine-millimetre, which she had dumped, in its holster, on the hall table next to the door. It was gone. In that second she put it all together: the sounds in the kitchen, the water, Mausi being jumpy. She turned back to MacSwain, her head having to move from side to side momentarily to allow her to focus on his face, and she couldn't help drawing a comparison between his cold green stare and the frosty disinterest with which Mausi habitually regarded her. That's it, she registered dully, he's something other than human. That was what she'd tried to explain to Fabel: that some unseen, conclusive element essential to humanity was missing. She staggered and made to grab for the edge of the kitchen cabinet. Instead MacSwain stepped forward and scooped his hands under her arms.

'Careful now,' he said, without a trace of solicitousness. 'I think you need another drink of water . . .'

As the drug cocktail that MacSwain had hidden in her drinking water began to close the curtains around Anna's consciousness, she somehow felt compelled to speak.

'I . . . I don't feel too well . . .' she said for only MacSwain to hear, and couldn't remember why it was she had to say it.

Saturday 21 June, 9.40 p.m. Polizeipräsidium, Hamburg.
Maria, Werner, Paul and Van Heiden were all there when
Fabel arrived. Maria had also called in the two officers from
the expanded task team who were still on shift. Fabel, the
book gifted to him by Otto tucked under his arm, strode
purposefully into the incident room and stood before the
inquiry board.

'Let me get straight to the point,' said Fabel. 'We have
a new prime suspect. Or at least *another* prime suspect:
John MacSwain, twenty-nine, a British national resident in
Germany.'

'What about Vitrenko?' asked Van Heiden.

'Vasyl Vitrenko is still very much part of this. I believe
what we are dealing with here is a master and his apprentice. Or high priest and acolyte. Vitrenko is a consummate
manipulator of people. His men follow him with a slavish
devotion that is founded on a half-assed re-spinning of old
Norse myths and beliefs. But it's not just his men he controls:
he uses all types of people to achieve his ends. And that
includes the psychologically damaged. John MacSwain is an
example, just like the guy in the Ukraine who was executed
for a series of similar crimes in the mid-nineties.'

Fabel paused. There was a total silence in the room.

'Vitrenko has had access to material that I have written
on a serial-murder case in Hamburg. He has also studied at
one of the world's leading criminology institutes . . . a
Ukrainian institute, and, as we know, the Ukraine has one
of the highest incidences of serial murderers in the world.
That is why everything we have dealt with so far has seemed
like a textbook case. Because it *is* a textbook case. Vitrenko
probably met MacSwain through the Eitels, for whom
MacSwain works. The Eitels are involved with Vitrenko in
a property scam that also involves the Odessa Mafia and
Norbert Eitel has been directly involved in the drugging,
abduction and rape of young women in some kind of ritual.

He has a very distinctive scar on his left hand that matches the description given by one of the victims. I believe that Vitrenko is using these rituals as some kind of binding thing. And I believe we will discover other powerful individuals caught up in all of this.'

Fabel paused again. It felt strange to give voice to it all; like he was externalising what had been, until now, a purely internal process. His audience sat almost motionless and totally quiet. There were no questions, so Fabel continued.

'As for the murders, Ursula Kastner, as a property lawyer working for the city, must have stumbled on irregularities in property deals relating to the Neuer Horizont partnership. My guess is she uncovered some kind of high-level involvement and decided to go to the press, instead of the authorities. And the press, in this case, was Angelika Blüm. Tina Kramer, the BAO-BND operative, was killed because she was identified as a front-line contact for Klugmann, whose cover had been blown by two officers from this force. Officers who were on the take and who murdered Klugmann in the Schwimmhalle and left a Ukrainian security-services firearm behind to confuse the issue. Three victims; one killer. John MacSwain. The apprentice.' Fabel gestured to the images of the three murdered women. He then moved across to the photographs taken in Afghanistan.

'These, on the other hand, are the work of the master. And I have seen his handiwork with my own eyes. The murder earlier today of Vitrenko's father and his assistant was a signature piece, and Vitrenko is egotistical enough to have wanted me to see that before he destroyed the evidence. This was his own father and the sister of one of the Kiev victims. Vitrenko would not entrust this to MacSwain. This was a masterpiece.'

'But other than this most recent killing, you claim MacSwain is the murderer?' Van Heiden asked.

'Yes. Vitrenko knew how to press all the right buttons with MacSwain. MacSwain is clearly sociopathic. Vitrenko realised that. It takes one to know one, I suppose. Anyway, John MacSwain had a very poor relationship with his own father. My guess is that Vitrenko has stepped into the paternal role, and wrapped the whole thing up in some kind of Viking mumbo-jumbo. MacSwain was probably first enlisted to find women for the rituals Vitrenko organised . . . which were, in reality, nothing more than disguised gang rapes. Vitrenko must have seen how deep MacSwain's psychopathy went. It was then that Vitrenko gave MacSwain his sacred missions to carry out. My guess is that MacSwain sent the e-mails but the wording was supplied by Vitrenko.'

'But why do you suspect MacSwain?' asked Maria. 'Now – after all this time?'

'It's his name. It's been in front of us all along.' Fabel flipped open the book on the table before him. 'The origins of the name "MacSwain". It is an Anglicised form of an Irish and Scots Gaelic name. The prefix *Mac* is patronymic . . . it stands for "son of". The Swain part comes from the Viking invaders who settled on the western isles of Scotland. It is a Gaelicised and then Anglicised form of the Old Norse name *Svein*, meaning boy.'

Fabel paused. He could sense the electricity in the air. They all knew what he was going to say next, but they had to hear him say it.

'MacSwain means "Son of Sven".'

'I knew it!' Werner said. 'And so did Anna. There was something didn't gel with MacSwain.'

'I've just had a chat with Norbert Eitel,' continued Fabel, 'who is still in custody downstairs. I told him that I knew all about Vitrenko and MacSwain's part in the rapes. He didn't answer me, mainly because his lawyer told him not to, but the look on his face said it all. The look of a man who has got in too deep. MacSwain's our man all right.' Fabel turned to Maria. 'We still have that team on him?'

'I've sent an extra officer over, but the surveillance guy

who's been watching MacSwain says he hasn't moved all evening.'

'Okay,' said Fabel, 'I want everyone ready to roll in twenty minutes. Maria, tell the surveillance team to stand by.'

A uniformed policewoman knocked and stuck her head around the conference room door.

'There's someone in reception to see you, Herr Hauptkommissar. A Frau Kraus . . .'

Margarethe Kraus could have been any age between forty-five and sixty-five. She was one of those women for whom the compensation of having looked middle-aged in youth was that she would probably still look middle-aged when she was in her late seventies. Whatever family resemblance there had been between mother and son must have been erased from Hansi's features by his years of drug abuse. Frau Kraus had a round, empty face and smallish brown eyes that wore a look of immeasurable weariness, as if she had never left a moment of her life behind her, instead carrying it with her everywhere she went.

She was sitting in the reception waiting room, by the window, which gleamed obsidian against the night outside. Her small hands were folded over a small envelope. She stood up awkwardly when Fabel came in.

'Frau Kraus?' Fabel smiled and extended his hand. 'I'm so sorry about your loss.'

Margarethe Kraus smiled bitterly. 'I lost Hansi many years ago. The difference is now we have a body to grieve.'

Fabel found he had no words. He nodded with a careful balance of sympathy and understanding. After a silence that seemed longer than it was, Fabel said:

'You wanted to see me, Frau Kraus. Was it about Hansi?'

The eternally middle-aged woman did not speak, but handed Fabel the envelope. Fabel made a confused expression.

'It's from Hansi,' she said.

Fabel opened the envelope. The letter had been written in pencil, but remarkably neatly. It was as if some distant memory of schoolroom discipline had invested itself into the writing. For Hansi, this had obviously been an important letter. It made painful reading. The majority of the letter was of a highly personal nature: basically, Hansi was apologising to his mother for the worry and distress he had caused her and his sisters. Fabel had begun to wonder why Frau Kraus had chosen to share this intimacy with him when he reached the closing paragraphs.

The reason I write now, Mutti, after so many years, is because I think my troubles are over. I don't want you to be sad or frightened, but I have to tell you that I think someone may be coming after me. If I am right, then I don't think we'll ever see each other again. If something bad happens to me, I want you to take this letter to Kriminalhauptkommissar Jan Fabel at the police Präsidium. He is an honest policeman, I think, and he will be able to get the people who have done whatever it is they have done with me.

There were two policemen in the Präsidium canteen when I was there with Herr Meyer. They sat down behind us and to the left. They were an older man and a younger man. The younger man had very short blond hair and was built like a muscleman or weightlifter. I asked Herr Meyer who the muscleman was. He said it was Lothar Kolski. Lothar Kolski is the man I saw shoot the man in the swimming pool. The older man at the same table is the man who told him to do it. I did not say anything at the time because I was so shocked to see them in police headquarters. I thought that maybe the police were behind the killing but I know now that isn't true. Herr Fabel will know what to do.

I am afraid, but not as afraid as I thought I would be.

I am no good. I never have been. It is better this way.

I am so sorry, Mutti. I was not the son you deserved, and you were a far better mother than I deserved.

Lovingly yours

Hansi

When he had finished reading, Fabel stared at the letter for a long while. Then he looked up to Margarethe Kraus.

'I am so very, very sorry, Frau Kraus. Thank you for bringing this in.'

'Was Hansi really killed by a policeman?'

'Hansi was murdered by criminals, Frau Kraus.' Fabel fixed her with an earnest stare. It wasn't a lie. 'But I promise you we will get them.' He held up the letter. 'And this is what we'll get them with.'

Margarethe Kraus smiled politely, as if someone had just given her directions to the bus station. 'I'd better go. It's very late.'

Fabel shook her hand. It was cold and a little moist. 'I'm afraid I'll ask you to stay a little longer. I need to get an officer to take a full statement from you. Then we'll have someone drive you home. I'm afraid we'll need to have someone watch over you for a few days . . . just until we get this sorted out.'

Frau Kraus shrugged her small shoulders resignedly. 'I'll wait here then,' she said and sat back down where she had been, refolding her hands over her lap, this time without having the last letter from her son beneath them.

Van Heiden was waiting for Fabel as he left the reception room. Fabel handed him the letter and pointed to the relevant paragraph.

'I take it I can leave this to you, Herr Kriminaldirektor?' asked Fabel. Van Heiden didn't respond, but Fabel could read the near future in Van Heiden's furious gaze: Buchholz and

Kolski didn't know it, but there was an express train heading straight for them.

'I came to give you this, Fabel.' Van Heiden handed him an e-mail.

Polizei Hamburg Mordkommission

From   SON OF SVEN
To   ERSTER KRIMINALHAUPTKOMMISSAR JAN FABEL
Sent   21 June 2003, 21.30
Subject DAUGHTER OF DAVID

YOU THINK YOU ARE CLOSE TO ME, BUT IT IS I WHO COME CLOSER TO YOU. I HAVE GIVEN YOU SO MANY MEMORABLE EXPERIENCES, HERR FABEL. THIS IS THE ONE YOU WILL NEVER FORGET. I AM GOING TO ENJOY THIS ONE MOST OF ALL.

IT IS IN THE NATURE OF A WOMAN TO DECEIVE. THEY ARE BORN POISONED WITH GUILE AND FALSITY AND SPEND THEIR LIVES REFINING THEIR SKILLS AS LIARS AND DECEIVERS. IT IS POETIC, IS IT NOT, THAT THE SON OF SVEN WILL SPREAD THE WINGS OF THE DAUGHTER OF DAVID.

SON OF SVEN

Saturday 21 June, 10.00 p.m. Harvestehude, Hamburg.
Fabel had fought to keep the team within the boundaries of urgency without crossing over into outright panic. The meaning in the e-mail had been crystal clear. The Daughter of David. The deception she had attempted on MacSwain. He was going after Anna. Maria had tried to get Anna on the phone. No reply. Fabel ordered a team to go round immediately to Anna's apartment in Eimsbüttel and force entry if necessary. In the meantime, Fabel led the assault on MacSwain's home.

The surveillance officer outside MacSwain's apartment block confirmed that the Briton had not come out since he returned at 5.56 p.m. There had been no obvious movement in the apartment other than the lights coming on at 7.30. The surveillance officer had even wandered over to check that MacSwain's Porsche was still in its parking bay in the Tiefgarage. Fabel sent half the team, led by Maria, up the stairwell while he and Werner took the other half, plus the heavy door-ram, up in the brushed-steel elevator.

There was only one door in and out of the apartment. The only other way out was onto the balcony and the three-storey drop to the pavement outside. Two body-armoured MEK officers swung the metre-long door-ram between them, silently counting out the beats until, on the fourth swing, it slammed into the door and splintered the lock. MacSwain's door flew inwards and the armed MEK team burst in, fanning the empty space of the apartment with their Heckler and Koch sub-machine pistols.

Fabel knew instantly that the apartment was empty. Within three or four minutes the team confirmed his feeling.

'Fuck!' said Werner. 'How could this happen again?'

'Because we were looking the other way,' said Fabel. 'I should have listened to Anna and kept a full surveillance team on the bastard.'

At the mention of her name the two officers exchanged a

knowing, almost frightened look. 'Chase up the team and see if they've found Anna.'

Werner snapped open his cell phone.

'*Chef* . . . come and see this . . .' Maria beckoned him over to a small box room, more a large storage cupboard, off the main living area. MacSwain had managed to squeeze a small computer table and chair into the tiny space. The walls were covered with photographs, cuttings and handwritten notes. Two ceiling spotlights illuminated the mural displays, as if they were some kind of museum exhibit. The focus was a carved wooden mask. It was a close replica of the carving Fabel had seen in the book that Otto had given him. The book that MacSwain had too. The bearded mouth was twisted in a berserker's snarl, the one eye hole shadowed black by the angle at which the spotlights cast their beams.

Maria had to move back to allow Fabel access to the box room. He imagined the door closed behind him and a spanner ratcheted up the claustrophobia in Fabel's chest a notch. Fabel could see that this was more than a space allocated for a special purpose. This was another dimension: a world away from the world outside. This was where MacSwain would sit, the closed box-room door as dense and impenetrable as an iron drawbridge, immersed in a universe of alternative truths and morals and beliefs that had been conjured around him. How much MacSwain had conjured himself, and how much of Vitrenko's hand could be seen in it, Fabel was unsure.

Something shone bronze-gold in the spotlights. The oval shape of an embossed Kriminalpolizei shield hung by its beaded chain from a panel pin. It was this shield that had been the key to Angelika Blüm's flat, to her trust; it was this shield that had deceived Blüm into believing that her killer had been Fabel. Maria leaned past her boss and indicated a newspaper cutting that was pinned on top of the layers of others.

'Christ,' she muttered, 'it's you.'

The article, a year old, had been cut from from the *Hamburger Morgenpost*. Fabel's photograph sat at the top of a couple of columns about his arrest of Markus Stümbke. Stümbke had stalked and murdered a female member of the Senate, Lise Kellmann. The article was obviously a follow up to the main story, because it went into greater depth, as the headline promised, about Fabel's background and history with the Polizei Hamburg. MacSwain had underlined a reference to Fabel's mixed British-German parentage and the fact that he was occasionally referred to as *der englische Kommissar*. Fabel scanned the rest of the display. It was almost all devoted to Viking mythology and history. A map of northern Europe showed the routes taken by the Vikings: down the Volga into the heart of the Ukraine, alone the North Sea and Baltic Coasts and, again highlighted in red, the route they took to raid and settle on the coasts of northern Scotland. With that red felt-tipped pen, MacSwain had sewn a thread of spurious personal history; a thin but unbreakable web of perverted justification for his actions.

'Notice something missing?' Fabel asked Maria. She nodded.

'No pictures or details of the victims . . . no trophies.'

'Exactly.'

Serial killers habitually sought a 'relationship' with those they murdered, even if the first contact had been the act of killing itself. There were no references here. Not to Ursula Kastner, not to Angelika Blüm, not to Tina Kramer. There were no surreptitiously taken photographs of the victims prior to death. There were no articles of clothing. There were no trophies.

'It's because he didn't pick his own victims,' Fabel said. 'They were selected for him. The object of MacSwain's obsession isn't his victim, it's the person who is guiding him. His spiritual father: Vitrenko. It's Vitrenko who fills the gap left by a natural father who didn't give a shit.'

Something else struck Fabel.

'There are no files from Angelika Blüm's apartment. And the missing video camera isn't here either. He's passed them on. He was told how to perform the murder and what to take from the scene.' Werner appeared at his shoulder. With Maria and Werner now both behind him, he felt trapped in the tiny, airless space. He turned around and indicated the open space of the living area with a determined nod of his head. They all moved out.

'It's Anna, *Chef*,' Werner's face was clouded with worry. 'It's not good. She's not in her apartment and she's left her bag and cell phone behind.'

Saturday 21 June, 10.00 p.m. The Elbe near the Landungsbrücken, Hamburg.

The day that had been was trying to be remembered in a sky spun through with red and in the pleasant, lingering warmth of the night air. Franz Kassel lifted his cap and smoothed back the fine strands of sandy hair over his scalp. His shift was nearly at an end and he was looking forward to a cold beer. Or maybe a few. It had been a quiet shift and Franz had been able to savour what had attracted him to the Wasserschutzpolizei in the first place: hearing the delicate sounds of the water and the gentle creakings and ringings of boats at moor; watching the ever-changing light, passing beneath the vast, looming hulls of ships as he patrolled. Most of all, there was the different perspective it offered. Things always looked different from the water. You saw more. The Hamburg he saw every day was totally different from the one seen from dry land. He felt privileged to have this unique viewpoint.

He knew not everyone shared his sense of privilege: like Gebhard, the Polizeiobermeister who had the helm and was guiding the WS25 back towards the Landungsbrücken

station. For Gebhard, the WSP was just a job; he had only
been in the WSP for three years and already he talked inces-
santly to the other crew members about training and transfer
to a land-based MEK.

Kassel watched as Gebhard steered towards the shore.
Gebhard was competent, but he clearly lacked the feel for
the water that Kassel believed was essential for any true river
cop. It was something that lay within the natural sailor: the
awareness of the river as a living entity. Gebhard, on the
other hand, treated the Elbe as a water-filled autobahn on
which he was no more than a traffic cop. Kassel left him to
it and went to stand on the deck. The breeze cooled his face
and he sighed the contented sigh of a man who has found
his place and knows it. It was then that he spotted a boat
he recognised exit from the moorings by the Überseebrücke.
Kassel raised his binoculars. It was the Chris Craft 308
Cruiser they had been asked to watch the other night. He
slipped quickly back into the cabin and ordered Gebhard to
follow the cruiser, but at a safe distance.

'But it's end of shift, *Chef*,' protested Gebhard.

Kassel replied by staring emptily at Gebhard who shrugged
and wheeled the WS25 back out into the Elbe. Kassel had
no idea if the young lady from the Mordkommission still had
an interest in this vessel, but he thought he had better check
it out. He picked up the radio phone and asked to be patched
through to Oberkommissarin Klee at the Mordkommission.

Saturday 21 June, 10.00 p.m. The Elbe, near Hamburg.
There was no dominant form to Anna's consciousness. If
confusion can be defined as a form, then that would be closest
to the shape her mind took. But even confusion connects with
other feelings, other emotions. You get confused and angry,
or confused and frightened, or confused and amused. But
Anna's confusion was of itself, totally unanchored. A moment

of lucidity would come. Then it would pass. It was like flying through patches of dense cloud; every now and then the plane breaks free and the brightness of the blue sky dazzles for a moment, then is lost.

She was awake. She recognised the interior of MacSwain's boat. Her hands were tied behind her back and she lay on her side on the bed. She knew now where she was and what had happened. MacSwain had drugged her. He had been in her apartment. He had mixed a cocktail of flunitrazepam or clonazepam and gammahydroxybutyrate into her drinking water. She didn't have her gun. She didn't have her cell phone. Fabel had given her time off so no one would miss her. She was on her own and she would have to make her own escape. In the space of a few seconds all of these facts were crystal clear to her. In the next instant they were gone. She had no idea where she was or what was happening to her. Then something like sleep enveloped her.

MacSwain's voice woke her. He was talking to someone. He was talking fast and breathlessly and without stopping. She could not make out what he was saying, she was so far beneath the surface of her own consciousness, but she pushed upwards, towards the voice.

She broke the surface. Her head resounded with a pain that reverberated against the sides of her skull. MacSwain continued talking. Anna opened her eyes. MacSwain was sitting opposite, his dead and empty eyes fixed unblinkingly on her, his mouth the only animated part of his face. It was as if someone had turned on a tap that could not be turned off until all of the contents of MacSwain's ugly mind had spilled out.

'He explained it all to me,' he continued, his voice urgent and excited. 'We make our own myths. We fashion our myths from our legends and we create our legends from our history. Odin is a god. He is the god of all Vikings because all Vikings believe he is a god. Before the myth said he was a god, the legends said he was a king. And before the legends made him a king, the history tells us he was probably a village chieftain in Jutland. But what he was isn't important. It's what he has become. Say the word Odin and no one thinks of a scruffy village chieftain. Say the name Odin and the world shakes. That is the truth . . . that is the truth. That is what Colonel Vitrenko explained to me. He showed me that we are all variations on a theme and we are all connected to our history and to our myths.'

He stopped abruptly. Anna had begun to ease herself up to a sitting position. MacSwain stood up and in two steps he was above her. His fist slammed hard into her temple and the pain in her head exploded. The world darkened a little for Anna, but she didn't pass out. She lay back down on her side and looked across to MacSwain, who continued talking as if he had simply taken time out to swat a fly.

'Colonel Vitrenko showed me how there are those to whom we are linked. Like the Colonel and me. He said our kinship is in our eyes, that we must have had the same Viking father somewhere back in time. And me and Hauptkommissar Fabel. Colonel Vitrenko showed me that Herr Fabel and I share the same mix of blood. That we are both half German, half Scottish. That we have both chosen our place. That is why Herr Fabel has been chosen for me as an opponent.'

Anna felt some of the strength come back to her. Her thoughts swam more freely and quickly through the thinning sludge in her head. She eyed MacSwain. He was big and powerfully built, but, although his punch hurt, it lacked power. There were no sounds from the boat other than the lapping of water. Anna guessed that MacSwain had switched the engine off and had come down to have his little heart-to-heart with her. Maybe this was it. Maybe this was her where and when. But she wasn't as drugged as he thought she was. She would fight. She would fight and fight until the last. He was not going to take her life easily.

'But we're not just connected to those who share our time.' MacSwain continued his monologue. 'There are those who have come before and those who will come after. And we are the history of those who will come after. And they will make legends of us. I shall become a legend. Colonel Vitrenko shall become a legend. And then, in time, we will take our places next to Odin.' MacSwain's eyes suddenly filled with a glacial malice. He stood up and made his way across to Anna. 'But first sacrifices have to be made.' He bent over her.

Anna's first kick caught him on the side of the head, but her awkward position and the enervating effects of the drugs sapped the power from the blow. MacSwain staggered back, more shocked than injured. It bought Anna the time to swing her legs off the bed and stand up. But as soon as she straightened up, her head swirled. She was aware of MacSwain pulling himself upright. The cabin was small and narrow and more of a handicap to the tall MacSwain than to Anna. He rushed her and she brought her foot up hard and fast into his chest, her heel slamming into his sternum. MacSwain's lungs emptied and he sank to his knees, sucking at the air in the cabin as if trapped in a vacuum.

Anna stepped forward and to the side, her movements hampered by her bound hands. She took time to aim carefully and swung her foot in a vicious kick onto MacSwain's temple. He was thrown sideways by the force and smashed into the small galley. He groaned and lay still. Anna ran towards the hatch and slammed her shoulder against it. It didn't budge. She remembered that it was a sliding hatch and she wriggled her arms and wrists down and below her bottom. Squatting first and then sitting, she slipped her hands behind her knees and looped them over her feet. She cast a sideways glance at MacSwain. He groaned again. Anna scrabbled with her still-bound hands to slide the hatch door open. She was going to make it. Out and over the side. Her chances would be better in the water than half doped and trapped in a boat with a psycho.

The hatch door jammed. Anna summoned up every remaining reserve of strength and will and wrenched at it. It slid open and slammed against its housing. The cool, oil-tainted smell of the river flooded the cabin. Anna lunged upwards towards the night.

There was an animal scream behind her. She felt MacSwain's full weight crash into her. Her face smashed down hard onto the top step that led to the hatch. The thick iron taste of blood filled her nose and mouth. MacSwain seized a fistful of hair and snapped Anna's head back hard and pulled her back into the cabin. His fist came down hard against her neck; but Anna realised it wasn't a punch. She felt the cold metal in her neck and the hard sting of a hypodermic needle. Then the night she had so desperately reached for reached back to her and claimed her.

Saturday 21 June, 10.15 p.m. The Elbe, between Hamburg and Cuxhaven.
Franz Kassel watched the cruiser stop. It was out of the main navigation channels and properly lit-up, unlike the WS25 that had stealthed along behind it. He watched the tall young man emerge on deck. Kassel could not be sure, in the dark and at such a distance, but, when the young man wiped his face with a towel, he could have sworn the towel was stained black. As if with blood. He snapped the binoculars from his eyes and turned to Gebhard.

'Try to reach Oberkommissarin Klee again. And if you don't get hold of her, I'm going to pull chummy over just for the hell of it.'

He looked back to the cruiser. There was a plume of foam, white against the black silk of the river.

'He's moving . . .'

Saturday 21 June, 10.25 p.m. Harvestehude, Hamburg.
The white tiled walls of MacSwain's bathroom glittered anti-
septically and the expensive taps and drying rails had a sharp,
cold, scalpel gleam. Fabel, Maria and Werner stared at the
shape of a man. A dark blue and red diver's drysuit hung
from the shower rail, dripping onto the bright enamel. It had
the unnerving appearance of a cast skin. Something that had
been sloughed off after a transition. A dive hood was draped
over the bath's rim.

Werner pointed to the drysuit with a small movement of
his chin. 'This what he wore, you reckon?'

Fabel peered into the bath. Another two drips drummed
echoing beats against the bath. Fabel thought he saw the
drips bloom a faint pink against the bright white enamel. He
took a pen from his pocket and pushed up the lever to close
the plug.

'If it is, then it's a bad choice for getting the blood out.
A drysuit may have an impermeable body, but the collar,
ankle and wrist cuffs are neoprene. No matter how often
he's rinsed it through, there will still be blood trapped in the
neoprene. No one touches anything in here until Brauner
arrives.'

Fabel decided to re-immerse himself in the claustrophobia
of MacSwain's tiny, windowless box room. There were layers
and layers of stuff pinned or taped to the walls. Rather than
sift through them methodically – a task he would assign to
Werner – Fabel let his gaze run its own route across the landscape of MacSwain's madness. A psychotic topography that
Fabel explored whole, not in part. There were articles on the
Soviet–Afghan war and cuttings from magazines and books.
One in particular caught Fabel's attention; what struck him
as odd was that it was only a segment of what must have
been a much larger piece. It had been carefully cut out, yet
began and ended in the middle of a sentence:

ensuing discord. Unable to find among themselves a suit-
able ruler, the Krivichians, Chud and Slavs agreed to
seek out a foreign prince or king to govern and establish the rule of law. They looked amongst those Vikings
of France that are known as Normans. They sought
amongst the Angles of Jutland and England. And they
sought amongst the Svear or Swedes of Sweden. These
Swedes are also known by the Moors as the Rus, and
from their number three brothers, Rurik, Sineus and
Truvor, came forth with their families and established
dominion over the peoples of the Dnieper. Rurik, the
eldest, became ruler of Novgorod, and the lands and the
people of that region became known as Russian. Rurik's
brothers both died soon after and Rurik became sole
ruler. It was brought to his attention that there was a
city to the south that was in great peril. It had been
founded by the Polianian ferryman Kii, his brothers
Shchek and Khoriv, and his sister Lybed. This city had
taken Kii's name and was known as Kievetz or Kiev and
had been governed wisely and well. However, after the
death of Kii and his kin, the city had fallen into great
peril and was suffering at the cruel hands of the Khazars.
Rurik was moved by the plight of the

Fabel reread the segment. Was this how MacSwain saw
himself and Vitrenko: Vitrenko as some latter-day Rurik and
MacSwain as his loyal kinsman? He roamed further across
the landscape of meticulous psychosis. Another cutting. This
one concerned the warlord lieutenant of Prince Igor, a
Varangian called Sveneld or Sveinald. A name, distant in time
and geography, but from the same root as MacSwain's own
and brought close under the magnifying glass of MacSwain's
insanity. He travelled further. Numerous depictions of one-
eyed Odin. A one-page pantheon of the twelve principal gods
of the Aesir. Another on the Vanir, headed by Loki. There

were fragments of downloaded Internet pages on Asatru. The largest item was a reproduction of a woodcut illustration of a giant ash tree, its branches and roots writhing and stretching like tentacles to loop through representations of a dozen different worlds. A vast eagle sat in its uppermost bough. This, Fabel knew, was Yggdrasil, the tree of the universe and the centrepiece of Norse beliefs. It was Yggdrasil that connected all things: mortal men with gods, the past with the present and the future, heaven with earth with hell, good with evil.

Maria's voice made him jump.

'The unit we sent down to the harbour has reported in. MacSwain's boat is gone.'

'Shit!' Fabel spat the English word into the small space of the box room.

'But there's good news too, *Chef* . . .' said Maria, her pale blue eyes glinting. 'I've had Kommissar Kassel of the WSP on the phone. He was the guy who helped us out when MacSwain took to the water the other night.'

Fabel nodded impatiently.

'He's trailing a boat at the moment. It's heading west along the south coast of the Elbe. He's sure it's MacSwain . . .'

Fabel rushed forward and Maria had to step back swiftly to avoid being knocked over.

'Paul, Werner, Maria – I want you to come with me.' He turned to the other two Mordkommission officers 'Landsmann, Schüler – you wait here in case he turns up.'

Fabel snapped open his cell phone. He spoke as he walked briskly out of MacSwain's apartment, Werner, Paul and Maria in his wake. 'Put me through to Kriminaldirektor Van Heiden,' he said. 'And do it right away.'

Van Heiden had arranged for the helicopter to be waiting to pick up Fabel and his team from the pad at Landespolizei- schule, next to the Präsidium. Buchholz and Kolski were both in custody and, as Fabel had asked, Norbert Eitel's lawyer had been informed that a police officer had been abducted by MacSwain. As Fabel had predicted, Eitel's lawyer was very keen to allow his client to make a statement as soon as possible.

Fabel and the others crouched low as they ran towards the helicopter, the rotor blades of which were already slicing through air thick with the smell of aviation fuel and the roar of the helicopter's engines. Once they were buckled up, the co-pilot handed Fabel a large-scale map of the river as well as a microphone and earpiece headset, gesturing for him to put it on. Fabel could now communicate with the flight crew.

'You know where we're headed?'

The pilot gave a sharp nod of his helmeted head.

'Then let's go. And patch me through to the WSP launch commander.'

Kassel's current position was close to the south shore of the section of the Elbe known as the Mühlenberger Loch. They were coming up to Stade and would soon be entering the section of river where the Elbe widened its arms to embrace the North Sea. Kassel explained that they had lost visual contact with MacSwain's boat – it was just too fast for them – but he was tracking it on radar, and he had scrambled two launches to assist from the WSP Polizeidirektion at Cuxhaven.

Fabel processed the information. They would soon be passing along the shore of the low, flat lands where the drugged girls had been dumped. The thought hit him like a steam hammer. He beckoned for Maria, Paul and Werner to lean in closer. Fabel pushed the microphone arm of his headset down from his mouth and shouted against the whine of the helicopter's engines.

'They didn't take the girls to wherever they were raped by car: MacSwain probably brought them there in his boat and afterwards he or someone else at the ritual took them by car and dumped them nearby.' He snapped the mouthpiece back to his lips. 'Patch me through to the Polizei Cuxhaven. I need to speak to Hauptkommissar Sülberg and I need to speak to him now.'

They were far out from the city by the time Sülberg's voice came on the other end of the radio. Fabel explained that MacSwain was unaware he was being tracked and he was probably heading towards the general area where the other two had been abandoned.

'Except this time,' added Fabel, 'he's got a police officer who can identify him. He has no intention of letting her walk away from this, drugged or otherwise.'

'I'll get units out there right away,' said Sülberg. 'We'll get into position and wait for your instructions.'

As soon as Sülberg was off the line, the co-pilot informed Fabel that Kassel had been in touch again. MacSwain had stopped. Somewhere just past Freiberg.

Fabel consulted his map. 'The Aussendeich area,' he said in a voice that the others could not hear above the thunder of the rotors.

Sunday 22 June, 00.10 a.m. Aussendeich, between Hamburg and Cuxhaven.

MacSwain's boat was moored at an old abandoned wooden jetty that looked like the wake of a passing boat would send it tumbling in pieces into the dark water. Kassel estimated that it had been there a good ten minutes before the WS23 had reached it. Time for MacSwain to have lugged Anna off the boat and out across the marshy fields that glistered coldly in the moonlight. Kassel and Gebhard had disembarked, weapons drawn, and slipped quietly into the bushes that fringed the field beyond. As they crouched in the scrub, Kassel could sense Gebhard's electric excitement; this was the kind of action he had dreamed about. Kassel cast a look in his direction.

'We take this easy, Gebhard, okay? I've radioed the Hamburg KriPo and they'll take it from here. We just watch out that this guy doesn't head back this way and try to escape on the boat.'

Gebhard nodded impatiently, like a teenager being denied permission to go to a party. Kassel scanned the field through his binoculars. The carelessly cast light of the moon was not bright, but Kassel could be pretty certain that there was no one there. MacSwain must have passed over to the other side. He lifted the binoculars the smallest degree and opened his horizon out by a hundred metres. There were two derelict buildings behind the far hedgerow: they looked like disused barns. He held them centre frame for a moment before recommencing his sweep back along the dark fringe of the field. Something snapped his focus back to the barns. A light. A faint, moving light inside the building to the left. Kassel slapped Gebhard twice on the shoulder with the back of his hand, then handed him the binoculars and pointed across to the barns.

'Over there!' he hissed. Raising the radio to his lips, he pressed the transmit button and spoke the helicopter's call sign twice.

Fabel found himself juggling radio conversations: he was keeping the Präsidium informed: an MEK unit was already on its way, but it would take nearly an hour before they were there. He told Kassel to sit tight and passed on the details of the location to the helicopter pilot and also to Sülberg and the Cuxhaven SchuPo units. The pilot confirmed that they would be able to land near the barns.

'No. I don't want to alert MacSwain to our presence too early. It could cost Anna her life. Fly clear of them and come down close to the main road. We'll join up with Sülberg there.'

Fabel radioed Sülberg, who gave him a map reference. He

turned to Werner, Maria and Paul. Each of them had a look
of hard determination on their face. Paul had something extra:
an anxiety that jarred with Fabel's instincts and made him
feel decidedly uneasy.

The helicopter set down in a clearing close to the main road.
Fabel realised, as he ran, half crouched, from beneath the
slicing blades of the chopper, that they were very close to
where the two girls had been dumped. The untidy, squat form
of Sülberg came running towards Fabel and the others.

'Our cars are on the main road. Let's go.'

Sülberg ordered the patrol cars to kill their headlights as
soon as they hit the dirt track that led to the barns. A driver,
Sülberg, Fabel and Maria were in the lead vehicle. The track
was pitted and clearly seldom if ever used; the green and
white Mercedes lurched wildly as it engaged its erratic topography. They approached a bend where they were shielded
from the barns by a high, unkempt hedge. Sülberg ordered
the driver to stop. The other three patrol cars pulled in behind.

Sülberg and Fabel went on ahead, crouching to keep their
bodies concealed behind the hedge. There were two large
BMWs parked, empty, in front of the barn. MacSwain was
not alone.

To one side of the building was a largish window that
spilled a cheerless, pale light out into the night, but its angle
prevented Fabel and Sülberg from seeing inside. They carefully made their way back to where Werner, Maria, Paul
and the four Cuxhaven SchuPos were waiting. They huddled
into a circle, like some American football team choosing a
gameplan.

'Werner, you and Hauptkommissar Sülberg go around to
the back and see if there's a way in there. Paul, you and I
will take the main door. Maria, you take a position out to
the side, with a view of that side window, in case anyone
makes a break for it that way.' He looked at Sülberg before

addressing the Cuxhaven officers. Sülberg nodded his consent. 'You two cover the other side of the barn. Just make sure, if anything comes out, that it's not one of us before you start shooting. And you two –' Fabel indicated the remaining SchuPos – 'take up positions on either side of Ober-kommissarin Klee. The WSP have the route back to the boat covered.'

A silver-edged, untidy clump of cloud drifted lazily in front of the moon and the shadows around the barns and on the surrounding fields seemed to stretch and soak out into the night, like black ink on an already darkened blotter.

'Okay,' said Fabel, 'let's go.'

The night seemed to empty itself of all other noise, making Fabel painfully aware of the sounds of their breathing and the crunch of their feet as they scuttled in a half crouch towards the parked BMWs. Fabel drew his Walther from his holster and snapped back the carriage to place a round in the firing chamber. Paul, Werner and Sülberg followed suit. Fabel nodded to Sülberg and he and Werner headed off around the side of the barn that had no window. Fabel gave them thirty seconds that seemed like an eternity, then nodded to Paul.

They were on their feet and across to the barn in seconds. Paul and Fabel positioned themselves, weapons readied, on either side of the door.

Fabel applied the slightest of pressure on the heavy door. It gave way. Of course they hadn't locked it. They felt secure in their seclusion.

Now was a time for cool professionalism, but they had Anna in there and Fabel felt anger and hatred hot in his blood. Paul's jaw was set hard, the sinuous muscles in his face like cables beneath his skin. A vein pulsed visibly in his neck. He turned to Fabel and his eyes burned with a dark fury. Fabel made a face that silently asked, *You okay?* Paul nodded in a way that did not reassure his boss. Fabel lifted his radio to his lips and whispered one word.

'Go!'

Paul slammed the door wide with the sole of his boot and Fabel burst through first. He took in four figures. There was a makeshift altar arrangement constructed out of an old oak table and Anna lay on top of it. She had a bathrobe flung around her and was unrestrained except for the bonds the drugs had wrapped around her will to move. MacSwain was half bent over her, his hands reaching out to her. He stared blankly at Fabel and Paul and then snapped his head around as Werner and Sülberg burst in through the other doorway. Fabel and Paul spread out, ensuring their line of fire wasn't directed at the two policemen opposite.

Fabel registered the other two figures. One of the men had the look of trapped, violent energy in his short, squat, powerful frame: Fabel recognised him from the surveillance images as Solovey, one of Vitrenko's lieutenants. The other figure was taller, dressed in a long black overcoat. And, even at a distance, his eyes burned an almost luminous green in the dim light.

Vitrenko.

Something gleamed in Vitrenko's right hand: a broad-bladed knife. Its blade was the thickness of a sword, but short and double edged, sweeping to a sharp tip. Fabel had no doubt that he was looking at the murder weapon.

Fabel heard his own voice high and tight. 'Police! Place your hands on top of your heads and get down onto your knees.' The three men didn't move. MacSwain from shock and indecision. The other two, Fabel guessed, as some kind of strategy. Paul Lindemann obviously shared the thought.

'Pull anything and I'll blow your fucking heads off. I mean it.' Paul's voice had the same spring-loaded tension in it that Fabel had heard in his own. And he had no doubt that Paul meant exactly what he said.

'I'm sure you do,' said Vasyl Vitrenko, the green eyes locking with Paul's.

It happened so fast that Fabel barely registered it. Solovey dropped as if a trapdoor had opened beneath him, his hand disappearing underneath his black leather jacket as he fell. There was the loud crack of a pistol and Fabel heard a sound like a slap beside him. In that instant, and without turning his head to see, Fabel knew that Paul was dead. Vitrenko made a swift move sideways, seemed to bounce on the balls of his feet, and dived at the window. Fabel fired at the floor where Solovey had dropped. The air fumed with the smell of cordite and filled with a deafening chorus of shots as Werner and Sülberg opened fire as well. MacSwain threw himself into a corner, where he curled up in a foetal pose.

Fabel turned to where Paul had fallen. He lay staring blankly up at the ceiling, the fury swept from his face by death. His broad, pale forehead was punctured dead centre by the entry wound made by Solovey's bullet.

Werner and Sülberg rushed forward. Sülberg kicked the prone Solovey, who lay face down on the dirt-covered floor; he eased his foot under the Ukrainian's shoulder and took a couple of heaves before flipping him over. He was clearly dead. Werner was already over to where Anna lay. He ran his hands swiftly and firmly over her body, his eyes searching frantically for any signs of blood. He looked up at Fabel, then briefly down at Paul.

'She's okay, Jan. She's not been hit.'

Fabel snatched the radio from his inside coat pocket. The aerial snagged on his jacket and he wrestled with it in a pointless fury that ripped the lining. Once it was free he pressed the transmit button.

'Maria . . . Vitrenko is making a run for it. He's jumped from the west window and is heading your way.'

'I see him! I see him!' The shrillness of Maria's voice was accentuated by the radio's static hiss.

'Maria, watch out for yourself. I'm on my way. All units assist Oberkommissarin Klee.'

He released the radio button and walked swiftly across to MacSwain, who still cowered in the corner. There was a deadly decisiveness in Fabel's movements. When he reached MacSwain he snapped his arm out rigid, jabbing the muzzle of his Walther into the flesh of MacSwain's cheek. MacSwain whimpered and squeezed his eyes tight shut, waiting for Fabel's shot to blast his face and his life to nothing.

'You fuck . . .' said Fabel in a slow, quiet voice. He looked across at Werner and Sülberg, both of whom said nothing. Fabel looked down on MacSwain. He eased and then re-tightened his grip on his pistol, his face twisted in a sneer. In a single second, a dozen images sped through his mind. Michaela Palmer's scared, hunted look. Four innocent women, ripped apart, prepared for death the same way. Paul Lindemann's dead eyes. But this was the apprentice, not the master. MacSwain's was a sick mind manipulated by a greater, even more twisted intellect. It had been Vitrenko who had killed the Ukrainian girl and the old man. His own father. Not work to be given out to an apprentice. A signature piece. Fabel snapped his gun away from MacSwain's head.

'Watch him!' he snapped at Sülberg, who nodded grimly and moved over to MacSwain. 'Werner, you look after Anna.'

'What about Vitrenko?'

'I'll deal with him,' Fabel said and sprinted towards the door.

Fabel burst out into the night. He stopped and scanned the low, wide fields. He snatched his radio to his mouth.

'Maria?'

Silence.

'Maria? Answer me.' Still no reply.

Sülberg, back in the barn, must have heard. His voice came on the radio asking each of the four Cuxhaven units if they had seen either Vitrenko or Oberkommissarin Klee. Three responded negatively. The fourth, like Maria, did not respond. Fabel narrowed his eyes and scoured the night for any movement against the green-black fringes of trees and scrub at the far end of the fields. He saw something. Indistinct, not even identifiable as a person. He burst into a sprint in its direction.

'He's heading towards the water! Away from the boat!' Fabel screamed into his radio between breaths. 'I'm going to lose him in the trees!'

Fabel's lungs began to sear. His heart hammered in his chest.

He found the Cuxhaven SchuPo first. The policeman lay on his side, his SIG pistol still in his hand, caressed by the long grass in the depression made by his own falling, dying body. The posture of the dead uniformed policeman reminded Fabel of the mummified bodies of ancient sacrificial victims that archaeologists would occasionally reclaim from the peaty earth of this part of Germany. From just below the ear, sweeping across his throat immediately beneath the jawline, a wide, sweeping gash sparkled in the dim moonlight and blood glistened black on the grass. Silence and death had come to the young SchuPo simultaneously, and he had been robbed of his right to cry out as his life left him.

'Maria!' Fabel bellowed into the darkness. Silence. Then something like a sigh. Fabel turned sixty degrees to his right. Maria lay, about ten metres away, half hidden in the grass. Fabel ran across to her and dropped to his knees beside her. She lay on her back, her face towards the dark sky, in a posture that looked almost relaxed, as if she had sought solitude to gaze up at the moon and stars. She moved her eyes to look at Fabel without turning her head. Her lips were drawn tight and she was breathing through her mouth in short, shallow breaths. The hilt of the broad ceremonial knife jutted hideously from her abdomen, just below the sternum. The entire blade had been driven into her body, deliberately missing the heart and an instant kill, but causing enough internal damage to throw Maria's survival into a perilous balance.

Fabel leaned over her and placed a hand gently on either side of her face, bringing his face kissing-close to hers.

'I don't want to die, Jan . . .' she said in a little girl's voice. 'Please don't let me die.'

'You're not going to die, Maria,' Fabel's voice held gentleness and determination in equal measure. 'Look at me. Listen to me. Think this through. Vitrenko could have killed you if he had wanted to. But he didn't. He didn't because he wanted me here, tending to you, instead of coming after him. You're not one of his victims, Maria. You're a diversion. A delaying tactic.' He could feel her small breaths on his face. 'You're not going to die.' But he was not at all sure he was telling the truth. Maria smiled and a small rivulet of dark blood escaped from the corner of her lips.

A voice from beyond the universe that was Fabel and Maria and the small circle of dark grass. A radio voice. Werner.

'Anna's okay, *Chef*. Repeat . . . Anna is okay . . . Have you got Vitrenko? Over.'

Fabel hit the transmission button. He heard his own voice, dead and flat, reporting the murder of the Cuxhaven policeman and that he had a seriously wounded officer in need of immediate airlift by Medicopter.

'Help will be here soon, Maria. You're going to be fine. I promise. We've got MacSwain.'

Maria smiled weakly. Her breath was becoming more laboured.

Fabel raised his eyes. He thought he could see a tall figure at the extreme far corner of the field. Vitrenko, heading into the woods. As he ran, Vitrenko's raincoat flapped behind him, like dark wings. Fabel leapt to his feet, drew his pistol and fired, knowing that Vitrenko was out of range. Out of reach. As the magazine emptied, and Fabel heard the repeated, impotent clicking of the firing pin on an empty chamber, he again recalled the words from the e-mail. The words that MacSwain had written, but that Vitrenko had dictated.

You can stop me, but you will never catch me.

THANKS AND ACKNOWLEDGEMENTS

I have a lot to be grateful for. And there's a lot of people to whom I am grateful: Wendy, my wife, for all her comments and edits on the first draft and for her unwavering support and belief in Jan Fabel; my children, Jonathan and Sophie, for their patience while I devoted so much time to this book; and my mother, an avid and expert crime thriller reader, who provided comments on the manuscript.

I wholeheartedly thank my agent, Carole Blake, for her enthusiasm, energy, commitment and hard work, as well as Oli Munson and David Eddy of Blake Friedmann Literary Agency. I would also thank Paul Sidey, my editor and a true literary gent, whose suggestions have made this a better book; Tiffany Stansfield, his assistant editor; and Neville Gomes, my copy-editor, for his painstaking attention to detail. I would like to thank Mark McCallum and Ron Beard, as well as everyone else in Random House marketing and sales departments, for their enthusiastic support.

I have to single out Dr Bernd Rullkötter, my German translator, who has gone above and beyond the call of duty in helping make this as authentic and accurate a book as possible in English as well as in German (even if this has involved telling me where to stick my *Umlaut*). I also owe thanks to Dr Anja Lowit, for her time and her comments on the original draft.

In my opinion, the Polizei Hamburg is one of the world's finest police services. I have also found it to be one of the most open and accessible. I have sought to remain, as far as possible, within the real operational and organizational structures and procedures of the Polizei Hamburg, but this is, after all, a work of fiction, so any licence taken or errors made are entirely mine. I would, however, like to make special mention of Erste Polizeihauptkommissarin Ulrike Sweden of the Polizeipressestelle, for all of the information, help and contacts she supplied. I would also like to offer my gratitude to Dirk Brandenburg and Birte Hell, both of the Hamburg murder squad, for devoting so much of their valuable time to me. Special thanks go to Peter Baustian of the Davidwache police station and to Robert Golz, from the control and operation room division of the Polizeipräsidium. Boris Manzella, Andre Schönhardt and Rene Schönhardt, all serving officers in the Polizei Hamburg uniform branch, offered invaluable opinions on the first draft of *Blood Eagle*.

I am enormously grateful to Katrin Frahm for all of her help in making me sound less stupid when I speak German. I would like to thank Dagmar Förtsch, of GLS Language Services (and Honorary Consul of the Federal Republic of Germany in Glasgow) as well as Duncan McInnes.

Special thanks also to my editors and publishers around the world for their faith and commitment.

And, of course, if this book has a hero, it's a city, not a person . . . *Vielen Dank, Hamburg!*